LIGHTS DOWN

Also by Graham Hurley

The Faraday and Winter series

TURNSTONE
THE TAKE
ANGELS PASSING
DEADLIGHT
CUT TO BLACK
BLOOD AND HONEY
ONE UNDER
THE PRICE OF DARKNESS
NO LOVELIER DEATH
BEYOND REACH
BORROWED LIGHT
HAPPY DAYS
BACKSTORY

The Jimmy Suttle series

WESTERN APPROACHES
TOUCHING DISTANCE
SINS OF THE FATHER
THE ORDER OF THINGS

The Spoils of War series

FINISTERRE
AURORE
ESTOCADA
RAID 42
LAST FLIGHT TO STALINGRAD
KYIV
KATASTROPHE

The Enora Andressen series

CURTAIN CALL *
SIGHT UNSEEN *
OFF SCRIPT *
LIMELIGHT *
INTERMISSION *

* *available from Severn House*

LIGHTS DOWN

Graham Hurley

SEVERN
HOUSE

First world edition published in Great Britain and the USA in 2022
by Severn House, an imprint of Canongate Books Ltd,
14 High Street, Edinburgh EH1 1TE.

Trade paperback edition first published in Great Britain and the USA in 2022
by Severn House, an imprint of Canongate Books Ltd.

severnhouse.com

British Library Cataloguing-in-Publication Data
A CIP catalogue record for this title is available from the British Library.

ISBN-13: 978-0-7278-5003-4 (cased)
ISBN-13: 978-1-4483-0930-6 (trade paper)
ISBN-13: 978-1-4483-0924-5 (e-book)

All Severn House titles are printed on acid-free paper.

Typeset by Palimpsest Book Production Ltd.,
Falkirk, Stirlingshire, Scotland.
Printed and bound in Great Britain by
TJ Books, Padstow, Cornwall.

To
Martin Anderton White
1948–2021

Imagination decides everything.

Blaise Pascal

As soon as you write, you are asking for forgiveness.

Jacques Derrida

ONE

London
Sunday 30 May, 2021

Looking back, I missed all the clues, every single one.

'You sailed all this way because of me?'

'Of course.'

I'm on-board Rémy's yacht, *Caspar*, a much-loved survivor from the days before plastic took over from – in his words – sweat and seasoned teak. It's tucked up in a visitor's berth at a marina near Tower Bridge, and just now Rémy's hunting for the bottle of Saint-Émilion Grand Cru he promised me on the phone.

'The world is crazy,' he's telling me. 'France is impossible. Heathrow is worse. Even if I could get a flight, your guys would lock me up for a fortnight in some airport hotel. The food would kill a Frenchman quicker than Covid.' He glances up, still without the bottle, and gestures at the scene through the cabin window. 'Fifty boats? More? Who's looking? Who's ever going to find me here? I tested negative in Boulogne. I'm double-vaxxed and I can prove it. The guys in the office are happy. I'm paid up for three nights.'

I agree the world has gone mad. This country commits more time and effort to manning the battlements and being nasty to foreigners than anywhere else on earth. Given that he set sail from the French coast late last night, I expect they'll have tracked him across the Channel every inch of the way.

'Nonsense.' He's found the wine at last. 'We need to talk about *Exocet*.'

Exocet is the new TV mini-series he wants to pitch me. Rémy Despret has long been my favourite director and he loves the grand gestures. Saint-Émilion Grand Cru costs a fortune, but he still needs to know I'm not an easy buy. We've known each other a long time, Rémy and I, and age gives me mothering rights.

'The Tower of London is five minutes away.' I'm nodding at the cabin window. 'If you're lucky they might release you in time for Christmas. If they get difficult, it could be much worse. Importing a French virus is a capital offence. Anne Boleyn lost her head for less.'

Rémy rarely smiles but it's nice when it happens. He's a big man, six foot three inches in his stonewashed jeans and faded T-shirt, and he holds my gaze for a moment, then sorts out a couple of glasses, leaving me with the view. I've never been to the St Katharine Docks marina before and I'm still wondering about the net worth of the yachts and motor cruisers nudging the pontoon when he proposes a toast.

'To *Exocet.*' He pours the wine and hands me a glass. The smile is even broader. '*À bas les Rosbiffs.*'

À bas les Rosbiffs means Stuff the Brits. It's a phrase that has always played well in certain circles in Rémy's native Paris, and just now I get the feeling it ties in nicely with the thrust of his new mini-series.

We settle at the table which is covered in navigation charts. I'm to think April, 1982. The Argies have landed on the Falklands and helped themselves to what little remains of the British Empire. Thatcher is outraged and has despatched a task force to reclaim her belongings. As a sizeable chunk of the Royal Navy steams south, the Argies have a couple of weeks to lay a trap or two and for that they'll need new friends.

'In Paris?'

'Of course. These people do things in style. They breed wonderful polo players and they're in love with speed. Put an Argie pilot in a fast jet and sell him a decent missile, and any navy on earth would be in trouble. This is the South Atlantic in mid-winter. The Brits have been at sea for weeks already, and in any case they've never taken foreigners seriously. That might turn out to have been a mistake.'

'How come?'

'Because we had an interest in making it hard for the Brits.'

'We?'

'Us. *Les Français.*'

'Are we talking reality?' The Grand Cru is delicious. 'This stuff actually happened?'

'Of course.'

'How do I know?'

'You don't. First you have to believe me. Then we have to make everyone else believe it, too.'

'We're talking audience?'

'Backers, first.'

'You haven't lined up the finance?'

'Not yet.'

'And that's why you're here? You think me on board will make a difference?'

'Enora Andressen? *The* Enora Andressen? I know it will. And by tomorrow, with you attached, I'm meeting a bunch of backers. This town is full of money that doesn't know what to do with itself. Covid has killed production. The cupboard's empty.'

Rémy's right. The week the BBC started to run repeats of repeats of repeats of *Dad's Army* was the week the nation rediscovered reading.

'So what happens in this series of yours?'

'Happened, *chérie*. Fact. The Argies have representation in Paris. They fly French aircraft, have done for a while. They think the world of the Super Étendard, and they adore the Mirage III. Strap on a French missile, a surface skimmer, and no Brit matelot will ever lay eyes on them. We're talking fire-and-forget. You're an Argie pilot heading for the task force. You're flying low. You release at seventy kilometres out, and then turn for home. The Brit radar sets see nothing, no trace, until our little Exocet baby's six thousand metres away. At those speeds, you've got less than a minute to react. Bam' – he drives his big fist into his open palm – 'sweet dreams.'

I was born in 1977 and I have the dimmest memory of watching news footage as a child on our family TV in Brittany. A British warship was wallowing somewhere in the South Atlantic, her hull blackened and torn open, smoke curling out of the wound. At the time, it was my mother who turned the set off. When I asked why, she said that lots of men had died.

'HMS *Sheffield*,' Rémy confirms. 'An Exocet did that and

a couple more sank a big container ship, which cost the Brits most of their helicopter lift. Later, the Argies fired one at a destroyer, big hole towards the stern. By then, the Brits knew they had a problem.'

'And the French? Us?'

'We loved it. This was the first time the skimmers had been used in anger. Half the world was watching. You can't buy an advert like that.'

'Horrible.' I reach for my wine glass. 'So where do I belong in all this?'

Rémy fingers his glass for a moment, then gestures me closer as if someone might be listening. I've been aware since I stepped aboard that something is different about him, and now I realize what it is. He's obviously tired, as he should be after sailing single-handed through the night, but he's nervous, too, a little brittle round the edges. I've never known him bite his nails before, just the lightest damage around both broad thumbs, and the battered Nike Air Zoom on his left foot appears to have developed a life of its own. Rémy, for me, has always been nerveless, the embodiment of directorial *calme*, but something, or someone, has got at him. I can see it in his eyes, in the way he keeps checking the pontoon through the window. This is a man, I tell myself, who's expecting bad company.

'Well?' I'm still waiting for an answer.

'The Brit task force is at sea. Buenos Aires has sent a small team to Paris. They only have so many Exocets, and they badly need more.'

'So?'

Rémy's looking at me again, impatient this time, as if I should be reading his mind, and when I insist on at least the outlines of the plot and just a clue or two about the character he has in mind for yours truly, he offers a slightly stagey sigh. The Brits, he says, have wised up about the Exocets. They've despatched Special Forces to neighbouring Chile to wreak havoc amongst various tucked-away Argie assets, and in Paris they've located the one French politician powerful enough to OK the delivery of more French missiles.

'This is the president?'

'No. But nearly.'

'This guy is real?'

'Of course.'

'And you're going to name him?'

'No way. We're calling him Alain. He's youngish, mid-forties, a high-flyer, a family man, a staunch Catholic. He's full of ambition, and the public love him, and even better he has a family debt to settle. A debt of blood.'

'Against whom?'

'The Brits. His grandfather died at Mers-el-Kébir. That's back in 1940. It's complicated Vichy stuff but he was blown up on a battleship called the *Dunkerque.* The Brits killed more than a thousand French sailors that day and he's never forgiven them.'

Rémy nods, and studies his big hands as if he, too, had taken the infamy of Mers-el-Kébir personally. Then he glances up at me and begins to explain young Alain's single weakness, a flaw that Brit Intelligence are determined to exploit.

'He likes middle-aged women with baggage,' I say lightly, 'which I'm guessing might be Enora's cue.'

Rémy has an acute ear for nuance, and he senses – quite rightly – that I'm not taking him entirely seriously. The Exocet missile, I can buy. Some of the historical stuff is genuinely interesting, especially when Rémy talks about the black-and-white footage of the Brits bombarding the French fleet anchored up at Mers-el-Kébir. This, he promises me, will launch the series, pictures of smoke boiling over the ruined hulls of French warships, images later echoed in news footage from the South Atlantic. So far, so good. But is there really space in this bloodfest for a middle-aged *femme fatale*, tasked with compromising the one screen-ready French politician who – in 1982 – can bring the Brits to their knees?

This is bullshit, and I hope we both know it.

'You're wrong.' Rémy is looking genuinely shocked. 'Your screen name is Honore. You're very close to Alain's wife. You know the family inside out. You've known them forever. Holidays? Saints' days?'

'And am I married?'

'Only to your job. You're a political journalist. National reputation. That's how the pair of you first hooked up.'

'Me and Alain?'

'Of course. You were the first to spot his potential.'

'And you're telling me this man is married?'

'Yes. To the comely Agnès.'

'Comely' puts a smile on my face. Rémy, who has a gift for languages, especially film, has always treated English like a hot bath. He wallows in it. He loves a splash or two of the more arcane words. Comely. Winsome. He once introduced me to a fellow thesp as 'reliably vulpine', and it took me a beat or two to realize he meant it as a compliment.

Now I want to know more about Agnès.

'She's become your best friend. You spend a lot of time together. Girlie weekends in Venice. She's having problems just now, and you're only too happy to help.'

'Problems?'

'She's menopausal. She doesn't recognize herself anymore. Vulnerable doesn't begin to cut it.'

'And me?'

'You're her rock. Tough love would come close.'

'Am I still working?'

'You are. You write for *Le Point.* Have done for a while. That's what took you to Alain in the first place.'

'Centre-right?'

'Exactly. A meeting of minds. What could be sweeter?'

I nod. Despite everything, Honore is beginning to come together in my imagination. I can picture her. I can hear her. She'd live somewhere interesting, somewhere off the beaten Parisian track. She might have a rural bolthole at the end of some TGV line. She'd swim, or run, or maybe both. She'd keep herself fit. When she had time, she'd worry about the planet. She might even abandon offal.

'And do I have any kids?'

'One. A boy. Louen.'

'That's a Breton name.'

'Exactly.'

'You named him with me in mind?'

'I did.'

'Isn't that . . .' I'm frowning now, '. . . a little presumptuous?'

'Not at all. The part is made for you, and so is Louen.'

'Age?'

'Twenty-two. And you know what he's done with his life? He's a fighter pilot. Just now he's based in Corsica, flying the Mirage. And you know what's best of all? The Ministry of Defence have offered all the help we're going to need. Whatever aerial sequences we script, they'll supply virtually unlimited access. That way, running the subplot, we can mirror the Argie pilots. They were flying the Mirage, too.'

'So what's in it for the Ministry of Defence?'

'*À bas les Rosbiffs*.' Another smile. 'One of the Air Corps generals has read the script. Total buy-in.'

I reach for my glass. The wine is truly wonderful, lingering on the back of the tongue, a series of delicious surprises in keeping with the best film scripts.

'This Louen carries the series?'

'No.' Rémy shakes his head. 'You do. Enora Andressen does, aka Honore. But the boy helps.'

'Describe him.'

'Short. Stocky. Gunfighter eyes.' He pauses. 'His friends call him Rouquin.'

'He's a redhead?'

'Sure. Just like Alain.'

I hold Rémy's gaze for a long moment. Alas, we're back in the pages of pulp fiction.

'He's Alain's boy?'

'Of course. He comes from the affair the pair of you had way back.'

'And now?'

'You live alone in the Tenth. You'll love the apartment I've found. It's a walk-up, no lift, with a view of Quai de Jemmapes. You and Alain still meet.' He shrugs. 'Is that a problem?'

'Only if you're thinking anyone in France would care. If this is our big reveal, we're in trouble.'

Rémy likes 'we', I can tell. He thinks I'm on the edge of saying yes to this new baby of his, and until the latest feeble plot twist he might have been right.

'No.' I shake my head. 'I'm sorry.'

'No? You won't do it? Won't even *read* it?'

'No, you've told me enough. This will be shot in France, am I right?'

'Yes.'

'How many episodes?'

'Seven.'

In my head, I tally the location commitment, the pre-shoot script conferences, the read-throughs, the post-production demands.

'That's a big chunk of time. Six months at least. I need to share something with you. Maybe I should have mentioned this before.'

'Before what?'

'Before you opened the bottle.' I'm trying to lighten the conversation. I've always had difficulty reading this man but now his disappointment is all too evident. No one ever says no to Rémy Despret. Especially me.

'Well?' He wants to know where this thing of ours has gone so badly wrong.

I gather my thoughts for a moment, wondering quite where to start, then I hear voices on the pontoon beside the yacht. Rémy is already on his feet, heading for the wooden steps that will take him out of the saloon. Through the open door I watch him steady himself beside the wheel. It's started to rain and the two figures on the pontoon want to come aboard. Rémy starts to argue, then shrugs and steps back as they clamber into the cockpit. Moments later, all three of them are down in the cabin. One of the visitors, an older man, is wearing a dark blue anorak with a smart St Katharine Docks logo. The other, much younger, has a yellow gilet and terrible hair and a lanyard with an ID I can't quite read. He appears to be in charge.

'And you are?'

I introduce myself. A friend of Monsieur Despret's. When he asks for ID, I query why that might be necessary.

'You sailed in with him?'

'Not at all.' I gesture at the bottle. 'We're having a chat.'

'Local, then? London?'

'Yes.'

He nods, produces a smartphone, taps in my name, waits to see what happens. Evidently satisfied, he turns to Rémy. He wants to know about Newhaven.

'You quarantined in the marina there. Have I got that right?'

'Yes.'

'And you left when?'

'Last night.'

Rémy is plainly uncomfortable, largely – I suspect – because of me. He raises a QR code on his phone and passes it across. Our new friend scans it, grunts something to the older man, and then asks for Rémy's passport. A brief flick through, and he's done. He even says thank you and makes a joke about the weather before clambering back up the steps and returning to the pontoon. Through the cabin window, we watch him taking shots of the yacht, fore and aft, kneeling briefly to capture a close-up of the name.

'Why *Caspar*?' I murmur. 'I've always meant to ask.'

'Caspar Friedrich? German artist? Big on Baltic landscapes? Google *Das Monch am Meer.* It'll change your life.'

'And why Newhaven?'

He doesn't answer me. He's still watching the figures on the pontoon and doesn't relax until they've gone. Only then does he turn back into the cabin. Rémy, to my knowledge, has never done guilt. Until now.

'You told me you sailed from Boulogne last night,' I point out quietly.

'I did.'

'Was that a lie?'

'Yes. I came straight from Newhaven.'

'So why not tell me?'

He gives me a look, then shrugs.

'It doesn't matter,' he says. 'Just business. The border people at the marina let me sit it out on board. There's CCTV everywhere in these places. They had me banged up.'

'And the business?'

'You don't want to know.'

'Meaning you won't tell me?'

'Meaning you don't want to know.' He manages to summon the faintest smile, then gestures at the bottle. 'You were telling me what a shit screenplay I'd written. There's enough left for a glass each.'

'Have I upset you? Be honest.'

'Not at all. These are very strange times. I'm sure you don't need me to tell you that.'

'You're right, I don't.' I take a step closer to him and put my hand on his arm. 'It's not the script. A couple of days and I'm sure we could put things right.'

'You're very kind.'

'I mean it.'

'So what's the problem? Why can't you sign on?'

'It's H. You've never met him, Rémy, but he's the father of my only child, and last year Covid nearly killed him. He's still ill, still suffering. They call it Long Covid, and in some respects it's worse because it doesn't go away.' I manage to summon a smile. 'Six months would be out of the question, I'm afraid, much though I like the idea of Honore.'

'You're looking after him? This H?'

'Helping to, yes.'

'Here? In London?'

'In Dorset. It's miles away. Flixcombe Manor.'

'Flixcombe?' Something has changed in his face. He's suddenly animated again. Flixcombe. He revolves the word in his mouth, enjoying it, tasting it, like a chocolate truffle he wants to last forever. Then he frowns. 'Flixcombe or Vlixcombe?'

'Flixcombe.'

'Wrong. It's Vlixcombe.'

'It's not.'

'It is, I promise you, and one day I'll explain why.'

'Tell me now.'

'No time. This afternoon's a wrap. *Ma chérie,* you're lovelier than ever.'

He's back in charge now, dependable, decisive, quite the old Rémy. He returns the cork to the bottle, puts the glasses in the tiny sink, checks his watch, and then gives me a brief hug before accompanying me into the cockpit and helping me onto the pontoon. This farewell, after our elaborate *pas-de-deux* over the script, feels unnecessarily brisk. Slightly hurt, I button my coat against the rain but when I lift my head to wave goodbye, he's gone.

TWO

It now gets complicated. I make my way home from St Katharine Docks, trying to work out why I feel so disturbed by Rémy. We've all lived through the last fourteen months, and I know only too well that Covid has put its smell on everyone, but the change in someone I always took for granted is deeply worrying. The old Rémy, the imperturbable presence on set, that acute master of dialogue and delivery who always teased the very best out of any casual on-screen exchange, the action director who could make a single perfectly framed camera movement do the work of half a dozen shots, the scruffy maestro we were all half in love with, appears to have downed tools and left for the big empty rehearsal hall in the sky. In his place is someone I barely recognize: clumsy, uncertain, nervous, prepared to settle for the dumbest of clichés in lieu of a grown-up script. Something's happened to a man I used to revere, and I need to find out more.

By the time I've made it to Holland Park, the rain is even heavier. I've been down in Flixcombe since the back end of last year, trying to spare H the worst of Covid's long reach, and London – like Rémy – feels like a presence I barely recognize. Lockdown, according to the good folk in charge, appears to be virtually over but old habits die hard. Strangers still carefully avoid each other on the street. Women, especially, are still wearing masks. And when I ride the 205 bus west, I have the entire front of the top deck to myself. Elements of this dreary urban shuffle are strangely agreeable because I happen to enjoy my own company, but I suspect that the government's breezy assumption that we'll all be partying by the weekend might be wide of the mark.

My apartment feels damp and abandoned. Malo has been making regular visits to sort the post, in search of anything pressing, but I've yet to get round to going through the rest. My lovely son, bless him, has been working for a food bank run by the Trussell Trust in one of the needier corners of south-west London. This, I suspect, was Clem's idea, but Malo's been honest enough to admit that it came as a relief after his post-Christmas week with H and me at Flixcombe. Coping with the unfed, he tells me, is a stroll in the park compared to the long, long days with the ghost that was once his father.

H stands for Hayden Prentice. Nearly two decades ago, we shared a bed on a superyacht in Antibes where I was on location. That night, both drunk, we conceived Malo and the following day I went down the coast to the Cannes Film Festival where I was up for an award. I never made it to the dais but I did meet a beguiling Scandi scriptwriter called Berndt Andressen. We were married within months, and when Malo arrived we both assumed that Berndt was the natural father. That turned out to be wrong and thanks to a DNA test Hayden – or 'H' – was able to claim paternity. By then, after years of ugliness, Berndt and I were in the midst of a messy divorce. By now I knew that H owed his wealth to the Pompey cocaine trade but we became friends. We've never slept together again, and we never will, but – like Malo – I was won over by his unflagging energy. In his own way, he's looked after both of us, and now is the moment when I'm happy to return the favour.

Why? Because H, through no obvious fault of his own, has found himself in the eye of the perfect storm. First the virus in its rude infancy, which nearly killed him, and now Long Covid, which threatens to do the same thing except much more slowly. Watching him struggle to surface from months of torment has been an exercise in patience as well as all the other Christian virtues. Life never endowed me with a huge supply of the latter, and on bad days I still try and roleplay my way through the worst of the crises, but there's no contesting the price we all have to pay.

No one could ever accuse the old H of keeping a low profile. For most of his working life, he dealt huge quantities of the marching powder, and when irritation or anger turned to violence he could be a real handful, but in our separate ways I now realize we all loved him. That love was unconditional because he had a big heart and limitless self-belief, and we all knew what to expect, but today's H is someone else, someone new, someone different. Surprise is a word I used to love. It sustained me through play after play, film after film, relationship after relationship. Now, alas, surprise is something I've learned to dread. Hence my eagerness to seize Rémy's offer of a decent bottle of wine and jump on the train to London. This will be respite care, I told myself. How wrong could I have been?

I settle on the sofa, trying to muster the energy to go through the mountain of unopened post. There's a message waiting for me on the landline. It's probably from Evelyn, who's bravely volunteered to keep an eye on H while I'm up here in London, but she's bound to have hit a reef or two and just now I can't face the conversation. Instead, I open envelope after envelope, making a neat pile of the charity appeals, still thinking about Flixcombe, about H, about those nightmare weeks in Portsmouth last year when the two of us – Malo and I – battled to keep him alive.

Covid, coupled with the aftershocks of one of H's long-ago feuds, took me to places even I could barely have imagined, but all the time – in the very back of my mind – there lurked a faith in a place called home. That's where everything would settle down, come good again. That's where we could queue up at Lost Property and reclaim the lives we'd once led. It might be Flixcombe. It might be Holland Park. It might, God knows, be a brand-new start somewhere hot and sunny and virus-free.

But none of that has happened. Instead, Covid has morphed, and morphed again, nimbler than any set of travel restrictions, more knowing than the vaccine programme, feasting on the old and the poor. Only yesterday, more than four thousand people died in India. Worldwide, that figure is way past three million. In this country, we take comfort in the vaccine roll-out, but our hapless government often seems asleep at the wheel, and in the face of a thousand unintended consequences, including H, I sometimes feel overwhelmed. A French *philosophe* whose name eludes me once said that we are all dust in the wind, and just now, in this exact moment in my life, I get the sense that he was right.

I finish the post and gaze at the phone. I badly need someone to talk to. It's barely four o'clock. Rosa, if she's working at all, might still be in her office. She answers on the second ring, and she seems pleased to hear me. Like a good agent, my tone of voice is the only clue she ever needs. Without me asking, she's insisting on a meet, a drink, maybe something to eat. I tell her I'll pick her up at her office. Give me an hour and I'll be there.

'No point,' she says. 'The office has gone. It's history. I'm camping in a mate's stationery cupboard, or at least that's the way it feels. Long story, my precious. Prepare to be bored.'

She tells me she's got a couple of comp tickets for a river cruise with dinner thrown in.

'Half six at Tower Pier,' she says. 'They still insist on Covid spacing so the evening belongs to us.'

THREE

Tower Pier is a five-minute walk from St Katharine Docks. I arrive early, with half an hour to spare before I'm to meet Rosa, wondering whether I might tempt Rémy to join us afloat, but *Caspar* has gone. At the marina office they dismiss his departure with a smile and a shrug. Sure, he paid for three nights but people change their plans. The tide began to ebb a couple of hours ago and Monsieur Despret should be way down the river by now. I digest the news in the rain outside, eyeing his empty berth. What about tomorrow's meet with his financial backers? How come he's simply sailed away?

By the time I get back to Tower Pier, Rosa has arrived, joining a handful of fellow diners waiting for permission to file on board. She spots me at once and gives me a wave. She's a big woman and has always made me laugh. She has a passion for second-hand fur coats and knee-length lace-up boots, but her negotiating skills are legendary and over more years than I care to remember I've owed her most of what makes me so contented.

Regardless of Covid, I give her a big hug. To my delight, she's invested in a fizzy perm, an explosion of curls that rather suits her. Rosa has always had the happy knack of plunging into every conversation as if the last one never ended, and now is no different.

'How's that gorgeous boy of yours? Married yet?'

'No. But Clem's expecting.'

'Good for her. When do we celebrate?'

'October the fourth, give or take.'

She holds me at arm's length, murmurs something absurd about the world's youngest granny, and gives me another hug. Behaviour this reckless has begun to attract attention, and when we finally get aboard, everyone gives us a wide berth. This suits us just fine. Rosa has already laid claim to the best table in the house, plumb in front of the view forward over the bows. Victory, as she's always told me, always belongs to the bold.

There's a rumble from way below our feet, the boat gives herself a shake, and the crew cast off. We make a wide turn across the tidal stream and head downriver under Tower Bridge. Rosa has already caught the eye of one of the waiters and demanded the wine list. We agree that a bottle of Greco di Tufo will make an acceptable start.

'This is on me.' She taps the menu. 'The more I think about you and Portsmouth, the guiltier I feel about not lending a hand.'

'It doesn't matter. There's nothing you could have done. We were lucky. Money will buy you anything, as long as it doesn't run out.'

'And did it?'

'Nearly. A bit. We were lucky. H pulled through, or so we thought at the time.'

'And now?'

'Now H is probably sicker, but in a different way. Covid never leaves some people alone, and H is one of them.'

I hold her gaze. Rosa always wants the full story, no edits, and so I take her through our weeks in that hideous flat overlooking the empty spaces of Southsea Common. H had lost a very good friend to Covid only days before he developed symptoms himself. He'd watched a video of a corrupt cop who helped H make his fortune saying his goodbyes to his wife on Facetime, and the experience had shaken him to the core. No way was he following Fat-Dave Munroe into the Pompey ICU, and it fell to me and Tony Morse, my all-time favourite lawyer, to sort out private provision. The weight of nursing care was enormous, as were the sums involved, but we thought at the time that H had sent the virus packing, for which we were all grateful. Other stuff happened too but given H's profile in the city I'm guessing that was inevitable. You don't blag millions out of the cocaine biz without making an enemy or two and one of them decided to settle his account with Pompey's legendary drug lord. In the end it was Malo who was hurt, and not his wayward father, but that – as they say in showbiz – is another story.

'And you wrote a book. Am I right?'

'I did. *Curtain Call.* There's a launch in the offing. Late summer? Might you be free?'

Rosa nods. She wants to know about serialization rights, about screen potential.

'This book's about you, my precious? *Roman-à-clef?* Have I got that right?'

'Sort of. I needed to sort out my tussle with the Grim Reaper. All the dramas with the tumour. Breaking up with Berndt. Finding out about Malo's real dad. Getting involved with the media guys and all the Brexit nonsense. Ending up shipwrecked on the Isle of Wight. Never a dull moment? If only . . .'

'A confession.' Rosa's hand has settled over mine, another flagrant breach of Covid etiquette. 'Truth is, I cadged a bound proof from your publisher, and I have someone sensational in mind for the lead role. Might you be up for it?'

I shake my head. Dark moments have come and gone over the last five years, far too many for my own comfort, and the last place I want to take this promising evening is back to any kind of retrospective. Rosa and I have always belonged to somewhere much sunnier, and I want to keep it that way.

'You're serious?' She's disappointed. 'It's a great read. You should be proud of yourself. Proud first, and then rich, and then even more famous, and then richer still. I can think of three producers who'd die for a sniff at it, and that's just in the Beeb. I mean it, Enora. All you have to say is yes.' A winning smile.

Rosa very rarely calls me by my Christian name. This is a sign that she means business. Literally.

'Later,' I say. 'Maybe tomorrow on the phone. Tonight, we get drunk. Tonight, you tell me why you haven't got an office any more. How's Kurt, by the way?'

Mention of Rosa's husband has the desired effect. Suddenly we've abandoned *Curtain Call* for something much closer to home.

'He's in Hamburg. His papa succumbed ten days ago. His poor mother's in pieces.'

'Covid?'

'Of course. Does anything else ever kill you these days?'

I think briefly of the shrunken tumour in my brain and then tell her how sorry I am.

'So how is he?' I ask. 'Kurt?'

'Bored, if you want the truth. I've always had the impression he never really got on with his dad, and I think it's the same with the Fatherland. He once told me that Germany was a bad habit he was lucky enough to shake off and now he's back in the belly of the beast, writing helpful notes for the local pastor's eulogy. Hamburg's thick with virus and they're in trouble with vaccine supplies. To be frank, it sounds gloomy. Germany's on the amber list, thank God, so I'm spared the funeral.'

'And Kurt?'

'He'll have to be there. Deep down he's a good German. Orders are orders.'

'I meant quarantine. On the way back.'

'A week or so of inappropriate movies in some desperate hotel. He'll be rampant for weeks afterwards. I might have to move out until he calms down. Oh look, look!'

Something out in the rain has attracted Rosa's attention. I peer through the window, following her pointing finger. All I can see is the huge spikey Dutch cap that is the O2 centre. In the murk, one shade of grey blurs into another.

'No, *there* . . .'

At last, I get it. Cable cars hang from wires suspended between two enormous pylons. Most of the cars appear to be empty.

'That was Bo-Jo's doing.' Rosa has spotted the waiter approaching with our bottle of Di Tufo. 'Lovely man.'

'The waiter?'

'Johnson. I've met him a couple of times. He gets a bad press. He's charm on legs.'

Boris Johnson? Charm on legs? All I can think about are those sausage fingers stabbing out across the despatch box when Starmer has got under his skin. Until the last three months I've never bothered with Prime Minister's Questions in the House of Commons but these ritual weekly exchanges are the one piece of television guaranteed to keep H's attention, and he insists on us watching them together. Something about Johnson puts a smile on his face, though I've still to work out what.

The waiter, young, English, and far too cool for his own good, is wrestling with the corkscrew. Rosa sends him away for a couple of menus and finishes the job herself. The cable cars are closer now, black silhouettes against the rumpled grey duvet that should be a summer's evening.

'The locals call it The Dangleway.' Rosa's pouring the wine. 'A lot of people think it's pointless but that's Johnson's *schtick.* Everything he does defies gravity. He's a born meddler but his dreams and schemes have the lightness of air. They amount to nothing. He gets other people to pay for them, one day an airline, the next day a steel billionaire, and when it all goes wrong there's never any sign of him. Whisper it quietly, but I think the man's a genius.'

I raise an eyebrow but Rosa hasn't finished. She passes me a glass and beckons me closer. Last week, she says, she got a call from a client. Like everyone else Rosa represents, this actress has been starved of work, and therefore money, but thanks to lockdown she's had the time and the incentive to write a book.

'About what?'

'A love affair.'

'With whom?

'A top politician.'

'We're talking Johnson again?'

'She says not. Most of the time, she calls him Mr Big. We gather that's some kind of compliment. The working title is *My Place or Yours?* Are you getting the picture here?'

'They're having a scene?'

'So she wants us to believe. She says they bonded over her take on some Shakespeare play or other. Apparently he adores private performances, especially in the early evening after work. She says he knows his Shakespeare inside out, and apparently he's unforgettable in the sack.'

'And she can prove all this? You believe her?'

'Not entirely, no. I suspect it's much more complex than that.'

'Complex how?'

'I think she mixes in bad company.'

'Criminals?'

'Russians. Probably the same thing. Either way her money troubles seem to have vanished for the time being, and she hasn't been near a publisher. Russians have the serious wealth in this city, and they can be very playful.'

'But the book?'

'Hard to put down. In fact, impossible to put down. She's written stuff before, good stuff. She can capture a voice, and she's got a certain kind of politician pitch-perfect. The way he speaks. How physical he can be, how charming, all that. She can put us in the room with him. We're there.'

'Watching them at it?'

'That, too. In fact, lots of that. And if I was Mr Big, I'd demand a second edition, and a third, and limitless fucking reprints down the line. The way she tells it, her lockdown shag is a god between the sheets.'

I'm toying with my glass. Something doesn't quite make sense here. Mr Big? An artful little swerve when it comes to the real name?

'She might be making the whole thing up,' I point out.

'She might.'

'Does that bother you?'

'Not really. It's a terrific read.' Rosa nods and takes a sip of the wine. Di Tufo should be properly chilled, which this most definitely isn't, but something else has occurred to me.

'You're a theatrical agent. Showbiz, not books. So why is she giving the book to you?'

'She wanted an opinion.'

'And?'

'It's good, like I say. In fact, it's great.' She smiles and puts her hand over mine. 'But not as great as yours, my precious.'

We drink our way downriver, barely pausing for mouthfuls of what might once have been lasagne. With the wine done, it's starting to get dark. The young waiter has supplied us with paper place maps showing the course of the Thames as it wriggles out of London and makes for the sea. I'm staring at this ever-fatter little worm, trying to picture Rémy at the wheel of his precious yacht. Then it occurs to me that Rosa might hold a clue or two about what's really going on. When I casually mention his name, she nods at once.

'I gather you saw him this morning,' she says.

'How do you know?'

'He phoned me. *Exocet*? Have I got that right?'

'You have.'

'And?'

'Tosh. Tripe. And the saddest thing is, he didn't seem to realize it.'

Rosa nods, says nothing. Then she catches the young waiter's eye and signals for a second bottle, Merlot this time. When he points out that we'll be docking in half an hour, she shrugs.

'Is that your problem, or ours? Just bring the bottle and a corkscrew. We'll take home whatever's left.'

The waiter disappears. One or two of the other diners are asleep, slumped on their banquettes, but once again, Rosa is keen to keep the conversation to ourselves.

'I'm best buddies with Rémy's agent,' she murmurs. 'You probably didn't know that. Wonderful man. Half Algerian, proper Arab stock, rare in our circles, even these days. His name is Habeeb. His friends call him Bee-Bee.'

I nod. I've heard Rémy mention the name but never realized the connection. That Rémy should chose someone from the Maghreb to represent his professional interests is entirely in character.

'And?'

'I talked to him last week. One of his clients is a wonderful French stage actress who's desperate for profile in the West End. I said I'd do my best, put the word round, then we fell to talking about Rémy.'

'His idea? Yours?'

'His. We have to cut to the chase here because a lot of what he said was confidential and I have to respect that, but the thrust of the conversation was pretty plain.'

'Rémy's in trouble?'

'Yes.'

'We're talking narcotics?'

'Yes.' She smiles, a gesture of applause. 'How did you know?'

'I guessed. We were together for a couple of hours this morning. He lied to me when he didn't have to and then the lie fell apart.' I'm watching the waiter return with the new bottle. Rosa settles the bill, and I wait until the youth has gone.

'What kind of drugs?'

'Guess,' Rosa says. 'Think H.'

'Cocaine?'

'Of course. And sizable quantities of North African *kif*.'

'Rémy is shipping this stuff in his own yacht?'

'I'm afraid I can't tell you.'

'But why is he doing it? Why get involved in the first place?'

'Because he needs the money. Or at least he thinks he does. Which I'm guessing is probably the same thing.' Rosa is toying with the corkscrew. Finally, when I shake my head, she slips the bottle into her bag. 'We all have fantasies. Mine happens to be Johnson, which is deeply disturbing. Rémy's taken Route One, which may turn out to be a better call. Either way . . .' She stifles a yawn. 'I'm blaming Covid.'

It's nearly midnight by the time I make it back to Holland Park. I settle on the sofa, too tired and too depressed to shed my sodden raincoat, wondering where this strange, strange period in all our lives will take Rémy next. At length, I spot the message waiting for me on the answerphone. I'm right. It comes from Evelyn. Her voice is light, barely a whisper, and I have to rerun the message three times before I can be absolutely certain what she's telling me.

'I've been watching H very carefully,' she's saying. 'And in my opinion it's more than Covid. Your H has dementia. Horrible news, I know, but there it is.'

FOUR

Dementia.

The word, the very *idea*, haunts me throughout the night. Dementia means letting go. Dementia means surrendering to some strange extra-terrestrial force that steals the you that you've always taken for granted and leaves the rest beached, something beige and poorly folded that you fail to recognize, the discarded cardigan that will be the rest of your life. The old H would answer the door to dementia and laugh in its face. The old H would take it aside for a cautionary word or two and send it packing.

By the time I'm properly awake, a grey dawn has washed across West London, and I can hear the patter of yet more rain at the window. I lie still, trying to drive the D word out of my teeming brain, then I realize that there's another noise, as well, that I'm listening to, someone moving around next door. I think I can make out footsteps on the lounge carpet, then a whisper of curtains being drawn. I do nothing for a moment or two, wondering whether I'm still asleep, then comes a movement as the door opens and a face appears. Malo. My lovely son.

'I woke you up?'

'No. Yes. I don't know.' I peer at my bedside clock. 'It's not six yet. What on earth are you doing?'

'I had to go to a warehouse place out in Essex. Picked up a bunch of Chinese stuff. You should see the back of the van.' He laughs. 'I'm Noodle Man.'

The Trussell Trust, it seems, has put him in charge of replenishing food banks across London. A Chinese entrepreneur, he says, has contributed massive stocks of everything from sacks of rice to boxes of fish sauce. The recent stranding of a huge container ship in the Suez Canal has messed up the delivery schedules and the Chinese management need to clear space for a delayed flood of incoming stuff. En route back to West London, he's called in to check the post.

This is far too much detail so early in the morning but it's nice to see Malo so cheerful. I struggle into a dressing gown and put the kettle on. Should I share Evelyn's news about H? I suspect not.

'How's Clemmie?'

'Brilliant. She had a scan yesterday. There's a little me in there. Amazing.'

'It's a boy?'

'Hard to say. Huge head. Cute little feet. Funny that. What a way to start your life.'

For a while now, I've been wondering how Malo and Clemmie are making ends meet. Clemmie used to work for a courier company, but lockdown killed most of the business and in any case pregnancy has made her cautious about wresting her precious Harley-Davidson out of the garage. Malo, of course, is still working full-time for the trust but only recently have they begun to pay him, and even now he's only getting minimum wage. So how are they meeting the mortgage payments?

'Mateo,' he says. 'Since he came out of hospital, he can't do enough for us. He's started a trust fund for the baby, and he's bunging Clem two grand a month. Food's never been a problem because there's always fresh veg left over at the end of the day at the trust, but it's nice to have a buffer.'

Mateo is Clemmie's father, a Colombian businessman, fabulously rich and seriously charming. He contracted Covid last year when we were all down in Portsmouth, and it put him in hospital for nearly three weeks.

Malo, as I expected, wants to know about H. He phones occasionally but he doesn't trust anything his dad says.

'Very wise. He's still low. Aches, pains, fatigue, always out of breath. Some mornings he can barely make it out of the front door.'

'But he copes, right?' Malo taps his head. 'In here?'

'He does his best but I think he's in denial and, if I'm honest, I don't blame him.'

Malo shoots me a look. He's always regarded H as a super god, a figure of awe, and one of the things I realized when we were all banged up down in Portsmouth was the importance of this myth. Malo needs to believe that his dad is immortal, and the battle he put up against the virus seemed to prove it. But appearances lie, and after Evelyn's little bombshell I suspect H is in deep, deep trouble.

'I'm thinking about power of attorney,' I say lightly.

'You mean for Dad?'

'Yes. Just now he's not thinking straight. He calls it brain fog. There's still a pile of cash left over from last year but that won't last for ever and there doesn't seem to be much movement on the other issue.'

The other issue is code for a series of woeful business decisions H has made over the last few years. One of them, a bid to start a business offering cut-price insurance for oldies fit and daft enough to tackle extreme sports, quickly collapsed under a flood of expensive claims. Malo is aware of all this but his attention span is even briefer than his father's, and just now he can only think about the baby.

'Technically, your dad is already bankrupt,' I explain. 'We may need to take steps to protect him.'

'How?'

'I'm not quite sure, and that's rather the point. Power of attorney would give me access to the right advice. Otherwise, everything will have to go through H, and just now this stuff is beyond him.'

'Then do it, yeah?' He checks his watch, and then gives me a brief peck on the cheek. Moments later, his tea untouched, he's gone.

I settle on the sofa, which is still damp from my raincoat. I'm wondering whether to go back to bed but in the meantime, I'm nursing my favourite mug, an end-of-shoot present from Rémy after we'd done the last takes on a long-ago series called *Trahison*. I very badly want to stop thinking about H, and the traffic jam of challenges that so obviously lie down the road, and so I try to imagine Rémy at sea in his precious yacht, somewhere in mid-Channel, yet another of Covid's castaways. If I'm to believe Rosa, he's abandoned what he does best – better than any other director I've ever worked with – for a walk-on part in a movie for which he's seriously ill-equipped. *Exocet* was a career suicide note but even the implausible Honore offers more promise than trying to score an easy win in today's drugs biz. Rémy, for all his undoubted talent, will be meat in the fat gangster sandwich. I know I have to do something but, to be frank, I haven't a clue what.

It's half past seven by the time I lift the phone. Dessie Wren is a big, bluff, interesting ex-submariner I met down in Portsmouth last year. He joined the police after leaving the Navy and strictly speaking his CID days are over, but he has a wealth of intelligence experience – much of it in the drugs field – and a career-long commitment to putting H behind bars. That never happened, and last year I discovered other surprises in their long relationship, but during that first lockdown Dessie looked after my best interests when I was desperate for help, and I know – to put it bluntly – that he'd very much like for us to stay friends. He lives alone. He has a young son he doesn't see as much as he should. And we make each other laugh. Three reasons why he might mark my card about Rémy.

When he finally answers, I know I've woken him up.

'No problem,' he says as I start to apologize. 'It's very good to hear you. How can I help?'

This is vintage Dessie. No messing. No small talk. Cut to the chase. I ask him how much he knows about drugs stuff beyond his immediate patch. Dessie's based in Hampshire.

'Where are you thinking?'

'Newhaven.'

'Why?'

I hesitate for a moment, then tell him enough about Rémy for him to get the drift.

'This guy's important to you?'

'He's the best director I've ever worked with. He's a close friend, too, and he's never let me down.' I pause. 'So why Newhaven?'

'Good question. You'll know the M25. There's a services place at Cobham. The food's crap but I'll buy you lunch. Twelve OK? We might need to beat the rush.' He laughs, then asks me to bring a photo of Rémy, and if possible the yacht. 'Midday,' he says again. 'The safest option is the noodle bar.'

The conversation over, I finish the tea, and then browse my

phone for location souvenirs that might feature Rémy. I have nothing recent but there's a particularly lovely shot of the pair of us sharing a booth at the main exhibition hall in Cannes. A younger Rémy, heavily bearded, has his arm round me and we're both gurning for the camera. Rémy had just got word that he was in the running for Best Director, and the bottle of Krug on the table is empty.

I tag the photo and despatch it to Dessie. 'I'm the one without the beard,' I add. 'In case you've forgotten what I look like.'

I leave London in mid-morning. Traffic is clogging the M25 once again, which is supposed to be a sign of the economy back on its feet, and it's two minutes past twelve by the time I've got to the services at Cobham. Dessie is on his feet the moment I step into the seating area closest to the Chozen Noodle Bar. He was far from lean last year, but he seems to have put on a few extra pounds. The weight suits him. In his baggy jeans and battered leather jacket he has a physical presence which most women, including me, find oddly reassuring. It speaks of someone who knows his way around, someone undaunted by life's sharper corners. The French call it *calme,* and Rémy used to have it too.

'You look great.' Dessie takes off his aviator sunglasses and gives me a generous hug.

'Never trust appearances. Where did you get that tan?'

'Gibraltar.'

'Abroad is illegal. In your trade you're supposed to know that.'

'Green list, your honour. Two Covid PCR tests, both negative.'

'And Gibraltar? Business or pleasure?'

'Business *is* pleasure, otherwise you're in the wrong job.' He escorts me to the noodle bar. 'Time is short, I'm afraid. And that's not an excuse.'

This, I assume, is a clue that he's back in harness with the police on one of those short-term civilian contracts they've started to use, an arrangement that makes perfect sense for someone with Dessie's experience. For whatever reason he's put the sunglasses back on again and now he buys me red Thai veggies with noodles, with a modest bowl of salmon rice soup for himself.

'Less is more? Are you trying to impress me?' We've settled at the table again. To my slight surprise, the glasses suit him.

'Always.' He plainly has no time for small talk. 'Tell me about your friend.'

I describe meeting Rémy again, how crap his pitch was, and then the nonsense he told me about shipping out from Boulogne.

'Why would he do that?'

'I've no idea, but I'm suspecting drugs. He's never lied to me before. That's not the way we were. Like I say, he seemed different. Maybe out of his depth. This is speculation. I simply don't know.'

'But he obviously matters to you.' Dessie has his phone out and is studying the Cannes shot again.

'Of course he matters. And the answer is no, if that's what's on your mind.'

'Never?'

'Not once.' I'm trying to be stern. 'Sometimes in life, Mr Detective, there are more important things, believe it or not.'

'Really?'

'Really. What can you tell me about Newhaven? Am I right to be worried?'

'Alas, yes. A lot of gear comes in off the ferry from Dieppe. It's not my patch but I'd guess major importations every week. I can think of a number of interviews where we've ended up talking about Newhaven.'

'Gear?'

'Good quality cannabis, most of it Moroccan. Plus serious quantities of cocaine, the bulk shipped across from Aruba. Your friend should be thinking private yachts from the Caribbean putting into tiny coves in Galicia. Sealed kilo blocks end up in the backs of trucks before they head north to Dieppe.'

I nod. This makes sense. A couple of years ago I was foolish enough to open my heart to a property developer down in Exmouth. He turned out to be a major player in the drugs biz, exclusively cocaine, and that was another story that didn't end well.

'You can make an enquiry or two?' My veggies are better than I expected.

'I can try. When did he leave Newhaven?'

'The day before yesterday. In the evening.'

'How long was he there?'

'I don't know. He didn't say.'

Dessie nods, says nothing. I get the impression he doesn't believe me, but when I ask, he changes the subject.

'How's H?'

'Terrible.' I tell him about Long Covid. H, like the rest of us, thought he was cured but nearly a year later the virus won't leave him alone.

'That must be tricky.'

'For H?'

'For you.'

'You're right. It's remorseless. There are moments when you think it might be over, mornings when he wakes up with a smile on his face and doesn't need help getting dressed, but those moments are getting rarer. It's a bit of a nightmare, to be honest, and it never seems to end.'

Dessie nods and mops the last of his soup with a curl of bread roll.

'You're still at Flixcombe, have I got that right?'

'You have.'

'I might drive down once I've put something together. Cheer the old bastard up. Would that be in order?'

'Of course. I'll warn him to expect you. Best bib and tucker.'

Dessie holds my gaze for a moment, a smile playing on his lips, then gets to his feet, taps his watch, makes his excuses and leaves.

Best bib and tucker. Back on the M25, every lane choked with traffic, I realize the impact Evelyn's brief message has made on me. Consciously or otherwise, I'm already making adjustments to the H I expect to find on my return to West Dorset. Someone slipping his moorings. Someone perhaps already adrift. Someone who might one day end up in a wheelchair,

hair neatly combed, fingernails trimmed, tie carefully knotted, best bib and tucker. The thought appals me, and only a klaxon blast from the truck behind returns my full attention to the road.

Another message from Evelyn is waiting for me when I get back to the flat. This time it's longer and much easier to follow. H, she says, has become a bit of a handful. At three in the morning, he was beating on her bedroom door, apparently in the belief that I was inside. Thankfully, she'd locked it, and in the end he gave up. She knows it's unforgiveable to be this much of a wimp but if there was any possibility of finding myself back at Flixcombe sooner rather than later, I'd have her undying gratitude.

'Maybe we should do this thing together,' she says at the end of the message. 'Maybe there's safety in numbers.'

She's right, of course, and for some reason her message puts a smile on my face. The old H, the old curmudgeon, the volcanic presence in all our lives, is familiar territory. That, at least, I can cope with.

FIVE

Evelyn's plaintive message leaves me no option but to hit the road again. I stuff a handful of clean clothes into my bag and depart before West London has a chance to clear its throat and spit out the beginnings of the rush hour. This works fine but the worm that is H, and dementia, is eating away at me, and I badly need to talk to someone I can trust. Past Stonehenge, I pull off the road to make the call. Mitch Culligan is an investigative journalist I've known for years, and I count him as a friend. He dresses like a tramp, and carries far too much weight, but that doesn't matter. More importantly, he smells corruption everywhere and has a particular loathing for the Tories. He's also fearless, and in conversation I've always admired the way he cuts to the chase.

'How are you?' he says.

'Not great.'

'You want to talk about it?'

'Only if you want to listen.'

Mitch knows about last year down in Portsmouth because we talked on the phone around Christmas time. What he doesn't know about are the latest developments at Flixcombe.

'H may have dementia,' I say carefully.

'That's bad shit. H? Losing his marbles? I wouldn't wish that on anyone. Even him.'

H and Mitch have history. One night way back, aboard an ancient Brixham trawler in the middle of the English Channel, H was minded to throw him overboard. A party of us were returning from France and Mitch had smuggled himself aboard to continue an awkward conversation he and H had started months earlier. The scene played itself out and the fact that Mitch wasn't the least bit intimidated by the threats of violence stayed H's hand. H has always had a soft spot for people who stand up to him, but that cuts no ice with Mitch, who will always regard H as a thug.

'What goes round, comes round,' he says. 'So who does the looking after?'

'I'm guessing me. At least for now and probably forever.'

'Have you come across this before? Early-onset dementia? Alzheimer's?'

'Never.'

'It's seriously weird. I shouldn't be telling you this but you're watching someone disintegrate in front of your eyes. Think onion. Think skins. Layer after layer peels away until what's left bears no resemblance to anyone you've ever met before.'

'Nicely put. How's Sayid?'

'Busy as hell. He's got a proper job now with the NHS. Mainly dealing with dementia.'

Sayid is Mitch's long-term partner, a beguiling, slightly built Syrian refugee who'd once been one of Syria's most promising gerontologists. He and Mitch share a lovely house in Hither Green, where Sayid used to bake some of the most delicate cakes I've ever tasted. Back in the day, as a warning to Mitch, H had him ambushed and badly beaten up, another reason why Mitch will never forgive him.

'Tell me about my options,' I murmur. 'Cheer me up.'

'Specialist care. It costs the earth but it softens the landing. My old mum got the D word. I blamed it on the sherry to begin with but then Sayid took a good look at her and told me she was losing her wits. I found a nursing home out in the country, sold her house, and most of the winnings bought the couple of years Sayid thought she had left. The rest we invested in Tio Pepe. She was a gifted liar, which was the other thing that kept her going. When her mind went blank, which it did most of the time, she just made it all up. If you were looking for a plot line, there wasn't one, but I think she died happy.'

'Lovely. Any other tips?'

'Yeah. Buy H a rail ticket to Zurich. Last time I checked, Dignitas were charging a baseline seven thousand five hundred Swiss francs for an assisted death. That's nearly six grand and it doesn't include funeral arrangements or VAT. If you're ever tempted, it might pay to check the exchange rates before booking.'

Dignitas is a Swiss organization that will relieve you of the chore of committing suicide. With euthanasia still illegal, they do a brisk trade in Brits at the end of their tether.

I thank Mitch for the thought and make a mental note to resist bothering their website. The thought of H succumbing to a cocktail of lethal drugs is wildly implausible, no matter how gone he might be, and I – for one – wouldn't have it. But then another thought occurs to me.

'How come you know so much about Dignitas?' I ask Mitch.

There's a longish silence on the line, then I hear him laughing.

'I wanted to check whether they sell gift tokens,' he says. 'I was going to send a bunch to this fucking government.'

I get to the Flixcombe gates in time for one of Evelyn's cream teas, and turn into the drive. This slow reveal through a succession of carefully sited trees is the perfect *hors d'oeuvre* to the banquet that is H's pride and joy. I must have driven this winding avenue umpteen times over the past year, but the views of the house have never failed to enchant me. The way the perfect Georgian proportions sit in the enfolding landscape. The glint of late-afternoon sunlight on the tall windows. The peacock Andy bought for Jess's last birthday, strutting madly around Andy's newly dug pond.

I spot Andy riding H's motor mower along the strip of grass that edges the drive. He and his partner Jess occupy a cottage on the estate. They're both Pompey, both devoted to H, and without them my life would be near impossible. I slow, and then stop beside him. I've been away less than forty-eight hours, but it feels like half a lifetime.

'How is he?' I ask. H needs no introduction.

'Mad as a frog. You shouldn't have gone. He thinks you're never coming back. I've told him he's out of his head but I'm wasting my breath.'

'My fault, then?'

'Of course. Jess agrees he's much livelier though, which makes a nice change.'

'Is Evelyn coping?'

'Not really. I think H frightens her. In fact, I know he does. Did she tell you about last night?'

'She did. She left a message on the phone. Very graphic.'

'I'm not surprised. He was raving, proper mad. Any more of that and we'll have to tie him down and give him a good spanking.'

I eye Andy for a long moment, wondering whether Evelyn has shared her diagnosis with him, and it's almost a relief to realize she hasn't. I gesture Andy a little closer and reach out to give his shoulder a little squeeze.

'A spanking might do the trick,' I tell him. 'Nice idea.'

I find Evelyn in the kitchen. I can't be certain, but I think she's been crying.

'What's the matter?'

'Look.' She gestures wordlessly at the open kitchen door. H is standing in the middle of the herb garden, his back turned to the kitchen. He's wearing a dressing gown of mine. An empty saucepan dangles from one hand and he appears to be urinating on to something bubbly and white scattered over a stand of mint.

'What on earth's all that about?'

'It's my scone mix. He appeared from nowhere a couple of minutes ago and grabbed it off the stove. I suspect it's some kind of punishment.'

'For who?'

'Me.'

'For what?'

'For not being you.'

She tips her head back and blows her nose on a sheet of kitchen roll before succumbing to a long hug. Evelyn has been a pillar in my life for more years than I care to remember. When she occupied the next-door flat in Holland Park, I could always count on her for support during the collapse of my marriage. Even when times got really difficult – Bernt, the tumour, our wayward son – she never gave up on either me or Malo and the knowledge that her door was ever-open was the one thing that kept me going. As a gifted editor, she scaled the heights of the London publishing world, and her recent retirement to Budleigh Salterton, home to a much-respected literary festival, prompted an entire evening dedicated to her stewardship of countless A-list authors. Now, it's my turn to offer comfort and all I can muster is the word sorry. Sorry for inviting her over. Sorry for leaving her with H. Sorry for exposing her to a scene like this.

'It's not your fault.' Her eyes are shiny. 'Don't blame yourself.'

I hold her gaze for a moment longer, and then step into the garden. H hasn't moved, hasn't turned round, but I know he's heard my voice. I stand behind him, tell him to make himself respectable. For a moment or two, he says nothing. Then he clears his throat.

'What kept you?' he grunts. 'I've been out here all fucking day.'

SIX

H is sulking. I can find no other word for it. I've taken him back to his bedroom. I've told him he's a disgrace. I've even threatened to get back in my car and drive away. For ever. None of this has made the slightest difference. On the contrary, he's slotted his favourite DVD into the player at the foot of his bed and stretched out on the rumpled counterpane, seemingly exhausted. He has the indoor look, thin and pasty after days of insistent rain, and he hasn't bothered to shave since my departure for London. He's still wearing my dressing gown, his bony ankles sticking out, and he ignores me as I circle the room, tidying up the litter of clothes on the floor. He must have watched *The Battle of Britain* a trillion times.

'We win, H, before extra time.' I nod at the screen. 'No need for penalties.'

He ignores my little joke and I settle briefly on the bed for what I imagine might be a chat but he waves me away. This flutter of his thin hand has a slightly imperious feel which, once again, I interpret as a good sign. The old H, back in charge.

Downstairs, Evelyn is debating whether or not to make a fresh start on her scone mix. I tell her that it's unnecessary, that the hour has come and gone, that this evening we'll all settle down and have supper together, and that I'll cook, and that she can have a stiffish gin, maybe two, and that everything will be absolutely fine. I can tell at once that she doesn't believe me, that a couple of days of H have taken her to a place she never wants to revisit, and that my current responsibility is to make her final evening at Flixcombe a pleasure.

No problem. Except I need to find out why she thinks Malo's father is losing his wits.

'You used the word dementia,' I say carefully, 'when you left that message.'

'I did.'

'Why?'

She flinches, and I know at once that I've been over-blunt. This is my ex-neighbour from the apartment block in Holland Park. This is a woman to whom I owe a huge debt of gratitude. She's frightened enough already. Don't make it worse.

'Please . . .' I cover her hand with mine. 'I just need a steer.'

'About dementia?'

'And H, yes.'

'I'm not a doctor. Maybe you should be talking to someone who really knows.'

'But there has to be a reason, surely, why you used the word. Words matter . . .' I force a smile. 'Don't they?'

Of course they do. Evelyn built her entire career on the power of language and she acknowledges the cliché with the faintest smile.

'He's upstairs?' She's eyeing the door.

'He is, and that's where he'll be staying for a while. We're safe down here. Just give me a clue or two.'

She nods, still uncertain, then she starts to tell me about something called the Now and Then Café back in Budleigh Salterton. She found out about it from an article in the local paper and popped down to take a look. It's run by a tiny bunch of fabulous people, she says, and they meet for a couple of hours every fortnight.

'The Now and Then Café? It's a great phrase.'

'Exactly. That's what took my fancy in the first place.' She taps her head. 'If you think you've got a problem up here, or maybe someone else has noticed something changing, it can definitely help. It's a bit off-putting to begin with. In fact, the first time I went along it felt like being in a *crèche.* There's lots of kids' books, lots of big smiley faces, big fluffy clouds, rainbows, even an abacus, but there's no sense of threat, nothing judgemental. It's a bit like AA. The big thing is to admit you're not quite as sharp as you were. That's a kindness, of course. Many of these folk have dementia or Alzheimer's, and they tend to be medical referrals. But once you realize you're all in the same boat, it really seems to make a difference. Dementia cuts you off. The Now and Then Café is there to put you back in touch. The whole thing's really about memory, and it certainly helps.'

I nod. I'm getting the picture. The Now and Then Café's latest volunteer will have absorbed a great deal about dementia's hidden secrets.

'You think H fits the picture?'

'I do, yes. I'm not sure you'd ever get him to a place like that but I'm afraid he's got all the signs.'

'Like?'

A frown clouds her face. She knows H is important to me and she wants to do this moment justice.

'It was his eyes first,' she says at last. 'One moment you can see him concentrating really, really hard. Then it's gone, just switched off, nothing there, a total void. I've seen it countless times at the café. Then a couple of days back, after you'd gone, I found him in the hall. He'd just put his coat on, and he was standing there, utterly bewildered.'

'Why?'

'He couldn't remember what he was supposed to do next.'

'You mean where to go?'

'I mean what to do. He couldn't remember putting the coat on. He hadn't any idea when it had happened – passive tense – or even why. I could see that it frightened him, this not knowing.'

'So what happened?'

'I made him a cup of tea in the kitchen. We had a little chat.'

'He still had the coat on?'

'Yes. When I suggested he took it off, he just ignored me. In fact, he wore it for the rest of the afternoon, sitting in that wicker chair he likes in the corner of the kitchen. But that wasn't the point. There was something else, too.'

'We're still in the kitchen?'

'Yes. Still here. He was staring at the fridge. He couldn't take his eyes off it. Then he pointed.'

'At the fridge?'

'Yes. I asked him what was wrong and he said nothing. All he wanted to know was where it led.'

'*Led?*'

'Yes. He thought it was a door. He thought it opened to some corridor or other. When I showed him it didn't, he just shook his head, as if he'd never had the thought in the first place.'

This is troubling. I press Evelyn a little further, wanting more of those tiny vignettes which can tell us a great deal more than any formal medical prognosis, and after some thought she nods. That same night, she says, she'd seen him up to bed.

'He'd lost it, Enora, completely lost it. He didn't know where he was, who he was, who I might be, or what to expect next. I remember him halfway up that first flight of stairs, just where he'd hung that portrait he had commissioned.'

'Of me, you mean?'

'Yes. It's rather lovely, if I may say so. I've no idea how well you knew the artist but he's captured you completely, not just the obvious stuff on the outside but the inside, too.'

Evelyn's right. The artist was a woman called Austral and I'd never met her before in my life, but she'd seen most of my better films and I like to think she'd drawn the appropriate conclusions about what makes me tick. In any event, we gelled through the three long sessions and we still meet for the occasional drink and catch-up. My grander thespy friends liked the portrait a lot and Austral has been a busy girl ever since.

'And H?' I enquire.

'He was looking at the painting. He seemed to be hunting for a name to put to the face, and I sensed . . . I don't know . . . a little wistfulness as well. I was still in the hall at the foot of the stairs and I remember him glancing down at me and shaking his head. He wanted to know how much time he had left. And he wanted, as well, to know what had happened to the rest of it. I don't know why, but I found that intensely moving. Later, of course, he got completely out of hand but if there's one word that applies to all these good folk it's bewilderment. They don't know what's happening to the insides of their heads, and that frightens them.' She nods. 'Even H.'

Picturing H on the stairs in front of my portrait, I'm starting to believe Evelyn. H really is losing his mind, a process that

Covid – in a rare display of goodwill – has done its best to camouflage. While we were all looking the other way, and worrying about chronic fatigue, and brain fog, and still not being able to breathe properly, the neural circuits in H's failing brain were beginning to self-destruct. I happen to know a lot about all those trillions of cells, largely because some of them betrayed me and stealthily grew into a tumour, and listening to my consultant before and after the key operation that undoubtedly saved my life, I began to fathom the darkness and mystery we all carry inside us. The brain is an enormous storehouse of memories. Those same memories, like the impressions we file away every waking minute, define who we are. But once those shelves are empty, there's nothing left. Whoever we thought we were, has stolen away.

I lie awake into the small hours, trying to read. Tomorrow, I shall be running Evelyn to the station at Yeovil Junction. By midday, *inshallah,* she'll be safe home in her Budleigh bungalow. It will be a comfort to know that she'll always be at the end of a phone line. I may even tap her up for more tips from her sessions at the Now and Then Café. But it's now beyond dispute that the immediate responsibility for Malo's broken father lies with me, which means that Flixcombe – at least for now – will become my home.

I abandon my much-thumbed copy of Rebecca West's *Black Lamb and Grey Falcon*, knowing that my long-promised trip to the Balkans won't be happening any time soon, and then I check my watch. By 01.56, H should be asleep.

One peek, I tell myself. H's bedroom door lies across the corridor. Last time I was in the south of France, I picked up a decent sketch of the harbour at Antibes where H and I first met. The sketch was done in chalks, heavy on the artfully smudged blues, and I had it re-framed before I bore it to deepest Flixcombe. It was H's decision to hang it beside his bedroom door, a small token – he told me at the time – of how life can take you by surprise. This was as close as H ever got to sentimentality, and it made me very glad that I'd bought the thing in the first place, but looking at it in the light from my open bedroom door, it's impossible not to be doubly moved. So much water. So many bridges. And now the news that Malo is also to become a father.

Very softly, I open H's bedroom door. To my surprise, his bedside light is also on. I stand immobile, not wanting to disturb him. The black-and-cream chequered rug, a present from Clemmie, still hangs over the end of the bed, and I recognize my own dressing gown, discarded once again on the threadbare carpet. For a moment or two I'm still thinking he's asleep, but then his eyes flicker open and he struggles upright, peering towards the door. I step into the room and approach the bed, thinking maybe we might have a chat, then I recognize the bewilderment Evelyn has already talked about.

He hasn't a clue who I am.

SEVEN

Next day I run Evelyn to Yeovil Junction and put her on the train. I know she's relieved to be away from H, but she has the grace not to labour the point. As we say goodbye, she puts a motherly hand on my arm and wishes me luck.

'Anything I can do,' she says, 'you only have to ask.'

We both know that's not true, but I give her a hug and tell her I'm truly grateful. Wherever this story goes next, she'll be the first to know.

'You mean that?'

'I do. The way through this is to pretend it's fiction. All I need is a prompt or two on the script.'

Tony Morse is a solicitor based in Portsmouth. He's known H since the years when cocaine brought him serious money, and it was often Tony's quiet advice that kept H one step ahead of the Major Crimes Team. He has a chaotic love life, an expensive litter of ex-wives, an exquisite taste in bespoke suits, and a deep appreciation for fine wine (mainly Bordeaux reds). Coupled with a sharp legal brain, this list of virtues makes him a wild anomaly in the grimness that is Portsmouth. We bonded on sight many years ago, and nothing's changed.

'Demented? You're serious?' I can tell Mr Morse is shocked, which is a very rare event.

I canter through yesterday's list of symptoms. Evelyn's story about the fridge makes him laugh.

'Friday nights after the second bottle,' he says. 'I know exactly how he feels.'

Tony, like Dessie Wren, is a busy man. Time is money, and while he's always been more than generous with yours truly, I never want to push my luck.

'I should have seen this coming,' I say, 'but somehow I didn't. Too close, too familiar, and you start missing the obvious. Just now, H can't find his way out of a room. Any kind of financial decision is beyond him which is why I'm thinking about power of attorney.'

Alas it isn't that simple, as Tony immediately points out. To become entrusted with someone else's money, you have to acquire that person's consent, and that person has to have – in Tony's phrase – 'full mental capacity'.

'But he hasn't,' I tell him. 'That's the whole point.'

'In which case we have to go a different route. There's something called the Court of Protection. It's cumbersome, and a pain in the arse, and should have been put to sleep years ago. It can also be wildly expensive. They appoint a deputy to ratify every decision you take, and it costs much more than it should. My darling, you should have nothing to do with it. Not yet, at any rate.'

'So what do I do?'

There's a brief silence. Last year, when H contracted Covid down in Pompey, it was Tony Morse who put me in touch with the private medical team who could keep him out of the ICU. It cost a small fortune, and Tony knows that H's reserves – securely hidden – are diminishing by the day. It was Tony's advice to keep that money in cash, and Jess has been guarding it with her life. Even I don't know where she's stashed it.

'So how much have you got left?'

'Seventy-eight thousand pounds. Jess had a count-up last week.'

'And how much are you getting through a month?'

'Less than you might imagine. Malo's not here for one thing, and I pay for myself. H eats like a sparrow these days, and we keep the heating off. For utilities and council tax Jess budgets eighteen hundred a month, and H has always paid them another three thousand for looking after the place. So five thousand a month might cover it.'

'Call it six,' Tony says. 'In fact, call it seven. Ten months down the line, H is skint.'

I nod. I can't think of anything to say. Tony Morse was always good with figures, but it's about to get worse.

'And the claims on the business?'

'Unresolved. H has refused to talk about it. I used to think he was in denial but now it's probably beyond him.'

'And the estate? I remember the price he paid back in the day. Two and a half million? Am I right?'

'Nearly. It was two million six five. That's a figure he never let me forget.'

'And today's market?'

'I've no idea. Prices are crazy round here. Maybe double it. Treble it. Whatever.' I shrug. The thrust of this conversation is suddenly beyond depressing. How can anyone put a price on the views? On the birdsong in the early morning? On the thick yolky spill of early sunshine over the hills to the east?

Even on the phone, Tony has always been able to read my mood – one of the many reasons women find him irresistible.

'Don't worry, my darling. Two things. Number one, get a couple of valuations. Number two, get someone you trust to take a proper look at H. This diagnosis could be wrong, in which case you still might qualify for LPA.'

'LPA?'

'Lasting power of attorney.'

'Meaning?'

'We could do something creative. Buy ourselves time. It's never over until it's over, *capisce*?'

You understand? Tony's back in his familiar world of smoke and mirrors, of delicious complicity, of canny masterstrokes which confuse the enemy and might keep our heads above water, and both these prospects please me immensely. He knows I'm pledged to *omertà,* the Mafia vow of silence. Nothing on paper. Nothing attributable.

'I love that brain of yours, Mr Morse,' I tell him. 'I'm here to do your bidding. Depend on it.'

'If only . . .' He's laughing now. 'Just keep me in the loop. *Si?*'

'*Si.*'

Moments later, he's gone, and I'm left alone at the kitchen table, watching the motes of dust dancing in the morning sunshine. I love the old house at moments like this, the way it creaks and adjusts as the warmth of the sun seeps into its ancient bones. It's been this way for centuries, I tell myself, and the least I owe H are my best efforts to keep it off the market.

I make myself a little breakfast. Of H, there's no sign. Mid-morning, I fire up my tablet and Google local estate agents. Two familiar chains, both of them upmarket, get a call and both are only too eager to attend for a valuation. The first will arrive tomorrow morning. The second wants to know whether outline planning position has been granted for any portion of the estate. When I enquire why he's asked the question, he chuckles.

'We need to talk,' he says.

'Gladly,' I reply, and we agree a date and time.

My second errand for Tony Morse is trickier. Prior to Covid, H has always been in rude health and while I know he's signed up to a medical practice in Bridport, I doubt he's ever troubled them. What I'm asking for feels deeply personal and I'm still scrolling aimlessly through various websites when I suddenly remember yesterday's conversation with Mitch Culligan. Mitch's partner is Sayid. Sayid is now working in the NHS as a gerontologist. Gerontologists, to the best of my knowledge, know all about the old. Sayid is one of the gentlest men I've ever met. It is, at the very least, worth a shot.

Mitch Culligan, when he finally answers my second call, can't believe it.

'You want Sayid to take a look at H?'

'I do, yes. He'd be perfect.'

'I'm sure you're right but that's not the issue. Has your memory gone, too? Have both of you lost your fucking marbles?'

Rather late in the day, I remember the evening when H had Sayid ambushed and beaten up. I visited the poor man in hospital afterwards. His face was sutured, his jaw was wired up, and he ate nothing but soup for nearly a month. This was meant to send a message to Mitch Culligan to abandon an investigation that involved H, and failed completely.

I apologize to Mitch, who is far from placated. Sayid, he points out, took a full year to properly recover. Why on earth would he now lift a finger to help out the guy who had him nearly killed?

'Because he's a lovely man,' I mutter. 'As you well know.'

It sounds pathetic, and it is. More to the point, it cuts no ice with Mitch. H, he says tersely, is a psycho and a thug. Just now he's being served his just desserts, a full helping, and he's deserved every bloody mouthful. This tirade goes on and on, Mitch at full throttle, but my attention has been drawn to a figure who's appeared in the walled garden.

It's H. I can see him through the kitchen window. He's wearing my dressing gown again, and he looks old, and shrunken, and altogether pitiful. Just now he's stooped over a bush of some kind. He has a pair of scissors in one hand and when he unbends, he's carrying a single rose. The rose is red, not yet in full bloom. He lifts it to his nose and then smiles to himself before tucking it behind his right ear. This little scene has an almost Shakespearean poignancy.

Mitch has finally run out of expletives. I'm still watching H as he drifts amongst a stand of gardenias.

'There's a story I came across the other day,' I say idly. 'Something I thought might interest you.'

'Like what?' Abrupt change of gear. Definite interest.

'Like a top politician in bed with an actress.'

'Anyone I might know?'

'The actress?'

'Very funny. She's named this guy?'

'No.'

'But?'

'You might like to make up your own mind. She has a written account. It's book length. She wants to go into print.'

'You're kidding.'

'I'm not. My best to Sayid. Is he still a veggie, by the way? I just need to know.'

EIGHT

Sharing news like this, of course, is unforgiveable. I haven't checked it out with Rosa, which is a hanging offence, but I don't care. I know which of Mitch Culligan's buttons to press, and the merest scent of a story like this will put him in my debt. He hates the Tories with a Jesuitical passion, and he has extra loathing for the clown who's led the latest coup. That the likes of Boris Johnson should find himself behind the prime ministerial desk is, in Mitch's view, evidence of a *coup d'état*. The ultras have seized power while the rest of us were looking the other way.

As expected, Mitch phones me back in the early afternoon. I've conjured up a little soup for H and installed him in a deckchair in his favourite corner of the kitchen garden. The veggies and the bed of herbs are flourishing in the blaze of sunshine and in the absence of a name H has settled for treating me as a member of the staff. He's still wearing the rose behind one ear, but already it's beginning to wilt.

Mitch needs more information. Evidently he's made some cautious enquiries and drawn a blank. This would put most journalists off, but Mitch is old school when it comes to nailing a story, and the fact that no one's heard of this phantom shag simply adds to the story's exclusivity.

'You wouldn't have a name, by any chance?' He's sounding almost plaintive.

'You mean the politician?'

'The actress.'

'I'm afraid not. Give me a day or two and I might be able to come up with something. In the meantime, it might help if Sayid paid us a visit. I was thinking of doing marrow stuffed with wild rice. Hints of ginger and chilli. How might that sound?'

Mitch has the grace to laugh. It turns out that he's just talked to Sayid on the phone. The pressure on NHS gerontologists just now, he says, is unprecedented but he managed to catch him on his lunch break.

'And what did he say?'

'The man's crazy, and far too nice for his own good. You're in luck, Ms Andressen. He's free tomorrow. We'll drive down.'

'We?'

'We. I've found Flixcombe on Google maps. We'll be there for lunch. You still owe me a name.'

Mitch rings off and when I check the kitchen garden again, H has disappeared. A brief search finds him spread-eagled on the front lawn, flat on his back, his face to the sun, my dressing gown thrown back. I stand over him for a moment or two, worrying about the weight that he's lost.

Broad in the chest and shoulders, H always had the stocky build of a weightlifter, ledges of muscle at the base of his neck, but Covid has stolen everything he possessed in the way of sheer physical presence and now he looks frail and old. I shake my head, careful not to disturb him, and then steal away. At the back of my mind, there survives the belief that tonight, just the two of us, we might take advantage of a decent meal, something involving fillet steak, and a glass or two of red to go with it, and that afterwards we might have a proper chat, but the more I see of him, the more certain I become that Evelyn's probably right. H has slipped his moorings. He's no longer available for conversations.

My next call finds Rosa at her borrowed desk. Before I have a chance to broach *My Place or Yours?* she has good news for me.

'I got a call from Bee-Bee this morning,' she says. 'Bee-Bee? Rémy's lovely agent?'

'Ah . . .' For a moment I was lost. 'And?'

'Rémy's been in touch. He has another property he needs to discuss.'

'With who?'

'You, my treasure, but Bee-Bee's playing the canny agent. To be honest, I got a bit lost on the details but it seems to be a period piece, Second World War. You'll be glad to know this isn't *Exocet,* but that's not the point.'

'It's not?'

'No. Bee-Bee asked me whether Vlixcombe means anything to you. I'm simply asking the question, my precious. Yes or no?'

Vlixcombe? I know I've heard the word recently, very recently, then I remember saying *au revoir* to Rémy on the pontoon at St Katharine Docks. He'd confused Vlixcombe with Flixcombe. Or so I thought at the time.

'Wrong, my lovely. Apparently that lovely house of yours was used as some kind of recording studio during the war. According to Bee-Bee, a bunch of crazy Free French moved in, de Gaulle's people. Our lot had tasked them to produce hours of scurrilous nonsense to broadcast to the Motherland. I'm not quite sure how, but all this mischief was supposed to wrong-foot the Boche and give them a hard time. It didn't work, of course, but Rémy's dug up diaries and scripts and all sorts and he thinks the story's irresistible. Bittersweet. Funny-sad. Lots of sex. Lots of laughter. To be honest, my precious, that might do the trick just now. It certainly sounds a lot more fun than the Falklands bloody War.'

'So what does he want to do? Rémy?'

'Bee-Bee says he's going to put it in writing. Formal pitch.'

'To who?'

'To you, my angel. I get the impression he thinks he's pissed you off. This is him making amends.'

I nod. This, at last, feels like the old Rémy.

'Pissed off is wrong,' I say. 'Disappointed is much closer. Tell him to email an attachment. I can read it tonight.'

'That might be a little hasty, my treasure. I suspect he hasn't written the thing yet. How's H, by the way?'

'Off the planet. Deep space. That thespy scribe you mentioned. The one who wrote the kiss and tell. Does she have a name, by any chance?'

'Of course she has a name.'

'Might I have it?'

'I'm afraid not. But I can go one better.'

'Like how?'

'I'll send you the script. I'll anonymize it first but it's for your eyes only. Expect it tonight instead of Rémy. Deal?'

Deal. Rosa's favourite word. The mission statement that's brought her both fame and fortune.

'Deal,' I hear myself agree. 'Ping it down. I can't wait.'

NINE

The second of the two estate agents phones less than an hour later. His name's Simon and he's sitting in his car at the end of the drive. This takes me somewhat by surprise.

'What are you doing here?'

'I had a viewing nearby. Two birds? One stone? Lazy, I know . . .'

He's obviously lying but these days, as I understand only too well, you need to stay at least one step ahead of the opposition.

'You want to take a look around *now*?'

'Just a first assessment. Wet finger in the wind. Half an hour, tops. If it's a pain, just say. I'm sure we can re-schedule.'

'Really?' I'm gazing out at the sunshine. 'Give me ten minutes. Best to see the place on a day like this.'

Simon turns out to be younger than I expected. He's wearing a lovely linen jacket, acceptably rumpled, with a Garrick Club tie. His shirt carries the lightest blue stripe, and his smile has a warmth I can only describe as close to sincere.

'You're an actor?' I'm looking at the tie.

'I am, for my sins. And you're in the same game, Ms Andressen.'

'You've Googled me?'

'I've gone one better. I've seen some of your work. *Trahison* I liked very much. And that Montreal movie, too. You absolutely nailed the Quebequois accent. *Quelle triomphe, quoi?*'

'Vous parlez français?'

'Un peu, oui.'

'Excellent.'

When I ask him what he's doing in estate agency, he shoots me a rueful grin. 'I had a couple of *Holby*s lined up, plus an audition for a new C4 pilot. My agent was promising three weeks in rep in Harrogate, with maybe another stint towards Christmas. Covid killed the lot. Two days after that first lockdown I was at the Job Centre.'

'And they turned you into an estate agent?'

'I got a driving job for a month or so, Asda deliveries. House rules say you have to leave the goodies on the doorstep, no physical contact, and seconds later the whole lot's been lifted. Total nightmare trying to sort it all out. My family's from down here.' He nods at the badged Range Rover. 'My pa knows the guy who owns the agency.'

'So you just slotted in?'

'Sort of. You play a role. It's thesping without the laughs. The technical stuff can sometimes be a challenge, but in today's market houses sell themselves. Sometimes I'm tempted to tell clients to back off for their own sakes, but the commission settles that argument.'

'You miss acting?'

'Of course I do. If I stuck at this game, I could make a fortune. It's really not hard. But acting often frightens me, and I like that.' He pauses to gaze out at the view. 'This is your place?'

'No. But I'm in charge just now.'

'It's wonderful. And I mean that. Shame, really.' He glances back at me.

'Shame how?'

'Having to sell it.'

'Having' is a curious word. It somehow contains an assumption that I don't much like, but of course he's right. He opens the passenger door of the Range Rover and I direct him around the accessible parts of the estate. Whenever we stop, he asks sensible questions and makes notes on what little information I can muster.

At length, we find ourselves back in front of the house. H, mercifully, is nowhere to be seen.

'You have time for a brief tour?' I nod towards the front door.

'No need. This is going to be ballpark. Just list the accommodations.'

The accommodations. I half-close my eyes, going through

the house floor by floor, room by room. The period features. The views. The feel of a place that umpteen generations have called home. Simon scribbles himself more notes, his fountain pen racing from line to line on his leather-bound pad. In a certain kind of movie, the pen would be a Mont Blanc, but this one is a top-of-the-range Parker, which is perfectly acceptable. When my mental tour comes to an end, he lifts his head, staring out at the house through the windscreen.

'Condition? Be honest.'

'Good in some places, less good in others. Everything important works, but the word you need to remember is old.'

This is meant as a health warning and raises a smile. Then comes a precautionary check, as he turns to the estate.

'Three hundred acres. Have I got that right?'

'Near on.'

'So let's start there. Prime arable land round here is going for £10,000 an acre; prime pasture land can make £8,000. I doubt any farmer would grow crops on this land, so you're probably looking at around two and a half million for the estate.'

'And the house?'

'It's lovely. Ballpark, I'd say two million. I can see a barn there. Any other properties?'

'A cottage. Currently tenanted.'

'How many bedrooms?'

'Two.'

'Let's say another half million. I'll obviously need a proper look to be sure, but including the land I suspect we're talking around five million. If I had the money, I'd buy it tomorrow.'

I nod. Five million pounds. Tony Morse will be thrilled.

'There's more.' Simon hasn't finished. 'The government want to drive a horse and cart through the planning laws. They're trying to make life easy for the developers. I don't want to bore you but the technical term is de-coupling.'

'What from what?'

'The planners from the people. The people want somewhere to live. The planners often make that hard but the people is where the votes are, and the developers and the builders know which strings to pull when it comes to central government.

Think Wild West, think Klondyke. Everyone has a right to a place of their own.'

'Here, you mean?' I gesture at the view, the peace, the solitude. I'm astonished.

'God, no. This is a premium site. This is the *crème de la crème.* Find the right developer, the right architect, plus a builder who can deliver to spec, and you'd be looking at million-and-a-half-pound properties, minimum, each one unique, each one with the right degree of privacy. A setting like this sells itself. All you'll need are plans on paper, and a developer with a decent track record. We can help you with the latter, *pas de problème.*'

I'm trying to take all this in. Mitch Culligan is bound to be in the know about the planning laws but he's not here until tomorrow. In the meantime, I need to be clear about the figures.

'So how many of these properties might you anticipate?'

'A site this big would swallow twenty, each of them adding a little something extra.'

'At a million and a half?'

'Yes.'

'That's thirty million pounds.'

'It is, indeed. But you'd need OPP.'

'What's that?'

'Outline planning permission.'

'I see. And that would bring us how much extra? On top of the five million?'

I've put the question as bluntly as I can, and now I watch Simon punching figures into his smartphone. At length, he looks up. If this was on stage, I suspect we'd be nearing the end of the first act.

'In the hands of a decent negotiator,' he says, 'I suspect you could comfortably double that figure.'

'You're serious? Ten million pounds?'

'Yes. This is serendipity. This is the reverse of the perfect storm. For an estate like this, you couldn't have chosen a better time to sell.'

I nod, sobered and a little shamed by the ease with which I appear to have doubled H's money. It feels like a conjuring trick, the blackest magic, an extra five million pounds banked without the slightest effort.

I turn to Simon to thank him for his time and effort, but his gaze has settled on a tall window on the first floor of the house.

'There's a guy up there with no clothes on,' he says thoughtfully. 'Shall I put him down as the Flixcombe ghost?'

The Flixcombe ghost. Over supper in the kitchen, I'm trying to figure out ways of making H behave. He's already toyed with the steak I've defrosted and grilled, and now he's expressing a lively interest in dousing my wedgies with ketchup, but his listening skills – never great – have deserted him completely. When I point out how much he frightened Evelyn the night he tried to break into the guest bedroom, he simply lifts his head to offer the blankest stare. Unless I'm mistaken, he hasn't the slightest memory of either Evelyn or the guest bedroom and the very idea of contrition is therefore a non-starter. This is frustrating enough but when I suggest very tactfully that keeping his clothes on might avoid needless offence, he starts to bridle.

'It's mine,' he insists. 'Fucking mine.'

'What's yours, H?'

'Mine,' he confirms, as if the conversation is done.

It's my turn to be confused. I haven't a clue what he's talking about, and what makes it worse is the big fat comma of ketchup at the corner of his mouth. He looks like the stroppiest child at the birthday party of your worst nightmare. All the other guests have fled. So what happens next?

To be frank, I'm running out of options, but H comes to my rescue with a fresh burst of madness. He's not in the mood for steak, and now he wants to know what's happened to the fucking dog.

'There is no dog, H.' I break the news as gently as I can. 'And there never was. Not here. Not at Flixcombe.'

'You're kidding me. Jericho. I love that animal.' He pokes the steak with his fork. 'He'll have the lot. Woof woof. We're calling him Jerry now but there's no need. He always answered to Jericho and he always fucking will. So where is he?'

The question carries the force of an accusation. In H's head, I obviously know about Jericho, and my silence on the subject is therefore an act of the deepest treachery.

'Well?' he grunts.

I hold the madness of his gaze for a long moment, and then gesture vaguely towards the door.

'He's upstairs, H, in your bedroom, where you left him.'

He nods, emphatic, and his sagging face suddenly creases into a broad grin. I've understood at last about Jericho and his world is back in one piece. He gets to his feet, swallows the last of his wine, and then makes unsteadily for the door. Once he's opened it, I watch him heading upstairs, one step at a time, his breathing still laboured, the hint of a tuneless whistle on his lips. Living with H has become surreal but in this small moment I realize that this new life of mine has its consolations. By the time H gets to his bedroom door, he'll have forgotten all about Jericho.

TEN

Rosa's email arrives mid-evening. I haven't heard a peep from H, and so I close the kitchen door, wedge a chair beneath the handle, and settle down in front of my tablet.

The manuscript, Rosa warns me, has been deliberately written to erase any verifiable trace of the authoress. Just to be certain, Rosa has skimmed through it for a second time and now she's more than happy to give me a peek. It's still in Word format, so if I fancy making any improvements, the floor is mine.

This playful help-yourself confirms the suspicion I first had on the river cruise: that this whole project may be nothing more than an elaborate scam. Either way, a couple of hours in the company of Mr Big's alleged mistress will be a welcome break from the multiple challenges of early-onset dementia.

I pour myself another glass of Médoc and open the attachment. The MS is double-spaced, 198 pages in all, and already I can picture this slender offering on the front table at countless Waterstones, a sexy little duckling amongst the season's worthier offerings. Every book, as I know only too well, owes much of its success to the opening pages. Get those wrong, and you'll lose the reader by the end of chapter one. In *Curtain Call*, I plunged in at the deep end, sharing the moment my consultant warned me to expect a visit from the Grim Reaper. This turned out to be a clumsy way of telling me that the tumour in my brain might well prove terminal, a poorly framed metaphor which I later found hard to forgive, but the moment I managed to capture the essence of that exchange and put it on paper, was the moment that I knew *Curtain Call* would work.

Something very similar happens in this book. *My Place or Yours?* begins in a borrowed flat in Clerkenwell. The one-bedroom apartment is tiny and belongs to our narrator's best friend, a fellow actress who's on a long location shoot in Andalusia. It's gone midnight. Our scribe has returned in a state of some euphoria after the opening night of an unnamed Shakespeare play. Comedy? Tragedy? One of the history epics? We have no idea. What's more important is the presence of a household name in the taxi home, and now on the falling-apart sofa, where he's busily attending to various parts of her nether regions.

Our narrator is drunk enough not to mind, and she's amused by his efforts, *inter alia,* to declaim random passages from a number of other Shakespeare plays. The timeline here is far from certain. Is this bang up to date? Or does it belong to those tormented years when half the Cabinet were making life difficult for Theresa May? Either way, as the scene develops, details like this are of no consequence. What matters is that our top politician comes across as thoughtful, funny, and – above all – inventive. In the small hours, after multiple couplings and another bottle of Australian Shiraz, the narrator falls into bed and begs for her new lover to join her but when she awakes next morning, there's no trace of his presence beyond a scribbled note. The note is in Latin, and it takes a fumble or two on Google to get a translation. *Bliss on the battlefield is rare,* her new *beau* has written. *As old campaigners can attest.*

This playful *adieu* brings the first chapter to an end and our scribe is honest enough to admit – as chapter two gets under way – that she doesn't know quite what to make of it. She's been flattered by his compliments on her performance, both on and off the stage, and despite a savage hangover she thinks she's caught a hint of someone truly vulnerable behind the stagey charm, but the real issue is what to expect next. She has no means of getting in touch with him, no personal contact details, and the thought of trying to run him to earth wherever he spends his waking hours doesn't appeal at all. She's an actress, for pity's sake, not some deranged stalker, and as the days slip by, she has to make do with the occasional glimpse of her one-night stand in the pages of the *Daily Telegraph* or the opening titles of some TV news show.

By now, she's checked out what the rest of the world knows

about this man. Yes, he has a complicated love life. Yes, he's no stranger to divorce. And yes, he has his eye on the biggest desk in 10 Downing Street. That, of course, makes him one of a small army of aspiring Tories, drunk and reckless on their own ambition, and she's beginning to wonder whether she's made this whole thing up when there comes a late-afternoon phone call. It's her passing *beau*, a voice she recognizes at once. He's just leaving some dull fucking function and he could do with a little cheering up. Might she spare the old warhorse a glass of something palatable and maybe an hour or so of light relief?

Taken by surprise, she hears herself saying yes of course and moments later the line goes dead. He's at her door within ten minutes, bottle in hand, Sauvignon Blanc this time, and only later does it occur to her to wonder how on earth he'd got her number, and – just as important – how he can have been so sure that her best mate hasn't returned from Andalusia to reclaim her flat.

Neither query gets in the way of more furious coupling, but this time she's sober and she realizes that he's really quite good at it. Her love life lately has been cursed by a relationship that should never have got anywhere near the sack, but did. The guy happens to be a fellow actor. She really likes him, respects him, admires him. He's fearless in argument, brilliant on stage, and world-class at poker. He's even learned to juggle five balls for minutes on end, but he's never quite figured out what makes a woman happy in bed.

Mr Big, on the other hand, has what she terms 'a piratical instinct for what works'. He boards her, he ravishes her to a decent standard, and minutes later he's able to do it all over again. The raw simplicities of their lovemaking come as an enormous relief after months of hopeless fumbling, and when he departs with most of the bottle undrunk, she makes him write down his phone number. *I'll give you a key to the door*, she texts him later. *Delete this*.

And so the relationship develops, no real commitment on either side, nothing written down, no letters, no anguished emails, no hint of a future the other side of the next shag, just the barest exchange of dates, times, and locations. *Meet me at Number 17,* she texts him on one occasion towards Christmas. *Rehearsals start at ten sharp. I can give you an hour if you can make it by eight.*

Does she feel a whore? The thought doesn't cross her mind. Does it matter that he's probably seeing umpteen other women? Not in the least. In a thoroughly modern way, she writes towards the end of the book, it's become the perfect relationship, wilful on both parts, richly satisfying, a glimpse of what might be possible if you keep both eyes wide open.

The latter thought briefly preoccupies her for a paragraph or two. How openly self-obsessed this man is. How honest he can be about his physical needs. How easily politics, and hustings, and all the drudgery of trying to nail some poor sucker's vote can bore him half to death. Life really is a battlefield, he keeps telling her. People are out to get you, out to hurt you, out to leave you prostrate in the mud, and all that matters are the scalps hanging from your own belt.

In the smallest hours, as the surprise and delight of the sex begins to falter, she begins to wonder whether one of those scalps might be hers. She is, after all, an actress with a reputation. She's very good at what she does and she knows – in his phrase – that she's easy on the eye. She's also been very quick to understand what pleases him in the cut and thrust of conversation, and what teases him in bed. These are talents that matter to someone as finely tuned to performance as Mr Big, and when the end of whatever it is they've enjoyed comes to pass, she makes sure it's on nobody's terms but her own.

In the book's final pages, her inamorato has just spent far too long at some godforsaken constituency event, trying to put the Tory ultras back in their kennel. And now he'd like to fuck her stupid.

Nice idea, she texts back. *Alas, the lady's not for fucking.*

A reply arrives within seconds.

Never?

This is the moment that ends the book. She writes of staring at the screen. Of feeling a hot flush of pleasure she describes as beyond sexual. She's enjoyed this man, appreciated his many talents, even grown to like him. They've helped themselves to the best bits of each other and laughed a lot. But enough is enough, and now is the time to take a bow and drop the curtain.

And so that final despairing question goes unanswered.

My Place or Yours? Nice. I like the title, and I love much of the writing. This is a woman prepared to take a risk or two, never doubting that she can deal with the consequences. The more intimate scenes have the ring of truth, and while I'm no closer to knowing whether she made the whole thing up, it's a satisfying read. It speaks of self-awareness and of something else, a playful riff on where life – and your imagination – can take you. Rosa's right. Properly lawyered, edited, and fattened for market, it could sell millions.

It's now nearly midnight. In around twelve hours, Mitch Culligan will be here, doubtless eager for more news of the rogue MS. Do I betray Rosa and let him take the whole thing away? Do I confiscate his phone, lock him in the library, and give him a couple of hours with the text in order to draw his own conclusions? Or might there be another option?

I pour the last of the evening's wine into my glass and scroll back to the book's opening lines. *Never believe an audience who rise to their feet*, she writes. *Standing ovations feed the worst of you. Beware compliments.*

Wise advice, seldom taken. My guide and mentor in the world of publishing has always been Evelyn. One of the many reasons she became the doyenne of London literary editors was her uncanny instinct for mapping the arc of a story, and then identifying the elements that made the book tick. This was a reductive process, compressing hundreds of pages to their essence. She could sit down first thing and fillet any manuscript before lunchtime, extracting key passages, identifying what worked and what didn't, and she did exactly this – unbidden – to *Curtain Call.* At first, like any apprentice novelist, I was aghast by the bruises inflicted on my precious infant, but in time I realized how clever, and how acute she'd been, and by the time we'd fought our way to the end of the second draft, my little tome was vastly improved.

Now, I want to do something similar to *My Place or Yours?* Not to improve it but to offer Mitch a taste of what will lie between these covers and thus keep my side of the bargain we've struck. Sayid, *inshallah,* will take a good look at H and tell me what's really going on, while Mitch will read my précis and draw his own conclusions.

The editing goes very smoothly indeed, and within an hour I've cut and pasted a careful selection of passages that do the book ample justice. It runs a shade under five thousand words and will take Mitch no time at all to read but by the end of it he'll be able to make a judgement about the book's authenticity. For me as well, second time round, the editing process is invaluable. The narrative voice has lodged itself in my head. It has a confidence, and an earthiness, it would be hard to confect. Whoever this woman's been fucking, she was definitely there.

Pleased with the final version, I go up to H's office to print off the results of my labour. The office is at the top of the house, a smallish, intimate room dominated by a big desk that H lifted years ago from the Naval Dockyard down in Pompey. The desk had been used by Harry Prentice, H's dad, who'd clerked all his life for the Admiralty. Leather-topped, with a stack of deep drawers on either side, the desk has always been a favourite of mine. Nowadays, H seldom uses this room, chiefly because Long Covid has made the stairs almost impossible for him to climb, but I've been coming up here a lot recently, not least because the view out over the Flixcombe estate is sensational.

I settle at the desk and plug my tablet into the printer. I've a feeling that it may have run out of paper and it turns out that I'm right. H always kept reams of A4 in the bottom left-hand drawer but when I tug it open, it's empty. I try the drawer above. Same result. Only when I start on the right-hand drawers do I find what I'm after but by now I'm deeply curious. Someone, presumably H, has been up here. But why? What possible reason could have dragged him up those stairs?

The two topmost drawers are full of business files going back years. The third has been emptied, except for a scatter of photos. I pull them out, recognizing the odd Pompey face, enlisted men in H's private army. One of them, a career psychopath called Wesley Kane, I got to know very well indeed, and

I spend a moment or two staring at the shot. Wes, as H always called him, is a tall, fit-looking brawler from the Caribbean with a scary reputation and an inexplicable fondness for the colour pink. Last year, with some reluctance, he saved H's life when a figure from the past was trying to kill him, though now I doubt that H will have any memory of what happened.

I study the photo a little longer. In the right mood, Wesley could always make me laugh, and I never ceased to marvel at the way he kept his looks. Seldom have I ever seen an Afro that wild and only lately have I realized how perfectly that explosion of curls mirrored what was going on inside.

Last drawer, then the copier. I tug the drawer open, still curious, and find myself looking at the travel version of a Scrabble board. This, I know, was one of H's treasures. He always went to great lengths to present himself as the authentic Pompey mush, unschooled, a creature of the streets, a serial truant, totally ungovernable. The truth of course, as his dad was the first to confirm, was very different. H did well at school, and afterwards he sat a number of accountancy exams before the cocaine trade won his undivided attention.

I reach into the drawer. The box of Scrabble lies open, the lid off, and the board itself, unfolded, is partly hidden by another photo. H was always good at Scrabble. He had the talent to conjure a host of words from a handful of those little plastic tiles, and when his vocabulary failed him – which was rare – he simply made words up. Now, I lift the photo. The board beneath is bare except for a line of four tiles.

At first glance, the word makes no sense. Then I realize what's happened, what those four letters are telling me, and the board begins to blur.

HLEP, H has carefully spelled out. Just that.

ELEVEN

Next morning, after a couple of hours sleep, I'm up early. I leave a mug of tea at H's bedside but he appears to be still asleep. Downstairs, back in the kitchen, I sort out a filling to stuff the discs of marrow I'll be roasting for lunch, and then put another call through to Tony Morse. He says he's at home, looking forward to the weekend off, and that Corinne – his latest passion – has the breakfast well under control.

I met Corinne last year. She's half Tony's age and clearly besotted. She's also exceptionally good looking and terrifyingly bright. Tony told me that her reading list during the first period of lockdown extended to Elena Ferrante's Neapolitan novels in the original Italian, a dense biography of Martha Gellhorn, and – for light relief – a copy of D.H. Lawrence's *Sea and Sardinia.* For the first time in his chequered love life, Tony Morse appears to have realized how he's finally lucked in.

When he asks about the valuation, I describe the conversation with Simon. The news that Flixcombe may be worth ten million pounds sparks an expletive.

'This is bad news?' I'm bewildered.

'Almost certainly, my darling. The estate is still in his name? He hasn't gifted you a portion? Wrapped it up in something tasteful and left it under the Christmas tree?'

'Alas, no. I'd have noticed.'

'Shame. I'll need to have a think about this. The moment H liquidates the estate is the moment all those creditors help themselves. I can smell bacon, my darling. Leave it to me.'

Leave it to me? The line has gone dead. I have a million questions but all of them will have to wait.

The rest of the morning passes more quickly than I'd expected. It's a battle getting H out of bed, and I can see a dark stain where he's soiled the bottom sheet, but I'm determined to have him looking spruce for the moment when Sayid takes him aside for a little chat. In this respect, and many others, I've begun to feel like H's mum. He's my charge, my responsibility, more of a handful than ever, and certainly more challenging than our wayward son. When I finally get him downstairs, he stares at the kitchen table I've just laid. I can see him counting the place mats and the readied wine glasses and trying to frame the obvious question.

'Friends of mine, H.' I'm here to help him out. 'People you won't know.'

Mitch and Sayid appear nearly an hour early. West Dorset has laid on a flawless day, barely a cloud in the sky, and Mitch struggles out of the car to light himself a cigarette. He's always been a bear of a man, perpetually dishevelled, zero dress sense, and since we last met he seems to have put on even more weight. Sayid, on the other hand, is as lean and winsome as ever. He has the softest brown eyes, and a melting smile, both coupled with a natural grace and diffidence I've always found irresistible.

Back in the day, once I'd earned his trust, he told me a great deal about those last years when Syria tore itself apart and his beloved Aleppo became a tomb. An experience like that can change a man forever and the miracle – for me – was that Sayid's essential decency has somehow remained intact. The beginnings of middle age have settled gently on his slender frame, and his taste in clothes is impeccable. According to Mitch, he still runs daily and the blessings are obvious. When God invented skinny designer jeans, he must have had Sayid in mind.

Already, he's taking me aside. Leaving London early was his decision. Lunch sounds a fine idea but first he needs me to tell him as much as I want to about H. 'Want to' is pure Sayid. This man truly understands the word respect. Mitch, by now, is gazing out at the view, enjoying his cigarette. There's no sign of H, and so I steer Sayid round the side of the house and settle him on the bench at the back of the walled garden. In the late-morning sunshine, we can feel the heat from the ancient bricks.

I tell him about the long weeks down in Portsmouth last year, about H's battle with Covid and the private nursing team that managed to keep him out of the ICU. Since then, we've been back here at Flixcombe, waiting for the recovery that never arrived. He's still breathless, still unsteady on his feet, still sick.

'Sick up here?' Sayid touches his forehead.

'Yes. Definitely. I put it down to brain fog to begin with. Google Long Covid, and that's the word that hits you first, but now I'm not so sure.'

I tell him about Evelyn's visit, and H's furious assault on her bedroom door, and then the moment when she watched him urinating on her precious scone mix. Evelyn, I explain, has sensibly fled but H shows no signs of reining himself in. On the contrary, he's taken to appearing naked at the most unfortunate moments and seems to have no sense of shame or restraint.

'Evelyn thinks he's got dementia and I'm starting to think she's right.' I'm eyeing the house, wondering what H has done with himself. 'He's just not there anymore. He can't follow an argument, can't engage. You can see it in his eyes. He's absent without leave, he's gone. And he gets so *angry*.'

'How old is he?'

'Fifty-five. That's young, isn't it?'

Sayid doesn't answer. Mitch has appeared at the corner of the house. H is with him, dwarfed by Mitch's sheer bulk. The pair of them approach our bench and then stop. H is looking up at Mitch and for just a second I think I catch a flicker of recognition in his eyes. Then Mitch steps away, gesturing at H but looking at me.

'Yours, I think.'

H and I swap places. I introduce Sayid as a good friend of mine, and watch his hand settle delicately on H's arm. I've dressed H in a long-sleeved training top I know he loves, a Christmas gift from the Pompey FC shop, and I marvel at the smile that spreads slowly across his face as he stares down at this stranger's hand. H normally hates being touched, but not now, not with this man beside him.

Mitch and I beat a retreat to the kitchen. Mitch has his back to the view of the garden but I can't tear my eyes away from the two figures on the bench. Not so many years ago, H had this man fighting for his life. Now, in ways none of us could ever have anticipated, the tables are turned. Mitch appears to be disinterested. I think it pleases him when God pays a debt or two but you'd never guess by looking at his face.

'You don't think this is remarkable?' I ask him. 'On Sayid's part?'

'Of course I do. That's why I told him not to come, not to get involved, but he wouldn't hear of it. That man has a faith in human nature it's hard to credit. How can you have lived in Aleppo and not believe in evil?'

'You think H is evil?'

'No, but I know he was one of those vicious little tossers who helped push us out of Europe and that comes close.'

When I first met Mitch Culligan he was exploring where the anti-EU headbangers got their money from, an investigative trail that led to Pompey drug lord Hayden Prentice. To be honest, I've never fully understood why H decided to mix profit with politics but whatever the answer, it's now academic. Sayid is probably asking him to name the numbers on his watch.

'He's going to lose everything, Mitch,' I point out. 'Doesn't that matter?'

'It was never his in the first place. He was a criminal then, and nothing's changed.'

'That's harsh. He's my son's father. In the end it's blood.'

'Sure. But whose blood? You want to ask Sayid? That man took a beating he'll never forget.'

'Of course. I was there. I saw him in hospital. But look at him now. Maybe most of us have lost the knack but I suspect Sayid hasn't.'

'Knack for what?'

'Forgiveness. We all bang on about pressure and stress and our precious mental health but I'm guessing you have to be Syrian to be any kind of real expert. Just look at him. Unless I'm mistaken he's got H involved in a conversation. That's rare, believe me.'

Mitch at last takes a glance through the window. For a

moment, he says nothing. Then he edges round the table and stands physically between me and the view. He's not here to trouble himself with a washed-up Pompey villain. First, he'd quite like a drink. Then we need to talk about *My Place or Yours?*

I pour him a glass of Médoc. The pages I printed are lying on the dresser. I flick briefly through and then hand them over.

'And this is?'

'Something I did last night. The book runs to 78,000 words. These are a handful of prime cuts. Think trailer for the main feature.'

'You've got the whole thing?'

'Yes.'

'So why can't I read that?'

'Because I promised to show no one else. All the clues you need are in that précis. Technically, I'm breaking my word already but a girl has to answer to her conscience.'

'Really?' A brief smile ghosts across Mitch's face. Then he bends to the first page. Seconds later, his head is up again, the smile much broader. 'Shit,' he says. 'Who *is* this woman?'

'I've no idea. My source used the word "de-coupled". The narrator's obviously a woman but she's gone to a lot of trouble to cover her tracks. In the end, it's about the writing, isn't it?'

Mitch stares at me, then his hand strays across the table to find the glass of Médoc.

'Wrong,' he grunts. 'In the end it's about whether it's true or not.'

Sayid and H remain on the bench for the best part of an hour while I attend to lunch. By the time the stuffed marrow is out of the oven and cooling on the side, Mitch has read my précis three times and disappeared to make what I suspect are a couple of calls. Should this bother me? Just at the moment, I don't care. Sayid and H are picking their way back across the garden from the bench, and while the conversation is obviously over, H has chosen to hang close to his new friend. This degree of trust is something so totally unexpected that I can't quite believe it. Even when I first met him, more than two decades ago in Antibes, H seemed wary of everyone. When it came to money, he was always first to the bar. But ask him to risk a friendship or two, he was always a man apart. Remarkable.

Sayid is first into the kitchen.

'Mr Prentice would quite like a nap. I'm afraid these sessions can be exhausting.' Sayid smiles, then taps his watch. 'Mitch and I have to be back in town by five, I'm afraid.'

H has already edged past him. Without sparing me a glance, he makes for the door and disappears.

'He's OK?'

'He's tired. Can we talk over lunch? Will that be OK?'

I nod. I know that Sayid doesn't drink but I have some farm shop elderberry in the fridge. I pour him a glass while he takes a seat at the table and leave the kitchen to find Mitch. We rarely use the dining room these days and it's the last door I try. Mitch is sitting at the long walnut table. He must have fetched his laptop from the car and now he's concentrating hard on some kind of report.

'Well?' I nod at the scatter of pages marked in red. Absurdly, I feel a tickle of authorship.

'Bloody interesting.'

'You believe any of it?'

'I need to know who wrote it. And why.'

'Are you hungry?'

'Starving.' For the first time, his head comes up. 'I'll eat in here, if you don't mind. Best if you and Sayid sort the business.'

The business. Me and H. Neatly put.

I deliver a plate of stuffed marrow and the rest of the Médoc to Mitch and return to the kitchen. Sayid, it turns out, has also been making notes. Sensibly, as he delicately spoons my ratatouille onto the marrow, he wants to be sure about my immediate interests.

'Mitch tells me you might have to sell this place.'

'Mitch is right.'

'You're thinking of lasting power of attorney? You representing Mr Prentice's best interests?'

'Yes.'

'Then I'm afraid it's far too late. You're right. Your Mr H is a sick man. Not just Long Covid, which must be bad enough, but I'm afraid his mental impairment is serious. I can't be absolutely certain at this point, but everything points to a condition we call frontotemporal dementia. You want me to go on?'

I gesture for him to eat. The food won't stay warm forever. Frontotemporal dementia? I'm trying to picture that first centipede of a word on H's travelling Scrabble board. Is he up in his office as we speak? Having a second go at HLEP?

'The condition originates up here, in the frontotemporal lobes.' Sayid taps his forehead and then reaches for a napkin to mop the corner of his mouth. 'It often presents as disinhibition, inappropriate social behaviour, stress, rage, and perhaps a slackening grasp of the meaning of things.'

'The meaning of things?'

'Yes. In cases like this, you might remember I wear glasses for reading but you have no idea of what glasses are. You'd gaze at the sugar bowl and the spoon and the waiting cup of tea and get no closer to the idea of what might connect them. This is a kind of dissociative incomprehension, and it spreads and spreads until you have no idea of what anyone is talking about. It sounds horrible, and I'm afraid it is. In the end, the very idea of meaning evaporates and by that time you can't reach out to anyone. All empathy, all the you-ness of you, and the me-ness of me, and the us-ness of us, has gone.'

I nod but say nothing. I can't help thinking of H weeing on Evelyn's scone mix, of H half-naked on the lawn, of Malo's gangster dad exposing himself in the upstairs window. Might any of this qualify as 'inappropriate social behaviour'?

'So you think he's got this thing? Frontotemporal-whatever?'

'I think that's the road his brain is taking. The mind is like the body. In the end, it will betray you. In the meantime, it's important to keep talking.'

'Why?'

'Because one day, your H won't be able to say anything.'

My H.

I've yet to start on my meal, but any scintilla of appetite I might have had has gone. I feel confused and frightened because I never expected the news to be this bad. I also feel faintly sick, maybe on H's behalf, maybe on mine. This lovely man across the table, so thoughtful, so patient, so gifted, must have seen hundreds of patients like H, most of them much older, and perhaps much sicker. He'd recognize the symptoms and understand the absolute need for frankness. This thing, these empty spaces in H's brain, aren't going to disappear. *Au contraire*, they're going to get worse. Not only can H remember very little, but it seems he can't make new memories, either.

'You're sure you've got this right?' I'm frowning now. 'Might there be some other diagnosis?'

'I'm afraid not. I toyed with bipolar, but that's a non-starter. I was also hoping H might have some form of mild cognitive impairment but I'm afraid he's some way beyond that.'

'So what do we do? What do *I* do?'

Sayid frowns, slips another morsel of marrow into his mouth, takes a delicate sip of elderberry. He's plainly been expecting this question, and he glances at the jotted notes beside his plate.

'The issue of stimulation is important. There are residential homes in Dresden where the owners have recreated the world of East Germany in the sixties and seventies, primarily for the benefit of their dementia patients. Think décor, wallpaper, furniture, curtains, music, even recorded movies on the TV. I don't think anyone's gone quite that far over here, but there are certainly help networks I can put you in touch with.'

I nod and try to summon a bright smile, but my heart is sinking. The thought of H in the Now and Then Café is too scary to contemplate. Singing along with a bunch of mad oldies would destroy what little is left, as would an afternoon of bingo. He'd be naked within minutes, and with a full bladder that could have the darkest consequences.

'Anything else?'

'Indeed. Psychotherapists have reported surprising results with adventure activities, as long as they're carefully monitored.'

'Like?'

'Gliding. Hot-air ballooning. Scuba diving. Anything that inverts the normal laws of physics. Patients like H need to be taken by surprise, to be set free. These things aren't cheap but anything that fills the void would be more than welcome.'

The Void. I have a sudden vision of daily life – that torrent of impressions, snatches of conversations, and all the other nonsense that seems suddenly so precious – sluicing through the empty scaffold that is H's brain and leaving absolutely no trace. I try and voice the thought, badly needing help, and Sayid understands at once what I mean.

'We call that the celebration of the now,' he murmurs. 'Your H needs to know that the now is all he's got, but that the now can be enough, that the present moment is a wonderful moment, entirely sufficient. It won't survive. It won't become a memory. But that doesn't matter in the slightest. This amounts to surrender, of course, or perhaps an accommodation with the disease, and I get the sense that neither have figured much in H's life, but nowness is worth his total concentration, if that isn't oxymoronic.'

Oxymoronic. A contradiction in terms. A tribute to the hopeless tangle of non-firing brain cells that is H's fragile hold on life. At this point, I become aware that Sayid is watching me carefully. Alas, he hasn't quite finished.

'There's something else that became quickly evident out there.' He nods towards the walled garden. 'You've become very important to him, very important indeed, and my best guess is that he may need you around. All the time.'

'Why?'

'To feel safe.'

'From what?'

'Excellent question. If we knew the answer, we'd all be in a better place.' He pauses, and for a moment, I think he's going to reach for my hand, but mercifully he doesn't.

'There's something else?'

'I'm afraid so. This is in the nature of a health warning. The shorthand for what you may choose to become is a carer, but caring isn't curing and you should never confuse the two. The cured get better. Caring, I'm afraid, can be forever.'

I nod. This man is seriously gifted and even I, never famous for learning my lines on time, have let him shepherd me gently to the very same conclusion. The outcome, alas, appears to be incontestable. H, bless him, is on a journey to the vanishing point. He's a drying puddle of memories and he'll evaporate until there's nothing left. *Nada. Le Grand Rien.* The onset of darkness. The Big Nothing. The implications of sharing that journey are beyond depressing but I know I have no choice. What will living with an older, madder, sadder H be like? Will he end up in nappies with a QR code and a whistle round his neck? Will he still have the nerve and the energy to strip naked and piss on something inappropriate? Or will the onset of that darkness feel exactly the way it feels now: full of dread?

It's at this point I realize that I'm crying, and when Sayid gets to his feet and tries to comfort me I do my best to fend him off. I know he means well but equally I know I have to face this terrible, terrible thing alone. Because thing it is. The void. *Le Grand Rien. Nada.*

'Here.' Sayid again.

I take the proffered Kleenex and blow my nose. Gradually, Sayid ceases to be a blur. To my surprise, his smile feels unforced.

'How do you make God laugh?' he asks.

'I don't know.'

'Tell him your plans.'

TWELVE

That night, with Sayid gone, I dream of Pavel. His real name was Paul Stukeley. He was a scriptwriter of genius, which is how come I met him in the first place, and by the time our paths crossed he was already blind, the victim of an inherited condition. This was bad enough but a handful of years later, thanks to a drunken, small hours plunge into a hotel swimming pool, he broke his neck and became a quadriplegic. By now, before the hotel accident, we'd become lovers, and with Pavel both paralysed and sightless, it fell to me to try and turn despair on both our parts into something more positive.

I needn't have bothered. In some respects, as I've later realized, Pavel had been rehearsing for this moment of total deprivation all his life. Already, he lived in his head. He wrote sublime scripts for the radio and for the screen. He lived for classical music, and for his beloved Prague (hence his adopted name of Pavel). He had an inner resource a trillion times the depth of the hotel pool that robbed him of all control and sensation. Bedbound, with the merest encouragement from little me, he continued to flourish.

With H's money, and Malo's help, we moved him down to a specially adapted apartment in Exmouth, in East Devon. There, he could map the gleaming expanse of the estuary outside the open French doors in his bedroom simply by listening to the wind, and the rattle of halyards in the nearby boatyard, and the chorus of birdsong from the waders out on the mudflats. He kept up with the world – politically, culturally, and in a million other ways – by listening to the radio. When work permitted, I sat with him day after day, evening after evening, and learned more than any book could ever have taught me. When I had problems in my private life, Pavel resolved them. He had a wisdom, a patience and a confidence that is vanishingly rare these days, and I write of him now because – in so many respects – he was blessed by the reverse of dementia. His body didn't work any more. And so he moved upstairs and lived in his teeming brain.

Next morning finds me enjoying a peaceful coffee on that very same bench in the walled garden where Sayid had taken H under his wing, checked him over, and drawn the key conclusions. A good night's sleep, enlivened by a conversation with Pavel, has softened the dread I felt last night and now I'm reliving those moments on the King Charles Bridge in Pavel's beloved Prague when I watched his ashes settle on the turbid waters of the River Vltava. Pavel died after a massive stroke two years ago. His inert body had finally given up, but I always knew there was something immortal in that vast brain of his, and it's good to know he's still available in times of acute need.

His take on H had always intrigued me. Pavel lived in the no man's land between fact and fiction and he always regarded H as a figure from one of the better-constructed TV series: full of the rudest vigour, intensely watchable, and addicted to conjuring plot surprise after plot surprise. Invent a character like H, he once told me, and your days at the keyboard acquire a magic and a delight of their own. You never know what to expect, and at the end of every working day you retreat from the PC, slightly anxious about leaving this monster to his own devices. Praise indeed from one of the country's top scriptwriters.

Monster? That's never been my word of choice for H. Over time, I got to know a great deal about his background, about the many scalps he'd taken, about the multitude of grudges he still kept, and about the masterstrokes that had tightened his chokehold on Pompey's access to the marching powder. In business, as he liked to call it, H was never less than ruthless but face to face, especially with women he respected, he could be both generous and funny.

He had a certain gruff charm for people who won his attention, but once I'd got to know him properly it was impossible not to sense the neediness and uncertainties that lay behind his gangster *schtick.* He needed to be listened to. He was desperate for that quiet inner peace that comes with the knowledge that someone loves you. His mother, I now realize, never loved him, but Malo – at a very impressionable age – most definitely did, and still does, and that unconditional acceptance of H's waywardness goes for me, too. So, in a way, Pavel was right. On stage, even in the most wooden of scripts, the sheer magnetic force of H's presence – offensive, loud, reliably dangerous – would be enough to keep the show on the road. And that, both in the theatre and for real, is very rare indeed.

I'm uncomfortably aware that most of this description is in the past tense but that very admission, I choose to think, signals an acceptance that Sayid is right, that H has fallen victim to an illness, a disease, for which there is no cure. He's looking for me now, stepping out of the kitchen, shading his eyes from the brightness of the sunshine, a frail figure, old before his time, one cautious foot in front of the other as if he's feeling his way in the dark. He's got my tablet under his arm, and at length he settles beside me on the bench, not saying a word.

I take the tablet and fire it up. I'm familiar enough with this new life of ours to understand that conversation is strictly optional, and in a way that realization offers possibilities I've rarely had the opportunity to explore. Most of the time, meeting friends or strangers, we often exchange a non-sequitur or two in order to bump-start whatever might follow, largely – I suspect – because it feels rude not to. But with H, the kinder option is to let silence do the talking, and oddly enough I vividly remember being part of something similar at Pavel's bedside. We only ever talked when there was something to say, or when he'd raised a conversational hare I couldn't resist pursuing. Otherwise, I was perfectly happy to sit there and stroke his thin pale hand, despite the fact that he couldn't feel or see a thing. Just an awareness of the physical presence of another human being can be a huge comfort, as I suspect H is beginning to discover.

My tablet must have signalled an incoming email to attract H's attention. Half-expecting a terse update from Mitch, or perhaps something more teasing from Dessie Wren, I find myself looking at a long message from Rémy. It comes with a sizeable attachment, not huge but still beguiling, and with H offering his face to the sun, I settle down to read.

Rémy, it seems, is back in Paris. Thanks to Covid, the city of a million kerbside café conversations is still largely empty, resigned to a state-enforced *confinement.* This, says Rémy, has turned out to be something of a blessing because he's had the time and space to give Vlixcombe the attention it deserves. Hence the attachment. At this point, he urges me to read what he's sent me and I break off to do his bidding. This, I suspect, is the project Rosa has already mentioned, and given the link to Flixcombe I'm curious to know exactly what Rémy has in mind.

Flixcombe Manoir, he's written, was bought in 1938 by champagne importer Max Gulliver who was then living in London. His wife, Hélène, was French. She came from Reims and they had three kids, two girls and a boy. Gulliver, who'd made a lot of money during the thirties, purchased Flixcombe as an insurance policy to keep his family safe in the event of war with Germany. They had many showbiz friends from the worlds of theatre and broadcasting, both in London and Paris.

I look up for a moment, aware of the deadweight of H leaning against me. The warmth of the sunshine has put a smile on his face, but his eyes are closed and he seems to be asleep. I wait a moment longer, then return to Rémy's account.

In May 1940 came *le débâcle.* The German *blitzkrieg* encircled whole armies, and hundreds of thousands of British and French troops were evacuated from Dunkirk. Many of them were wounded, some seriously, and Gulliver offered Flixcombe as a temporary convalescent home. Army tents were erected in the grounds. Nursing help arrived. Most of the casualties were French, and Hélène was in charge.

So far, so good, but by the year's end, with France divided between the Germans and the Pétain regime in Vichy, most of the eighty-odd convalescents had left, most deciding to return to *la patrie*. The BBC, meanwhile, had been invited to submit proposals for a massive expansion of foreign programming, including broadcasts to France. Free French talent who'd chosen to join De Gaulle in the UK applied for posts at Broadcasting House. They came up with idea after idea. The first regular programme to be beamed into France was called *France parlent aux français*. They were bombed out within weeks, and finally settled in Bush House.

By now, according to Rémy, the French service was mostly left to its own devices. Already it had attracted anarchic talent from the pre-war Paris arts scene. These are names that mean nothing to me but Rémy is promising a lot more detail in his next despatch. In the meantime, he assures me that de Gaulle's gift to the Brits had the twin talents of mischief and malevolence and were pledged to wage a war of their own against the hated *Boches*. Whatever came to hand – satire, comedy, music, ridicule – was ladled onto broadcast after broadcast to rally listeners on the other side of the Channel.

I'm smiling now because this makes perfect sense. As I know from my own grandmother, there was no real *résistance* in France until the German invasion of Russia gave the French communists a shake, and in the meantime it must have fallen to this wild bunch of broadcasters to get the French back on their feet. Or so they hoped.

Max Gulliver, it seems, knew most of these people through Hélène, and when the bombing made life impossible in Bush House, he offered Flixcombe as a kind of satellite radio studio. The French talent who made the service tick could live in the house, or in a handful of the tents the army had left behind. There would be about a dozen of them in all, mainly writers and performers, plus a few technicians to make the recordings. This strange little tribe quickly acquired a reputation for wild partying amongst the locals, who didn't know what to make of them. The French called Flixcombe *Le Bled*.

I pause to check on H again. He's still leaning against me, as light as a feather, and his breathing tells me he's definitely asleep, and so I return to my tablet. Rémy's sketch of life in wartime West Dorset already has me hooked. *Le Bled* means the back of beyond, which is exactly the way all these arty Parisians would regard Flixcombe. Already, I sense the despair at Broadcasting House, more cautious heads shaking as the French Service gleefully explored their new-found freedoms. There's definitely something new and rather wonderful in this pitch of Rémy's, and it crosses my mind that my favourite director might be relishing the chance to stake out controversial French territory at exactly the moment when the Brexit pot is boiling over. Neat, I think, and an immense improvement on *Exocet*.

I return to the attachment. In 1941, a former Belgian justice minister recruited by the BBC had stumbled on the letter 'V'. 'V' for *victoire* in French. 'V' for *vrijheid* (freedom in Flemish). 'V' for victory in beleaguered Britain. It wasn't much of a stick to shake at the Germans, but Churchill was quick to see the potential, as were the outlaw broadcasters revelling on our wonderful Dorset estate. It cost nothing, and week after week patriots in every corner of France were urged to paint the 'V' sign on barn doors deep in the country, to trace the letter with a fingertip in the dust on the back of German trucks, to chalk the promise of freedom on random bits of urban France. And – according to Rémy – it worked.

First irritated, then enraged, the Germans declared war against the rebel daubs. There were threats of mass imprisonment, even reprisal executions, but nothing deterred patriots swept up in this new game. Returning pilots crossing the French coast reported Breton fishermen holding up their oars in the 'V' sign. Farm labourers working in the fields of Picardy held up their arms in the 'V' sign at approaching Allied aircraft. Like a clever advertising campaign, the Victory brand swept the continent.

The French broadcasters were delighted, and it was at this moment – according to Rémy – that Flixcombe was renamed 'Vlixcombe'. By now, Hélène had been much impressed by the work of a *Daily Express* journalist, Sefton Delmer, who was producing a nightly show called *Der Chef,* beamed directly into Germany. This tricked the audience into believing that they were eavesdropping on a real conversation between disaffected Nazi high-ups, and Hélène persuaded her pet thespians to do something similar at Vlixcombe.

These new broadcasts centred on a pretend *résistant* dubbed *Le Patron,* whom listeners would happen across and tune in to. The tone, Rémy writes gleefully, was by turns scurrilous, outspoken, and frequently pornographic, a spontaneous conversation between like-minded *confrères,* though in reality it was carefully produced. Much to the satisfaction of Hélène's hard-living *artistes*, these broadcasts quickly acquired a sizeable audience. Vlixcombe played Vichy for fools, mocked the Germans, and cautiously looked forward to the return of all the cherished Gallic virtues. It made Broadcasting House uneasy, and upset de Gaulle, but – according to the creatives down in the wilds of West Dorset – had an ever-growing French listenership in stitches.

'*Voilà . . .*' Rémy writes at the end of his pitch. '*Ça vaut la peine d'y penser?*'

Do I think it's worth thinking about? I scroll back through the attachment, re-read a paragraph or two, then lift my head to gaze at the house. Flixcombe basks in the late-summer sunshine. Already, I can hear the music through the open windows, discs imported from Paris, the best of Fréhel and Chevalier. With it comes laughter and an expletive as some luckless thespian makes a late entry or fluffs a line. Then a roar of laughter and wild applause as he finally gets it right.

I shake my head in admiration, a small private tribute to Rémy. The tone of his pitch reminds me slightly of *Mash*, the craziness of war refracted through a bunch of front-line medics in Korea. Behind the ongoing battles between propaganda, anarchy, and the starchy bureaucrats in London, there'd be plenty of scope for subplots. Local women, attracted by the sheer presences of these exotics. Secretaries and leggy script assistants down from London. Maybe even a *tendresse* between Hélène and one of the older thesps. Stumble on the right core situation, as Rémy so clearly has, and the ongoing plot possibilities are endless.

H, by now, is awake. I draw his attention to the final page of the pitch. The words will probably make no sense to H, but that doesn't matter.

'Brilliant,' I tell him. 'We have to make it happen.'

He stares at me, and then he nods. Looking back, I suspect this was the last moment when there was any real glimpse of the old H. That may be fanciful on my part but either way I get up from the bench and extend a hand. Like Sayid, Pavel had access to life's darker secrets. He never mentioned God laughing at whatever plans we might have but he once told me that we should imagine the Almighty as the dancing partner of our wildest dreams. He knows all the moves. He probably wrote the tune. And he's endlessly forgiving when we tread on his toes.

H is on his feet now. He seems to understand the invitation, even welcome it, and I coax him a little closer. In front of the bench is a patch of gravel big enough for us to try a slow twirl or two. H has always been a softy when it comes to waltz music. One of his favourites is 'The Sleeping Beauty' and I start to hum it now. Pavel would have been appalled. He loathed anything to do with Tchaikovsky – too sentimental, too *easy* – but H picks up the tune at once and begins to sing it himself, 'da-dera-da, da-dera-da', way too loud. A blackbird, alarmed, flaps away, then a couple of pigeons do the same, and H cranes his head back, watching them heading for the safety of a nearby tree.

'Dance, H,' I whisper. 'We need to dance.'

H blinks at the word. His singing has suddenly stopped. We're standing in the sunshine, still close, our bodies still entwined, but looking into the blankness of his eyes, I know that the moment, like the birds, has fled. I turn our embrace into a hug, and kiss him lightly on the forehead, a gesture he has trouble decoding.

'Dance?' he says again.

THIRTEEN

Rémy phones me that night. At the very least, it's good to know that he's still intact but I can tell at once from the warmth in his voice that something has rekindled that fire within that has always been Rémy's trademark. I have a shrewd suspicion what that something might be, and I'm not wrong.

I tell him I love the pitch he's sent. In fact, I've just spent a very happy hour doodling ideas.

'Hélène?' he says. '*La châtelaine de Vlixcombe? C'est toi*. The part is yours.'

'I'm flattered.'

'Don't be. You'll be perfect.'

This puts a huge smile on my face. Future tense positive, no mights, no maybes, nothing conditional. Rémy will make this wonderful project happen.

When I ask him where he found the idea, he plays shy, mumbling something about conversations with an old friend. She'd been researching an idea for a documentary about the early years of the German occupation and had come across the Vlixcombe *émissions*. I'd already bothered him with descriptions of H's spread in West Dorset and – *voilà!* – he'd made the connection.

'This is doubly fantastic,' he says. 'Number one, no one really knows about your lovely *manoir* and what happened there, and number two, it still exists. Not just that but the leading lady is already in residence. Have you made lots of changes?'

'Very few.'

'It still looks the way it was?'

'More or less. I'll have to check but H really wanted to leave the old place alone. That surprised me at the time because he's a born meddler but I think it was pure respect. The place tickled him pink.'

'Tickled him what?'

I explain the phrase, which makes Rémy laugh, then I ask him about backing. At first sight, given the single location, this isn't big budget but given our current circumstances I'd be asking for a sizeable fee on H's part.

'*Pas de problème.*' Rémy has it covered. 'I have meetings with potential backers scheduled for next week.'

'That's what you told me on the boat a couple of days ago. They never happened.'

'But this is different. Different property. Different prospects. You were right. The script was shit and *Exocet* would have been a nightmare to shoot. Never work with babies, animals, or fast jet fighters. *Vlixcombe?* Your lovely Dorset in the late summer? All that period detail? All that music? Scripts drenched in red wine and *grivoiserie*?'

Grivoiserie means sauciness. Whether Rémy's planning for these to occur on or off set, deliberately or otherwise, is academic. From where I'm sitting just now, the prospect of a little fun, a little laughter, is a tonic of its own.

'You said scripts. Does that mean a series?'

'Of course. We want to build *Vlixcombe* into a major event. We've got to make the nation sit down at the same time every week and tune in to a different take on those bloody awful years. It's got to be funny, and true, and absurd. *La combinaison parfaite française, non?*'

The perfect French combination? Rémy's absolutely right, and as I mouth those four words to myself, I know that this thing is getting better and better. *Vlixcombe.* A chance to kick *la débâcle* in its sorry arse, as Pavel would have put it, and take a fresh look at recent history. Laughter, wit, tenderness, plus the best kind of remembrance. And the entire series fronted by yours truly.

'You're a genius, M. Despret. I've always thought so, and now I know.'

Rémy chuckles at the compliment, and then asks about H. I tell him the truth. Flixcombe's owner has been diagnosed with early-onset dementia and just now I'm wondering quite what to do about it.

'He needs a little stimulation,' Rémy says at once.

'That's exactly what a consultant said.'

'We'll give him a job. He can join the circus. You say he's demented? Mad? *Fou?* The perfect qualification, *quoi*?'

The prospect of H coping with a troupe of thesps and everything that goes with them on location is an arresting thought. In his pomp, he'd have had no time for showbiz, largely because he wasn't in control, but now might be very different. Give him an accordion and a stool and a guide to the simplest chords, and he might be happy as Larry. Add a regular supply of decent wine, and his journey into the darkness might feel very different.

I share these possibilities with Rémy. He has the grace to agree but already he wants to know who has the legal right to sign an access contract when the time comes.

'That would be you, *chérie.* Am I right?'

'It might be. I'll make some enquiries. Trust me. It's only money. There's bound to be a way.'

This sparks a genuine laugh. Rémy, it turns out, is just putting the finishing touches to a brief video which will accompany his pitch when he's talking to potential backers and the French media. He'll send it as soon as it's done.

'Like when?'

'Tonight, maybe. Tomorrow morning latest. It just needs a handful of edits.'

'You're a genius,' I say again. 'You've no idea how happy this makes me.'

'*Un plaisir, Hélène. Dors bien . . .*'

FOURTEEN

I sleep, as instructed, like a baby, and awake to find the promo video on my tablet. I check in on H, who's still asleep, and then take the tablet back to bed. Rémy has obviously been raiding the newsreel archives because his video is entirely in black and white.

Scored for Maurice Chevalier singing 'J'aime Paris', German tanks thunder across the belly of France while flights of Stukas plunge out of the sun and feast on columns of refugees plodding south. In Paris, meanwhile, anyone who's elected to stay nervously awaits the arrival of the French and the British armies to defend their precious city. This never happens, of course, and the video ends with the uniformed figure of Hitler, the new Emperor of France, arms akimbo, standing *en plein Paris*, surveying his latest conquest.

Chevalier's voice, jaunty, romantic, proud, gives these images a savage piquancy, and over the final image of Hitler Rémy has cleverly faded up a brief excerpt from a sample *Vlixcombe* broadcast. It has the authentic tinniness of the era, swelling and fading as the fictional Le Patron speculates on the relationship between some top Nazi in Paris and a gay French actor, famous for his conquests amongst senior Third Republic politicians.

Rémy's line about No Entry rules makes me laugh, and I re-cue the video to watch it again. As a come-on for potential backers, and as bait for the media, this treatment is near perfect, and I tap out a brief message to Rémy to tell him so. Within minutes, I'm looking at a reply. He's already appointed a location manager, a no-nonsense Serbian guy he's worked with on a recent shoot. Ratko, he says, is living in London *au moment*, and Rémy would appreciate him spending half a day on-site to take photos of Vlixcombe inside and out.

No problem, I tap back. *I'll pick him up at Yeovil Junction if he's coming by train.*

* * *

Ratko doesn't come by train. Instead, next morning, I have a text on my mobile telling me he's an hour away on the A303. This is slightly awkward because I've just agreed to let Simon, from the Bridport estate agency, take a proper look at the property. He'll doubtless be wanting photos too, and as I answer Ratko's text, telling him the coffee's already brewing, I'm starting to wonder what H will make of all this activity.

Vlixcombe, of course, has rather changed our prospects. Assuming it actually happens, and that Tony Morse can find some way of setting up a company to negotiate the location fee and keep the proceeds away from H's creditors, then we may be able to hang on to the estate. Given the flood of publicity that would follow series transmission, I can imagine all kinds of ways we could cash in. Cornwall, after all, is full of German fans of Rosamund Pilcher's novels, as well as Poldark obsessives. Decent screen exposure never did any estate owner any harm.

Simon is the first to turn up. To be fair to him, I briefly mention the possibility that Flixcombe might soon be featuring in a French TV series and the mention of filming perks him up no end. The attractions of estate agency, I suspect, are beginning to flag and the prospect of a part so close to home is clearly welcome.

'I can do any accent,' he assures me. 'And that's a promise.'

I leave him to drift from room to room with his smartphone and his Distance-Meter, warning him that the estate may not come onto the market after all, but he simply shrugs.

'Any accent,' he repeats. 'And I'm great at playing the drunken cad.'

I tell him I'll keep the thought in mind, and moments later I hear the growl of another car on the gravel outside. This has to be Ratko. I stand at the top of the steps, Lady of the Manor, very happy to be enveloped in this sudden swirl of visitors. Sayid was right when he talked about the dangers of solitude for carers, wrong when he hinted about support groups like the Now and Then Café. In this world, I tell myself, you make your own entertainment.

Ratko I judge to be in his early thirties. He's stocky and broad in the chest, built like a younger version of H. He has the Pompey swagger, head down, lots of shoulder action, as if you've spent half your life wading into a strong headwind. He's wearing a new-looking leather jacket and has a delicate silver ring in his left ear. Indigo tatts in the shape of a jagged skyline surface above the collar of his denim shirt, and close-up he smells of money. Pricey aftershave and soft expensive leather have never done much for me, but the fact that I might be spending a great deal of time with this man prompts a precautionary smile.

When I offer a late breakfast Ratko shakes his head. 'Done already.' He pats the flatness of his stomach. 'Happy Eater. Shit for brains, me. If you'd offered earlier, I'd never have given the place a second look.'

He has a strong accent, and I get the feeling he doesn't smile very often, which is often the way with good location managers. Thespians are notoriously undisciplined, and it never pays to indulge them.

'You speak French?'

'*Oui. Avec Rémy, ç'est obligatoire, non?* I'd prefer to speak Serbo-Croat but it doesn't travel well.'

I nod, say I understand. His French accent is appalling but I love the implication that no one in the real world has the first clue about Serbo-Croat.

'You know Rémy well?'

'Everyone knows Rémy well. Nice guy. Clever. Plenty up here.' He taps his head. He has the hands of a navvy, thick-fingered, strong, but strangely well-cared-for. Two silver rings, one on each thumb.

I take him into the house. Simon is measuring the hall while H sits on the staircase, watching him. When I do the introductions, Ratko declines a handshake.

'Too early,' he grunts.

'In the day, you mean?' I'm lost. Do Serbs only shake hands after dark?

'Covid, yeah?' Ratko shoots me a pitying look. 'You mentioned coffee.'

I make a fresh brew. Simon has finished in the house and is looking for the perfect angle to showcase the walled garden. It's at this moment that I hear the murmur of voices from the hall. One of them is Ratko, whom I've left to get the feel of the place, the other is H.

There's a mirror on the kitchen wall that offers a view of the staircase through the open door. Ratko and H are sitting together on the same carpeted step, as if they'd known each other forever. Ratko is telling H something about London, about some bar he especially likes, and H appears to be hanging on his every word. He's nodding from time to time, even offering the odd thought of his own. The old H was never good with strangers. His gut instinct was to mistrust anyone he didn't know. This H appears to have thrown caution to the winds, much as he did with Sayid. For just a second or two I'm tempted to invite Ratko to move in. Anyone who can tug H into a conversation would be more than welcome.

Moments later, Ratko is back in the kitchen. He jerks a thick finger in H's direction.

'Yours?'

'Mine,' I agree.

'Sweet old guy. Reminds me of my dad.'

'Did he go crazy, too?'

'Yeah.'

Ratko, too, has madness in his eyes. I accompany him around the house, gently quizzing him about his months with Rémy on location. If anything, he's amused by my efforts to tease the odd story out of him. Yes, he enjoys working with Rémy. Yes, as he's already said, he has respect for the man. And yes, actors and technicians can be a pain in the arse, as can script executives, finance directors, and people like me who ask far too many questions.

In the end, he says, he's on set to make sure the job gets done. This is by far the bluntest description of trying to make a movie, or a TV series, that I've ever heard, but as we move from room to room, and he raises his smartphone to take yet another snap, I sense that someone like Rémy would be only too eager to give this man the job that truly matters. Like H, oddly enough, he cuts to the chase. Rémy is in good hands. And it shows.

By mid-afternoon, I have the house to myself. Ratko has left to tackle the A303 again, while Simon – after giving me a verbal canter through his glittering thesp career – has returned to his desk in Bridport. It now remains for me to try and coax H to deliver a verdict on his new friend. God willing, he'll be seeing a great deal more of Ratko once the money is in place and the production team moves in. So what did he make of Rémy's location manager?

The question appears to floor him. He gazes at me, uncomprehending, the bewilderment back in his eyes. We happen to be in the hall.

'There.' I gesture towards the staircase. 'You were sitting together. You and Ratko.'

His head slowly turns towards the staircase. I know he's trying really hard but those moments that I took for conversation have obviously gone. His gaze settles on me again, and then his hand plunges into the pocket of his jeans and emerges with my phone. I've been looking for it since Ratko and Simon left. And here it is. Has H heard an incoming call, the way he did with my tablet, and made it his business to play secretary? I'll never know.

I'm staring at the screen. The WhatsApp has come from Rosa, and couldn't be more blunt. *Phone me,* she's written. Just that.

I thank H for the phone and watch him climbing the stairs to his bedroom. He's taken to napping at odd corners of the day, or maybe he thinks it's bedtime. Either way, I'm glad of a little privacy to muster my thoughts before ringing Rosa.

This has to be about *My Place or Yours?* Has to be. I dread to think what Mitch Culligan has been up to, and it turns out I'm right.

'We had an agreement,' she says as soon as she picks up the phone. 'That draft was for your eyes only.'

'It was,' I counter, 'and it stayed that way.'

'So how come I get your journalist friend on the phone? He's read all the best bits. He was quoting me passage after passage. He's learned the fucking book *by heart.* That's bad enough, believe me, but it gets worse. He says he's been talking to contacts. These are people with access to the Cabinet fucking Office. And he's come up with a name.'

'Who?'

'You mean he hasn't told you?'

'Exactly.'

'Then ask him yourself. This is the woman, he's reliably informed, who's been shagging our Mr Big and keeping notes about the best bits.'

'And is he right?'

'You want me to tell you? You have to be joking. Journalists are animals, Enora. They hunt in packs. They think of nothing but the kill and now we'll all pay the price. What on earth possessed you to do it? A fucking explanation. That's all I want.'

Two clues here. Number one, Rosa never calls me by my Christian name. Number two, she never – or very rarely – uses the 'F' word. My lovely agent has the lowest blood pressure of anyone on the planet. And here she is, about to combust.

'I'm sorry,' is the best I can manage.

'Sorry doesn't cut it, my lovely. Sorry is pathetic. I was given the fucking book in good faith and now look what's happened. Just tell me why you did it. That's all I want to know.'

I gaze at the phone, desperate to muster some kind of explanation. Before Rosa gets a chance to start shouting at me again, I tell her about Sayid, and his relationship with Mitch, and my desperation to get someone qualified to take a proper look at H.

'So you used the book as leverage? Is that what I'm hearing?'

'It is, yes. I gave Mitch a tiny précis, five thousand words at the most. I've still got it on my tablet. I can send it to you. It was a taster. And I made him promise that he'd keep it to himself.'

'But journalists keep nothing to themselves, my precious. That's why they exist. To spread the fucking word and make life tough for the rest of us.'

This is unarguable, as I'm forced to admit. I'm tempted to put the blame on Rosa, given that she was the first to let the book out of her sight, but a moment's reflection suggests this might be less than wise. The fact is that she trusted me, and I let her down.

'So what happens next? Is that a question I'm allowed to ask?'

'Ask all you like – the fact is no one knows. The book's out there in the wild as we speak, and anything can happen.'

I nod. By now, it's begun to occur to me that the woman

Mitch has fingered as the scribe may be anything but. The waters around the upper reaches of the Tory party, I suspect, are never less than turbid and even someone as cynical as Mitch can get sucked under.

'One question,' I mutter. 'Am I allowed?'

'Just one. Because, believe it or not, I still love you. I shouldn't but I do. Go ahead, my precious. No guarantees I'll give you an answer.'

'This name Mitch has come up with. Is he right?'

'No bloody comment.'

'I'll take that as a no.'

'Take it any way you like. You're on your own now. And so is your pushy friend.'

'No clues?'

'Absolutely none.'

'But we still think your actress didn't make it up?'

'No comment. Whatever happens next is between me and the good lady scribe. If you'd like to pass that on to Mr Culligan I'd have absolutely no objections. He should keep his distance. Difficult, I know, but there it is. Reckless is a way of life for certain kinds of politicians. It's my job to turn that into a decent advance.'

'So you really think it's true?'

'I have no idea. And neither do you. And neither does Culligan. So is this where we pull stumps and wander back to the pavilion? No bloody way.'

After a brief silence, Rosa and I declare a truce. I promise to be stern with Mitch, and to forbid him to pursue the story an inch further. Rosa is pleased that I share her enthusiasm for the writing and at this point, I change the subject and bring her up to date with Rémy's new project. My description of his video pitch wins her full attention, not least because she's such a fan of Maurice Chevalier.

'Send it to me,' she says. 'I promise not to show another living soul.'

'Don't make promises you'll never keep,' I tell her. 'We live in a wicked world.'

FIFTEEN

A week goes by. I hear nothing more from Rosa, from Rémy, even from Simon, whom I'm half-expecting to bring a coachload of eager developers to the waiting opportunity that is the Flixcombe estate. As for Mitch, who owes me at the very least a conversation, I draw a total blank. My calls go unanswered and my texts are unacknowledged. To all intents and purposes, Mitch Culligan is off the radar.

H and I, meanwhile, circle each other daily with occasional interventions from Andy and Jess. Jess, in particular, is really worried about H. 'He used to drive me nuts,' she tells me one morning, 'and that's something I could rely on. Now, just the sight of him makes me sad. I never thought I'd miss the old H, but I do.'

I know what she means. H, like me, has risen to the challenge of strangers in the house. Whether it was Sayid or Ratko, they parted the heavy curtains in his failing brain and caught his fleeting attention. They beckoned him briefly into the daylight and offered the possibility of a conversation. One of the saddest legacies of that brief spasm of human contact was H's absolute failure to remember either of them. When I enquire gently about Sayid, H blanks me. Ratko's name already means nothing, and when I mention the leather jacket, and the tatts, and the single silver earring, he simply yawns and looks away.

This is important because somehow H and I have to find a way of getting by together. I hate the word carer. I loathe that sense of utter dependency, one person the keeper, the other the kept. As a novice mother, with a wailing Malo, neither of us had any choice in the matter, and in any event, I suspect that Mother Nature programs women to throw their arms around their newborn and fend off all-comers, but looking after a man of fifty-five is utterly different. Nonetheless, we've been through a lot these last few years, especially with Malo.

We're old campaigners. We've won our stripes, and I don't want to lose that kinship.

'I know it sounds funny but believe me it isn't. Some of this stuff breaks my heart. He's just gone, pushed off, and the worst thing is I've no idea where to find him.'

I'm talking to Malo. I've told him the story about H and the fridge door and I've shared one or two other glimpses of the void that used to be his dad. The challenge here is trying to connect all these terrifying dots, and thus chart a pathway forward. Sayid has been more than generous with his time, but his diagnosis still ends in the 'c' word – 'carer' – and something within me says there might yet be a different outcome.

Malo appears not to have been listening to a word I've said.

'You could bring him up here,' he says breezily. 'Clem could take him to Regent's Park. He always loved the zoo. He could stay for a week, give you a break. I'm sure Clem wouldn't mind, and maybe he could spend a day or two coming to work with me, give us a hand packing the food boxes, see how the other half lives. Stick him on the train if you don't fancy the drive. I could pick him up at Clapham Junction.'

'He wouldn't know where to get off.'

'There's a map thing, a route map, station names. All he has to do is look out of the window when the train stops.'

'It doesn't work that way, not anymore. Everything's in a muddle in his head. Then he panics.'

'So ask someone to keep an eye on him. Do they still have guards? Talk to him, her, whatever. And tell him not to forget a mask, and a spare in his back pocket just in case. People get funny about masks up here. You'd be amazed.'

I shake my head. It's sweet of my son to come up with an offer like this but he clearly has no idea how bad it's got. The last time he saw H was at Christmas. Long Covid, I now realize, was masking the onset of dementia and five months later the H we're all living with is barely recognizable from the sturdy H who carved the turkey.

'This isn't a summer cold, Malo,' I tell him. 'This thing is forever, and it'll probably get much worse.'

'Really?'

'Yes, really.'

There's a longish silence. At last I suspect the truth about H has started to dawn on his cherished boy.

'You want me to come down?' he asks at last. 'Would that help?'

'It might, but you'd have to be ready for a surprise or two.'

'Like?'

'He might not recognize you.'

'*What?* You're serious?'

'I'm afraid so.'

Another silence, even longer this time. Then he's back on the line, much sobered, with a question I've been privately mulling for a day or two.

'So does it kill you in the end, this thing? Do you die of being mad?'

The Dorset History Centre is in the middle of Dorchester. It's a Friday, and I've managed to book a couple of hours in the early afternoon, lodging a request for any information on Flixcombe Manor. Since talking to Malo the night before last, I've been thinking hard on how we can ambush dementia and somehow bring it to its knees.

Most case histories I've read on the internet – and there are hundreds of them – seem to end in a nursing home, and the guilt-ridden testimony from carers and other family members are beyond depressing. Dementia is like a bad attack of damp. The mould is visible on wall after wall, the smell is ever-present, and finally you have to do something about it. We, the sane, always start this journey with the best of intentions but I'm beginning to sense how easy it might be to consign the resident ghost to the care of strangers.

Except that H is – just – still H. Last year, we spent weeks and weeks and a vast sum of money to keep him out of ICU because he'd seen what it had done to poor Dave Munroe, and he couldn't face the aloneness of a similar death. Now, under very different circumstances, I know in my heart that we have to see off the dread prospect of a nursing home. Same logic. H was never built to be banged up, either in ICU or on a dementia ward. There isn't an institutional bone in his body.

Close the door, lock it for his own good, and he'd go even madder.

And so here I am, bent over a modest pile of documents in a big sunny room overlooking a railway line. By now I'm convinced that Rémy's wonderful *Vlixcombe* idea has immense potential for keeping H distracted. I know a great deal about the uncertain chemistry of location film shoots. With the wrong director in charge they can be a disaster, breeding an atmosphere that often shows in the rushes, but Rémy has a rare gift for keeping the location pot bubbling at exactly the right temperature, and anything I can do to help him get the project financed and scheduled must surely help. Three birds with one stone, I tell myself. First of all Rémy, then H, and then me. *Vlixcombe* might turn out to be salvation for all of us. Here's hoping.

I've asked for everything specific to Flixcombe since the house was built, and anything that might set the scene for its arrival in – as far as I'm aware – the early 1790s. The latter material has a fascination of its own because it addresses a question I've often asked myself: how did people in these parts build fortunes that led to so many grand houses, expansive estates and fabulously show-off churches? The answer, it turns out, is twofold: sheep and smuggling, both of which boiled down to trade.

Sheep, it turns out, have been grazing on these hills and pasturelands for centuries. They account for the bright greenness of the landscape in early spring, but it's a surprise – for me, at least – to learn that West Country wool was in such huge demand abroad. The wealth from this trade settled on parish after Dorset parish, financing ever-grander churches as the rich did their best to secure a perch in the afterlife, but what catches my eye is the occasional reference to travelling exorcists, mainly itinerant Anglican priests who would – doubtless for a fee – chase out devils and poltergeists from the afflicted.

This has nothing to do with wool and churches but just now, were we living a couple of hundred years ago, I can imagine the travelling exorcist arriving at newly built Flixcombe to attend to H. He's not himself anymore. He's been possessed.

His mind is no longer his own. I sit back from the spread of documents before me, hearing the clatter of a passing train. Are exorcists still around? Do they advertise their services? Might I be able to Google a couple and check out their credentials?

I scribble myself a note – any port in a storm – and then turn to smuggling. The literature here is extensive, the stories colourful. Many of them I've read before in various magazines, but I'm struck by the sheer wealth of references to the same name. A successful smuggler with steady nerves and the right connections quickly became a wealthy man and by far the richest was a smuggler called Isaac Gulliver. It seems that he ran a fleet of no less than fifteen luggers, sailing from France to remote beaches the length of Dorset and Devon with cargoes of wine, brandy, silks, salt and tobacco, plus asylum seekers in the shape of titled aristos fleeing the Revolution.

I pause for a moment, trying to imagine midnight shadows in the lanes around Flixcombe, and the whisper of muffled wheels bearing the contraband inland. Were the revenue men lying in wait? And were these long-ago Dessie Wrens outwitted by the likes of Isaac Gulliver? According to one document, he was active at the time Flixcombe was built and ended his days as a church warden in Wimborne Minster. The minster's communion wine, according to one source, came directly from Gulliver's illegal stash, but the king of the Dorset smugglers made no charge.

Gulliver. In Rémy's pitch for *Vlixcombe*, this is the name of the uber-resourceful wine importer who bought Flixcombe before the war, the wealthy merchant who married Hélène and turned H's pride and joy into a convalescent home for wounded French soldiers. A coincidence? Undoubtedly.

It's at this point that I unearth the earliest print of Flixcombe. It's dated 1810. It's a pen-and-ink sketch, not entirely successful, but it does ample justice to the wonderful symmetry that became the hallmark of Georgian architecture. The elegant, multi-paned windows across the front of the house. The main door plumb-centre. The columns at the entrance, a proclamation of wealth, and the glazed panels flanking the door itself. The house has been drawn from the final bend of the approaching drive, H's favourite view, though many of today's trees are missing.

I gaze at this sketch for a while, only too aware of the historical irony. Houses like Flixcombe were a celebration of perfect balance, of one architectural element exactly counterpointed by another, of the calm and poise and confidence of the Georgian moment. How strange that our poor, wrecked H should find himself falling apart in a house like this.

I take a shot on my phone, meaning to show H when I get back. The History Centre closes at four thirty and already the neighbouring tables are beginning to empty. After spending far too much time on smuggling and sheep, I've yet to get to the twentieth century, let alone the Second World War.

I leaf quickly through the remaining documents, surprised to find so little reference to Flixcombe. In 1937, a cutting from the *Bridport News* reports on a successful Flixcombe garden party to celebrate the coronation of George VI, but I don't recognize any of the names. After that, to the best of my knowledge, comes the steady tramp to war, but of Gulliver and Hélène, and everything they did on the estate following the Dunkirk evacuation, there's no mention. This omission I find odd, though I suspect the wartime mania for secrecy may explain it. Why draw attention to a bunch of renegade French patriots when West Dorset may be thick with German spies?

I'm last to the central desk before the History Centre closes. The staff have been more than helpful, and I hesitate for a moment before returning my documents and security pass. The woman behind the counter is already aware of my interest in Flixcombe, and even knows where it is.

'Find everything you needed?' she asks.

'Not really.' I briefly explain about Vlixcombe, and the French broadcasts to the Motherland, and the very real possibility of a TV series.

'Vlixcombe with a "V"? How strange.' The woman is checking her watch. 'First time I've heard about it.'

SIXTEEN

I carry this little health warning back to Flixcombe, and by the time I'm halfway up the drive I've convinced myself that a French talent for blending into the historical landscape has to explain this gap in the county archives. I was right to be thinking secrecy. The essence of the BBC's wartime presence in the middle of our sleepy landscape was obviously discretion. Under the threat of being returned to their native France, the scriptwriters and the sound engineers and the thesps would have been sworn to silence. Thus Rémy's latest baby, baptised with his trademark brilliance, will come as a surprise as well as a delight. I'm thinking scoop, which in the world of historical drama is very rare indeed.

It's at this point, rounding the last bend in the drive, that I register a newish VW estate parked in front of the house. I've a feeling I've seen this car before, way back last year, when we were all down in Portsmouth. I draw up beside it and a glance at the aviator sunglasses abandoned on the passenger seat confirms my suspicions.

I step into the house and stop to listen. Nothing, except the slow tick-tock of Flixcombe time from the nearby grandfather clock. Then comes the low murmur of a voice from somewhere above. I creep upstairs, one careful step at a time, until I'm outside H's bedroom. The door is an inch or two open and Dessie Wren is doing his best to prepare H for the forthcoming Euros, the football fest, which opens this evening. This first game is in Rome, which is news to me, and I'm fighting a wave of the deepest guilt for assuming that just a little of the wall-to-wall media pre-hype might have got through to H. He's always loved football, which is odd really because it leaves both Malo and I stone cold. There's a guy who plays for Spurs who has the naughtiest grin and thighs to die for but I've yet to meet a man, even sober, who can explain the offside rule.

'Turkey?' H's voice is barely a whisper, though the question is thickened with wonderment.

'It's a country, H. Muslims. Eighty million of them. The manager's shit but they can be useful on the night.'

'Yeah?'

'Yeah. It's a home tie, though, for the Italians. Christ knows how many they'll let into the stadium but they haven't lost for years and they have to be favourites. Ask me nicely and I might stay for the game. Eight o'clock kick-off? Bite to eat? Few beers?'

'Yeah?'

'Yeah.'

'But you're carving, right?'

'Carving . . .?'

Dessie has every reason to have lost the thread of the conversation but from my side of the door it's all too clear. H has got stuck on Turkey. He struggles in the breaking waves of any conversation and just now he's clinging onto the word for dear life. Turkey means Christmas, redcurrant jelly, dollops of stuffing, roasties hot from the oven, and probably his dad's special gravy he once told me about. This is stuff he remembers, everything in the sharpest focus, unlike the strangers who suddenly appear in his life, bothering him with details that refuse to stay still and explain themselves. Turkey, H understands. Turkey speaks to him. Dessie has the carving knife and Dessie will do the honours. Job done.

I muster a polite cough and open the door. H is lying in bed, the sheets tucked up around his skinny chest. Dessie is sitting on the edge of the bed. On the pillow beside H's head lies an open copy of a book I recognize. I bought it for Malo when he was a kid and had trouble getting off to sleep and it's somehow found its way to Flixcombe. Malo really took to *The Sandman*, and even now he still picks it up. Has Dessie been reading it aloud to H? I suspect the answer is yes.

'Just in time.' Dessie is on his feet. 'H thought you must have done a runner.'

H is inspecting the face at the door. Who is this stranger at the Christmas feast? Will there be enough turkey to go round?

I make light of everything. There's no point, just now, asking Dessie what on earth he's doing here because there's no way

– in H's presence – he'll give me a sensible answer. I know he wants to stay and I'm very happy to make that happen. I'll rustle up something to eat. We'll have a drink or two. And at eight o'clock we'll all settle down to watch the football.

'Perfect,' this from Dessie. 'My money's on the Italians. How about you, H? What's your call?'

H is still staring at me, eternally curious. Who *is* this woman?

H doesn't make the football, or even the meal. Alone in the kitchen, I conjure a spaghetti marinara from frozen prawns, onions, a big tin of tomatoes, and as many cloves of garlic as I can find. I've despatched H to give Dessie a tour of the house and from time to time I cross to the open door and listen for voices from above. I can hear the shuffle of footsteps and the sigh of various doors opening and closing, but the only voice is Dessie's. At length, the meal nearly ready, he's back in the kitchen.

'Where's H?'

'I put him to bed. We were about to come down, but he decided he was tired.'

'Really?'

'Really.' Dessie is gazing at the sauce bubbling in my Le Creuset pan. 'Big double bed? Green panelling? Lovely full-length mirror?'

'That's *my* bedroom.'

'That's what I thought.'

'You put him in there? In my bed?'

'His decision, I'm afraid, not mine. One minute I'm looking out at the view. The next he's tucked himself up, eyes closed, out for the count.'

'And you left him there?'

'I did. Even now, he's got a mind of his own.'

I nod, giving the sauce a final stir, not knowing quite what to say. To my knowledge, this has never happened before. Getting inside what remains of H's head is a very big ask indeed but I'm beginning to wonder whether he's trying to protect me. Maybe he's scented Dessie's interest in yours truly. Maybe, in some corner of his failing brain, this is an act of protection, or even – God help me – ownership.

'So what do you think?'

'I think it's a fabulous house.'

'I meant H.'

'I know you did.'

Dessie has settled at the table. I've readied three glasses beside a newly opened bottle of Muriel Rioja and I tell him to help himself. When I ask about H again he seems reluctant to venture an opinion, but when I turn from the stove and look him in the eye I can see why.

'This upsets you?' I ask.

'H? The state of the man? Of course it does.' He's staring at me now, as if I've touched something very precious. 'H led us a dance for years. If I was running a masterclass for quality criminals, he'd be up there with the best of them, Exhibit One. You want the truth? We never laid a finger on him. Why? Because he was that good. It was blokes like H that made the Job worthwhile. There's not a lot Pompey can be proud of but H was in a class of his own, and this lovely house and the estate and the views are the living proof. A hundred acres? Two hundred?'

'Three.'

'Three . . .' he repeats softly. 'Three hundred acres. None of that happened by accident, believe me. At H's level the drugs game was never for beginners. You needed to be canny, you needed to take the right advice, and you needed a great deal of nerve. H had all that. In spades. And now look at him. Shit . . . I'm sorry . . .' He shakes his head.

For a moment I'm tempted to comfort him, to give him a hug, but I'm aware that Dessie inhabits the same Pompey darkness that has been so kind to H over the years. Nothing in that world is ever quite what it seems. Every gesture, every half-sentence, is loaded with a significance you might not quite catch. Beware detectives and top criminals, because the best of them come from the same egg. Last year in Pompey taught me that, and it's a lesson I'm unlikely to forget.

I drain the pan, dish out the pasta, and pour sauce over the tangles of spaghetti. As hard as I try not to, I can't help thinking of H curled up in my bed. Dessie tells me the prawn sauce is tops. Then he reaches for his glass. He's calmed down now and not for the first time in our relationship, he seems to have read my mind.

'You still sleep together? You and H?'

'Christ, no. It happened once, a very long time ago.'

'Really? So all this?' He gestures round. 'The woman's touch in all those rooms? You being here?'

'He's the father of my only son. Apart from my mother, H and Malo are the closest I get to family.'

'So what's he doing in your bed? Now?'

'Is that any business of yours?'

'Yes, in a way it is.'

'How come?'

'Because I need to know how close you are.'

'We're very close, in fact I'm probably all H has got left. I'm not sure he knows that but it happens to be true. I've had him checked out. Dementia robs you blind, Dessie Wren, and that's an irony I never saw coming. H is oddly spared because he knows nothing any more and so it's my job to play the good shepherd. I've had some tough roles in my life, believe me, but nothing . . .' I close my eyes a moment, reaching blindly for my glass, slightly shocked at my own vehemence, knowing that I shouldn't expose myself like this, but when I catch my breath and take stock, Dessie hasn't moved.

'So . . .?' The loose gesture he makes with his right hand could mean anything.

'So the man in my bed isn't a man at all. It's not H, it's not the guy you seem to miss so much, it's someone else. Think child. Did he want a story earlier? Before I arrived? Be honest.'

'He did, yes.'

'And?'

'I did the honours.'

'Good. That was kind. Did he say thank you?'

'He didn't say anything. All he wanted to do was look at the pictures.'

'Clouds of sleepy dust? The fairies in the forest?'

'Both.'

I hold his gaze a moment, aware of a prickling behind my own eyes, and then stare down at my plate. My appetite has deserted me. The last thing I need are coils of pasta, already lukewarm.

'More wine?'

Over the next hour or so, we talk at much greater length about the world H has left behind, about the small army of Pompey villains, important and otherwise, who still think the world of him, and about the muddle that Dessie himself has spent half a lifetime trying to untangle.

Before he joined the police, Dessie was in the Navy. His years of service in a hunter/killer submarine – his precious HMS *Courageous* – taught him a great deal about detecting the bad guys, about ghosting along in the wake of Soviet missile submarines, about the need to stay invisible in the depths of the ocean at the height of the Cold War. Many of these lessons he later used to good effect in the badlands of Pompey, first as a detective constable, then a detective sergeant: the same emphasis on patience and raw cunning, the same need to lay a trap or two, the same knowledge that any mistake could be worse than costly.

Much of this I'd heard before last year when H, very sick with Covid, became a sitting target for an old enemy with a serious grudge. Over those weeks down in Pompey, Dessie and I became briefly close. He was there when I needed him, and he never once took advantage in any physical sense, and I was more than grateful for all his support and protection. But deep in his DNA, like H, Dessie is always on patrol, listening for Soviet submarines, plotting moves on Pompey villains, and I'd be naïve to ever think otherwise. Which is why, in the end, I insist on talking about Rémy Despret.

By now, we're next door in H's den. I've got the TV on, tuned to the Italy vs Turkey game, and I've broached another bottle of Rioja.

'Newhaven,' I murmur. 'Anything to tell me?'

'Yes. Plenty.'

'And?'

'You were right.'

'About what?

'To be worried. That friend of yours has been keeping bad company. He arrived on Tuesday the twenty-fifth of May. He radioed ahead for a visitor berth. He was carrying a French certificate for two Pfizer jabs, and he'd also taken a PCR test in Jersey a couple of days earlier. The test was negative but the people in Newhaven insisted on another before allotting him a berth. That was negative, too. He stayed in Newhaven from the Tuesday until Saturday the twenty-ninth. He left in the morning.'

I nod, trying to do the sums. By the following Sunday morning, Rémy was tied up in St Katharine Docks, where he did his best to sell me *Exocet.* I've no idea about the tides in the English Channel but it would be a longish haul from Newhaven, hence the need to sail through the night.

'So what was he doing in Newhaven?' Dessie's attention has drifted back to the game, but our conversation is far from over.

'Your French friend had a number of visitors,' he says. 'Three of them turned out to be of interest. One was a trucker with previous for carrying. Another used to work for the Border Force before they sacked him.'

'You've seen these people?'

'On-screen, yes. The marina has lots of CCTV, especially the visitor berths.'

'Previous for carrying what?'

'Narcotics, in this case cannabis. He was stopped on the A23 a while back. The guy was on the salad run from Murcia. Amongst the lettuces, the rummage crew unearthed half a dozen blocks of Moroccan resin, nothing over-ambitious but enough to put him away for four years.'

'And the man from the Border Force?'

'He got on the wrong side of a bribery investigation. The accusation had him trousering a couple of grand for looking the other way on several documented occasions. Nothing was ever proved but the fact that he didn't fight the sacking told the Home Office he was better gone.'

'And he paid Rémy a visit?'

'He did.'

'Why would he do that?'

'I've no idea. Except he'd know the border operation by

heart. If Despret's planning serious importations, he could do a lot worse than Newhaven.'

I reach for my wine. Dessie's use of Rémy's surname is slightly chilling. This has ceased to be a cosy chat.

For a long minute, I half-follow the football action out in Rome, doing my best to resist the obvious implications. That Rosa is right. That Rémy has somehow got himself involved in the drugs biz and is way out of his depth. Easily done, I'm thinking. A career in cutting-edge gangster movies is no guarantee you'll ever succeed at the real thing.

'You mentioned three visitors,' I murmur at last. 'Who was the other one?'

Dessie doesn't answer. Instead, he reaches into the depths of his leather jacket and produces his smartphone. A couple of swipes takes him to a particular shot in his gallery. He gazes at it for a moment or two, and then passes the phone across before the game recaptures his attention.

'Three-nil at least,' he murmurs. 'The Turks are wasting their time.'

I'm staring at the face on the smartphone. A middle-aged man in jeans and a football top is sitting at a café table. He's alone, a cigarette in one hand, his phone in the other. On the table, alongside a small cup of expresso, is a battered-looking leather cap. In the background, slightly out of focus, are dozens of superyachts, most of them a study in bad taste.

'Where was this taken?'

'Marbella.'

'When?'

'Yesterday.'

'And this man has a name?'

'Vuk. It's Serbo-Croat for "wolf". You're going to ask me next whether he paid Despret a visit, and the answer is yes. Not once, but twice, and on the second occasion he stayed a while. Just swipe to the left' – he's nodding at the phone – 'and tell me what you see.'

This, it occurs to me, is like an audition without a script, a free-form exchange of dialogue that could literally go anywhere. Slightly mesmerized, I do Dessie's bidding and find myself looking at the same man, probably in the same jeans. The weather looks awful and the quality of the CCTV image is far from perfect, but there's no disguising the thickset figure pausing beside Rémy's yacht.

'This was taken in Newhaven?'

'Yes.'

'So tell me more about this Wolf person.'

'He's a top player in the cocaine business. He's rich already but he wants to get much richer. Respect matters a great deal and just now he's building alliances over here. I get the feeling he values peace and quiet. Unlike some of these tossers, he's got no time for the toys.'

'Toys?'

'Superyachts. Crates of Krug for breakfast. Shouty mates he needs to impress. An executive jet with his name all over it. H, oddly enough, would approve but it might be a bit late to check.'

I nod. I've swiped to the right on Dessie's phone, and my gaze has returned to the lone figure at the waterside table in Marbella and something very cold has stolen into the very middle of me. I met this man barely ten days ago. He told me his name was Ratko, and he said he was to be the location manager on Rémy's next production. He also took lots of photos of H's precious house.

Peace and quiet, I think. Fat chance.

SEVENTEEN

I wake up to the spill of fierce sunshine next morning, hearing Dessie's voice from the kitchen garden below my open window. Dessie and I had stayed up after the football, me trying to find out more about the man I'd known as Ratko, but Dessie hadn't been in the mood for more revelations and in the end we'd both shepherded an unprotesting H back to his own bed before tucking him in.

It was Dessie who'd volunteered to keep an eye on Pompey's drug lord overnight, and I dragged in a mattress he positioned on the floor at the end of H's bed. I chose to interpret this as a gesture of genuine concern, though it took me a while to realize it was for my sake rather than H's. This morning, Dessie is trying to interest H in a replay of key moments from last night's game, but H barely glances at his phone. Maybe the sun's too strong, I think. Or – more likely – the tiny figures on Dessie's screen have ceased to make any kind of sense. What does three-nil mean?

Saturday mornings I've always enjoyed. Covid has made a nonsense of the working week but there's still something liberating in the thought of a weekend to myself, but the latter, I'm starting to realize, has become a cherished memory. I pledge to keep H out of the hands of strangers, and every next day becomes a repeat performance of the last: looking after my sorry charge, tracking his every movement, trying whichever way I can to catch his attention, to stir a response from whatever's left upstairs, to delay that moment when he folds in on himself like some dying star and ceases to exist. This prospect is beyond horrible, and I later share it with Dessie over a glum breakfast.

'How much time has he got?' Dessie enquires.

It's a good question, and I take a while to answer it. I tell him about Sayid's diagnosis, about the mysteries of frontotemporal dementia, about the long goodbye which will probably be the shape of the weeks and months to come.

'But he's still in his fifties,' Dessie points out.

'I know.'

'So it could be much longer.'

'You're right. There but not there. Mr Invisible. Can you imagine that? H, of all people?'

Dessie nods, and then turns his head to stare out of the window. H is still in the kitchen garden, still in his pyjamas, slumped in one corner of what's become his favourite bench. He might be asleep, he might not. It might be Long Covid, it might not. Truly, there's nothing to say.

My phone starts to ring. I glance at Caller ID. Mitch Culligan. He tells me he's sitting in a café in Camden Town. He's just had breakfast with Anoushka, and now she's gone.

'Anoushka?'

'Your Mr Big's alleged shag. The phantom scribe. I think she's decided I might be useful when it comes to nailing a contract. A whisper or two from the cheap seats might end with an auction.'

'This is the name you got from your contact?'

'Yeah.'

'And?'

'I think she's full of shit.'

'Right.' I'm looking at Dessie. 'So why are you telling me?'

'She claims to be a thesp. It's there in the book. I can find no trace of any track record but I need to be sure. She's heard of you and she's happy to meet.'

'For what?'

'A chat. You'd suss whether I'm right.'

'About the bullshit?'

'About whether she's ever been near a film set, or a stage, or anywhere else. A favour for a favour? Sayid sends his best, by the way. If you're lucky he might bake you a cake to take home.'

My gaze has drifted to H, still on the bench. How can I go to London? How can I leave him like this? Jess would step in, I know she would, but that wouldn't be fair on either Jess or H.

Mitch is waiting for an answer. I close my eyes a moment, then feel the lightest touch on my arm. It's Dessie.

'I'll stay.' He's heard everything. 'I can give H a couple of days.'

Dessie takes me to Yeovil Junction to catch a mid-morning train. H is in the back. The journey from Flixcombe through the deep country lanes has always felt like a return to an older England – butterflies, and a wash of wildflowers, and that heavy warmth I remember from my first reading of *Cider with Rosie* – and I can tell that Dessie is impressed. Every time we crest another hill, he slows to appreciate the view, even stopping on one occasion to step out of the car and take a photo on his phone. H joins him, stooping to inspect a stand of pale pink dog roses amongst the roadside explosion of cow parsley and honeysuckle. With Dessie watching attentively, he's still locked in some kind of private decision, his chin in his cupped hand, his eyes slowly tracking a bee from flower to flower.

By now I'm starting to worry about missing the train but Dessie tells me to relax. Finally H nods and grunts to himself and stoops to pick the biggest of the roses. This isn't as simple as he seems to assume. On his knees in the long grass, he wrestles with the stalk, pulling, half-twisting, still determined to liberate the rose. Dessie has produced a penknife, which he ignores. At length, H tilts his head at an awkward angle and attacks the stalk with his teeth. This is painful to watch, so God knows what it's doing to H. Moments later, he's at my window.

'Yours.' Blood is trickling down his cheek from where the rose fought back. 'Can we go for a walk now?'

I thank him and take the proffered rose, exchanging glances with Dessie. With H reluctantly back on board, we make it to Yeovil Junction with a couple of minutes to catch the train and as I hurry towards the station entrance, I'm aware of H watching me. He seems bewildered that I'm leaving, but I've seen him with Dessie and I've sensed the bond between them. Never did I suspect that dementia could bridge half a Pompey lifetime on rival sides of the law, but if friendship any longer means anything to H, then Dessie is a lucky man.

'Take care, guys,' I murmur to myself as I wave goodbye. 'Enjoy.'

* * *

I buy a paper in time to greet the train as it arrives. Thanks to the Gods of Covid, I have a choice of seats in a near-empty carriage, and I settle at a table I have entirely to myself, plunging into the *Guardian* as the train begins to move. Journeys like this – unexpected, solitary – have always held a special magic, burying my head in the paper for a minute or two, then glancing up for another leisurely gaze at the ever-changing view, but my luck only holds as far as Sherborne where the platform is thick with kids. The train has only three carriages, and with some reluctance I move my bag to make space on the adjoining seat.

The kids, mainly girls, pile on. Most of them are in their early teens, and they're overwhelmingly loud. The names, I tell myself, are the clue. Sherborne is seriously monied, hence Tansy, and Allegra, and Béatrice (pronounced the French way). Phones in hand, they grab seat after seat in a torrent of girly excitement.

Mercifully, the seat opposite mine falls to a woman I judge to be in late middle age. At first, I mistake her for one of the teachers in charge of the pack, but then she stores a violin case on the overhead luggage rack and I decide I must be wrong. She's wearing a light summer jacket in a lovely shade of drab olive. The jacket has a slightly military cut which goes well with her cap of greying hair, artfully feathered. Above the mask, she has the face of a much younger woman, not a trace of make-up, perfect bone structure, and as she produces a book from her bag, I become aware of her hands, long fingers, trimmed nails, no rings, and a playful twist of something loved and African around her left wrist. The kids are still pressing down the central aisle, looking for somewhere to sit, but there's a sternness in this woman's face, a sense of purpose, and after one look the kids drift on.

The train begins to move again, quickly gathering speed. We're on the sunny side of the carriage and the constant flicker of light through the trackside branches makes the print of my newspaper dance in front of my eyes. This is wearying, and it's all too easy to transfer my attention to the book my new companion is reading. The cover features a wash of the richest reds and blacks, pricked with what I can only describe as points of brilliant gold. As for the title, I'm completely in the dark. Thanks to Pavel, I have a passing acquaintance with the Czech language, especially those little tell-tale upside-down circumflexes, and I'm still trying to figure out the author's name when – with a sigh – she puts the book down.

'Do you have daughters?' she asks me. 'So eager. So loud. So damn *noisy*.' Foreign accent, possibly Czech.

I tell her I have a son but no daughters. She nods, studying me with some care. Then she produces a flask and a single cup.

'Coffee.' She takes her mask off. 'Expresso. Good coffee. You're welcome to take the risk.'

'You mean the coffee?'

'I mean sharing the cup.' The smile is transformative, warming the space between us. 'Me? Two jabs.' She mimes a hypodermic in her upper arm. 'You?'

'The same. And, yes, I'd love a sip or two.'

She pours the coffee, which is very good indeed with just the right measure of oily bitterness, and I ask her about the instrument lodged on the overhead rack. It turns out she's a professional musician. Just now, she's occupying a desk amongst the first violins in the London Symphony Orchestra, and she's been summoned to attend an afternoon of rehearsals at a venue in the heart of the City. In August, the LSO are guesting at the Edinburgh Festival and today is their first go-through for pieces from Martinů, Ibert and Richard Strauss.

'And your favourite?'

'Ibert,' she says. '"Divertissement". It's a crazy piece. Crazy rhythms. Crazy intentions. Crazy everything. If it lived next door, you'd invite it in when life got boring. Definitely a soufflé. Never a pudding.'

I return her smile. Dialogue of this quality, I tell myself, is a windfall on any train journey. I especially love 'crazy intentions'.

'You live up the line?'

'Exeter.'

'Any daughters?'

'None. I had a husband until recently but he's gone now.'

'You mean he died?'

'I mean he's gone. He's English, thank God, and he's happy not to divorce so that makes me a lucky girl. Otherwise, the way things are going in this country, I'd be back in Prague. Never marry a percussionist. They get ideas above their station. He never did the ironing, either, but that's another story. And you?'

This is a question I'm determined to keep at arm's length. A proper answer would ruin a promising day and so I tell her I work in the travel business and then – in search of common ground – fasten on dearest Pavel who is, of course, dead. I skip the blindness, and the midnight plunge into the hotel pool that left him paralysed, and pretend that he's still alive, still in love with all things Prague, the calm centre of my giddy life. At this point, briefly formal, a hand extends over our shared expresso.

'Johana,' she says. 'And you?'

'Enora.'

'That's a Breton name.'

'How do you know?'

'We have a Breton in the orchestra. A bassoonist. Maiwenn. A lovely, lovely girl.'

We go back to Pavel, and to Prague, and to keep the conversation afloat I invent all kinds of stories based on my sketchy knowledge of the Czech capital. The last time I was there I emptied Pavel's remains into the river from the Charles Bridge, a thinning cloud of black ash that drifted with the wind, but I remember the graffiti that now disfigures so many of the finest buildings, and this appears to prove that I've actually been there.

'Disgusting,' she says. 'Most Czechs I know blame the tourists but that's nonsense. The kids are all the same these days. They all think they're artists but that's nonsense, too. Art demands effort. Ask Maiwenn. Ask me. Ask anyone.'

This quickly develops into a rant, and by the time we're racing through the inner suburbs, minutes from Waterloo, I know a great deal about the kids down the road from the house Johana has managed to rescue from the wreckage of her marriage. They, too, are handy with the spray can but it might help, she says despairingly, if they could bloody spell.

This parting shot puts a smile on my face, and as the train pulls into Waterloo, I get to my feet and extend a hand.

'It's been a pleasure,' I say. 'And I mean that.'

Johana looks up at me for a long moment, ignoring my hand.

'It's been a while since I last saw *The Hour of Our Passing*,' she says. 'But you were unforgettable.'

'Really?' I'm staring at her now. I've just spent the last two hours making a complete fool of myself. *The Hour of Our Passing* is a World War Two movie produced a while back. I play the lover of an eager young French *résistant*. It was the first time I ever appeared nude, and the script required me to make love to my doomed lover on the eve of his arrest. The sequence, beautifully lit, did me more than justice. It was the first time, oddly enough, that I ever worked under Rémy's direction.

'You remember that scene?' I ask.

'Of course. Everyone does. You were sensational. You know you were.'

'Pavel loved it too,' I tell her as the carriage begins to empty.

'Loved?'

'He's dead. I'm afraid I never mentioned that.'

'*Tant pis*,' she says. Too bad. 'We make up stuff all the time. Sometimes it helps, sometimes it doesn't.' She pauses. Then looks me in the eye. 'Do you mind me asking something personal? Are you in a bad place, just now?'

I hold her gaze, then nod. 'Very bad,' I tell her. 'How clever of you to guess.'

'It wasn't a guess. It's there in your face. I can see it. A little advice?' Her hand is on my arm. 'In Africa, they have a saying. It goes like this. After the rain, we drink at the waterhole. It's natural. It's what we do. Otherwise, we'd all die.'

EIGHTEEN

I float down the escalator to the Underground, still wondering about the waterhole, and the drenching African rains, but buoyed by the company of a woman who'd known from the start exactly who I was. To pretend otherwise, to put all the showbiz nonsense to one side, to take our conversation – instead – in a very different direction is seriously unusual, and seriously cool.

When I get to the Camden café and spot Mitch looking grumpy at a corner table, I give him a full account, and then get one of two things off my chest.

'You took liberties with that script,' I point out. 'And left me to clear up afterwards.'

'Liberties?' The word puts a scowl on his face. 'I'm here to defend them. It's what I do. Does freedom from our masters come at a price? Of course it fucking does. Should I have asked nicely first? Sought your permission? No way. That's not how it works, and you – of all people – know it.'

This little scold appears to bring our contretemps to an end. With nowhere to go, it's my turn to shrug.

'So tell me about Anoushka. Where does she live?'

'Round the corner.'

'And she's still happy to see me? Even if she might not be a thesp?'

'Right. Strange doesn't start to cover it. Bizarre might be closer. The woman is feral. That's the closest I can get.'

'*Feral?* You mean that?'

'I do. I've done my best to get to the bottom of her but I'm the wrong kind of journo. She wants celebrity, not someone in her face asking too many questions. She doesn't see the point of my kind of person, but at least she's honest. The real question is the bloody book.'

'You still don't think she wrote it?'

'No way. Forget the guile. Forget the craft. Forget the putting of one word after another. Even if she laid hands on a pen, she wouldn't have the patience. All she's after is the money, and whatever else comes out in the wash.'

'Like?'

Mitch studies me for a long moment. For the second time in three hours, I'm under the microscope. Finally he checks his watch and nods towards the street.

'I'll walk you round,' he says, 'and do the honours. After that you're on your own.'

Anoushka's apartment is five minutes away, two upper floors in a Georgian five-storey terrace off the Euston Road. Mitch warns me she'll call it a duplex, a nod to the fantasy life she dreams about in New York, and it turns out he's right. Introductions, he effects through the entryphone. A woman's voice, thickened by what sounds like a heavy cold, tells me to make my way to the third floor. She sounds unsurprised but slightly impatient as if time is short and I'm already late. Listening beside me, Mitch rolls his eyes. There's a pub on the corner called the Crown and Anchor. He'll be waiting at one of the tables outside when I've finished with Anoushka.

I push through the front door and climb the first flight of stairs. The temptation, to which I succumb at once, is to pretend I'm someone seriously big in government. Did he, too, finger that little button on the entryphone? Cradle his fuck-me bottle of Shiraz? Wait to be admitted? I pause on the first landing to admire the Thomas Rowlandson prints that adorn the walls. Rowlandson, with his playful contributions to eighteenth-century soft porn, has long been a favourite of H's, chiefly because of his take on Portsmouth Point.

H adored the scrum of drunken bodies and buxom whores making merry while the fleet waited to sail, and a framed print I gave him several Christmases ago made him very happy. There are more Rawlinson prints as I make my way up the next flight of stairs, and I pause on the third-floor landing to inspect a nest of naked beauties attending to their latest customer. The etching is a festival of empty glasses, rumpled sheets, wandering hands, and – on the face of the lucky client – something close to bliss.

I'm still trying to understand the role of the third woman, her fleshy rump in the air, when I hear the door behind me open.

'You approve?' It's the voice on the entryphone.

I glance round. Anoushka must be in her early forties. She's wearing a man's dressing gown, belted at the waist, and she must have just washed her hair because she's wound a towel around her head. Her feet are bare on the sanded wooden boards. A thin silver chain loops around one ankle and she's painted her toenails black.

'Very much,' I say. 'Can you imagine the research that man must have done?'

My comment sparks a smile. She has a big, handsome face and one hand has strayed to a silver orthodox cross that nestles in her ample *embonpoint.* Aware of my interest, she tells me the cross is a recent gift from a Russian friend.

'They're crazy, these Russian guys. More money than fucking sense. Do them a favour and they're all over you. Sergei won't leave me alone. Thank God he's fat. The stairs knacker him and I'm dreading the day he gets an elevator put in.'

'He owns the place?' I gesture round.

'Christ, no. That's not the way it happens. Russians start with where they want to get to and then work backwards. In this case, it's lucky me, and if an elevator will make him a happier man, then he lifts the phone. Every Russian has an army of little helpers. Some do elevators. Others buy flowers. A couple will see to people you don't much like, no questions asked. Beware of these guys. They can ruin your day.'

'And Sergei?'

'Lots of flowers, lilies especially. All Russians are in love with death. That's something else you have to get used to.'

I nod, not quite sure how to respond. In a way this is a kind of audition and for once in my life I'm not the one in the spotlight, but I sense already that this woman will be very hard to pin down. For whatever reason, she talks at a thousand miles an hour, bombarding me with a torrent of free association, her head tipped slightly back as if she's trying to get the range exactly right. An actress? Just possibly.

I follow her into the flat. Soft carpets underfoot in the tiny hall. A scatter of Kelim rugs on the polished wooden floor in the living area. Low black leather sofas. And – yes – a stand of lilies in a rather nice vase that might be Scandinavian. A flight of steps in the corner leads to an upper floor, which gives the apartment a space and lightness unusual in buildings this age, and I can smell fresh coffee. The walls look newly painted and someone – Anoushka? – has a real gift for using various colours in daring counterpoint. I'd never dream of asking Hague Blue and Day Room Yellow to live together, but somehow it works.

Anoushka has found a hairdryer. She's about to plug it in when I catch sight of the laptop on the desk in the far corner of the room. It's already fired up and the image on the screen is all too familiar. Rémy left what he called the key scene in *The Hour of Our Passing* to the very end of the shoot. This decision, he later confessed, was driven by the hope that by then me and my brave young *résistant* would have established an on-set rapport that might show in the rushes. How right he was. Anoushka has frozen the action seconds before I collapse on my lover's chest. Immodest, I know, but the expression on my young face puts Thomas Rowlandson to shame. No wonder it made such an impression on Johana.

'You Googled me?' I ask. Anoushka is unwrapping the towel around her head, revealing a tangle of blonde curls.

'Of course. Couldn't resist.'

I go across to the desk and close the laptop, aware of Anoushka watching.

'But you were so good,' she says. 'If it turns me on, fuck knows what it must have done to the men in your life. Were you really screwing? Do you mind me asking?'

'You're supposed to be an actress. Are you telling me you don't know? Can't guess?'

'Actress?' she says archly. 'What gave you that idea?'

'That book you wrote. The one that went to Rosa. The one that Mitch has read.'

'*My Place or Yours?*' She cackles with laughter, and then throws her head back, shedding tiny droplets of water. 'Fiction, darling.'

'You mean the actress bit?'

'Of course.'

'And the rest?'

'The rest is as true as we can make it.'

'We?'

'Me and a friend of mine.'

'I see.' I gesture down at the desk. 'And this is where you wrote it?'

'Christ, no. Writing's not my thing. I'm in PR, run my own outfit, put people together in crazy combinations and then step well back and see what happens.'

'These are Russians?'

'Some of them. I speak the language, and that puts me ahead of the fucking pack. Russians sweat money. It oozes from their pores. The English can smell them a mile away, especially politicians. These days, nobody has any dosh. I could lift that phone now, promise a tame Russian or two with readies on tap, and most of Westminster would be knocking at my door. It's sad, really. The PR game used to be more subtle than that.'

I nod. There's just a hint of Mitch Culligan in the way this woman settles on a passing target and gives it a thorough kicking and I'm tempted to enquire further but that's not what I'm here for.

'So who wrote the book? Who put the words in the right order if it wasn't you?'

This time, I'm spared another volley. Instead, Anoushka sits herself on the arm of the smaller sofa and offers me the hair-dryer. The belt securing her dressing gown, already loose, has come undone but she doesn't bother to hide what's underneath. Full breasts. Slightly too much belly. Plus a rich thicket of blondish pubic hair. Very Rowlandson.

'Do you mind?' She turns her head away. 'I can never get the back properly dry.'

I've no idea where all this is leading but I start to hose a stream of hot air onto the nape of her neck. Beneath the tangle of curls is a small, discreet tattoo. A delicate wreath in dark blue cups a date. 23.6.2016. This has to be deliberate. She wants me to see it.

'Interesting,' I murmur.

'What?'

'This tattoo of yours. Twenty-third of June? 2016? Am I intruding here?'

'Not at all. I don't know about you, but I was casting a vote.'

I pause a moment, mussing her hair with my spare hand. It's thick and warm and it isn't hard to imagine our Mr Big doing something very similar.

'You don't get it?' She sounds slightly disappointed. 'June? 2016? Voting booths? Maybe you were out of the country. Very wise. They'd killed an MP just days earlier. Do I need to spell any of this out? That Culligan knows. He definitely knows.'

'The referendum.' At last I've got it. 'You think something died that day?'

'Too right.'

'And is that what's behind the book? Revenge on the Brexiteers?'

Another cackle of laughter. She twists round on the arm of the sofa, staring up at me.

'*Revenge?* How does that work? We love Brexit. My little tatt is a celebration and that book bigs the lucky bastard up. He's a class shag. He knows how to make a girl grateful. Plus, he laughed a lot. That's very Russian, too. They're either weeping with laughter or weeping for real. Maybe that's this guy's *schtick.* Maybe Mr Big's a closet Russian. Odder things have come to pass. Either way, that girl lucked in, believe me.'

'*That* girl? Meaning it wasn't you? Meaning you didn't write it?'

She shrugs, picks at a nail, says nothing. Coy isn't her style. She does it really badly. In the interests of my imminent conversation with Mitch, I decide to start again.

'So you're telling me it was ghosted? By this friend of yours?'

'That's right. More or less.'

'But it really happened? Here? Upstairs? Wherever?'

'What do you think?'

'I think nothing. I have no opinion. I'm asking you.'

'Why?'

Good question. I hesitate for a moment, and then plunge in. I tell her that my agent will be fronting the book. And I explain that a very good friend of mine – Mitch – has interests of his own. One of them, after the earnings drought of the Covid months, wants to earn a big commission. The other has a burning urge to make life tough for top Tories.

'So what's your motivation?' I ask.

'I don't need motivation,' she says. 'All I need is opportunity. The opportunity comes along' – she shrugs – 'I take it.'

'With Mr Big?'

'With anyone, anything. Life never waits for you. You grab it, or it's gone.'

I nod, trying to assess the evidence. This woman says she's in PR, which would certainly bring her to the feeding trough that is UK politics, and that – in turn – could easily put her within touching distance of the centre of power. But why would she want to court the publicity that would come with joining the long list of casual top Tory shags?

'I happened to like the man . . .' she says at last, '. . . and I think he gets a bad press.'

'You're still in touch?'

'No way. The guy cuts you off like that.' She snaps her fingers. 'It's a turn-on, believe it or not. He's ruthless. Some women love that. It's a kind of honesty. Would I like to see him again? Yes. Would I like to lie him down and fuck him witless? Of course I would. But it won't happen.'

I nod. This woman belongs in a very dark part of the forest, lying in wait for any – in her phrase – passing opportunity. Feral, I'm thinking. Culligan's right.

'Proof?' I enquire. 'Notes you might have kept? Recordings of calls? Little presents he might have given you?'

'No way.'

'No way you're going to show me? Or no way, because they don't exist?'

'Just no way. Read the book. It's all there.'

'But you said you were an actress. And that was a lie. So why should I, why should anyone, believe you?'

'The actress thing was a little bit of extra. Not my idea, if you're asking.'

'You're blaming this friend of yours? Whoever actually wrote it?'

'Of course.'

'Man? Woman?'

'Woman. Very talented. And she needs the money, like we all do.'

I nod. I can only agree about the talent. *My Place or Yours?*, from the title onwards, is brilliantly done.

'So you briefed her, gave her the details, the chronology, the way it happened, the way it *felt*, all that?'

'Correct. I explained what I wanted her to write.'

'And she went away and turned it into a book?'

'Yes.'

I nod, putting the hairdryer to one side. My next question is all too obvious.

'So who is she, this woman? And how do I get to meet her?'

Anoushka gets up at last and goes through the motion of a lazy stretch. Then she sheds the dressing gown until it heaps around her ankles. She smells of bath oil, and something slightly earthier.

'You look as though you could handle a long massage.' Her face is very close. 'How does that sound?'

NINETEEN

I'm outside the pub minutes later. I like to think of Mitch Culligan as a good friend. I owe him for bringing Sayid down to Flixcombe, but no way does my gratitude extend to a horny afternoon with Mr Big's alleged lover.

Mitch is on his phone at a table on the pavement, bent over something yellow and fizzy which he's barely touched. Panels of Covid Perspex seal him off from neighbouring drinkers, most of whom are also on their phones. I take a seat across the table from Mitch. When the barman arrives, I show him my QR code and order a large gin and tonic. Escaping death by massage gives a girl a thirst.

Mitch at last brings his conversation to an end, his eyes still on the phone. He wants my take on Anoushka.

'The book wasn't her doing,' I say at once.

'She never wrote the thing in the first place?' Mitch at last looks up from his phone.

'She says not. She says the book was ghosted by a friend.'

'She never told me that.'

'Maybe you didn't ask nicely.'

'Yeah, maybe I didn't. What else did she tell you?'

'That she has lots of Russian men friends, and no shame. She also told me she's in PR. Beyond that, she was at full throttle most of the time and to be frank I lost the thread.'

'PR?' Mitch has produced a pen. 'Her own company? Someone else's?'

'She wouldn't say.'

'Did you ask?'

'No.'

Mitch nods. I can tell he's disappointed but he has the grace to try and hide it.

'If she's really in PR, she'd spend most of her life bending the truth,' he says. 'Spin is their game, fiction under a different name. These people are gatekeepers. Beyond them is the real money.'

'That's exactly what she told me. Most of it's Russian but I'm guessing there's oodles elsewhere.'

'Too right. Set yourself up in PR, plug yourself into the networks that matter, and for fees you won't believe you can put any lie into the public domain and watch it grow. That's why God invented social media. Junk news for the lazy. Junk news for the gullible. Never bloody fails. And you know why? Because most people have forgotten what truth tastes like, smells like, why it even matters.'

Mitch sighs and reaches for his glass. One day, when times get even stranger, he'll probably take the cloth and find some urban intersection to preach hellfire sermons to the passing traffic. Until then, he's got an audience of just one. Me. A touch of the Covid? Or simple despair? Probably both.

At length, he gestures at his phone.

'A friend of mine does occasional stuff for the *Telegraph*. The address you visited rang bells. He just told me the whole house belongs to a Tory MP, idle twat from the leafy shires. He's put tenants in a couple of the flats, mates of his, but the third-floor duplex has never been let. This guy organizes discreet orgies from time to time, two grand a pop, mainly Slav girls. Most of them, from what I can gather, are Russian.'

'Takers?'

'He thinks chummy's spoiled for choice. Ten grand up front buys you a place in the queue and after that you keep your credit card handy and wait for the call. These events last most of the weekend so you need stamina as well as deep pockets. These little get-togethers always coincide with the full moon, so that's a help, diary-wise.'

'How does he know all this?' I'm looking at the phone.

'He got a freebie a couple of years back, before all the Covid stuff kicked off. He says he was there to road-test the talent but I'm guessing he was invited to spread the word afterwards. Covid wasn't a problem, by the way. They all wear masks in any case, leather mainly, so it was business as usual. Screw or be screwed. It's a Tory thing.'

My gin and tonic arrives. Nine pounds seventy, even with two slices of lemon, is a brutal reminder of London prices. I take a sip before the gin surrenders to the flotilla of ice cubes and tell Mitch once again about the ghostwriter. It's occurred to me that she might be the actress, in which case there's just an outside chance that Rosa can supply contact details.

'Call her now.' Mitch pushes his phone towards me. 'I need the loo.'

With Mitch gone, I do his bidding. My call finds Rosa at home in Deal, anticipating – she says – the next in the recent sequence of storms.

'Frogs and locusts by teatime, my precious.' She's laughing. 'What's on your mind?'

I offer a brief account of my afternoon. I also need to add a little self-justification.

'Mitch needed a second opinion,' I tell her. 'He seems to think he's met your client, the one who wrote the book. Her name is Anoushka. She says she's in PR. She eats wealthy Russians for breakfast and they lovebomb her with flowers and I expect lots else.'

'And the book?'

'She says it was ghosted by a friend of hers. Maybe your actress.'

'Describe this woman.'

'Big where it matters. Mouthy. Blonde.'

There's a longish silence on the line. A male voice in the background at Rosa's end suggests that Kurt has returned from Germany. At length, Rosa's back on the line, newly brisk.

'Right. So here's the thing, precious. I'm afraid this woman is a fake. Russians love games like this. Clever you for spotting it.'

'You're telling me the Russians put her up to it?'

'More than possible. They bore easily.'

'And the real scribe?'

'No way.'

'Why not?'

'Because you'll set Culligan on her.'

'I won't. I wouldn't dare. Not after the last time.'

'You promise?'

'I promise.'

Another silence, even longer, while Rosa has a think.

'Cropped black hair and the chest of a child,' she says after a while. 'I doubt she's ever bought a bra in her life.'

'So definitely not Anoushka?'

'Not a chance.'

'But she's an actress? And a client of yours?'

'Right on both counts. And she writes like a dream. As we both agree.'

'So how do I find her?'

'You don't, my precious. This girl is very shy. I wouldn't dream of disturbing her.' There's another pause, briefer this time, then she's back on the phone. 'I forgot to mention it but we're both in quarantine just now, thanks to Kurt, and the bloody man won't leave me alone. Happy days, eh?'

The phone goes dead and I have a moment or two to compose my thoughts before Mitch returns from the loo.

'And?' He's looking at my phone.

'Anoushka takes us nowhere. I've no idea where she belongs in all this but I doubt she had anything to do with that script. Nor with Mr Big.'

Mitch sinks back into his seat. He's beginning to look disappointed.

'And this mate of Anoushka's? The one who did the writing?'

'Rosa wouldn't comment.'

'You pressed her?'

'No.'

'Why not?'

'Because I've let her down once, badly, and twice would be unforgiveable.'

'So you didn't even ask?'

'Of course I didn't. I need a good agent, believe it or not. Rosa keeps my fridge full. Without her, I'd go hungry.'

'Thanks a bunch.'

'Pleasure.'

We stare at each other for a long moment, then Mitch grins. He's always thrived when a story disappears under a swamp of false leads. He has a huge appetite for following the stench of something dodgy upwind, and happily couples this with a lifelong belief that all Tory politicians, the entire tribe, are deeply venal. *My Place or Yours?*, he grunts, shows every sign of blowing up in some important faces and he can't wait to be there and applaud the fifth act. In fact, he's so pleased he nods at my glass and offers to buy me the other half.

'I'll spare you.' I show him my debit card receipt. 'One day you'll be rich, and then I'll say yes.'

After toying with a peaceful night in Holland Park, I make my way back to Waterloo. I know H is in good hands but Dessie's never less than busy and guilt puts me on the 19.20 Exeter train. The least I can do for the men in my life is to show up when they need me, and so I make the call. The moment Dessie answers, I can tell that I've done the right thing. H, he says with commendable understatement, has been a bit cross. He'll be very pleased to see me and it will be Dessie's privilege to pick me up at Yeovil Junction. Any hour, no matter how late. Just as long as I come home.

I've made a note of the arrival time at Yeovil. It turns out that Wales have managed to hold Switzerland to a draw in Baku, a small miracle, but Dessie tells me that 22.05 is the best news he's heard all day.

'You'll be there?' I ask him.

'Bet your life.'

'Alone?'

'Yes. Jessie's on call if needed. Once I've got H to bed I don't want to mess with his head any more. Plus he's knackered anyway.'

I say goodbye and retrieve my copy of the *Guardian* from my bag. G7 leaders have mustered at Carbis Bay, with Boris Johnson gurning for the world's press. I gaze at the photo the *Guardian* has selected. The blond mop. The rogue tie knot. The hint of belly beneath the buttoned jacket as he stands on the beachside plinth and raises his hand against a backdrop of the world's leaders.

Would any of these men be remotely surprised by the brief presence of an Anoushka beneath our leader's bulk? I'm looking at Macron, at Biden, at the handsome guy in charge of Canada. Aren't they all at it? Isn't an early evening frolic one of the perks of office? Wouldn't we humble punters be just a tad disappointed if demigods like our Boris didn't help himself? This, of course, implies that *My Place or Yours?* has no commercial value, that serial disloyalty is already priced in as far as top politicians are concerned, but I know for certain that this isn't true. People love detail, the small print of adultery. Rosa, who never underestimates the public's hunger for trash, wouldn't be wasting her time unless there's a major killing round the corner. Amused, but none the wiser, I turn the page and settle into a glum piece about Californian wildfires. We'll all expire beneath a thin cloud of falling ash, I'm beginning to think. And not before time.

The train divides at Salisbury. I abandon the *Guardian* and buy a gin and tonic from the trolley. There's a tempting two-for-one offer on miniatures of Gordon's, and I say yes. The trolley gone, we're on the move again. I decant the first of the miniatures into the little plastic glass, add half the tonic, and stare out into the thickening dusk.

West of Salisbury, especially in this light, England is at its most beguiling and its most mysterious, and as the train gathers speed I realize why I could so easily abandon Holland Park for the lush pastures of West Dorset. After spending so much time with H, it's impossible not to acknowledge that every life has its natural end, including mine, and as the train plunges into the roaring darkness of a tunnel I become aware of my own reflection in the window. Has dementia left its mark on little me? Am I visibly ageing as H's behaviour becomes ever more bizarre? And if I'm spared a death by falling ash, what kind of shape might I be in by the time H has finally gone?

I demolish my gin and tonics far quicker than I should and decide to pay a visit. The nearby loo is already occupied and so I make my way through the adjoining carriage to find another one. I'm weaving unsteadily down the aisle when the sight of a couple sitting side by side at a table brings me to a brief halt. They've emptied two small bottles of red wine, and demolished a couple of sandwiches, and now they both appear to be asleep. The woman has her head nestled on the man's shoulder, and they're holding hands. A glance at the rack above their heads confirms two violin cases, and I shake my head, not quite sure what I'm feeling. The woman is Johana. She plays for the LSO, lives in Exeter, and made this morning's journey a real pleasure.

The man begins to stir. Then, through his patterned mask, he plants the softest kiss on Johana's forehead and goes to sleep again. I hurry on down the aisle, reaching for support from empty seats. Safely locked in the loo, I steady myself over the hand basin. Only when I'm certain I've got the words in the right order, do I try the line for real. I'm thinking of the bracelet on Johana's thin wrist.

'After the rain, we drink at the waterhole,' I whisper to the face in the mirror. 'It's natural. It's what we do. Otherwise, we'll all die.'

The train is a couple of minutes early getting into Yeovil Junction but I spot Dessie's VW the moment I emerge from the station. He flashes the headlights, and I fight to steady myself as he steps out of the car to greet me. Much to his surprise, he gets a proper hug.

'That's for coming,' I murmur. 'And for looking after H. Are we still friends?'

'Is that a real question?'

'Yes, it is.'

'Then the answer's yes. Yes, here and now. And yes since the day I first laid eyes on you.' He looks at me for a long moment, then smiles. 'You're drunk.'

He's holding the passenger door open and gestures for me to climb in. I do as I'm told, watching the train depart, the row of carriages disappearing into the darkness down the line. I'm thinking about the lovebirds from the LSO again, about hundreds of thirsty Africans converging on some muddy waterhole, about the smell of dry earth after rain. I shot sequences for a movie on a game reserve in Botswana years back and the memory of that smell has never left me.

Dessie has yet to start the engine. I glance across at him, my hand trying to find that little lever that adjusts the seat. When I finally work it out, I put far too much pressure on the back of the seat and end up nearly horizontal.

'Here?' Dessie is laughing. 'Now?'

'Later,' I tell him. 'Somewhere dark.' I reach up for his hand. 'As long as you don't tell H.'

'You're serious?'

'I am.'

'About H?'

'Yes. And about everything else, too. Like I said, somewhere dark, somewhere private.'

'You mean that?'

I'm gazing up at him. In the Navy, as Dessie confided last year, everyone has a nickname.

'I do, Mr Jenny Wren. And I'm serious about H, too. Why? Because he'd probably kill you first. Then me.'

Dessie nods, says he understands, then ducks his head to kiss my hand.

'Do that again.' I'm staring up at him. 'Can you hear the rain?'

TWENTY

In the end, we don't stop on the way home. It's Dessie's decision, his call, and when I press him for a reason, feeling slightly hurt, he says it's because I've been drinking.

'That's not a reason. You're calling me out.'

'Nothing of the sort. Do I want it to happen? Of course I do. You know that. I know you know that. But I want it to happen for real.'

'Not because I've necked a couple of gins?'

'Exactly.'

'Sweet. I mean it. Do you mind me saying that?'

'Not at all. I'll get you home. Rain or no rain.'

When I put the comment in context, explaining about Johana, and seeing her again on the train, he chuckles softly in the darkness. It's a truly lovely sound. It tells me we're friends, nothing hidden, a cheap advantage offered but not taken, and I realize just how much I respect this man. When things got tough down in Southsea last year, he was kindness personified. He listened to my troubles, he offered sound advice, and though he never stopped being the policeman, he somehow managed to occasionally fence that part of him off. It was a quiet word from Dessie ahead of a police raid that enabled Jessie to bury a great deal of H's money before they arrived. For that reason alone, the man has earned my trust.

When we arrive at Flixcombe, a light is on in H's bedroom. Not a good sign. Dessie kills the engine and we exchange glances.

'You or me?' he asks.

'Both of us.'

'Top call.' Dessie is laughing again. 'Start the way we mean to go on.'

We let ourselves in and mount the stairs in the half-darkness. Dessie opens H's bedroom door but I'm first in. H is sitting up in bed, a phone in one hand and a corner of the sheet in the other, tucked beneath his chin. His face looks gaunter than ever and he badly needs a shave. He stares at the pair of us, blank incomprehension, and then holds out the phone. This is a scene from a movie I was expecting to shoot decades later, H banged up in some nursing home, utterly adrift, but it's happening now, within his own four walls.

I take the phone, and dial 1471. A recent call has come from Rémy, timed at 21.54.

'Did you talk to him?' I've settled on the edge of the bed. H is looking vague. 'Talk?' I nod at the phone and mime a call, two spread fingers to my ear. This gesture serves simply to complicate things. H seems to think I'm trying to address an itch. Finally, it's Dessie who resolves the impasse.

'He might have left a message,' he suggests reasonably. 'Worth a shot?'

I check on 1571. Dessie's right. Rémy, to my relief, sounds relaxed. He wants to know whether I've had any further thoughts about *Vlixcombe*. And he needs me to get myself to Jersey for a meet. More clues when I phone him back.

Jersey? I'm looking at Dessie. He's heard every word.

'Phone him,' he says.

I check my watch. It's nearly half past eleven but Rémy is a night owl. He answers at once, while I'm still heading for the door, as if he's been awaiting the call. I ask him whether he means it about Jersey. He says yes. He's been looking at maps. My nearest airport is Bristol and there's a Blue Islands flight that leaves at one o'clock tomorrow afternoon. He'll take care of everything once I've landed.

'But why do you want me there?'

'There's someone you need to meet. *Inshallah*, he'll be funding *Vlixcombe.* Nothing happens without you being there.'

'You're serious?'

'*Oui*.'

'And does this person have a name?'

'He does. Georges Monsault. I've known him a while. He's a good guy and he loves some of our movies.'

I nod. The name rings a bell but for the life of me I can't think why. I'm still at the bedroom door. A glance over my shoulder confirms that H, and doubtless Dessie, have been listening in. H is looking more fretful than ever.

'And me?' he's trying to say. 'Can I come, too?'

It's gone midnight. Dessie has tucked H in and has joined me in the kitchen. Under the circumstances, now that the gin has worn off, a glass or two of Greco di Tufo seems a companionable proposition.

'Monsault?' I'm thinking aloud. 'I've a feeling he was big a decade or so back.'

'You're right. He spent a lot of time chasing the ultimate high. He wanted to give weed a bit of class. He started in the Himalayas and ended up with hundreds of acres in Morocco.'

'Of course . . .' It's coming back to me. 'And everyone said he was a fascist when it came to dope. Monsieur Impossible. He had lots of fans in showbiz and ran a kind of subscription club. If you had serious money, and lots of people I knew did, then M. Impossible could make you very happy.'

'You had that kind of money?'

'I did. I also had gin, which was much cheaper.'

Dessie has taken a seat across the table and accepts a glass of white wine. I've got the feeling there's more to come about Georges Monsault, and I'm right.

'Your friend knows him?' he asks.

'I'm sure he does. Rémy knows everyone. He's also been partial to the odd joint, which would probably help. Monsault brought in a kind of certification scheme. It was AOC for dope heads. People said he was crazy, putting that kind of lipstick on the pig, but I thought he was smart.'

'AOC?'

'Appellation d'Origine Contrôlée. Think of the best Bordeaux reds and you're halfway there. I seem to remember the paperwork was too much for him in the end, but I might be wrong. Is he rich, now? If not, he should be.'

'Very rich.' Dessie is sipping his wine. 'You don't get to live in Jersey without a great deal of money, and he has other properties elsewhere.'

'This is drug money?'

'He says not but then he would. One of his talents is choosing the right professional advice, plus a tax regime that won't rip the shirt from his back. Hence Jersey. In his prime, the way French cops describe his MO, he reminds me of H. Same attention to the bottom line. Same coolness under fire.'

'And he's still at it?'

'Not really. He's made his fortune already, and now's the time to enjoy it. He's nearly seventy but from what I hear, he still wants to give the guys at the top a bit of a shake. *Le gratin*? Have I got that right?'

I nod, delighted. *Le gratin* is a phrase the French lifted from gastronomy. Literally it translates as 'the upper crust' but coming from the likes of Monsieur Impossible, it means the elite. Back in the day, Monsault always did contempt and envy really well, and I admired him for that.

'So how come you know so much about this guy?' I ask.

Why Dessie shakes his head is beyond me but it's what he says next that really matters.

'I need to come with you,' he says.

'To Jersey?'

'Of course.'

'Am I allowed to ask why?'

'Because things might not be the way they seem.'

'With Monsault?'

'With Rémy Despret.'

'You don't think it's about *Vlixcombe* at all?'

'I don't know anything about *Vlixcombe* but I know a lot about Monsault, and about your friend. Someone else we should bear in mind is Ratko.'

'You mean Wolfman?'

'Too right. He and Monsault are partners just now. This is business, because everything's business, but there's only one clue you really need. Your friend Rémy is out of his depth. Totally at sea. And he has been for a while.'

Totally at sea? Rémy, at the wheel of his precious yacht, would relish the choice of phrase. I toy with sharing the joys of *Vlixcombe*, Rémy's other baby, but decide against it. Instead, I want to know exactly why Dessie wants to come with me.

'Is this some kind of protection? You playing my guardian angel?'

'Close.'

'You think I'd be safer with you on hand?'

'Yes.'

'So we front up together?'

'Christ, no. We arrive on the same plane. I peel off, pre-book a hotel in St Helier. You have my phone number. That's all you need. These days Monsault rarely leaves his estate, especially in the evenings. That's where Rémy will probably take you. I can be in a hire car parked up two minutes away if needs must.'

If needs must. It's at this point it occurs to me that Dessie has been nursing this script for a while, that he's been expecting the call from Rémy, and when – as ever – circumstances demand he'll slip into his other role. Not the big, reassuring Jenny Wren who waited in the car park for the Waterloo train, but someone altogether more businesslike. Dessie never made detective sergeant by accident.

'This is where we parted last year,' I say quietly. 'I really wanted to trust you, and maybe I wanted more than that, but you could never stop being the cop.'

He nods, says nothing. In the hands of a good scriptwriter – someone of Pavel's class – this would be the key scene, but my defences are still down and I find it incredibly sad. So close, I think. Thank Christ we didn't stop on the way back from the station.

'What about H?' I murmur. 'Have you thought about him at all?'

'I talked to Jess this morning. She's happy to hold the fort.'

'So you were expecting the call from Rémy?'

'Yes.'

'And if H gets upset? Wanders off? Declares UDI?'

'Then we depend on this.' He digs something out of his pocket. It turns out to be an Apple Watch.

'GPS tracker? And you're telling me he'll wear it?'

'He has to.'

'Why?'

'It's the only way he can stay in touch.'

'With who?'

'Jess. She'll know exactly where he is.'

I nod. Dessie Wren, he of the soft chuckle, has thought of everything, which is doubtless his job. I reach for the bottle and return it to the fridge. Then I nod towards the door.

'The mattress is still on H's floor,' I tell him. 'I'm sure he'll be pleased to see you.'

TWENTY-ONE

I get up early next morning and Dessie keeps a low profile, which is probably wise. I toy with not going to Jersey, partly because I object to two men – Dessie and Rémy Despret – writing my script for me, but mainly because I'm genuinely anxious about H. He follows me around the house. He tracks my every move. A couple of times we get close to having a conversation about my impending departure but there's an expression on his face, the bewilderment of a child abandoned for no good reason, that he can't hide. This I find very hard to cope with, and it's only the thought that I might be able to help make *Vlixcombe* happen that takes me to the phone to book the ticket to Jersey. The prospect of this wonderful old house full of thesps and the best of dramatic intentions is a huge come-on. H, so isolated, so lost, would be the real winner.

Dessie, I assume, is making his own arrangements. For the time being, we're barely talking. The flight takes off at one o'clock. We leave at ten, Dessie at the wheel of his VW, H nowhere to be seen. Jessie, as ever, has been a tower of strength. She has an iPhone already so the workings of the watch H has consented to wear is no mystery. If he goes AWOL and becomes a neat little blob on the screen of her phone, she'll simply despatch Andy to bring him back. It is, we both agree, as near foolproof as we can manage. Restoring hope to the world of lost bearings might prove to have been Apple's greatest triumph.

Technology, as it turns out, has also become one of Dessie's best friends. We've set out for Bristol Airport but Flixcombe is still a fleeting presence amongst the trees, getting ever smaller, when he nods at the glove box.

'Leather wallet,' he murmurs. 'Take a look.'

With some reservations, I do his bidding. Inside the wallet is a mobile phone.

'And?' I'm mystified. I need a clue or two.

'It's been specially modified,' he explains.

'To do what?'

'To transmit.' He's slowing as we approach the gates to the Flixcombe estate. 'All you have to do is switch it on and then leave it somewhere sensible. It acts as a microphone. It'll pick up conversations and broadcast them on a particular wavelength. Anyone tuned in can help themselves.'

'Anyone?'

'Me, in this instance. As long as I'm within a mile or so, I'm there in the room, as good as. Clever or what?' He risks a smile, checking left and right as we come to a halt.

'And my role? What am I supposed to do?'

'I suspect your friend will meet you at the airport in Jersey. Odds-on, he'll take you to Monsault's place. He lives in the north of the island, fifteen-minute drive, max. My guess is you'll be staying the night. Am I getting warm here?'

I nod. On the phone, Rémy told me to get an open return ticket. Selling *Vlixcombe,* he'd warned, might take a while.

'So you want me to plant this phone in Monsault's house? Is that it?'

'Yes.'

'You're crazy. Why on earth would I do a thing like that?'

Dessie takes a while to answer, pulling in to make way for an oncoming tractor. Finally, we're on the move again.

'Two reasons,' he says. 'And only one of them's H. He has interests you might want to protect, incidentally.'

'Like?'

'The house. The estate. Everything, really.'

'They're under some kind of threat?'

'Yes.'

'Care to tell me why?'

Dessie shakes his head. Later, he seems to be saying. Once we're friends again.

'And the other reason?'

'Your friend Rémy. Narcotics these days is no place for beginners. If he's to stay in one piece, it might pay to lend him a hand.'

'By planting the phone?'

'By doing what I say. We need leverage here, and by leverage I mean evidence. Otherwise we're stuffed.'

'We?'

'All of us. You. H. Despret. Even me. Lesson one. Never underestimate the reach of big money.' Another smile, colder. 'But I'm guessing you know that already.'

I think about this proposition for a moment or two. Then I get it.

'You're telling me not to mention Ratko to Rémy? Is that what I'm hearing?'

'Exactly.' Dessie could soften this warning with a smile but doesn't. 'As far as Despret's concerned, you know nothing.'

We get to Bristol Airport slightly earlier than we'd planned. By now, to be frank, I'm starting to question the wisdom of going to Jersey at all but Dessie escorts me briskly to the check-in desk and sits me down for a coffee afterwards. The more I think about becoming his accomplice, the less the appeal, but a small voice insists he owes me at least the beginnings of an explanation. He's still on the phone at the counter, waiting to collect the coffees. Just who is he talking to? What does this do to my relationship with Rémy? And where on earth might Dessie and I go next?

When he joins me at the table, I beckon him closer.

'Confused isn't a big word,' I tell him. 'But here and now that's just what I am.'

'Confused about what?'

'About you. A cop or the guy I thought I could trust. Which is it?'

Dessie studies me for a moment, and for the first time I detect something close to exhaustion in the darkness beneath his eyes.

'Both.' He empties a sachet of sugar into his coffee. 'You asked me the same question last night when I met you off the train. If I didn't care about you, I wouldn't be here. You came to me, remember. You wanted the word on Newhaven. I was happy to oblige, and nothing's changed. It's my job to know about people like Ratko. I know what makes them tick and I know the strokes they're capable of pulling. You may take them at face value because that's the kind of person you are, in which case I'm doing you a very big favour.'

'And me?' I nod at the phone I've left on the table. 'I'm supposed to return the favour?'

'You're supposed to trust me.'

'And if I don't?'

'Then I have no business being here.' He gestures up at the nearest departure screen. 'My life would be a whole lot simpler if I called it a day now.'

'And did what?'

'Binned this . . .' His big hand settles lightly on his boarding card. 'Drove back to Pompey. Got on with my life.'

'You're telling me this is something extra, whatever it is? Something you've just taken on?'

'Yes. It breaks every rule to say so, but yes. In my line of work it's far too easy to stumble into something you never anticipated.'

'Like me?'

'Yes.'

'Are we talking the access I'm offering?'

'Partly, yes. But that I can walk away from, no problem. I'll still have a job. I'm on a civvie contract now but they still work me like a dog. Narcotics are forever, believe me.'

I nod. We're beginning to clear the air here, and it's a good feeling. All I want to know is where we stand. Cop or companion? Simples, as Malo might say.

'So tell me this, Mr Dessie.' I cover his hand with mine. 'What happens if I don't do your bidding? What happens if I don't plant the bloody phone? Will it make any difference?'

'To what?'

'Us.'

He studies me for a long moment, and then shakes his head. The smile this time has real warmth.

'What a silly fucking question.' He nods at the nearby screen, and then gets to his feet. The Jersey flight is open for boarding. 'We could pretend we're on holiday.' He extends a hand. 'Unless you've decided to bail out.'

* * *

I haven't. The flight is barely half full. Dessie insists on buying me a gin and tonic and I'm weak-willed enough to say yes. What I want, above all, is a little of that warm blush I felt last night. Rémy's *Vlixcombe* still means the world to me, and Dessie is heading in the same direction, but somehow, over the hours to come, I have to broker a peace between these warring voices in my head. I can recognize a great script idea when I see one, and despite his best efforts to prove me wrong, I want very badly to trust Dessie. Stay tuned, I tell myself. And go easy on the gin.

At Jersey Airport, everyone on the flight succumbs to a Covid test, which is gratifyingly free, before we're allowed to file through to the arrivals hall. Dessie has already joined the modest queue at the Hertz desk, and it's a moment or two before I spot Rémy.

'*Chérie* . . .' He enfolds me in a warm hug. For the first time ever, I can feel the bones of his ribcage under the rumpled T-shirt. Directing movies is far from stress-free but he's always carried a little winter plumage, so how come he's suddenly so thin?

We leave the terminal building and walk to the short-term car park. Dessie's right. We're off to Monsault's place, which appears to be in the north of the island. Monsault, it seems, runs an open house for all manner of waifs and strays and I'm to prepare myself for what Rémy describes as *une soirée magique.* A magical evening.

'You know Claudine.' Rémy is gesturing at a woman behind the wheel of a nearby Renault. For a moment, I fail to recognize her. She's wearing a slightly piratical headscarf, knotted at the back, and a pair of designer shades that are slightly too big for her face, but then she's stepping out of the car and extending her arms for a hug, and it all comes back to me. We first met on location in Montpellier an age ago when she camped in my hotel room after a fight with the Corsican actor she was bedding and we briefly became friends. Since then, I've heard that she's become Rémy's lover and now she wants to know about life on the other side of *la Manche.*

'It's fine,' I tell her. 'Nice and peaceful, if you want the truth. You should try it out. Very good for the blood pressure.'

'If only . . .' She pulls a face. 'Abroad is off limits. Even England.'

'A blessing, *quoi*?' Rémy has opened the rear door for me.

We leave the airport and plunge into a maze of narrow lanes while Claudine half-turns in the front passenger seat and offers titbits from the feast that used to be the Parisian media scene. How she's been trying to make ends meet. How disappointing are the rewards of private tuition. How even the Arabs won't pay decent money to have their kids schooled in Molière and Racine.

'Thank God for Rémy.' She shoots him a grin. 'No mortgage on the apartment? No rent to pay? How lucky are we?'

By the time we get to Monsault's place, she's pressing me on Flixcombe.

'Rémy raves about it.'

'He's been there?' This comes as another surprise.

'Of course not. I'm talking about the script. The old days. Ratko sent us his photos. I'm guessing nothing's changed.'

Mention of Ratko's brief visit to Flixcombe puts another temptation in my path but thankfully I resist it.

'You're guessing right,' I say lightly. 'Time stopped a while back in our part of the country, and some of us are very grateful.'

Rémy has come to a halt in front of a pair of new-looking gates, solid wood inlaid with iron studs. Tall granite walls stretch in both directions, and the gates are flanked with discreet cameras. Rémy extends a long arm through his open window and presses the entryphone to announce himself. I, meanwhile, am gazing at the name of the property, tastefully picked out on a shave of grey slate.

La Maison Blanche. The White House. Back in the day, H's army of little helpers on the Pompey drug scene were full of in-jokes like these. White as in cocaine? A casual nod to the source of all this heavy security? Very funny.

The gates open with the faintest whisper, and we're suddenly looking at two large Ridgebacks, both chained. One of them lunges playfully at the Renault as Rémy accelerates onto the gravel drive. The drive is flanked by small grey stones, waist high. To me, a Brittany girl, they look like a bonzai version of menhir, the Bronze Age eruptions that dot the Breton landscape and attract tourists by the thousands. There are more of them around the side of the property, and Claudine and I agree that we rather like them.

The house itself is solid and sure of itself, grey granite blocks edged in yellow where lichen has pushed through the mortar. There are tall windows on both storeys, with three dormers in the slate roof. The lawns around the property are patrolled by a brace of peacocks, and when we step out of the car, following Rémy, the house unfolds before us. To the rear is a swimming pool, fully decked on three sides, and the nut-brown figure bent over a pile of manuscripts must have been taking maximum advantage of the recent sunshine.

He doesn't get up. He's wearing an ancient pair of baggy shorts in a rather lovely red, faded almost to death, and the knotty plait of the black ankle bracelet reminds me once again of Africa. He has sun damage on the broadness of his chest and his hair falls in grey ringlets, framing a face I last saw in an ancient edition of *Rolling Stone.* He looks, I've already decided, like a man who owes his success to an appetite for risk and maybe mischief. H, for one, would love him on sight.

The vaguest gesture of a hand serves as a greeting. Rémy indicates the adjacent empty chair.

'For me?'

'*Toi, chérie.*'

Rémy does the introductions, and Monsault nods at the mention of his name as if he's saying hi to a stranger. We're speaking French, which under the circumstances makes perfect sense. Monsault examines the tip of his pencil, and then puts it carefully to one side. When a stir of wind ruffles the papers on the table, he tells them to behave.

'Books are like children,' he says. 'And the best of them are very naughty.'

'You write books? This is your work?'

'Alas, no. I publish books. You need an eye for the unusual and lots of nerve. Most of it's vanity, of course, but then vanity sells. I swore I'd never get into this game but it sometimes serves a man to break his promises.' The light falsetto giggle comes as a surprise but goes well with the rest of him. There are hints of Languedoc in his accent, and something else I can't quite place. He yawns, and stretches, and then begins to worry at his groin.

'Too much fucking.' He's talking to Rémy. 'You ever find that?'

'Never.'

'That makes you lucky, Despret. I tried talcum powder last night but it didn't work. This evening, perhaps, something different. In Bhutan they use urine collected first thing and left in the shadow of prayer flags all day. Never fails.' He giggles again and turns to me. 'Fill your bladder and think of me. I have prayer flags upstairs. Some people say you have to be a Buddhist to hang them out but they're wrong. The key is the wind. You have a favourite colour?'

'Green most days. Yellow occasionally.'

'Excellent. Water and earth. You might come back as a dam. Think of that. Wine? Tea? Something else? Despret is never less than generous but his taste can be *pénible*. He loves Rioja, which is a filthy habit, but I'm guessing you know that already. Our Serbian friend brought a crate or two of slivovitz. This is a spirit that knows how to look after itself. Very Balkan, don't you think?'

Pénible means tiresome. Our Serbian friend has to be Ratko. I nod, trying hard to follow the logic but mostly failing. Rémy has his eyes closed, maybe because he's heard all this before, and Claudine has disappeared completely. Rémy twitches and then rubs his eyes.

'Enora wants to talk about *Vlixcombe*,' he tells Monsault. 'She's been in the house full time for a while now. She's listened to it, understood it, tuned herself in. She's read the pitch, seen the video. She also knows what works on screen. *Chérie* . . .?'

Monsault hasn't taken his eyes off me. His lifted forefinger has stopped Rémy in his tracks.

'Slivovitz, I think.' He reaches for his phone. 'When God discovered truth, he celebrated with damson plums.'

TWENTY-TWO

Over the next few hours or so, Rémy and I work as a team. Rémy draws on all the research he's done about the madness of the *Vlixcombe* days, while I try and sketch the trillion ways he and I could put that troupe of madcap thesps onto the planet's screens. The seed idea, I tell Monsault, has everything: a period of history rich with memories, a bid to land a blow or two on the German occupation across the Channel, and – most important of all – the daily culture clash between rural Dorset and metropolitan Paris. Bittersweet doesn't begin to cover it. This is neither comedy nor straight drama. Every producer, every actress worth her salt, longs for a genre-busting vehicle. And this is it.

By the time we abandon the chill of early evening and make our way indoors, I've drunk a little too much plum brandy. Even if I could remember where I'd left Dessie's special phone, I wouldn't dream of doing his bidding. The game has moved on. Between us, Rémy and I have to coax a development budget from Monsieur Impossible. A million euros, Rémy has already confided, would do nicely.

Monsault, I sense, is intrigued. I've no idea whether Rémy has had these conversations before, and Dessie has taught me to accept nothing at face value, but Monsault has definitely warmed to the dramatic potential of a bunch of Parisian lefties marooned in deepest Dorset. The more Rémy and I play-act our way through potential episode themes, the broader his smile. He's still plucking at his sorry crotch, but it's become a kind of reflex side dish to the main course. He likes what he's hearing. And he has the money to make it happen.

We're now in what I take to be the sitting room. The detail is a tiny bit blurred, but I register oak-like beams on the ceiling, an impressive grandfather clock, etchings of Rouen cathedral on the walls beside the fireplace, and a Kelim the size of a football field on the floor. The Kelim is subtly patterned, a puzzle in lively blacks and blues, and I'm trying to plot my way from one corner to another when Monsault turns from Rémy and raises what I suspect might be a deal-breaker.

'H,' he says. Just that.

Rémy, who so far hasn't touched a drink all night, is staring at him. He and I have just been on a wild riff about Le Patron, the male lead in our little show, a crazy Rive Gauche import who is determined to lay siege to his hostess. The latter role falls to little me. On the one hand I'm flattered by the carnal greed of a man half my age, while on the other I have a husband and a reputation to protect. The chatelaine of Vlixcombe Manor has no business in a Frenchman's bed. Or so my conscience tells me.

'H?' I repeat.

'My Balkan friend tells me he has a problem.'

'Your Balkan friend is right. The Brits call it Long Covid.'

'Not just that. Upstairs, too.' One long finger taps his forehead. 'In here.'

I muster a smile and try to hold his gaze, which isn't as simple as it may sound. Bits of the room, including Monsault, keep slipping out of focus.

'He's mad.' This from Rémy. 'Crazy. He's an old man already. He's lost it.'

'But he still owns the place? The house? The estate?'

'Of course.'

'So who invites us in? Who signs the deal? With whom do we do business?'

Dimly, I realize that Monsieur Impossible is much sharper than he cares to admit. I'm also outraged by Rémy's casual dismissal of a man who still deserves, at the very least, a little respect.

'H is ill,' I concede. 'He's also the father of my only son. Did you know that?'

'Yes.'

'How?'

'Your H was a man with a reputation. Anyone who was serious about the business probably had dealings with him. He ran a very effective operation in Aruba. That place was never easy. The Colombians on the mainland would test any man. Your H secured deals some of us found hard to believe. You have to admire him for that.'

Monsault doffing his cap to *my* H. Sweet.

Rémy is now talking about a classy lawyer he knows in Paris. This man has representation in London and can evidently fix anything when it comes to the Court of Protection. Securing the all-important location, in other words, won't be a problem.

Monsault hasn't taken his eyes off me.

'H,' he says again. 'Tell me more.'

'He's rich. Clever. Like you.'

'And he had class, this man of yours. Everyone knew that.'

Had is a word I don't much like. Language matters, especially tenses. *Had* carries the smell of nursing homes and long, empty autumn afternoons enlivened by bingo cards and perhaps a bowl of Pringles.

'H is still H,' I tell him. 'And it's my job to keep him that way. If class means never giving in, then yes, he definitely has it.'

'And you?'

'I'm the mother of his son.'

'Of course. That's very brave. But you really think you can rise to the challenge?'

'What challenge?'

Monsault's finger taps his head again. He says nothing. Rémy, I know, is desperate to change the subject. He wants to get back to the bottomless potential of his little baby, the dollar signs at the end of the first series, and I can quite see why. If Rémy is battling some midlife crisis, then *Vlixcombe* might be his salvation, but Monsault and slivovitz have touched something deep in my soul and if he's serious about H, then the least I owe him is a proper answer.

'H has dementia,' I say carefully. 'Everyone I talk to tells me it's irreversible. Medical people, carers, they all say the same thing, but they're wrong, and you know why? Because they *have* to be wrong. H is still in there somewhere and it's my job to find him. Will that need a miracle? I've no idea. Will I therefore give up? Never.'

I sit back, very happy to have parted the curtains of slivovitz, if only for that single impassioned moment. I've always been able to read an audience, and I know that Monsault is impressed. Even Rémy has the grace to sit back and nod in a gesture of applause.

'I'd like to help you.' Monsault's hand has settled on my knee. 'Everyone should believe in miracles.'

Elliott, who appears to be a house guest of Monsault, turns up shortly afterwards. He's a bulky forty-something in a beautiful three-piece suit. Despite the weight he carries, he moves with the lightness of a ballroom dancer. The moment he enters the room, his gaze settles on Monsault and a strong London accent tells me he's English.

Monsault, also speaking English, wants to know how it went.

'Knock-out. They loved it. Businessmen can never get over themselves. They think they've got life cracked and then I come along. Never fucking fails.'

Elliott, it turns out, is a magician. This evening he's been entertaining the Jersey Chamber of Commerce at a ritzy hotel down the road. Tomorrow, he says, it's the turn of a bunch of Russian oligarchs aboard a superyacht in one of the St Helier marinas. He's insisting on his fee in dollars. He's been burned by roubles before. By now, I've abandoned the slivovitz for brimming glasses of Perrier, a decision I will never regret.

Elliott has an almost feral interest in new faces, something I've noticed before in performers. Maybe it goes with working a room full of strangers. Or maybe he's just nosey. Either way, he's pulled up a chair between myself and Monsault.

The ebbing tide of Balkan plum brandy has left me emboldened. First I check that he really is a magician. Then I ask for proof. The question delights him.

'Georgie tells me you're a famous actress.' He has a ready smile. 'True?'

'Actress, certainly. Not sure about the fame.'

'Care to prove it?'

'Silly question, Mr Magician. All you need show me is a trick or two. Me? I'd have to bore you to death with *King Lear* or one of those long silences from Harold Pinter.'

'Bang on.' The smile widens 'You win. We've just met, right?'

'Right.'

'No prior knowledge. No prior anything, more's the pity. So think of a card, any card, but keep it to yourself. Can you do that? Just nod.'

I nod. The three of diamonds.

'Done?'

'Done.'

He gets to his feet. From his jacket pocket he produces a pack of cards and checks again that I have a card in mind.

'I do. Can I change it?'

'Absolutely not.'

He has the cards out now, the whole pack, and he fixes me with the kind of look I can only describe as searching. This, of course, is stagecraft, part of the act, and when he asks me for the third time whether I'm happy with my choice, I invite him to get on with it.

He and Monsault, who appears to be bewitched, exchange glances before Elliott invites me to take the pack.

'Just go through them,' he tells me. 'One is face down.'

I do his bidding. Towards the bottom of the pack, I find the face-down card.

'Well?'

'Well what?'

'You want to turn it over? Only you're looking at a thirsty man.'

I hold his gaze a moment longer, glance across at Monsault, then reveal the card. It's the three of diamonds. I stare at it for much longer than I should. I've watched magicians before, and nothing should surprise me, but this is truly astonishing. This man has peered deep inside my brain. He knows the entry code. He knows everything.

'Do it again,' I hear myself say.

'Don't believe me?'

'Do it again.'

This time he's produced a dice. He insists I take it, inspect it, turn it over, give it a shake.

'You OK with it?'

'I'm OK with it.'

'So now chose a number, put it in the palm of your hand, and then cover it. Yeah?'

'Yeah.'

He does a stagey little twirl. With his back to me, I put the five face-up and shield the dice with my other hand.

'Done?'

'Done.'

He's back in my face, much closer this time. His aftershave masks the scent of a busy evening with the Jersey Chamber of Commerce, but only just.

'Five is very popular.' The dice is still hidden but there's a hint of mockery in his smile. 'You could have tried harder.'

We retire past midnight. Monsault has assigned me a bedroom on the first floor and accompanies me up the stairs. While he's been very happy to pour Chateau Yquem down Elliott's throat, and leave Rémy with a bottle of Johnny Walker Black Label, I've noticed that he's drunk very little himself. Rémy, on the other hand, is near legless.

The room is sweet and very simple: a scatter of rugs on the polished floorboards, a double bed with a thin summer duvet, and a beautiful campaign chest that may well have seen service in the Peninsula Wars. Half close my eyes, and the bare granite walls have the texture of muscles under the skin of this lovely house.

With Monsault making his way downstairs again, I perch myself on the edge of the bed, enjoying the scent of honeysuckle through the quarter-open window. At length, I get up to gaze out at the view. The single curtain hangs down on one side and I finger the heavy linen which I like very much.

The bedroom is in the front of the house and the lawn is bathed in the soft yellow light that comes with top-end security systems. Out there in the darkness beyond the walls, Dessie may be fighting the chill in his rented car, and I try to resist a brief pang of guilt for not doing anything with the phone he's given me. Would Elliott's tricks have the same impact without the accompanying visuals? Would Monsault's musings have any evidential value in whatever case Dessie is trying to put together? To both questions I have no answer. Monsault is playing his new role as gentleman-publisher to perfection, regardless of his darker past.

The residue of the slivovitz has left me in a slightly pensive mood with just a splash of the *tristesse* I remember from angst moments in my adolescence. Then, I was stressing about weight gain and the dread possibility of acne. Now, I'm worried half to death about H. I meant it downstairs about miracles. Somehow, I have to find a way for both of us to live with this terrible, terrible affliction that is eating him alive. Otherwise, he'll be out there in the darkness for ever, even chillier than Dessie, and he deserves far better than that.

I take a shower in the en suite, and slip into bed. The night wind is beginning to stir the linen curtain and I drift off to sleep with H still on my mind. In no time at all, I'm awake again, flat on my back, every nerve stretched tight. Something's disturbed me and I don't know what. Then it happens again, two voices out in the corridor, a murmur of conversation and then the softest of laughs. Their favoured pronoun is 'she'. She, I suspect, is me.

I'm wearing only my knickers. I reach out blindly in search of my bag on the floor beside the bed. I want very badly to find Dessie's phone. I've no idea what's about to happen, but it might be wise to share it. At last, I lay hands on the bag but it's too late. The door is already opening and in the flickering light of a candle I can make out two figures.

One of them is Monsault, the other is Elliott. Both of them are wearing tightish trackie pants, bare feet beneath, and both faces are masked. Monsault is naked above the waist, while Elliott wears a Marbella-badged T-shirt. They pause at the foot of the bed. I return their gaze, not bothering to feign alarm, or outrage, or even surprise. I've been in similar circumstances before and I know that the key to the next few minutes is to hold my nerve. No woman ever helped herself by losing control.

'We've come to say nighty-night.' This from Elliott. I can tell at once he's drunk. He's swaying slightly, which is tricky when you're holding a candle.

'Very thoughtful of you.' I'm looking at Monsault. '*Et vous?*'

'*Toi.*' We're back in French, and he definitely wants to be my friend. 'Elliott has another trick he wants to show you.'

'Excellent.' I pat the bed. 'You want to sit down? Make yourselves comfortable?'

'Alas, no. The trick requires that we remain standing, me especially. All you have to do is watch. Afterwards we'll leave you in peace. This is an intrusion, I know, but it's Elliott's favourite trick and I hate to disappoint the dear man.' He glances at the figure beside him. 'Am I not right, *chérie*?'

Elliott nods, and then does a passable imitation of Monsault's falsetto giggle. It's at this point that it occurs to me that these men are gay, and very probably a couple. True or otherwise, I begin to relax.

'Go ahead,' I say. 'I'm here to be impressed.'

Elliott nods, and then extends his free hand. Very slowly, palm-up, he draws his fingers inwards as though he's cupping something. He does this two or three times while I search in vain for the point of the trick.

'Me,' Monsault murmurs. 'Look at me.'

'Really?'

'Yes.' He starts to giggle. 'Spot the difference. It shouldn't be hard. Not in that sense.'

Now I'm completely lost but as my gaze moves on from Elliott, I become aware of a stirring beneath Monsault's trackie bottoms. Something's alive in there, moving, uncoiling, engorging, and seconds later I'm witness to the most enormous erection I've ever seen. It's huge. It has a life of its own, shrugging off the confines of the thin polyester. Under any other circumstances, this would be seriously troubling. As it is, I know they won't be offended if I laugh.

'Impressive,' I murmur. 'And a round of applause for the party piece, too.'

Monsault offers a modest little bow while Elliott does his best not to fall over. Monsault blows me a kiss, then guides his pet magician towards the door. Moments later, he evidently has a thought.

'Look in the top drawer.' He nods towards the campaign chest. 'I left it earlier. It's a present for H. If you're a believer, it might help. My regards, incidentally. Peace, sanity and a long life. One day we may even be friends.'

With that, and two more little bows, my guests leave.

TWENTY-THREE

One day we may even be friends? I carry this thought through a very long night. There's no lock on the door but, as quietly as I can, I wrestle a chair across the floor until it bars entry. Monsault's little *cadeau* I've already lifted from the top drawer of the campaign chest, and after I feel a little safer I return to the bed for a proper look.

The present is nicely wrapped in white tissue paper, and carries a symbol I don't recognize, carefully drawn in black Pentel. Even before I remove the tissue paper and put it to one side, I recognize the distinctively pungent aroma. This is quality cannabis resin, presented in a tiny china pot. The pot is white, as fine and light as a feather, and carries a single painted line on the body of the pot beneath the lid. Yellow, I think. The colour of earth.

I lift the pot and gaze at the dark ball of resin inside. The smell is much stronger now, close to overwhelming. Growing up in Brittany, we kids had a dabble or two with weed but money was always a problem, and by the time I was older and richer I was very happy with alcohol. Rémy, though, would understand the chemistry of this present. Only after the best advice, would I dream of offering it to H.

The best advice, as it turns out, comes not from Rémy but from Monsault. I'm down in the big kitchen by seven o'clock in the morning. My host is wearing a silk dressing gown decorated with dragons – all of them in yellow – and is supervising a pot of fresh coffee which we share at the long oak table. Neither of us mention the masks or the miracle of my host's nether regions, but he's very happy to tell me about the source of my little present.

The resin, he says, comes from the Parvati Valley in the foothills of the Himalayas. He discovered it first as a twenty-two-year-old, committed to finding the world's best terpenes.

'Terpenes?'

'Cannabis oils. They're in the live resin concentrate. Without terpenes, the weed stays a weed. Find the best terpenes, and you're mixing with the gods.' He smiles and gestures vaguely upwards.

In the Parvati Valley, he says, he was living in a wooden shack at the mouth of a cave. Below were thickets of wild cannabis plants and a local holy man had already warned him of their potency.

'You remove the fan leaves from the plant, and then caress the small green flowers. They contain the resin glands. The stuff leaves a thin layer of stickiness on your hand. It's clear to begin with, and then turns brown. This is where you find the terpenes. The holy man was right. Inhale the fumes like you'd take communion. It's a divine thing. Your body floats in the bosom of the valley. You're lighter than air, richer than any man alive. Wait . . .'

He abandons his coffee and leaves the room. When he returns, he's carrying a smallish cardboard box. Inside is an object in black glass which sits on a flat base. At the other end is a mouthpiece. It also contains a lead and an electric plug. This, it seems, is also for H. Plugged in, the device will heat little balls of resin until they vaporize. All H has to do is inhale the fumes.

'We call it a dabber,' he says, 'but tell H to take care. This stuff has a potency of eighty-five per cent.'

'So how will it help him?' I'm still looking at the dabber.

'It will remove toxins from his body and evil spirits from his soul. It will burnish his best memories and restore the rest. His energy levels will rocket' – he gestures down at his groin – 'so lock the bedroom door.'

When he asks me what I've done with the resin and the little china pot, I tell him it's stowed in my bag.

'You're taking it back today?'

'Of course.'

'Then you'll need the shield box. It's a hundred per cent aroma-proof. They have sniffer dogs at the airport. Be careful.'

I nod. I'm still thinking about the pitch he's made for the wild cannabis of the Parvati Valley.

'You guarantee this stuff? It never fails?'

'Never. And if it does, you call for Elliott. He can revive anything, that man. Believe me.'

Rémy drifts down to an alfresco breakfast an hour or so later. He's badly hungover but I make him scrambled eggs on toast and force him to eat them. Monsault has disappeared, I think upstairs, and of Elliott there's no sign.

'You've talked to Georges this morning?'

'I have, yes. He's been more than kind.'

'Kind how?'

'He's thinking of H. Like I am.'

'And *Vlixcombe*?'

'He thinks it's a great idea. I suspect he'll fund the development budget.'

'He *said* that?'

'More or less. He said we made him laugh last night. I get the feeling that's important. Too much shit in the world. That's his take, but it happens that I agree. Here . . .'

I've scribbled a name and an address on a copy of the *Jersey Evening Post*. Rémy studies it for a moment.

'His media lawyer,' I explain. 'The guy works out of an office in the Avenue Charles de Gaulle. You might pop in and see him.'

'And this?' Rémy's finger has found a symbol I've carefully transcribed from the tissue paper Monsault used to wrap my present.

'It's an invocation of the Goddess Shiva. If H asks nicely, she might take care of him.'

Rémy is staring at me. He clearly thinks I've been at the terpenes. 'This is bullshit,' he says.

'*Au contraire*.' I push the newspaper towards him. 'Believe in miracles and anything can happen.'

My return flight leaves at ten in the morning. After a curiously formal *au revoir* to Monsault and Elliott, Rémy drives me to the airport and drops me outside the departures hall. The news about the development budget, confirmed by Monsault that very morning, has banished his hangover and lifted his spirits. A little of the man I used to revere on location after location has returned, and for that I'm deeply grateful. When I ask about Claudine, he says she took a flight back to Paris last night. Today he has a lunch in St Helier, after which he'll be joining her at the apartment they share in the Fifth. This evening, he'll make final adjustments to the development budget and first thing tomorrow morning he'll push for a meeting with Monsault's lawyer. Before he drives away, I squat beside the driver's door, and reach through the open window of the hire car to give him a hug.

'Take care.' I nod at the steering wheel. 'The last thing you need now is an accident.'

Dessie is already in the departures hall. He looks knackered. The Bristol flight's on time and before we have a chance to talk he asks me to mind his holdall while he pays a visit. His holdall is at my feet. I watch him disappearing towards the toilets, and then unzip my own bag. By the time Dessie's returned, the shield box containing H's salvation is nestling beneath Dessie's smalls. If the guys manning the X-ray cameras in Security decide to take a closer look, it's ex-DS Dessie Wren who'll be handling the harder questions.

Dessie is back. There's already a queue for the security line and we join it. As we shuffle slowly forward, I enquire where he spent the night.

'Don't ask,' he grunts. 'What happened to that phone of mine?'

'I left it in my bedroom.'

'On purpose?'

'Of course. I was being grown up, making my own decisions. It happens sometimes.'

Dessie shakes his head, says nothing. When we reach the X-ray check, Dessie gestures for me to go first. I happily comply, waiting for him at the other end of the luggage belt. From where I'm standing I have a near-perfect view of the X-ray screen. I can see the shadow of neatly folded trousers, a fuzzy knot of socks, what looks like a paperback book, and the cube that has to contain Monsault's treasure from the Parvati Valley. Dessie's holdall appears from the machine, and the watcher bends to inspect the next image.

'All done?' I say brightly. 'Any chance of a proper conversation?'

We talk on the plane. In that quaint phrase which I remember from last year in Pompey, Dessie wants a full account of my doings. I tell him about La Maison Blanche, and the company I kept. I describe the relationship between Monsault and his magician house guest, and I hazard a guess that the guardian of the best dope in the world may well fund Rémy's *Vlixcombe.*

'And Ratko?'

'Nowhere to be seen.'

'Did they talk about him at all?'

'Not when I was around.'

'Just showbiz talk? A cheerful evening round the fire? It was bloody arctic last night. How they ever sell this place to tourists is beyond me.'

Dessie, it transpires, was parked up the road after nightfall, listening in vain for transmissions from the phone he'd given me. Without choice cuts from our conversation, I'm assuming he would have returned to whatever hotel he'd booked himself into but I'm wrong.

'I was there all night,' he grunts.

He shoots me a look. He's toying with a cup of thin coffee. The remains of an egg and cress sandwich are probably his breakfast. He's very fed up, and it shows.

'Ratko,' he says again. 'I don't believe you.'

'You think he was there?'

'He had to be. That's where he was staying. They've had him under surveillance for days. He was logged in yesterday morning and he never left.'

'You were part of this team?'

'I was on the night shift. There were four of us in all, every exit covered. Had he bailed out, we'd have seen him.'

I nod, thinking of the darkness beyond the loom of the granite walls. Four cars, four pairs of eyes. Then I remember the dormer windows.

'There were bedrooms under the roof. He could have been up there.'

'But you never saw him? He never came down? Joined the party?'

'Never.' I start to laugh.

'Something funny I said?' Dessie has turned to stare out of the window.

'Not you. I was thinking of the magician guy I mentioned. He was really good. In fact, he was exceptional. He could make anything disappear. Even Ratko.'

Dessie is shaking his head. He doesn't think any of this is the least bit funny and, in his shoes, I wouldn't either.

'I'm sorry about that phone of yours,' I say at length. 'You think I let you down?'

Dessie says nothing for a moment. Then I catch a faint nod. 'I thought you were better than that,' he murmurs. 'Turns out I'm wrong.'

It gets worse. After we land, he can't find a letter he needs before making a phone call. He pauses on the concourse and starts to rummage through his holdall. In truth, I'd forgotten about the precious nut of resin gifted to H but Dessie lays hands on it at once. He pulls out the aroma box, stares at it a moment, then glances up at me.

'What's this?'

'Quality cannabis. Monsault gave it to me. He thinks H needs cheering up.'

'But what the fuck's it doing in my bag?'

Good question. Maybe Dessie's right. I should be better than this.

'You're a cop,' I say lamely. 'Or at least a civvie cop. Cops never get searched. I was thinking of H, really. Needs must? Does that make any sense?'

Dessie is shaking his head again but this time it's looking terminal. He checks around and then passes me the box.

'This never happened,' he says. 'There's a bus outside that will take you to Temple Meads. You change trains at Exeter. Give my best to H and tell him good fucking luck with the weed. You got that? Or do you want me to write it down?'

Moments later, he's gone.

TWENTY-FOUR

When I finally get back to Flixcombe, five long hours later, I find H on the bench in the kitchen garden. Jessie is sitting beside him, shucking peas from an old wicker trug. It's a glorious day, hot sunshine at last, and H has obviously been making the most of it. He's acquired a light tan and the hollows in his face are filling out. He's always adored Jessie's cooking, and for the second time today I feel a stab of guilt. What's wrong with the meals I make? How come I'm not looking after the men in my life?

I'm watching this scene from the privacy of the kitchen and neither of them are aware I've returned. Jessie is doing all the talking while H has his head back in the sunshine. His eyes are half-closed and there's a contented little smile on his face and from time to time he gives her a pat on the thigh. Jessie can talk for England and I've no idea whether H is able to follow the usual torrent of celeb gossip sieved from the columns of *Hello!* magazine, but that doesn't matter. For the first time in weeks, I'm watching an H who seems at peace with the world.

I make a pot of coffee and carry it out to the garden bench. H looks up, shading his eyes, and there's a flicker of alarm when I stoop to put the tray on the nearby table. He's grabbed Jessie's hand and won't let go. He's loving this moment in the sunshine and he thinks I'm here to take him away.

'It's Enora, H.' Jessie pats his hand.

'Who?'

'Don't be silly. She's brought coffee. Be nice to her, H. She's been away.'

'Away?'

This is a word with which H now has some difficulty. I noticed it first a couple of weeks back when I was trying to explain how long it would take to drive to Pompey. A long way away made absolutely no sense to H. Pompey was down the road. Pompey was in the top drawer, where he'd left it. Pompey was a thousand memories, some of them still at his beck and call. Away was somewhere different.

'I've been to see a man about a movie,' I explain. 'It's going to happen here, H. Here in this house, here in this very garden. Lots of people. Lights. Cameras. It's going to be brilliant. Lots to see. Lots to get involved in.'

'You're kidding me.' This from Jessie. 'I know you've mentioned it before but it's really going to happen?'

'It is. Fingers crossed.'

I tell her about the house in Jersey, about the pitch that Rémy and I made, about a coachload of crazy French thesps descending on rural Dorset all those years ago, and about our success in nailing the seed money to get the whole project rolling.

'So who stars? Who will I get to meet?' Jessie's back in the pages of *Hello!*

'Bit early for that, Jess. Maybe you should have a think. Tell me who takes your fancy.'

'Anyone?'

'Anyone. Showbiz is dreamland. We all know that.'

'Dreamland?' H is back in touch. At first, he's looking solemn, then his face creases into a sudden grin. 'The Who. Pete Townsend. Great night. Had a ruck with some Chelsea scum off the boat.'

Jessie and I exchange glances. Then Jessie puts her hand on H's arm.

'That's Margate, H. Andy and I had a holiday there once. Crap decision. It pissed down all week.'

'Margate?' The blankness is back.

'Yeah.' Jessie gives his arm a squeeze. 'Dreamland's on the seafront. We might take you there one day but it's a long way away.'

It's nearly six by the time I find Andy. He's just driven back from Bridport with a trailer full of sand and is looking stressed. When I thank him for keeping an eye on H, he nods at the trailer and rolls his eyes.

'Jessie's idea. She wants me to build a sandpit for H. Fuck knows why.'

I muster a consoling grin. Jessie is famously impatient when it comes to projects. Just the word Margate would be enough to send her partner to our local builder's yard.

'That lovely woman is full of good intentions,' I mutter. 'Did you buy a bucket and spade as well? And some of those little flags for H's sandcastles? Or should I do that?'

Andy has the grace to smile. When I ask him about H when I was away, he simply shrugs. 'He's gone.' He taps his head. 'Packed up and left. Saddest thing I ever saw.'

'Was he any trouble?'

'None. Jessie made him kip in our spare room. I shouldn't be telling you this but he wet the bed, poor old sod.'

Poor old sod. Never did I expect any of the Pompey tribe to couple H with a term like this. When I ask Andy whether he's still doing weed, he nods.

'When I've got the money, yeah.'

'Then I need your advice.'

'Why? Has it got that bad?'

'Yes. Since you ask.'

We walk back to the house together. I've stored the aroma box and the glass dabber in a cupboard in the kitchen. When I get them both out, and lift the tiny china pot from the box, I've definitely won Andy's full attention.

'Is that what I think it is?' He's nodding at the pot.

'Open it. Take a look.'

Andy does what he's told. After one sniff he steps back from the table, shaking his head.

'One little taste? Do you mind?'

'Not at all.'

He picks up the pot, licks a finger, and rubs it lightly against the little knot of resin before teasing the end of his tongue. This piece of theatre has an almost religious feel. It speaks of something close to reverence.

'Jesus,' he says softly. 'Where did you get this?'

'It doesn't matter. I just need to know how to use this thing.' I fetch the dabber. Andy gazes at it.

'You plug it in,' he says. 'The resin goes into the base. It gets hot and you suck out the fumes at the other end. You're telling me you've never done this before?'

'Never.'

'And you're starting with *this*?' He's still holding the china pot.

'It's not for me, Andy. It's for H.'

'*H?* H was never into weed. This little baby will blow him away.'

'Maybe that's the idea. We need to stop him in his tracks. Bring him back home.'

'You're serious?'

'I am. All we have to do is get the setting right. Right time, right place.'

'You want me to road test it?'

'I want you to think about H, and about this stuff, and then tell me where and when and maybe how. I can't imagine that little lump will last forever. You'll do that? For H's sake?'

It's mid-June, and we're only a week off the longest day of the year. Sunset this evening is at half past nine and I know this because Andy has checked. He also recommends something light for supper, and after H and I have shared the simplest of salads, we join him on the lawn at the front of the house. An empty stomach, according to Andy, gives quality cannabis a clear run.

From the corner of the property, looking out across the rolling hills, we can enjoy H's favourite view of the setting sun. Here, on the gravel path that tracks around the side of the big old house, Andy has arranged three deckchairs in a loose crescent. An extension lead disappears through a nearby open window, and the dabber awaits on a low table I last saw in the room that serves as H's den. When Andy appears from nowhere, and invites us to sit down, I mime applause. All this little tableau needs, I think, is a proscenium arch, a curtain, and programme notes for the drama to come.

When Andy asks whether I want music, I tell him I'm not sure.

'Isn't this supposed to be meditative? Laid-back? Chilled out?'

'Of course it is. All that. I just thought . . .' He shrugs. 'I dunno.'

'You think music will help?'

'It might. Any suggestions?'

Andy nods, and hands me his phone. 'Check it out inside.' He nods at the house. 'See what you think.'

I step back into the cool of the hall. Andy has chosen a Santana track I recognize at once. 'While My Guitar Gently Weeps' is nice enough, and I can see him nodding along on a hot summer's evening in a cloud of dope, but I'm not at all sure it's right for H. Best, I think, to gracefully decline.

Back outside, Andy shrugs. *Tant pis.* Too bad. H is occupying the deckchair next to the dabber, and I settle down beside him. The sun is plunging towards the distant ridge of hills, and bits of the sky are already on fire, the deepest crimson that spreads and spreads. Sitting in my deckchair, I can feel the day's heat still radiating in waves from the ancient stonework behind me. The god of sunsets, at the very least, deserves a word or two of gratitude from yours truly, and I'm still trying to get the words in the right order when I catch Andy's eye. He wants to start.

'Go for it,' I murmur.

The dabber is already warm, and Andy plugs it in again before extracting the little ball of resin and seating it carefully inside. The blackness of the glass hides it from view but this stagey little bit of business has caught H's eye. He looks suspicious, even a bit cross. He has no idea what's going on, and even less idea how he might find out.

'It's a treat, H,' I whisper. 'A little present I've brought back for you.'

'Back?'

'Relax, H. Nothing's going to hurt you.'

The only word he appears to recognize is 'hurt'. He folds his thin arms across what's left of his chest, a gesture that couldn't be more defensive. I'm playing this scene like a novice, I tell myself. Rubbish dialogue. Totally the wrong vibe. I reach across, and try to offer reassurance, but the touch of flesh on flesh simply makes things worse.

Andy, crouched over the dabber, is getting excited. I can see shimmers of heat rising from the open mouth of the dabber and the scent of jasmine from the nearby bush is suddenly swamped by something infinitely more pungent. Andy shoots me a look. It's time for H to make his entrance, to cast aside his worries and his confusions and pay a visit to the Parvati Valley.

What none of us have thought through is how, exactly, to make this happen. Do we pass him the dabber, which is already hot? Do we encourage him to bend towards the oily breath of the resin? Is it self-evident that here is a chance to fix the wreckage of his neural circuits? To trust the wisdom and benevolence of the Himalayan gods? To start, in a word, afresh?

The answer is no. H wants nothing to do with what's happening on the table beside him. Instead, he's transfixed by the unfolding drama of the sunset. The sky is ablaze. Fat cattle are stirring in the corner of a distant meadow. Even a colony of rooks from a nearby copse of elm trees have taken wing and are now circling noisily for a better look. When Andy tries to tug H a little closer to the dabber, H pushes him away before leaning forward, his face to the dying sun. For a moment, there's nothing that any of us can do. H, or perhaps the sun, has taken charge.

Then I notice H's lips begin to move, and his knees too, keeping time, and next his clenched fists, and finally the whole of that wasting body, swaying awkwardly from side to side. From somewhere very far away he's managed to dredge the memory of a song, of a beat, even lyrics, and as the rim of the ball of flaming gas touches the distant treeline, he's trying to sing. It comes out as a growl, a raspy tribute to a lost moment of time, but that doesn't matter because both Andy and I can hear the words. Pete Townsend. 'My Generation'. Dreamland's finest.

Andy is grinning fit to bust. Both he and I know that the marriage of H and cannabis will never happen. Pompey's drug lord never had any time for the weed – too poncy, too fucking *lightweight* – and in his current state he won't go anywhere near it. But this isn't just weed, it's Monsault's weed, Shiva's weed, the best terpenes in the world, and unless I make a decision fast, a lot of it will go to waste. Andy knows this too because he's thought it through, and when I suggest he helps himself, he needs no second invitation.

H, meanwhile, has got to the end of the first verse, and – a smile on his face – considers that his work is done. Lying back, he watches the last of the sunset, his head turned away from the heavy fumes of the dabber, then his eyes close and he drifts off to sleep. Half an hour later, it might be more, it might be less, Jess appears around the side of the house and comes to a sudden halt. She can't believe her eyes.

'Christ,' she says. 'What have you done to Andy?'

TWENTY-FIVE

I'm in bed, nearly asleep, when my phone rings. It's Claudine, and I know at once that something is very wrong. As an actress back in the day, her self-control was legendary. On set, or in real life, nothing ever threw her. Now she seems to be hyperventilating.

'What's the matter?'

She won't say. She just wants me to stay on the line.

'Why? Where are you?'

'In Paris. I had a call just now. It's Rémy.'

'What did he say?'

'Nothing.' She's crying now. 'He's dead.'

Dead? I'm staring at an oblong of black that used to be my window. All of a sudden, nothing makes sense any more. Rémy? *Dead?*

'How?' I manage. 'When?'

'They found a body in a field. Georges identified him. He'd been shot in the head.'

'Where? Where did this happen?'

'Christ knows. Somewhere on that bloody island. We should never have gone. We should never have believed a word any of them said. I told Rémy. I said he was asking for trouble. But you know that man as well as I do. He never listens.'

Listened, I think.

'You have someone you can talk to?' I ask. 'Someone close? Someone to be with?'

'Of course. I phoned you first because . . .'

'Because what?'

'Because you're part of it.'

'Part of what?'

There's a long silence on the line, and then I lose the connection completely. It's tempting to blame a technical glitch, some outage on the network, but I know she's hung up on me. *Part of what?*

Still holding the phone, I realize that I'm trembling. It's still warm, even gone midnight, but news like this carries a chill like no other. Looking back, I suspect the proper word would be shock but just now I feel nothing but an enveloping emptiness. The world, or circumstances, or some cosmic evil has stood me on my head. I don't know where to turn, who to phone, what to do. H is crazy. Andy is out of his head. Jessie, bless her, is probably asleep. And now Rémy is dead. Shit.

I put the phone to one side, trying very hard not to think of Rémy prostrate in some field. He and I, in our separate ways, built whole careers on scenes like these, even on the kind of phone conversation I've just had with Claudine, but somehow neither of us ever dreamed that this stuff happens for real, and that one day it might happen to us. Was he shot in the face? And if so, what must he have thought when he looked down the barrel of that gun? Did it happen fast? Was he spared the choking fear, the sheer disbelief, that must accompany your own passing? Or did he try and fight back? Try and make it back to wherever he'd come from?

Before we'd said goodbye at the airport, he'd mentioned a lunch he'd organized. One person? Two? More? Did it happen before he made it to the resto? Or did he die on a full stomach? To these questions, I know I have no answer, but try as I might to make a brief peace with my teeming brain, the questions keep coming, irresistible, ever-louder, an unruly mob of mights and might-nots that defy my pitiful attempts at crowd control. Ratko, I suspect, must have something to do with all this, but again I can't be sure. The cops in Jersey obviously had doubts about him. Dessie was part of their surveillance operation. But why would Rémy's so-called location manager ever want to kill him?

I lie back and pull the duvet tight around my neck, an instinctive attempt to ward off yet more disasters. This reminds me all too obviously of H, faced with the world's most potent toke, but as my pulse settles, and my mind begins to clear, I know I have to regain some kind of control. With Rémy dead, everything is up for grabs: *Vlixcombe*, H, the estate itself. And all it's taken is a single bullet. Bang. Everything gone. Lights down. Cue applause.

* * *

Dessie must be asleep when I phone. He takes a while to answer. 'You,' he mutters.

'Me,' I agree. I tell him briefly about Rémy but it turns out he knows already. 'Then why didn't you phone me?' I ask.

'Maybe you're better off not knowing.'

'You really thought I wouldn't find out?'

'Of course not.'

'Then why not lift the phone?'

'Because it might help if I had something to say.'

'About what?'

'About what happened. About why it happened. About what might happen next. I'm due a conference call first thing tomorrow. After that it might make sense to have a proper conversation.'

I pause a moment. If Dessie's icy logic is meant to impress me, it doesn't. 'So what about me? Now? Here? I've known that man half my life. We've been through no end of stuff together, good stuff, bad stuff, the lot. And now he's gone and I'm all over the fucking place. Isn't that worth a phone call? Just for old times' sake?'

'That man?'

'Rémy. Don't be a prick, Dessie. It doesn't suit you.'

'Old times' sake?'

I stare at the phone, choked with anger, then hit the red button. Prick is right, I tell myself. I should have looked harder.

Dessie phones back within the hour. He's evidently been brewing himself a pot of tea, as well as making a couple of phone calls.

'I don't want information,' I tell him at once. 'I don't want to be briefed. That's not what this is about. I thought you were a friend. When you said you cared, I believed you. That turns out to be a mistake, and those kinds of mistakes don't do much for a girl.'

There's a longish pause on the line and for some reason I can't fathom I don't want him to hang up.

'That stunt at the airport was infantile,' he says at last.

'You mean the cannabis?'

'Yes.'

'If you want the truth, I thought it was funny. And I also thought you had it coming. You give me a phone I'm supposed to plant. No please, no thank you, just do it. That level of assumption reminded me of my ex-husband. You never had the pleasure of meeting him but believe me, you were spared.'

'Tit for tat, then? Is that what I'm hearing?'

'Sort of.'

'And now?'

'Now I'm wrecked. I know this sounds pathetic but I've been through some rough weather in my life. My marriage turned out to be the pits. My son bailed out on me. And then a nice man at the hospital put an X-ray up on his little light box and pointed out the tumour that would probably kill me. All that I've coped with. All that is history. It's gone. It's over. But this, believe me, is something different and just now I haven't a clue what to do next. If that sounds like mitigation, then so be it. My apologies for the rant, but Rémy dead has put me on the floor. It's two in the morning. You must have better things to do than listen to me.'

There's another silence, and then I hear the fanciful scrape of heavy furniture moving as we at last make space for each other. We talk for an hour or so and not once does Dessie play the cop. At the end of the conversation I warn him that I'm as needy and broken as the next woman he'll probably meet and he chuckles.

'That's the best news I've heard for a while,' he says. 'Just try and get some sleep.'

It works. A dreamless sleep, mercifully free of images of Rémy, leaves me rested and – I hope – strong enough to face whatever might now follow. I'm brisk with H, solicitous with Jessie, and when Andy asks whether I might find any more of the magic resin, I tell him he hasn't a prayer. The last place I want to re-visit just now, in my head or otherwise, is La Maison Blanche.

Dessie phones in mid-morning. Happily, we're friends again, and this time I sense it's for real. He tells me that Rémy never made it to the lunch he mentioned, and that it's far from clear whether the lunch ever existed. There was no trace of it on his phone, and under interview Georges Monsault said he'd never mentioned any rendezvous. Enquiry teams are checking every restaurant in the area for bookings but have so far drawn a blank. All Dessie knows for certain is that Rémy's body was found in the early afternoon by a pair of young BMX cyclists in one of the few semi-deserted stretches of the island. His hire car had been abandoned in a nearby lane and has so far yielded no evidence worth the name. The nearest properties to the crime scene were half a mile away, and no one had heard any gunshot. The incident, Dessie says, has all the hallmarks of a professional hit dressed up as a suicide: one bullet through his temple, the gun inches from Rémy's hand.

'Have they checked the gun for fingerprints?'

'Of course. Surprise, surprise, they're Despret's prints. It tells us nothing.'

Details like this I can do without but Rémy, I know, would expect me to be paying attention.

'And Ratko?' I enquire.

'Gone to ground. Jersey Major Crimes put a team into Monsault's place but Ratko wasn't there.'

'You think he did it?'

'To be frank, yes. He has a reputation for settling debts in person.'

'Rémy owed him?'

'For sure. That goes with the company he was keeping.'

I nod. This, very sadly, feels all too plausible.

'So how did Ratko give you the slip?'

'I've no idea. At this stage everyone has a to-do list as long as your arm. The post-mortem comes later.'

'Nice phrase.'

'I'm sorry. Ratko, incidentally, was never a location manager, whatever he might have told you. Major player on the Marbella drug scene? Definitely. Force to be reckoned with? For sure. But the rest was bollocks.'

'So he came here under false pretences? Taking all those pictures? Is that what you're telling me?'

'I'm afraid so.'

'So how come Rémy vouched for him?'

'Rémy was in deep with him. Just how deep we don't yet

know for certain but deep enough to get a bullet in his head. Why Ratko needed the photos we can't yet explain.'

'But you're really sure that Rémy dead was down to Ratko?'

'Odds-on, yes. Can we prove it yet? Sadly not. Ratko's no infant when it comes to settling debts. We think Marbella's where this thing begins and ends. It's the Wild West, believe me, and I have it on good authority that Ratko scares the shit out of everyone.'

'Hence Wolfman?'

'Exactly. Top dog.'

I nod. This is sobering news, all the grimmer for Ratko's evident ability to stage his own disappearance. For the second time, I'm wondering about Elliott's talents.

'There's a superyacht in some marina or other on Jersey.' Briefly, I tell Dessie a little more about Monsault's lover. Last night, he was due to entertain a boatload of Russians. 'Might they have some connection with Ratko? Comrades-in-arms?'

'It's a possibility. Your magician friend must be a disappointed man.'

'Care to tell me why?'

'The yacht sailed last thing yesterday afternoon. It was hired from an agency in Gibraltar. His audience had gone.'

'You know where it was headed?'

'Last time we checked it was out in the Western Approaches and turning south. That put it within chopper range of Brittany and Western France. There's a landing pad on board. Pay the right money, and you can get anyone flown off.'

'Golly. Very James Bond.'

'Exactly. There's something else you ought to know, too.'

'About?'

'Rémy. Don't you wonder what he was ever doing with a guy like Ratko in the first place?'

'Of course. And . . .?'

'It seems that lockdown got to him. All his projects had turned to shit and he needed to find the money to float a new idea.'

'Would this be *Vlixcombe*?'

'As it turned out, it would, yes. In the first place he had some other idea, something to do with the Falklands War.'

'*Exocet*,' I mutter. 'He pitched it to me. Total crap.'

'Whatever. Either way, he had a yacht. He was prepared to take the risk. He ran up a sizeable bill with Ratko, shipped lots of gear into Newhaven on extended credit, flogged it all but never paid up.'

'Because?'

'Nobody knows. Which is a shame because it might have saved his life. Ratko talks a good game but you'd never fuck with the man. Cross him once, like I say, and he'll have you. Rémy did just that, and look what happened.'

'But *Vlixcombe* was a great idea,' I say plaintively. 'So how come he was still after seed funding from Monsault?'

'That I can't fathom. Yet.' He pauses. 'You want me to come down? Moral support? Lend a listening ear?'

'That would be nice. I expect H would love it.'

'And you?'

'Me, too, Mr Dessie. If you can find the time.'

That afternoon, after pondering long and hard about *Vlixcombe*, I phone Rosa. Our sainted government are talking about lifting all Covid restrictions by mid-summer, and she sounds buoyant. There's laughter back in her voice, which is good to hear.

'I'm getting calls from the Beeb,' she says. 'From ITV Drama, from Channel Four. Lockdown has emptied their cupboards. Commissioning editors are snowed under, my precious, so now is the time to make their sad little lives even tougher.'

She starts to beat the drum for *Vlixcombe.* The French will do the heavy-lifting production-wise, so a rights negotiation should be – in her phrase – a doddle. The series will be a smash on whichever channel pays top dollar.

'But there's a problem,' I say.

'Impossible. The bloody thing can't fail.'

'Rémy's dead.'

'Rémy's what?'

'Dead. Someone shot him.'

'That's terrible. Is this some kind of joke?'

'Far from it. It's a long story and it's far from over and I'm one of those people who are going to miss him most, but that's not the point. Unless I'm wrong, there'll be no French production. In which case, we need to talk.'

'Christ.' There's a hint of admiration in Rosa's voice. 'You're even tougher than I thought you were.'

We agree to meet in Salisbury next day for lunch. Rosa knows a hotel off the market square that serves rare beef to die for. Salisbury is halfway for both of us, which seems more than fair, and if I'd be kind enough to email my latest thoughts on the project she'll make sure she's up to speed by the time we're squabbling over the horseradish sauce.

Next, I phone Dessie. He seems very happy to pick me up in Salisbury tomorrow once I'm through with Rosa, and drive me back to Flixcombe. When I ask him about Ratko, he says there's no news. The superyacht is still heading south, in international waters, and when it comes to a destination Dessie's money is on Marbella.

'If Ratko's on board, they could drop him there before returning the boat to the agency in Gib. We're trying to organize a reception party in Marbella but Brexit makes this kind of stuff bloody difficult, especially with the Spanish. Guys like Ratko run Marbella. The place makes them lots of money. They don't want to piss him off.'

Mention of the agency sparks a memory.

'You had a tan when we met in the services place.'

'You mean the M25?'

'Yes. And you said it came from a trip to Gibraltar.'

'That's right.'

'So you've been on this job for a while? Is that what I'm hearing?'

Dessie's chuckle makes me smile. He's rarely in the business of sharing secrets but in this instance it seems, in his phrase, that I'm bang-on.

'So I stepped into your operation? Is that right?'

'Yes. Not my operation. I'm very lowly. But . . . yes.'

'Doesn't that qualify as trespass?'

'Of course it does. And for the record, Ms Andressen, you're very welcome.'

* * *

The day's business comes to an end with a call from Simon, the thesp-turned-estate-agent. He's talked to his masters in Bridport and it appears that given certain moves on my part there's every chance of securing outline planning permission for up to twenty bespoke dwellings on various corners of the Flixcombe estate. Phrases like 'bespoke dwellings', we agree, have no place in any normal sentence but he offers to drive out and share the small print.

'This is good news, believe me,' he says. 'Paragraph seventy-nine could be a game changer.'

By now, he'd lost me completely and when he pushes for a meeting tomorrow morning I turn him down. I'm out all day, I tell him, and after that I've no idea what might happen. Both statements are only too true and before we part, I promise to make contact when life has settled down.

'That period movie you mentioned?' He's sounding excited. 'All those French guys off the leash?'

'I'm working on it. Stay tuned, eh?'

The conversation over, I open my laptop and write down a series of thoughts about *Vlixcombe* for Rosa's benefit. These include the slightly wild pitch Rémy and I made to Georges Monsault, the night we stayed at La Maison Blanche, and when I think I've nailed the essence of the idea, I ping it off. The email despatched, I'm thinking of Rémy again. To my shame, I have no idea who might be the most important person in his life and in the absence of a name I rummage for paper and pen to write to his agent, Habeeb. Rosa, I know, will have his address and tomorrow I can post the letter from Salisbury.

Trying to sum up my feelings about Rémy, now he's so suddenly gone, is near impossible. He turned out to be exactly the same age as me but the first time we met I assumed him to be much older. He had a lovely presence on set, an easy confidence salted with a wry wit, and he was very good at deflating the huge egos that plague our business without leaving a trace of resentment.

At the time, working at a studio on the edge of Paris, I was the callow provincial up from a seaside town in deepest Brittany. I had looks on my side, and a real determination to make it as a performer on screen, and I busked my way through a couple of auditions to secure a small but challenging role in a story about a blackmail scandal at the top of one of the many thirties' French administrations. This was only Rémy's second movie, something he never admitted, but he knew at once how much I had to learn and was happy to oblige.

The shoot, including location work in Deauville, lasted nearly a month and by the time it was done, we were buddies. We had the same sense of humour, the same eye for the absurd, the same urge to get something different and wonderful up there on the screen, and as the years rolled by that bond between us could only deepen. Rémy never touched any project he regarded as worthless, no matter how high the fee, and I admired him for that. He became a brother to me, I write to Habeeb, and in important ways I trusted him with my entire career, which in essence meant my life. He never let me down, not once, and now that he's gone I feel half the person I used to be. Diminished, I add, is too small a word. Rémy represented the best. He *was* the best. And the world will be a sadder place in his absence.

I put my pen down and sit back at the old wooden table, unaware that H has ghosted into the kitchen. He's sitting in the wobbly armchair in the corner, staring at me.

'Why are you crying?' he says at length. 'Is it something you've eaten?'

TWENTY-SIX

Next morning, I take the train to Salisbury. Andy drives me to Yeovil Junction, and an hour later, as the train begins to slow, I'm eager for that first glimpse of the cathedral spire that towers over the water meadows. This is one of my all-time favourite views, the assurance that objects of rare beauty can still survive the centuries intact, and when it finally appears it works its usual magic.

Thanks to Simon's phone call, I've been stressing about our finances. In a handful of months, H will run out of money. Neither mentally nor legally is he in any state to make his own decisions, yet I appear equally helpless when it comes to taking charge. Tony Morse has promised to come up with some kind of solution, but I've heard nothing. Another phone call, I think. And yet another challenging conversation.

I walk from the station to the market square, but it's only when I lay eyes on the White Hart that I remember I've been here before. Years back, after Mitch Culligan stepped into my life, we met for what turned out to be a difficult lunch. Mitch was in the process of investigating UKIP funding and to my shame I confirmed that H had written one of their candidates a sizeable cheque. It was an act of breezy defiance on H's part, two fingers to the London establishment, but I sensed that conversation would take us all to a dark place, and it turned out I was right. H and Mitch have had their difficulties ever since, but both men are still important to me, and I count that as a blessing.

Rosa has already commandeered the best table in the dining room. She's wearing a long coat with an extravagant floral motif and a hat that might have started life as a fascinator. Opening lines are important in any conversation, and this one is all too obvious.

'How was the wedding?' I enquire. 'Someone close?'

'You, my precious.' She extends a big hand, gets up for a

hug, and then nods at the empty seat. 'I thought champagne might be in order. I know Rémy would approve.'

She is, of course, right. We have a choice here. We can gloom about Rémy, or we could celebrate the good times. Rémy himself would opt at once for the latter.

The champagne arrives. Rosa has chosen Krug. The waiter pours, and we wait for him to leave before raising our glasses.

'A man with impeccable instincts.' This from me.

'And a man with a bum to die for.' This from Rosa.

Rosa has always had the knack of finding my sweet spot, and this lunchtime is no different. She makes me laugh, and like the cathedral spire down the road, she makes me believe that life is often a much brighter proposition than it might appear.

For not very long, we gossip. The government have given the sagging corpse of lockdown a poke or two and Rosa confirms that prospects in the media biz are definitely on the mend. Her phone has started to ring again, and next week she's moving into premises off Covent Garden.

'An office of my own again.' She's beaming. 'Now all I have to do is pay for the bloody thing.'

When I ask whether she's had the time to read my latest thoughts on *Vlixcombe*, she offers a vigorous nod.

'Lovely,' she says at once. 'I get it completely, and so will they.'

'They?'

'The Beeb. Or maybe Channel Four.'

'But this will be a French production. Made in Paris.'

'Wrong, my precious. I talked to Habeeb first thing. Without Rémy he doesn't think the thing will fly. *Vlixcombe* depended on him. It *was* Rémy. Finance will be tricky now he's gone.'

'But we got a pledge of development funding. A guy called Georges Monsault. Strange man, but seriously rich.'

'I know. Habeeb told me about that, too. Rémy had the number of his lawyer in Paris, and Habeeb gave him a ring. The deal isn't entirely what you might have assumed. Habeeb thinks the money's dodgy.'

'Dodgy how?'

I meet Rosa's gaze. She's a woman of insatiable appetite

and the tablecloth around her side plate is already littered with the torn remnants of her second bread roll.

'We won't go there, my precious.' Her hand is on mine again. 'Not for a while, at any rate.' With this, it seems, I must be content.

'So is the project dead and buried?'

'In Paris, yes. Here? Happily not.'

She has in mind, she says, three commissioning editors she rates highly. One, a mere girl, is a child genius. The other two are older.

'You'll need a proper pitch.'

'For the time being, I've got all I need. You know how these things work. It's a conversation for starters. I have to light a fire under these people, and that – believe me – won't be hard. It's a glorious idea. It's so different, and it's so fucking *fertile*.'

'Fertile?'

'Full of possibility. And mischief. And *brio*. And sheer bloody *fun*.'

'I know. That's exactly what Rémy said, word for word.'

'Then he's right. We'll be doing these people a favour. And that goes for the audience, too. We've all been banged up for far too long, and bloody Covid's only half to blame. We need to get over ourselves, lift our heads, try something *new*.'

'But it's an old story. It goes way back. That's the whole point.'

'Wrong, my precious. The setting is old, I grant you that, but we'll be treating it in a new way. You know the test of a truly great idea? That it touches a nerve in everyone. This isn't just about 1940. It's not just about the war and the fucking Germans and the French down on their knees. It's about a culture clash. It's about what happens when one bunch of strangers bump into another. It's a clusterfuck in the making. It's about sex and life and death and that rough country cider you all neck down there. And it's about Brexit.'

'Brexit?'

'Of course. Frame the series properly, get the emphasis just right, and we'll teach ourselves a great deal about just who we bloody are. Do I hear the word ambitious, my precious? And will you be able to cope with the next couple of years?'

Rosa, I know, is rehearsing for the conversations to come once she lifts the phone to the commissioning editors. I've seen her in this mood before, stoking the fire, raising the creative temperature, whetting the appetite until the only possible response is a big fat Yes.

'So who directs?' I say at last. 'Who plays Rémy?'

This, concedes Rosa, is a very good question. She's slept on it overnight, and this morning, on the train, she drew up a list of possible contenders for the Rémy slot. She has half a dozen names in mind. A couple, both men, are old campaigners with a lot of period drama under their collective belts. They know how to raise expectations, how to key a mood, how to beguile a million viewers into believing that time has gone backwards. They have a genuine feel for period detail, and they both work with designers of genius. *Vlixcombe*, in short, would be safe in their hands.

'But?'

'But they're not women.'

'And you think that's important?'

'I think it's vital. This little baby of ours needs a woman's touch. We're talking motherhood here, and guile, and nuance, and wit, and patience, and the whole nine yards. One of the other names on my little list is a girl. She's brilliant in almost every respect, but she's had an amazing press lately and she's begun to believe her own publicity and that makes her dangerous. *Vlixcombe* has to be about us, not her, about all of us, the way we were, and the way we still are.'

'So not her? Whoever she is?'

'Definitely not.'

I nod. 'The Rémy slot' is a phrase I like very much indeed. He is, of course, irreplaceable, as I've known all along.

'And the other names?'

'Boilerplate, my precious, and all men. Safe bets, the lot of them, decent track records, reliable when it comes to budget and deadlines, but no real energy, no real thrust. Our money would be safe, and the ratings might be half decent, but we're after so much more.'

'So where do we go next? Who else do you have in mind?'

She smiles at me, and cocks her head a certain way, and

I suddenly know exactly where this conversation has landed.

'You're looking at me,' I say slowly.

'I am, my precious.'

'You think I could do it?'

'I do.'

'You're serious?'

'I'm afraid I am. And you know something else? Our Rémy would be delighted.'

Our Rémy. I spend the next hour or so trying to get beyond the shock of her suggestion, of her faith in me, and explore exactly how we might make this thing happen. One obvious objection is that I have zilch directing experience, but Rosa doesn't think that matters in the slightest. In today's culture, she says, no one has a memory, and none of the normal rules apply. What people want is the bold and the unforeseen, some little passing jolt that makes them hurry through the pages of *Hello!* magazine and settle on a new story, a fresh face.

'But I'm old news,' I point out. 'I've been around forever.'

'But not as a director, my precious. Not as the commanding presence. Everyone's at it, starting with Angelina Jolie. You've got the experience, and you've got the scars to prove it. You know your way around, and you're tough as fuck. It's there for the taking. It's acres of publicity without lifting a finger. You'll be a smash.'

'And I'll perform as well?'

'Your decision. Your call. Think Clint Eastwood. Directs, produces, stars. *Bridges of Madison County* was to die for. And so was *In the Line of Fire*, Kurt's all-time favourite movie incidentally. If Clint can do it, so can you.'

'Really?' I'm less than convinced but the notion of occupying the Rémy slot is beginning to grow on me, and for whatever reason I suddenly think of Pavel. He, too, had a touching faith in my judgement and what he occasionally termed my special take on life. Whether or not that would equip me to coax decent rushes out of the chaos of a film location is anyone's guess, but there are other scents arising from this dish of Rosa's and one of them is the smell of money.

'So who owns this idea?'

'You do, my precious. You need to register the name soonest. I can help you with that.'

'Name?'

'*Vlixcombe.* Get it right, which we will, and it'll become a brand. Think spin-offs, books, merchandise. Contraception in those days was in its infancy. Tricolour Dutch caps? Available on Amazon? Can't fail. Those old wind-up steam radios? Music to nod along to in the dark winter evenings? Vera Lynn? Maurice Chevalier? This is a script that writes itself. All we have to do is let the snowball roll downhill. Avalanche time. A ton of the filthiest lucre.'

The key word in this little riff is, of course, 'we'. Rosa, after all, is an agent. She's spent an entire lifetime turning the dark arts of negotiation to her advantage, and when a decent proposition pops up, she recognizes it at once. The language of money, I've learned, opens every door and just now she's pushing hard at mine.

'You think I need to form some kind of company?' I enquire.

'We, my precious. This stuff can be complex. You're going to have your hands full. Between us we can sort it.'

'You mean clean up?'

'Yes. And I'm sure that would be a proposition we could both live with.' She reaches for her glass. 'Agreed?'

I lift my glass. Within the busy space of less than an hour, I appear to have become the must-commission movie director, the hot successor to our beloved Rémy. After yesterday's news from Jersey, and the near collapse of my dreams, *Vlixcombe* is back in the rudest health. For now, only one issue remains.

'So who gets to write it?'

Rosa favours me with a smile I can't quite interpret. On the one hand, it's slightly knowing. On the other, like me, she may have given the small matter of the script little thought.

'Good question,' she says, picking up the menu. 'We need to eat.'

The beef is delicious. The accompanying sweet potato mash leaks delicate tendrils of glistening red wine *jus*, and the *al dente* cauliflower florets are perfect. As an entrée to my new career, this is deeply promising. Over a dessert of Bakewell tart in a raspberry coulis, I drag our conversation back to the business of words on paper. Every great idea needs a scriptwriter to make it happen, as Pavel was always pointing out. A good pitch can only take you just so far. To unlock the money that matters, you need proper collateral.

'Who might you have in mind?' I ask. 'And don't look to me this time.'

'Her name's Hajira. She's Afghani.'

'Never heard of her.'

'I'm not surprised. I've kept her under lock and key.'

'She's a client of yours?'

'She is. She's wanted to be an actress most of her life, but to be honest she's wasting her time. She has the most astonishing face, truly beautiful, and she has presence, too. I got her a walk-on in *Holby* and a speaking part in a Channel Five dramatized doc. I'm told the crew couldn't get too much of her but when it comes to performance, the game's up. She's totally wooden.'

'So how does she make a living?'

'She has amazing hands. There's a market for hands like hers, believe it or not. She models for rings, watches, and one or two other markets.'

'So where does the writing come in?'

Rosa is looking briefly irritated. She wants this story to unfold at her pace, not mine, and I'm being far too pushy. By way of an apology, I signal to the waitress and order two large glasses of port before turning back to Rosa.

Hajira, it turns out, fled to the UK as a refugee back in the day when the Taliban made life in Kabul impossible for young women. Her mother, a gynaecologist, was beaten to death by a gang of jihadists. Her father, a university professor, died shortly afterwards.

'She was always bright,' Rosa murmurs. 'Perfect English.'

'Now, you mean?'

'Then. Her parents were hot on education. She topped up in a London comp. Books were always a big thing in her life and the writing followed. She has a truly wonderful imagination.'

The waitress arrives with the port. I gaze at the deep blush of red in my glass, trying to get a handle on this client of Rosa's. Beautiful hands. A tragic background. And doubtless piles of books beside her bed.

'She lives alone?'

'Mostly. She has a flat in Clerkenwell. Third floor with a view across a churchyard. She's crazy about flowers. I'm betting she spends more on freesias than food.'

'And her writing extends to scriptwork?'

'It extends to everything. She did a couple of original scripts after she'd had a go at a novel. The novel got close to publication but never quite made it. On the back of the scripts I pulled some strings and got her a jobbing contract on *Hollyoaks*. She says the dialogue writes itself which proves she has a sense of humour.'

'And all this is enough to get through? Keep the wolf from the door? Hands? *Hollyoaks*?'

'Not really, no. To be honest, she struggles for money and lockdown certainly didn't help.'

'And this is why you think *Vlixcombe* might be for her?'

'Yes.'

'How much does she know about the French? About the war? About rural Dorset?'

'Not much, but you could ask the same about life in leafy Chester. The script editor on *Hollyoaks* says she's the quickest study she's ever come across. You need to meet her, my precious. Don't take my word for it.'

I nod. I say I'm only too happy to once the smoke has cleared.

'You mean Rémy?' Rosa asks.

'Of course. There'll be a funeral. It'll be in Paris. I have to go. It's non-negotiable.'

'But I thought France was closed?'

I shrug and reach for my glass. Port always made me bold and now is no different. Rosa hasn't moved. So far I've been impressed, and slightly unnerved, by her enthusiasm for *Vlixcombe,* and her faith in little me. I happen to share her belief that it's a brilliant idea, but until now it's never occurred to me that we could make it happen here.

'Be straight with me, Rosa. You really think this thing would fly?'

'I know it will. What matters just now is laying hands on a first draft script. That means you getting together with Haj.'

'Is that what you call her? Haj?'

'Yes.'

'It's nice.' I try the word out again, and nod. 'Haj. I like it.'

'So you'll meet her? ASAP? Soonest? Top of your list? Numero uno?'

I'm gazing at my glass again, reluctant to make a promise I might not be able to keep. H. Rémy's funeral. Dessie. Simon's thoughts on the Flixcombe development. The need for Tony Morse and I to get together. Then H again. Always H.

'It's difficult,' I murmur.

'Everything's difficult, my treasure. If it wasn't we'd all die of boredom. Do you really want that? With *Vlixcombe* in the offing? Buses like this one don't come along that often. We need to hop on. Trust me. Meet Haj. Just say yes.'

Still I can't commit. Half close my eyes, take another sip of port, and I can see nothing but a wall of faces jostling for my attention. Then I feel the lightest touch on my hand. Rosa doesn't do light. This must be beyond important.

'Yes?' I ask. She's leaning across the table. Her face is very close.

'A secret, my precious. Strictly *entre nous*. Agreed?'

I nod. I can smell horseradish on her breath.

'Agreed,' I murmur.

'You promise?'

'I do.'

'Haj wrote *My Place or Yours?*' She gives my hand a little squeeze. 'Might that help?'

TWENTY-SEVEN

It most certainly does. Dessie arrives, as promised, at three. We give Rosa a lift to the station and I walk her to the ticket barrier. We've agreed she'll give Haj a ring and see how she's fixed for a meet over the coming days. When she suggests that it might be easier for her to come to me down in the West Country, I shake my head. I want to find out about this woman. I want to see where she's built her nest. I want to get to know her by the books on her shelf, by what she cooks, by the men in her life. And above all, I want to find out about Mr Big. Rosa is hanging onto her hat. I can tell she's pleased. She'll also be in touch with Habeeb about funeral arrangements for Rémy. I should expect a call tonight or – at the latest – tomorrow morning.

Dessie knows nothing about *My Place or Yours?* and I'm in no hurry to tell him. In Dessie's world, as I've already suspected, information is power and it pays to think very hard before sharing it. Dessie, I know, thinks I've wandered into someone else's swamp and has been kind enough to try and make sure I come to no serious harm. The reptiles are everywhere, and it appears that the meanest of them – Ratko – is still missing.

'They're expecting the yacht in Marbella this evening.' We're on the outskirts of Shaftesbury.

'They?'

'The operation has a couple of blokes down there. The guy in charge likes to call them assets but I suspect that's delusional. Ratko has an army of people on call, and we're not talking little helpers. Most of them are Brits, and some of them are psychos. Down there you used to watch your step with the Corsicans and the Turks. These days that's all changed. Most of the nastiest bastards have English accents. Violence is one of the few things left we do really well.'

I nod. My experiences over the last couple of years or so

suggest he's right. Violence and Class A drugs. Mayhem after dark and money for nothing.

'I might need to go to London over the next couple of days,' I say idly. 'You're welcome to stay as long as you like.'

'You want me to keep an eye on H?'

'I want you to treat the place as home.'

'*Home?*' He turns to look at me. 'Why would I want to do that?'

I'm normally a good judge when it comes to reactions, and I have the feeling his astonishment is genuine.

'If you think this is some kind of peace offering, Mr Wren, you'd be wrong. Neither am I trying to get you into bed. All I'm saying is that Flixcombe might be a bit too much for a single girl just now.'

'You mean H.'

'I mean Flixcombe. There are great things in the offing and I'd love a bit of support. No ties, no commitment. On a good day you can make me laugh, and that – believe me – is important.'

I tell him briefly about my lunch with Rosa. If anyone can take *Vlixcombe* to market, then I can think of no one better equipped. I describe Rosa's many networks across the media world, a wealth of contacts at every level. I make a big deal of the way people trust her, give her a hearing, put faith in her judgement. Speaking personally, I tell Dessie, this is a woman who's allowed me to flourish at exactly the level of performance I like best. She's never pushed me towards the really big money. She's always respected my quaint affection for a decent script. And she's always shown the dodgier producers the door.

'Impressive,' he says. 'Maybe she should move in, too.'

Flixcombe, when we finally arrive, is blessed with yet more sunshine. Dessie knows his way around now, and he chooses exactly the right spot to slow his VW to a halt on the drive. Through the stands of elm and oak, the house hides itself behind a shimmer of heat rising from the fields, and as we coast to a halt to savour the moment, Dessie lowers the window on my side of the car.

'Waterlooville this isn't,' he murmurs.

I can barely remember Dessie's little bungalow in the straggle of suburbs north of Portsmouth, but I can only agree. I can smell a hint of wild garlic on the stir of breeze. I can hear the soft buzzing of bees feasting on a nearby stand of verbena. Then comes a rustle of movement from Dessie's side of the car, and I know he wants to kiss me. I half turn to offer him my cheek, and then my lips, and moments later he's cupping my face. The feeling, I realize, is beyond good. I'm stirred, and I'm reassured, and I want more. Then I become aware of his eyes scanning the long fall of fields towards the house.

'Something's wrong,' he says, reaching for the ignition key. 'No one runs in weather like this.'

H has gone missing. Jessie made him a late lunch several hours ago and served it in her kitchen. Her macaroni cheese is a favourite of H's, and afterwards he took a nap on their sofa next door. At that point Jessie departed to Bridport on multiple errands, and when Andy looked in past mid-afternoon, H had gone. Thinking nothing of it, Andy checked in the kitchen garden behind the main house where H spends more and more of his days, but the bench in the sunshine was empty. Puzzled, Andy returned to the house and checked room by room, floor by floor. No H. He shouted his name, just in case he'd missed a vital clue.

Nothing.

Now, we've all mustered on the gravel in front of the house for a council of war. Just where might H have gone? Given three hundred acres to search, where should we begin? It's at this point that Jessie returns from Bridport. She's as bemused as the rest of us when it comes to making a start, and blames herself for not insisting that H keeps wearing what she calls his bloody handcuffs. Mention of the Apple Watch sends me up to H's bedroom. I know he keeps the watch in his sock drawer, but when I look I can't find it.

Back in the sunshine, Jessie consults her iPhone. A small red blob reveals that H has found his way to a copse of trees off the drive. Approaching the house, we must have been within metres of him. Andy fetches his Land Rover and we set off down the drive. No one's saying very much and unspoken is the fear that H may have done something very silly. Does dementia ever end in suicide? If you've lost your wits, might it be a small step to discarding the rest of you?

As we approach the copse of elms, the blob nearly marries with Jessie's phone. Andy pulls to a halt when she says stop and we all pile out. For a moment we're all looking at the shadowed turf beneath the trees and I fight the temptation to wonder whether we should be carrying a net, or a lasso, or some other means of hauling H in case he decides to bolt. But then I tell myself he's not some wild animal but Malo's dad. He still deserves, at the very least, a little respect.

It's Dessie who leads the way. It's an entirely natural move on his part, and I love him for it. He tramps into the trees, having sent us left and right to spread the search, but it's Jessie who spots H first.

'Over here,' she calls.

We join her at the foot of a huge elm. H is propped against it, his thin legs spread in front of him, his eyes closed. Dessie ducks to check for a pulse and confirms that he's asleep.

'I'm betting he was after the shade.' He gestures up at the huge spread of branches in full leaf. 'Can't say I blame him.'

H must have heard the voices because his eyes are open now and he's staring up at us. He doesn't seem the least bit surprised by the company of faces he probably doesn't recognize, but then I spot the photo he's clutching in his left hand. It's Dessie, once again, who stoops to gently retrieve it. He gives it a single glance and then hands it to me. H hasn't said a word.

I gaze at the photo. It's an old black-and-white print and I recognize the bank of pebbles on the beach beside Southsea Pier. It must be summer because families have spread rugs on the shingle and are enjoying the sunshine. Closest to the camera are a middle-aged man with a young boy. The baby is stark naked and can't be more than two. The man is dangling the infant by his tiny wrists. His bare feet are brushing the pebbles, and there's the widest smile on his little face.

Dessie is peering at the image over my shoulder. 'Who's that?'

I glance back at him, then my gaze returns to the photo. 'That's H and his dad,' I murmur. 'The day H took his first steps.'

We all have supper together. I muster yet another salad, and Dessie plays barman. The relief around the kitchen table is obvious, and we're all doing our best to include H in the conversation. The assumption seems to be that he's upset but from where I'm sitting there's absolutely no evidence that this is true. After we brought him back in the Land Rover, I had a sternish word about wandering off the way he did, but nothing I could say made any impression. If he understood me at all, I suspect he thought I was talking about someone else, some stranger who'd thrown a spanner in the Flixcombe works, so in the end I gave up. He'd taken his dad for a walk. They'd found, as Dessie has already pointed out, somewhere nice to have a sit-down. And now the pair of them are back again.

I met H's dad last year, down in Southsea. He's a Geordie, Harry, a lovely man, bright, kind, softly spoken. He spent his working life in Pompey dockyard as a clerk, though more recently he's taken early retirement. I liked him on first sight and now, amongst the million other items on my to-do list, I make a mental note to somehow get him down here for a visit. H never had any time for his mother and having met her as well I can understand why, but if H recognized his dad from the photo, who knows what might happen in the flesh.

It's Dessie who accompanies H upstairs to his bedroom. Jess and Andy, by now, have left. I wander round in a daze, first thinking about Rémy, and then about the lunch with Rosa, and finally I remember the punch in the gut when I realized that H had gone. None of this does anything for my peace of mind but Rosa's revelation about Haj has kindled a little spark in the darkness. All I can think of is the way her hands might look and the world she must have left to come to the UK. To lose both your parents under circumstances like that would probably frame the rest of your life. Quite why she'd ever open the door to the likes of Mr Big is, for the time being, beyond me.

Dessie is back downstairs in time for us to catch the late-evening headlines on *BBC News at Ten*. Aside from Covid jabs becoming mandatory for staff in care homes, the hot news features a pair of crayfish. Exposed to anti-depressants, they appear to behave more boldly. Dessie says he's never met a crayfish in his life, bold or otherwise, and is clueless about where all this research might lead. When I suggest it might somehow spill into dementia care, he simply shrugs. He's been watching H very carefully this hour or so, and he's beginning to wonder just how badly he's really affected.

'You mean he's pretending?' I find this hard to believe.

'Hand on heart, I've no idea. But I've a feeling he's still in there, pretty much intact. Odd? Definitely. Forgetful? Join the gang. But completely off his rocker? Somehow I doubt it.'

I press him for evidence. I, too, have been keeping an eye on H and all I can report is that whatever's wrong seems to be getting worse. H, as I remember only too well, was always in your face. Now he's a ghost.

I tell Dessie about Sayid's diagnosis. This is a man who's spent half his life dealing with the ravages of ageing, and he seemed convinced enough to give H's affliction a name.

'Frontotemporal dementia,' I tell Dessie. 'And he told me there's no turning back.'

'So maybe he's wrong. What else did he say?'

'He said that carers have a tough time, and I might think about getting H out of his comfort zone.'

'How?'

'Something physical. Something challenging. He mentioned gliding or scuba diving but I was thinking about a parachute jump. They do it locally, I know they do. You jump with an instructor and he does the biz. H could come, too.'

'You'd jump as well?'

'Of course.' I shoot him a grin. 'And you? Aren't you tempted?'

We go to bed shortly afterwards. It's a joint decision, absolutely no drama. I pause outside my bedroom door and when Dessie commendably checks I'm up for this I tell him not to worry. I'm a grown-up woman. I feel bloody old. The last few months have been beyond difficult and just now I'd quite like someone to put their arms round me and take me to bed and whisper in my ear and that someone sounds remarkably like Mr Dessie Wren.

'You're objecting?' I kiss him lightly on the lips. 'Or just being a wuss?'

He laughs. We share a shower and soap each other down. Dessie is running to fat but says he doesn't care. He's always been three meals beyond his recommended BMI and nothing's going to change that.

'Not even me?'

'Not even you.'

We step out of the shower and I apologize for the lack of hot towels. Dessie seems to think this is funny and when I ask why he says he hates the fancy stuff that comes with gym membership and spa hotels. Living with a hundred blokes on a nuclear submarine, he says, rubs the edges off civilized life. You get by as best you can and a return to dry land comes as a bit of a surprise.

'You object to clean sheets?' We're about to get into bed.

'Try me.'

We make love. Dessie is warm, and tender, and – for a big man – surprisingly agile. I drift off in his arms knowing I've earned a good night's sleep, and it turns out I'm right. By the time my phone starts ringing again, it's nearly eight in the morning.

Assuming it's Rosa, I find myself listening to Mitch Culligan. This is doubly problematic because Dessie can hear every word, and because Mitch thinks he may have a lead on whoever wrote *My Place or Yours?* I get out of bed and stand by the window with my back turned, shielding the phone. I'm trying to get Mitch to call back later but he's never been good at taking hints. He thinks we might be dealing with an actress who lives in Shoreditch or Clerkenwell or some bloody place. By all accounts she's a bit of a looker, and Mitch also thinks she's been punting scripts to some TV soap opera or other. I tell him that all sounds fascinating but it's still bloody early and I've just got out of the shower. Then I hang up.

Intent on the phone call, I haven't heard my bedroom door open. When I turn round, H is standing outside in the hall. Barefoot on the polished wooden floor, he's still in his stripey pyjamas. I ask him to shut the door and go back to bed but he doesn't move. He has his thumb in his mouth, and he can't take his eyes off the man in my bed.

Truly weird.

TWENTY-EIGHT

An hour or so later, Dessie and I are in the kitchen having breakfast.

'It's a game.' He's on his third slice of toast. 'H is dicking us around.'

'That's what you said last night.'

'I know. And that little charade just now tells me I'm right. This is calculation, not dementia. The old H was never less than artful. He could pull every trick in the book if it suited him and nothing's changed.'

'But why is he doing it?'

'I've no idea. He definitely got Covid. That was no act. But all this nonsense, going off by himself, that snap of his dad, sucking his thumb just now . . .' He's shaking his head. 'I don't buy any of it. It's contrived. He's putting on a show.'

'You really believe that?'

'I do, yes.'

I shake my head. Dessie has spent his entire working life not believing people because that's what cops do. He's also made it his business to be around H in his prime, to watch Pompey's top villain running rings around the Men in Blue, and I suspect that's bred something close to admiration when it comes to many of H's undoubted talents. I could make a case that no one knows the real H as intimately as DS Dessie Wren which makes him, at the very least, someone worth listening to.

'You think that was jealousy? Just now?'

'I think it was probably shock. He assumes he still has rights here. You don't have to sleep with someone to lock them away.'

'You think that's what he's done?' I'm slightly offended. 'Locked me away?'

'I think he wants sole access. If you won't be his lover, then carer probably comes close.'

'No life of my own?'

'None.' He's reaching for my hand. 'Are you telling me you haven't thought this thing through?'

It's a very good question, and to tell you the truth it's shaken me. H's rapid descent into dementia has been truly scary, both remorseless and irreversible. On his part, he appears to be helpless, while my duty is simply to cope, but now, thank God, someone new has marched into both our lives with another interpretation: that H may be writing a script of his own.

Just now I'll reach for any passing comfort, but I still owe a duty of care to H and for the life of me I can't work out how to put Dessie's take on events to the test. Do I confront H? Accuse him of play-acting? Of feigning insanity? Do I treat him like a child? Or the village loony? Or the grown-up ex-gangster that Dessie suggests he remains? The longer I try and chivvy these questions into some kind of orderly queue, the more muddled I get, and when Rosa finally rings just after lunch, I'm very glad to hear her voice.

'Done,' she announces.

'Done what?'

'Haj. We had coffee this morning. I talked her through *Vlixcombe* and she loved it. She can't wait to make a start, my precious, but first she needs to talk to you.'

This proposition has the merit of being really simple, and after the last twenty-four hours I can't resist it.

'Where?' I ask. 'When?'

Rosa's giving me Haj's contact details. She tells me our prospective new scriptwriter is awaiting a call and will doubtless invite me to pay her a visit. All I need do is get on a train.

'And you really think she can do it? I'm sure she's up for it, but is that enough?'

Rosa snorts down the phone. We're to be partners in this grand adventure. We both need it to take the media world by storm. Already she's beginning to spread the word about a super-special project in the offing. Would she really take a risk on someone like Haj if she had the slightest doubt that she couldn't deliver?

'You read that book she wrote,' she said.

'You're right. I did.'

'And?'

'It was great. She did a fabulous job.'

'Then I rest my case. Tell her hi from me. And take a carton of milk because I think she's running out.'

I make a mental note, then remember something I've been meaning to ask her.

'Does she know you've told me about the book?'

'No, she doesn't.'

'So do you mind if I bring it up?'

There's a long silence, which is rare in any conversation with Rosa. Then she's back on the phone again.

'Your call, partner. If needs must, then do it.'

I phone Haj minutes later. I've installed Dessie upstairs in the room H used to use as an office, and I know he has a ton of his own calls to make. The operation currently trying to find Ratko has a name – Palliser – and the fact that Dessie's been happy to share it is a very good sign indeed. Part of me can't wait to take him back to bed and I sense he knows this.

Haj answers on the third ring. She has a husky voice but I fail to find any trace of Kabul. When I introduce myself, she says she's just been watching one of my movies. Rosa suggested *Trahison* but she couldn't find it so she's ended up with *The Hour of Our Passing.*

'That's the second world war,' I say at once. 'Great place to start. Perfect choice.'

'It's very sad,' she says. 'You were great.'

'That's kind. It was a very long time ago.'

'I know. The black-and-white treatment works perfectly.'

'I meant the shoot. I've filled out a bit since then. Different woman, maybe wiser, certainly bigger.'

This gentle misunderstanding makes her laugh. She begins to tell me about all the period reading she intends to do, but I cut her short. I want to come up tomorrow. Can I buy her lunch?

'We can do better than that.' She gives me an address. 'I'll cook for you. Most of the OK restaurants round here are still shut. Halloumi cheese, OK?'

'Perfect.'

'You like wine?'

'I do.'

'Then I'll get some in.'

'You mean I'm drinking alone?'

'Yes.'

'Then don't. Water's fine. A girl needs to watch her figure.'

'I don't believe you. Not after that movie.' She has a very natural laugh, totally unforced, which is rare in the media world. Moments later, the conversation done, I look up to find Dessie raiding the fridge.

'Ratko's back in Marbella.' He's hunting for scraps from last night's supper. 'Two sightings an hour or so ago. He has company, which I must say comes as a bit of a surprise.'

'Anyone I might know?' I say lightly.

'Your friend Claudine. She must have come down from Paris.'

This is news I never expected. Claudine, to the best of my knowledge, was Rémy's lover. Claudine was the woman in tears on my phone. Claudine, on Jersey, was briefly my accomplice and comrade-in-arms the afternoon we drove from the airport to La Maison Blanche. What on earth is she doing with the prime suspect?

'Is this someone you've planted?'

'Not to my knowledge.'

'Meaning?'

'She has to be there of her own volition.' He pauses to fork a flaky chunk of tuna into his mouth. I'm getting to know this man. I suspect he's about to ask me a favour and it turns out I'm right.

'Habeeb?' he says. 'Rémy's agent? You know the guy?'

'Yes. Not well, but yes.'

'Might you give him a ring? Ask nicely about Claudine? Try and get a sense of what Despret meant to her?'

'Of course.' I nod. 'How's life in that study of H's? He never goes up there anymore. Can't make the stairs.'

'Really?' Dessie glances across at me. He has a curl of lettuce in the corner of his mouth. 'So why was he listening at the door?'

I stare at him for a long moment, and then step across. I lick a finger and look him in the eye before removing the lettuce.

'It must be nice being you, Dessie Wren, all those surprises life sorts out for you.'

He's smiling now, and he holds me at arm's length.

'Early night?' he murmurs. 'Do I hear a yes?'

It turns out to be a busy day in Habeeb's office, but he seems pleased that I've got in touch. It's obvious that he hasn't received my letter but we talk about Rémy for a while, what a bloody mess the whole thing is, and how the bad stuff always happens to the best guys. When I ask him about a possible date for a funeral, he tells me it's currently in the hands of the police. The Major Crime guys on Jersey have organized a post-mortem for tomorrow, after which the body will probably be released.

'Am I right to be thinking Paris? For the funeral?'

'Of course. Rémy had a favourite church. It's tucked away in the Fifth but I'm not sure it'll be available. You're coming over?'

'Absolutely, Covid permitting. Claudine will need all the support she can get.'

Mention of Claudine changes the conversation completely. Habeeb suddenly sounds guarded. When I press him gently about whether now is the right time to give her another call, he seems to have no opinion. Of course she's upset. All Rémy's friends have taken it hard.

'But Claudine especially, I imagine.'

'Of course.'

'You've seen her recently? Been in touch?'

'No.'

'She must be wrecked.'

'I expect she is.'

We're getting nowhere. Dessie is going to be less than pleased. Then Habeeb, all too predictably, changes the subject.

'I was talking to Rosa yesterday,' he says. 'I understand you're going to produce *Vlixcombe* over there.'

'That's right. It's a bit of a punt but we're going to try.'

'Sure. You mind me saying something?'

'Of course not.'

'Excuse me a moment . . .' Someone in his office has a problem. While he does his best to resolve it, I'm thinking hard about the obvious issues Rosa and I might have missed. Did Rémy have intellectual ownership on his idea? Did he register it with whichever EU agency deals with these things? Does it now belong to his estate? Are we, in short, fucked before we even begin?

None of the above. Habeeb is back on the phone. He has something, he says, he wants to share in confidence. He has absolutely no objection to Rosa and I picking up the *Vlixcombe* torch and running with it, but he thinks there's something we ought to know before we start that journey.

'Like?'

'Like the whole thing never happened. Not at Flixcombe. Not the way Rémy described it.'

'You mean he made it up?'

'Yes. The background's right. All the stuff about Broadcasting House and De Gaulle's people and transmissions into France is true but none of them came from Flixcombe. In fact I don't think any of the Free French broadcast lot ever set foot in Dorset.'

'And Rémy knew that?'

'Of course.'

'And you did, too?'

'Not until yesterday. I took him at his word. I believed him. Then I was talking to someone in the National Archives, here in Paris, and one thing led to another and he put me onto someone else who knew everything about these people, and that someone else said the whole thing was a fiction. London, yes. One or two other places. But never Flixcombe.'

I nod. No wonder the woman at the Dorchester archives was so surprised by my questions about Flixcombe's role in the war. The darkness is gathering again. I can feel it.

'So why did Rémy bother?' I ask at last. 'Why pretend?'

'I know he was very fond of you. You'd told him all about Flixcombe, shown him photos, described what it was like to live down there. You know Rémy. It just took one seed, one tiny idea, maybe even a single image, then he was off.'

I nod. Rémy, like Pavel, lived in his head. And it's true about Flixcombe. Face to face and on the phone I often raved about West Dorset. Some of that passion must have settled in his teeming brain, and produced a flicker of an idea, and then the roaring bonfire that had become a formal pitch.

Habeeb is a wise owl. You don't get to the top of the Paris media scene without iron nerve and perfect judgement.

'So what would you do?' I ask, 'In my shoes?'

'In the first place . . .' He's laughing now. 'Nothing. Then, if I had to, I'd own up. The best movies are fiction. Everyone knows that. As long as you get it right, as long as people believe it, no one will care.'

I share this advice with Dessie that same night. We're in bed by half past nine, and after we've made love again, I tell him about Habeeb and Rémy's fantasy *Vlixcombe*. To my surprise, unlike most men, he hears me out. More than that, he seems genuinely fascinated and once again I realize that I'm sleeping with a man who has devoted most of his career to various forms of fiction. Either cover stories he's doubtless had to adopt for undercover work, or the many lies he's had to unpick in the interview room.

When I gently press him on this, he admits at once that it's true. The blacks are never wholly black, he says, and the whites are never as white as you might have imagined but poke the grey bits in between and somewhere you might stumble on the truth. This modest *aperçu* seems to amuse him, and when I push him a little harder, he tells me that the tallest stories in Pompey always came from the likes of H. He'd tell lies so outrageous that you were convinced you were on a stone-bonker.

'Stone-bonker?'

'Guaranteed result. Banged to rights. Total wipe out. At that point you'd lower your guard and then H would have you because all along he'd been trailing his cape, acting like the dickhead he wasn't, simply to enjoy the moment when he came up with the proper story, lots of corroboration, fully thought through, and after that you were well kippered.'

I lie back, my head on the broadness of Dessie's chest, feeling him beginning to stir again.

'And is that what he's doing now?' I ask softly. 'Trailing that cape of his?'

'Too right.' Dessie has reached for my hand. 'You should be in my game.'

TWENTY-NINE

Next day happens to be a Friday and London is beginning to come to life again. By late morning, the tube from Waterloo is comfortably full, though everyone is still wearing a mask. I walk the half mile from Farringdon Station, following directions on my phone.

Haj lives at the top of an interesting-looking house in a side street across the road from a church. There's a Londis on the corner and a couple of Deliveroo boys locked in conversation at the kerbside. The hot news is the absolute need to delete their NHS QR codes. Getting pinged means losing more than a week's wages. In this corner of London, hunger is evidently a far tougher proposition than a dose of Covid.

Haj buzzes me in. I've bought a bunch of lilies from the flower seller outside Farringdon Station, and she seems genuinely touched. I follow her up flights of stairs to the top landing where she opens her door and stands back to let me in. Rosa's right. She has the kind of face which defies either description or a reasonable guess at her age. She obviously works out because her skin is taut and flawless, not a hint of make-up, and the longer I look at her the more I realize that there isn't one feature I'd ever change. Mouth? Lips? Those huge brown eyes? All perfect. Her hair is dark and lustrous, falling way below her shoulders and she moves her slight frame with the silky lightness of a trained athlete. She's wearing a pair of ripped jeans and a Manchester United top, and one of the first secrets she confesses is a passion for Paul Pogba.

'So clever, so cool' – she nods down at the TV – 'so *lazy.*'

I know very little about Paul Pogba so I can only agree, but what's taken my eye are her hands. She has the hands of an artist. She has hands that Rubens or Michelangelo would immortalize on a triptych behind some Renaissance altar. Long fingers, beautifully shaped nails, and a single ring in the thinnest gold with an inset baguette diamond. No wonder all those close-up jewellery shoots keep her in groceries.

I can smell garlic and something herby from what must be the kitchen, and she leaves the room while I make myself at home. The flat is on the small side but pleasingly bare: a low sofa that obviously doubles as a bed, a scatter of rugs and cushions on the floor, and a biggish table positioned for the fall of light through the sash window. Her open laptop is flanked by piles of books, and she's been scribbling pencilled notes on a big A4 pad. Two place names are underlined. Yeovil and Bridport.

I'm admiring a framed poster on the wall, a celebration of the Venice Biennale I last saw in a gallery on the Cote d'Azur, when she returns from the kitchen. She's carrying a glass of wine.

'It's Greco di Tufo,' she says. 'I checked with Rosa.'

'You shouldn't have.'

'You prefer something else?' She's looking alarmed. 'Something French maybe?'

I tell her that Tufo is fine. She really shouldn't have bothered, and she gazes at me for a moment before returning to the kitchen. Her hands are covered with a light dusting of flour, and there's more on the side of my glass.

No matter. When she calls through from the kitchen and asks me to make space for us on the table I'm very happy to oblige. I remove the laptop and put the books on the floor against the wall. One of them is a memoir by Rory Stewart, *The Places In Between.* It's an account of his journey over the mountains in the aftermath of the US invasion of Afghanistan back in 2002.

'You've read it?' Haj has reappeared with knives and forks.

'Last year. It's very good. He's a brave man. How many politicians take the trouble to really find out about stuff?'

Haj nods, says nothing. Moments later we're sitting down to lightly fried slices of halloumi. The dressing is exquisite, lime laced with soy sauce and delicate fronds of coriander, and it serves for both the cheese and the accompanying green salad.

I've left the Stewart book on the table. I want to find out more about Haj's childhood in Kabul.

'It felt very good. I was very happy. My parents loved me. My mother was a wonderful cook.'

'But the place was falling apart, wasn't it?'

'Of course it was, but I was too young to know that. Sometimes the water was off and there were always problems with the electricity. My mother had to wear the burqa when she went out and the Taliban had closed the schools, especially to girls, but my father turned all that into a game. I guess my parents wanted to protect me. They didn't want to see me frightened. We lived indoors. Everyone lived indoors . . .' She shakes her head, picking at the salad, and I get the feeling I shouldn't be pressing her any harder. What followed, according to Rosa, was indescribable, and certainly doesn't belong in this conversation. Your mother beaten to death in front of your eyes? Your father dying of a broken heart weeks later? Then, as a young adolescent, having to submit to a bunch of vile jihadists? Move on, I tell myself.

'*Hollyoaks*?' I murmur.

Haj is looking relieved. She says she knows the series isn't premium drama but she has one foot in a media door she'd never had the nerve to open. Thanks to Rosa, she got a short-term contract with the production company and she's evidently in with a chance of an extension. Joining a team of writers has been, in her phrase, a joy, and she says she's learned a lot.

'They're generous with me,' she says, 'Generous with their time, and generous with their advice. That feels very Afghani, believe it or not.'

'But you've been in this country a while, isn't that right?'

'Of course. But in here I'm always in a different place.'

A different place. Her hand has closed briefly over her heart, and then she laughs and says all this is being too serious. She wants to know about *Vlixcombe*. She thinks the idea is brilliant. She can't wait to find out what she can bring to the party.

I tell her about the house, and the estate. When she asks how I became part of it all I skip lightly over the small print of H's colourful past and simply say that he's a very good friend of mine. Just now, I tell her, he's slowly recovering from Covid and I'm happy to be there for him. She nods. She says she understands. Life can be tough. *Inshallah,* he'll get better.

'*Inshallah*,' I agree. God willing.

'And your friend Rémy? Rosa told me the news.'

'You know he's dead?'

'Yes. Killed, Rosa said.'

This comes as a slight surprise, partly because she seems so sanguine about someone being shot to death, and I briefly wonder how candid I should be, but I'm not here to play the protective parent and I know that if this thing is to work then we have to be honest with each other.

'Rémy gave me the impression that *Vlixcombe* had actually happened, that the French guys had been down there during the war,' I tell her. 'That turns out not to be true.'

This is news I've yet to share with Rosa, and there's no way that Haj could have known, but once again she's unmoved.

'So is that a problem?'

'Not for me. You?'

'It makes no difference. Nothing in *Hollyoaks* is true but millions still watch it. I have a script editor called Margit. She's wonderful. She's half-German. The other day she told me that reality is what you make it, is what you want it to be. Her grandfather worked for Goebbels, so maybe that makes her an expert.' She laughs and goes to the kitchen to fetch the bottle of Greco.

Watching her fill my empty glass, moments later, I marvel at her English, at her wit, at her seeming command of history, at those fabulous hands, and as she caps the bottle, I can't help thinking of the Mr Bigs of this world, how physically gross they can be, how totally consumed by their own careers, their own ambitions, their own *journey*. By now I have an image of this man in my head and trusting him with a woman like this, I think, would be trusting a child with a delicate piece of prized china. He'd drop her by accident, or forget where he'd left her. She'd become yet more wreckage in his boiling wake, a casual discard, one amongst many. Would she really get involved with someone so reckless? So louche? So obviously on the make? Having survived the trauma of losing both parents, and afterwards – unthinkably – the vile attentions of the Taliban?

We haven't finished with *Vlixcombe.* Haj has a list of plot possibilities based on her conversation with Rosa and after finishing the halloumi, we go through them. They all depend on strong characterization, salted with hints of the surreal, and I like them very much. It's obvious that her stint on *Hollyoaks* has taught her a lot about plot surprises.

By mid-afternoon, we've definitely bonded. Even before I arrived I had huge respect for what a woman like this has managed to make of her life, but now I've got to know her a little I suspect I can take a liberty or two. She's tougher than I thought. She's obviously a survivor. And I suspect she can – in the end – handle a direct question.

'*My Place or Yours? . . .*' I edge my chair back, reach for my glass. 'You wrote it here? At this table?'

She studies me for a long moment. I don't think she saw the question coming but it doesn't seem to have disturbed her.

'I did,' she says. 'Is that why you've really come?'

'Not at all. I've come to talk about *Vlixcombe*.'

'So how do you know about the book?'

'Rosa showed it to me.'

'You've *read* it?'

'Of course.'

'And?'

This is a question every writer I've ever met will always ask. What do you think? What did it *do* for you?

'I thought it was brilliant,' I say. 'And that's the truth.'

'Brilliant how?'

'It involved me from the start. You made me turn the pages. That, believe it or not, is a real skill.'

'You believed it?'

'Yes.' I hold her gaze. 'Are you saying it's not true?'

She smiles, shrugs, and I know at once she's not going to tell me. Yet.

'I was broke,' she says. '*Hollyoaks* had laid me off, and there was nothing from Rosa, and my savings wouldn't last forever. Bit part actors like me, trainee scribblers, none of us qualified for furlough. One day I knew I'd wake up and there'd be nothing in the fridge. I wasn't going to let that happen.'

'So you wrote about an affair with a top Tory politician?'

'Yes.'

'It felt very real.'

'Excellent. Music to my ears.'

'But what about the detail? The way he talks? His body language? What he gets up to in bed? All those little tics that make him leap off the page? Where did all that come from? It had to be real, didn't it?'

'If you say so.'

'Not me, Haj. You. Take this as a compliment. I believed you were there. And I believed this guy was, too.'

'Good.'

We look at each other for a long moment. Then I ask her another question.

'Do you know a woman called Anoushka? Big? Blonde? Runs a PR agency?'

Haj looks briefly troubled for a moment or two, then shakes her head.

'No,' she says.

'But this affair of yours, this liaison, really happened?'

Another silence, longer this time.

'I was broke,' she says at last. 'I just told you. I chose a top politician and dreamed up a silly name and called him Mr Big because that way it becomes a kind of guessing game. I thought any publisher would snap it up.'

'And?'

'They won't. They think it might be Boris Johnson and they're scared he'll sue.'

'So *is* it Boris Johnson?'

She looks at me, says nothing. I ask the question again, because passages in the book fit him like a glove, but she holds my gaze and won't volunteer an answer.

'Let's say it's not,' I suggest at last. 'Let's say it's someone else. Not Johnson at all.'

'Sure.'

'What does that mean?'

'It means you believe the book. It means I've *made* you believe what I've written. And that makes me very happy.'

'So this guy didn't exist? Ever? The whole thing's a fiction?'

At last, she smiles and then I feel her hand on my arm. It's a gesture of reassurance, or maybe thanks. It means that we share the beginnings of a secret, just a hint or two of exactly how this thing came about, but beyond that – for now – she's not prepared to venture any further.

By unspoken mutual consent, we change the subject. Back in the safety of *Vlixcombe*, we agree that Haj will prepare a pitch of her own for Rosa's benefit, and for mine. She'll detail her plot lines over the curve of the first three episodes and include a handful of sample scenes to offer a taste of her talents for dialogue and narrative twists. When I suggest a deadline of three weeks, she says it won't be a problem as long as I'm open to frequent emails when she needs prompts about the house. Everything that leaves her laptop will be copied to Rosa.

By now, I'm ready to head back to Waterloo but first I need to pay a visit. Haj tells me the way to the bathroom and makes a start on the dishes. The bathroom badly needs a little TLC but my eye is drawn to a collage of photos mounted in a clip frame. It hangs on the wall above the towel rail, and after I've washed my hands I take a proper look.

Most of the shots include Haj, and in every single one of them she's been snapped on a tennis court. Sometimes she's playing singles. In other games, she's partnered by a series of men, most of whom look a good deal older and some of whom could shed a pound or two. In tennis whites, Haj cuts an unforgettable figure – lightly muscled legs, perfect balance, hair tamed by a scarlet bandana. In one shot, she's on her toes on the baseline, about to serve. Her eyes are locked on the ball above her head, and her racket is raised, ready to smash it into the opposing court. In another shot, she's reaching for a low pass, her long legs splayed, a study in fierce concentration, and it's obvious from this and the other photos that her many partners are deeply smitten.

Back in the sitting room, she's already sitting at her laptop. When I mention the photo collage in the loo, she nods.

'Russians,' she says. 'They're mad about the game.'

Russians? I'm suddenly thinking hard about Anoushka again, and her borrowed Camden love nest. She, too, was in deep with the Russians.

'This woman Anoushka,' I say carefully. 'She seems to have read your book. In fact she claims to have given you most of the material.'

'Anoushka?' She's trying to feign bewilderment, as if she's never heard of the woman, but I hold her gaze until she shrugs.

'So . . .?' she says. 'You think I wrote the book for her? You think it's *about* her?'

'I've no idea. I'm just asking.'

'Then you're wrong, and so is this Anoushka woman. *I* wrote that book. It was my doing.'

'And did it really happen? The way you describe it?'

She looks down at her laptop for a moment, adds a word or two, and then smiles.

'The best things in life' – she touches her head – 'happen in here.'

THIRTY

Dessie, once again, meets me off the train at Yeovil Junction and drives me back to Flixcombe. This means more to me than I'd like to admit, largely because he's sacrificed watching England take on Scotland. He has the radio tuned into the game for the journey home, and with the score still nil-nil at full time, he tells me he's missed nothing. This is beyond generous on his part, and earns him a long hug the moment we get back.

The spread of meat awaiting incineration in the kitchen, together with a bowl of carefully cut chips, tells me my gorgeous man's back in the world of HMS *Courageous*. When I mutter something about love handles and maybe a bowl of salad, Dessie says he has no choice. H, it seems, has presented him with a bottle of brown sauce as a down payment on the evening's meal. This sounds like communication of a sort and I'm starting to wonder whether Dessie might be right about H faking it. H, like his son, has always adored brown sauce.

'Your agent phoned. Rosa?' Dessie's just broached a bottle of Pinotage.

'What did she say?'

'Zilch. No one tells the secretary anything round here.'

'Is that what you are? A secretary?'

He passes me the glass and I check to make sure H isn't around before I cup his big face for a second time and tell him that I'm thinking of falling in love.

'Is that a promise?'

'Certainly not.' I kiss him on the lips. 'And you ought to check the small print first.'

I phone Rosa from the privacy of my bedroom. It's nice to see Dessie's clothes scattered everywhere. He told me only yesterday that life underwater on a submarine makes you super tidy. Either he's talking nonsense or he's thinking too hard about the next instalment in our sex life.

Rosa explains she's just been talking to Habeeb in Paris. Rémy's family are still trying to book a church for the funeral.

'This is his brother?' Rémy's brother, improbably, is a serving soldier. Both his parents are dead.

'Theo, yes. Habeeb also told me how naughty Rémy's been about *Vlixcombe*. I've cut him some slack, and I'm guessing you have too. The fact that none of it ever bloody happened gives us the freedom to do exactly what we want script-wise. Agreed?'

'Agreed.'

'So what did you make of Haj? She phoned me, by the way, the minute you'd left. She loves you to bits, as she should do. She also thought you could nail that Nantes scene tomorrow if you ever wanted to re-shoot. How's that for a compliment?'

The Nantes scene has to be my first and only brush with full on-screen nudity, but something has super-charged Rosa. She's never been fussy about the many blessings of hyperbole, and I doubt very much that the Nantes quote had anything to do with Haj, but Rosa's always been in favour of the gaiety of nations and who am I to be the gloombag?

'I thought she was really interesting,' I say, realizing at once that this isn't much of an endorsement. 'She's also a brilliant cook, and we had great chats.'

'About?'

'Everything.'

'Including the bloody book?'

'Of course.'

'And?'

'It never happened.' I pause. 'I'm pretty certain she made the whole thing up. Did you know that?'

'No, I didn't.'

'And does it matter?'

'Not in the slightest. *Vlixcombe* isn't true, either, but do we care? Of course not.'

'Haj also told me no publisher will go anywhere near it.'

'That's true. I've circulated the anonymized MS to a handful I thought might have the balls to take it on. Sadly, I was wrong.'

Rosa very rarely pauses long enough to flirt with anything remotely reflective, and I'm not quite sure what to make of this little glimpse of wistfulness, but I get the feeling that *My Place or Yours?* is yesterday's business and she's already keen to move on.

'I've been trying to stir interest in a *Vlixcombe* development deal,' she says. 'And that's not going terribly well, either.'

'Isn't it a bit early?'

'God, no. You have to test the water. Big the idea up. The formal pitch comes later.'

'And?'

'People aren't getting it, mainly because they're all so fucking young. Recent history started with Spotify. One little girl I talked to this afternoon thought De Gaulle plays centre midfield for Paris St-Germain.'

'No upfront money, then?' This is sobering news.

'Not so far. Early days though, my precious. We must keep our nerve and find someone who's heard the rumour that we fought a war back then.'

I nod. Already I'm thinking there must be other ways of raising a decent development budget. I'm on the point of suggesting something imaginative in the way of venture funding when Rosa returns to Haj.

'So do you think she even knows a Tory arch-shagger?' she asks. 'Be honest.'

I've been giving this question some thought. To her great credit, nothing I saw in the woman who gave me lunch would ever answer the door to someone as gross as Mr Big. For one thing, she'd never believe a word he'd say. And for another, I suspect she'd have the pick of far tastier men.

'No,' I say finally. 'I think she did a Rémy. I think the whole thing's an invention. The real question is why? She told me she was broke but I don't entirely buy that.'

Dessie doesn't, either. In bed, we talk long into the night. Rosa has once again sworn me to silence as far as Haj's book is concerned, but I'm getting weary of having to sort all this stuff out on my own, and I'm very happy to have someone I trust to confide in. The book, strictly speaking, has nothing to do with little me, but that's not the point. The price of getting Sayid down to take a look at H was giving Mitch a taste of the thing, and after that all bets were off. For better or worse, I now have a stake in *My Place or Yours?* and it would help if I believed a word of it.

'You think she's made it up?' Dessie asks.

'I do, yes.'

'Why?'

'Firstly because she's virtually admitted it. And secondly because she's brighter than all this crap. She'd never stoop that low. You can have a look at it if you like.'

I still have a copy of Rosa's anonymized text. I fetch my laptop and hand it to Dessie. Being a cop obviously teaches you how to speed-read. Half an hour later, he's through.

'And?'

'Brilliant.'

'Brilliant what?'

'Brilliant read.'

'And do you believe it?'

'No.'

I study him for a moment or two, and then remove the laptop.

'Kiss me?' I say.

We talk at greater length in the middle of the night. It's a tribute to Haj's writing skills that Dessie can't leave me alone, and while he's deft and inventive I insist we have other business to transact.

'Like?'

'Russians.'

First I tell him about Anoushka, the woman with the Brexit tattoo whom Mitch first suspected of writing Haj's book. When I met her, she'd claimed to be an actress. The other lie suggested she'd authored *My Place or Yours?* Wrong on both counts.

'But she claimed to have shagged this Mr Big?'

'She did, to begin with. She was very loud, totally in your face, but then she played coy, which was a bit of a disaster, and after that she just talked about her Russian friends. One in particular was an older guy, all over her, seriously rich.'

'He has a name, this bloke of hers?'

'Sergei. The place where we met turns out to be a Tory love nest for weekend swingers. You can't make this stuff up.'

'And Haj?' Dessie nods at my laptop. On the final page, our heroine is celebrating her freedom after Mr Big has been denied visiting rights and moved on.

'She also mixes with Russians,' I say. 'Tennis seems to figure a lot. To be frank, these wouldn't be the kind of people to let her starve so I don't buy her claim that she was broke.'

'But she definitely wrote it?'

'I think so, yes. The real question is why she'd ever bother.'

Dessie nods, then reaches for the laptop and begins to scroll back through the book. From time to time, he pauses to re-read a passage or two, a smile on his face. Finally, on the first page, he nods as if he finally gets it.

'The Russians love playing games,' he says. 'They were at it during the Cold War, and they're at it again now. Underwater, they were bloody good at making life hard for us, and nothing's really changed. I'm thinking the first woman you met – Anoushka – was a cut-out, a kind of decoy. She was there to lay a scent or two. This lady' – he nods down at my laptop – 'is the real thing. Back in the day, those big old Soviet boats would lurk way down, stay hidden, then suddenly come at you and declare their hand. Nowadays, the Ivans don't care who knows what they're up to. They're disruptors. They have a ton of money to give away and they make bloody sure they put most of it to good use. This is black dosh the oligarchs have looted from Mother Russia but nothing happens without Putin's say so. Forgive the pun, but the Tory party would be dead in the water without it. Why? Because they've become addicted to free bungs, and they can't wean themselves off.'

Black dosh? Oligarchs? Free bungs?

'What's any of this got to do with Haj's book?' I ask him. 'Forgive me for being thick but I'm not sure we're on the same page here.'

'The UK is a free-for-all.' Dessie has put the laptop to one side. 'The Tories make a lot of noise about sovereignty and stricter immigration laws and all the rest of it, but if you have serious money London is the playground of your dreams. That can be cute if you live here and have residency, but Putin never left the judo mat. He's sworn to keep the West off-balance. Trump was the gift that never stopped giving. Johnson isn't in the same league but both guys were never wired for serious office and Putin can't believe his luck. Two guys at the very top with jobs they can't handle? Beyond perfect . . .'

I'm up on one elbow now, trying to follow the logic and beginning to succeed. It was Russian keyboard warriors, after all, who tried to game the American election, Russian agents who crept into Salisbury and coated a suburban doorknob with nerve agent. Is *My Place or Yours?* part of the same war? Has Haj rallied to the flag to chuck another boulder into the Westminster pond? I put the thought to Dessie and he nods.

'In a word, yes,' he says. 'Putin gets it that democracy can be our worst enemy. He gets it that we've voted a clown and an incompetent into office. All he needs to do now is keep him there.'

'By having Haj write a book?'

'Exactly. It doesn't even have to be published. All you need is the suspicion that Johnson is at it again, that the old shagger has found yet another love in his life. In any grown-up country, most people wouldn't bat an eyelid, but not here. We all love cakes and ale. Johnson is Falstaff. He's loud, and silly and ridiculous, but he makes us laugh, which in turn makes us love him. That's the trick. That's what put him into Downing Street. Putin's mission is to make sure he stays there, and this book of Haj's, which I suspect is the purest bollocks, will help him do just that. It might set tongues wagging. It might give us another laugh or two. And that's all the Russians are after.'

I nod. Bravo. I finally get it. Boris Johnson is a habit the Brits are finding hard to shake off, and Haj – doubtless for a helping of that looted Russian cash – has been only too happy to rally to Putin's flag. Thanks to our partying PM, we Brits – after Brexit and Covid – are in ever deeper trouble. Much merriment in Moscow. Plus a quiet round of applause from the upper floors of the Kremlin.

'You're a clever man, Dessie Wren.' I open my arms again. 'The more you sound like Mitch Culligan, the more I love you.'

THIRTY-ONE

H wakes up with a raging toothache. I find him downstairs at the kitchen table. He's got hold of a mirror from somewhere and now he's using his favourite knife to poke around in the far recesses of his open mouth. I offer to take a look for myself. All I can see is blood seeping from a self-inflicted wound in his gum.

'Don't.' I try and take the knife away. 'You need a dentist. God knows where that knife's been.'

H resists, seizing the knife back, and in the end I let him keep it. The tooth, I can see, is definitely loose. H nods vigorously when I ask him if it hurts and when Dessie appears he volunteers to try for an emergency appointment at the practice H uses in Bridport. This turns out to be impossible. Covid clean-ups after each patient have stretched every appointment to at least an hour and H would definitely be better off in the A & E department in Dorchester.

The pair of them push off after breakfast. H insists on holding Dessie's hand, which should be sweet but somehow isn't, and once again a tiny voice in my head suggests that H's dementia – one way or another – might not be quite what it seems. If the last few weeks and months turn out to be pantomime, a grotesque piece of theatre on H's part, then I – for one – will consider my duties to be at an end. If H is genuinely witless, then I'll do anything I can to help. If, for whatever reason, he has some other agenda, then I'll be gone.

Over a third cup of coffee I'm wondering how to put him to the test when I remember Sayid's advice about the blessings of a physical challenge, something bold to take H out of himself. A while ago, in very different circumstances I had dealings with a pilot called Cleggie. He was a bluff Northerner, lately of the Red Arrows, and looked wonderful in a flying suit. In many respects, he was the airborne version of Dessie Wren. He carried a pound or two of winter plumage but still radiated the kind of raw physical self-confidence that never fails to impress me. He was the best company in a variety of social situations, and when the going got tough one night in a Glasgow hotel car park, his steadiness under fire probably saved both our lives.

I finally get through to him on the third attempt and he apologizes at once, blaming a dodgy valve spring on a light aircraft he's thinking of buying. He's had it out twice and given it a seeing-to but the bloody thing still isn't right. The moment he laughs, I can picture the grease on those huge hands and when I enquire whether he's still available for hire he says he's mine for the asking.

'I can fly a bit, too,' he adds. 'If you're thinking light relief afterwards.'

'I want to make a parachute jump,' I tell him. 'Is that something you can help me with?'

'Solo or tandem?'

To my shame I haven't thought this thing through.

'I'm guessing solo takes a while. What happens with tandem?'

'You sign up with the guys who know. It's normally half a day. You jump with an instructor lashed to your back. They brief you on the harness and the small print and tell you what to expect when you get close to landing. Some people tell me it's the best four minutes of their lives but that makes me wonder what they've done with the rest of it. Speaking personally, you'd never catch me with another bloke up my arse but that's me being particular. I fly these guys sometimes. We've got a Skyvan we bring down from Staverton that does them very nicely when they've got a big list to get through.'

I haven't the first idea about Skyvans, or Staverton, but when I tell Cleggie there's going to be two of us he says no problem. The Jump School guys will be delighted, and afterwards – the job done – he knows a nice little pub ten minutes from the airfield where we can all celebrate. He gives me a name at the Jump School and contact details.

'Your oppo,' he says. 'That wouldn't be H by any chance?'

'The very same.'

'Then tell him it won't hurt.' Another bark of laughter. 'And give him my best.'

Dessie phones an hour or so later. He and H have made it to the A & E in Dorchester, but he needs H's National Health number. H doesn't seem to have a clue where to look but I promise to hunt it down and phone him back. The obvious place to start is H's office at the top of the house. I know he used to keep details like this in one of his desk drawers, and it shouldn't be hard to lay hands on it.

Dessie, of course, has been using the office only yesterday to make various calls, keeping in touch with Operation Palliser, and I find his open laptop on H's magnificent desk. Dessie must have been working again before he left for Dorchester because the machine is still fired up. I settle at the desk, unable to resist a peek at what Dessie's been up to.

His screen saver features a boy of eight in a black-and-white football shirt, grinning up at the camera. I've seen this shot before. The boy's nickname is Titch and he's Dessie's son from an affair he had a while back with another man's wife. Titch is much older now, quietly visible in the less peopled spaces of Dessie's life, but in his young footballing days he developed a knee problem that demanded specialist attention. The NHS queue was round the block, and it was H who paid for the operation to be done in Turin. The bill, H admitted later, came to five figures but at the time he considered it money well spent.

I've never really thought about the implications of that phrase, and given the fact that Dessie is now sharing my bed I'm not sure that now is the time to start, but one of the blessings of having Dessie around is the relationship that – even now – he seems to have with H. In some ways, the two men are so very different. They were at war for decades in the badlands of Pompey but that constant battle for advantage bred a mutual respect that became very evident last year when we were nursing H through Covid.

H always rated DS Dessie Wren. They were in the same hurry to match means with ends. They rarely cared who they upset. In their separate worlds, the rules were there to be broken. As a direct result they each pulled stroke after stroke and H never doubted that it was Dessie's intention to put him away for a very long time. That never happened, much to Dessie's frustration, but I know for a fact that they had a few laughs along the way and gazing at the little face in the screen saver I feel a warm blush of pride that Malo's dad should have been generous enough to put Dessie's boy back on his feet.

When I move on from the screensaver, the task bar at the bottom of the Word screen is showing two icons. One is Operation Palliser. The other, another operation, is tagged Limpit. Access to both is denied to me without a password, which is a shame, and after a final *adieu* to Titch I start hunting for H's NHS number. I've been in these same drawers only recently, looking for paper for the photocopier the day I discovered H's travelling Scrabble board, and the harder I look, the more it occurs to me that someone's been through the files he's stored here. They're not quite arranged the way I remember them, and when I look harder I notice the faintest pencilled question marks on one or two of the spines. There's a pencil on the desk beside Dessie's laptop, and I gaze at it for a moment or two, beginning to wonder.

H's address book is in the bottom drawer. In the back, along with other data, is his NHS number. I borrow Dessie's pencil to make a note, and lift an old envelope from the wastepaper basket. The stamp and postmark tell me it came from Gibraltar. Dessie Wren, at my invitation, is leaving his fingerprints all over Flixcombe.

Dessie returns with H in mid-afternoon. They've had to wait forever at the hospital but a trainee dentist finally extracted H's tooth and gave him a course of antibiotics. A thin dribble of pinked saliva is leaking from the corner of H's mouth but he happily succumbs to dabs from Dessie's wad of Kleenex.

Looking at the pair of them, I can't help thinking about H's office upstairs. What's incontestable is the bond between them that dementia – or maybe something more complex – appears to be cementing. I'd like to sit them down. I'd like to ask them exactly what's going on. But lives spent on separate sides of the law have bred an extreme reluctance to come clean and I realize yet again that I'm on my own in putting this particular corner of the jigsaw together. Dessie isn't faking it with little me. Of that, at least, I'm certain. But where H has really chosen to park himself, and why Dessie is poking around in his files, remains a mystery.

Supper, and a modest glass or two of Pinotage, come and go. Dessie and H retire to H's den to watch Germany take on Portugal in the Euros while I settle down in my bedroom to talk to Tony Morse. He, too, is watching the football and I offer at once to ring back but he won't hear of it.

'Multi-tasking is where it begins and ends,' he says. 'Tell me everything about yourself and I'll keep you in touch with why the Germans are on the back foot.'

'Back foot?'

'Ronaldo's just put them one-nil down. Ran the length of the field, took the pass, and stroked it into the net. The guy's a hundred years old, for God's sake. How does he do it?' He's laughing now. 'H OK?'

'Mad. Maybe.'

'Maybe?'

'Don't go there. Not yet. I think there's every chance we're about to become the location for telly's next big thing.' I'm lying, of course, but I need to keep Tony's attention.

'Tell,' he says simply.

I brief him about *Vlixcombe.* About the genius idea that may bring a drama production crew to H's estate. I don't bother him with Rosa's latest disappointments about the development funding but insist that we're looking at the real possibility of a prime-time smash hit, entirely filmed in deepest West Dorset. At the end of my little pitch, as ever, Tony cuts to the chase.

'So how much? In location fees?'

'Top six figures.' I'm inventing this. 'Maybe more. Just now I'm trying to get our ducks in order. Rosa is talking about a joint venture and setting up some kind of company but whatever happens, I assume someone has to assign location rights when it comes to filming.'

'H,' Tony murmurs. 'Because he owns the place.'

'But he can't. Because he's potty.'

'Indeed. There may be another way around it. Your joint venture sounds promising. Rosa is that agent of yours?'

'She is.'

'And you trust her?'

'Yes. I've known her for years. She's been with me every step of the way. So far, she hasn't put a foot wrong.'

'Then maybe a meet might be in order. Is she brave enough to take the train to Pompey? Are you?' He suddenly breaks off. 'Shit.'

'What's the matter?'

'The Germans just scored. Goodens and Havertz are putting the Portuguese to the sword.'

I wait for him to recover, then confirm that I'll get in touch with Rosa about a Pompey meet and keep him in the loop about Simon's thoughts on planning permission. About to hang up, I enquire about the lustrous Corinne.

There's a longish pause on the phone before he comes back to me.

'Shame,' he says. 'I was hoping you wouldn't ask.'

'Why's that?'

'She walked out about a week ago. Disappointment I can deal with but not when she's shagging a very good friend of mine. Bastard helped himself. He's made a fortune in the property world so I'm guessing he's never been troubled by conscience.'

I tell him I'm sorry and assure him she'll be back as soon as she realizes the error of her ways. This last thought, for some reason, sparks a dismissive grunt which isn't this man's style at all, but I'm not in the mood to pursue the conversation any further. Tony Morse was always world class when it comes to screwing up perfectly good relationships and I suspect nothing's changed. I'm thinking of phoning Rosa for the briefest chat when the door bursts open. It's H. Fresh blood is trickling down his chin but in his excitement he seems oblivious. His finger and thumb are just millimetres apart.

'Them Krauts again.' He's barely coherent. 'That fucking close.'

The Germans, as far as I can gather, finally win. Bed, in

this gathering madness, has become a kind of sanctuary. As has Dessie Wren.

'About H.' I've just stepped into my bedroom from the shower. 'Be straight with me.'

Dessie has been speaking to someone in France. His phone is lying on the duvet because he's expecting a call back.

'What do you want to know?'

'I get the feeling stuff's happening behind my back.' I'm still drying my hair. 'The pair of you seem to be up to something.'

'We go back a while. H hasn't forgotten everything.'

'And that makes you buddies?'

'That makes me valuable.'

'To H?'

'To you.' He reaches for my hand. 'You're right about me and H. I think I understand where he's ended up, and there are just tiny little moments when I think he does too. Dementia's never supposed to come and go but in H's case I'm starting to wonder. He was up for the game completely just now. He even recognized some of the players. Do I blame that on Fratton Park? On all those Saturdays wasted on the terraces? To be honest, I haven't a clue. I simply can't tell.'

'But you know the man,' I insist. 'You probably know him better than I do. Did you ever interview him? Properly?'

'Of course I did.'

'And?'

'He pissed all over us. He never walked into an interview room without a class lawyer and he always knew we couldn't lay a glove on him.'

'Why not?'

'Evidence. Everyone knew he was at the top of the heap, and he loved that, but he was scrupulous about covering his tracks. Sometimes that took a bit of doing.'

'You mean violence?'

'I mean Wesley Kane.'

I nod. Wesley was H's enforcer. His speciality involved an electric kettle and several spoonfuls of sugar. Pain you wouldn't believe with change from a ten-pence piece, a quote that came directly from Wes last year.

'We'd get whispers about H.' Dessie is gazing at the phone. 'We knew exactly what he was up to, his MO, all that, but you can't take a man to court on whispers. No one would ever go on the record and to be honest, given some of the photos I've seen, I don't blame them.'

'Yet you became friends?'

'Sort of.'

'Enough for H to fund the knee operation?'

'That was H's doing. He was always clever. He knew about my nipper and the knee. Titch lived with his mum, and H made it his business to get alongside her. When I got the quote from the Italian surgeon, I passed it onto Dawn. There was no way either of us could find eighteen grand but H got it sorted, dealt directly with the surgeon. I took the boy out there, stayed with him after the operation, and brought him back. When I asked the surgeon who'd paid he wouldn't tell me.'

'The Knee Fairy?'

'Very funny. I should have pressed him but I didn't. Just having Titch back in one piece was all that mattered.'

'And H?'

'He never told me, not directly. In the end I found out from another source, someone close to Dawn.'

'So why did H do it?'

'Good question. Some days I put it down to him being nice. He had oodles of money. He could be generous when the mood took him. And he liked Titch enough to sometimes turn up on Sunday mornings to watch him play.'

'And other times?'

'Other times he was the H we all knew. He had something on me. He'd given me a bung. That was a card he never revealed, never had to play, but it was there when he might need it. Like I say, clever.'

'And ruthless.'

'Of course. You don't get to live in a town like Pompey without taking a scalp or two. The drugs game was evil even then. When push came to shove, H could be the hardest bastard I ever met.'

The hardest bastard I ever met.

'H was always possessive,' I point out. 'He hated parting with anything.'

'Too right. And that's another reason he got so rich.'

'Yet you're sharing a bed with his son's mother. Under H's own roof. Doesn't that give you pause for thought?'

Dessie glances across at me. I've raised a smile.

'Nicely put,' he says. 'You think he's jealous? You think that word has any meaning for him?'

'More than possible,' I say. 'And if it does, he still might be capable of anything.'

'You think we ought to lock the door?'

'I think we ought to make the most of each other' – I reach up and touch him lightly on the cheek – 'while we still can.'

'That makes you reckless.'

'Not at all.' I lean into his kiss, peel off his dressing gown, and feel the warmth of his naked body. 'That makes me lucky.'

We gaze at each other, and then laugh. This is a truly lovely moment, a moment I'll treasure given what lies down the road, but then Dessie's phone begins to ring. A glance at caller ID reveals a French name. Marcel.

Dessie listens intently, and then grunts his assent before ending the call.

'That was about Ratko,' he mutters. 'He was at Malaga airport this afternoon, and boarded a flight to Paris. The French police arrested him at Orly and our guys will be sitting in on what follows.'

'This is good news?'

'The best.' He puts the phone down and then opens his arms. 'Madame Reckless,' he murmurs. 'I like that.'

THIRTY-TWO

The weekend comes and goes. The weather is gorgeous, and given the news about Ratko's arrest, Dessie is very happy to stay over. To my huge relief, everything seems to be settling down and even H is more peaceable than I've seen him for months. He and Dessie watch the Italy vs Wales game on the Sunday, and H buries his head in his hands when Gareth Bale nearly equalizes towards the end. One of the Italian defenders, I can report, has a grin to die for.

The weekend over, Dessie spends the Monday morning in H's study, conferring with various colleagues on Operation Palliser, and joins us for a light lunch around the table in the kitchen garden. He's looking sombre and when I ask why, he says that the French interview team dealing with Ratko have hit a brick wall. They've spent the weekend quizzing Monsault's Serb friend about his movements on Jersey around the time Rémy was killed, and it appears that Ratko spent the entire day on the Russian superyacht. As corroboration, he's produced a sheaf of photos from his phone, each of them time-stamped. Ratko helping to prepare lunch. Ratko hosing a bottle of champagne over one of his hosts. Ratko asleep in the Jersey sunshine, sprawled on a mattress on the yacht's helicopter deck. When I ask whether evidence like this is the end of the story, Dessie shakes his head.

'Apparently these weren't selfies,' he says. 'So what possessed him to lend someone else his phone? Why would he do something like that? Unless he knew he'd need the shots later?'

It's a good question but when I ask whether this is enough to keep Ratko in custody, he shakes his head again.

'He's got a shit-hot brief,' he says. 'Plus a couple of the Russians off the yacht are very happy to fly to Paris and vouch for him. As an alibi, I have to say it's looking foolproof. Ratko couldn't be in two places at the same time.'

'And Claudine? Is she involved?'

'No idea. There was no sign of her in the photos from the boat.'

It's at this point that I remember Monsault's lover, the magician I met at La Maison Blanche. He had a booking to appear on the boat that same night, so he obviously knew the Russians. It's tempting to suggest that he could have somehow tele-transported Ratko into Rémy's path, done the foul deed, and then conjured him back to the marina, but one look at Dessie's face tells me to keep this little bit of whimsy to myself. We're back in the murderous world of drug debts, and DS Dessie Wren is far from pleased.

This, as Malo would say, is a downer but my afternoon picks up with a call from Rosa. To my relief, she's sounding like the agent I've known and loved all these years. Good news is definitely in the offing.

'Have you read it?' she says.

'Read what?'

'Haj's stuff. She's done a draft ep. God knows how in just a handful of days but she's totally on top of it. I think we might be dealing with some kind of genius. I thought her Mr Big kiss-and-tell was a hooker but this is even better. Find yourself somewhere comfortable. Half an hour, that's all it'll take. Our troubles are over, my precious. There isn't a commissioning editor on the planet who'll ever turn this down.'

She's right. Haj's attachment is waiting on my laptop, and I fire it up, together with a two-line note to myself and Rosa. *I've done the reading and listened to Enora and come up with this. It isn't perfect but I hope it makes you laugh.* Just that.

I retreat to my bedroom and open the attachment. Thanks to her weeks on *Hollyoaks,* she's obviously familiar with the Final Draft software which makes it an easy read but what sparks this first episode is her effortless command of what Pavel used to call the Three Musts when it comes to a decent script: lots of business, little clots of sublime dialogue, and knowing exactly when to take a risk or two. In a script as newly hatched as this, the fault lines between these three elements are often all too visible but Haj, a mere apprentice at this game, has already arrived at a near-perfect result.

The job of the episode is to embed our motley collection of French thesps in West Dorset. This early in the war she's still calling H's estate Flixcombe, rather than Vlixcombe, which is historically correct. The French, after a wearying journey from Central London, pause for refreshment at a Dorset country pub. These are the glory days of the Battle of Britain, and the pub is a mile or so from a nearby airfield which is home for two hard-worked squadrons of Spitfires. The French, three women and five men, descend from their charabanc and eye the bicycles propped against the pub wall. In the distance they can hear the throb of Merlin engines. They exchange glances. This, they agree, is deeply promising.

A bunch of young super-god fighter pilots are already in the public bar, playing darts. Survivors of yet another day battling the Hun, they spend the rest of the evening partying hard with the surprise visitors from London and a great deal of bonding goes on in a nearby field behind the pub's scruffy car park. Taking the lead in these revels is a woman called Brigitte, a comely chain-smoking habituée of countless Left Bank cafés, and a couple of fellow thesps have peeled off with local girls summoned by phone by the pub's landlord. The latter's new wife, half his age, also extends a welcome of her own in an upstairs bedroom to the character who will play Le Patron in future episodes. Closing time comes and goes. The landlord declares a lock out, and broaches a couple of spare barrels in the name of *Fraternité*. By the time the charabanc finally makes it to Flixcombe, barely half an hour away, the thesps are legless.

The pub sequences occupy most of the episode. Beautifully written, artfully-paced, a beguiling mix of high farce, plus occasional moments of surprising pathos, these scenes will be beyond watchable but what – for me – takes Haj's script into a different dimension are her cuts to the carefully mounted welcome awaiting the French at Flixcombe. Max Gulliver and his wife are going to a great deal of trouble to make the house ready. Bedrooms have been prepared, food sourced, flowers picked. This painstaking attention to detail is in rich contrast to the rude anarchy developing in the pub down the road, and the episode's final scene is an absolute classic.

Husband and wife are getting anxious about the lateness of

the hour. Have the French come to grief somewhere? Might a telephone call to the local bobby be in order? Then comes the cough of an engine and a gear change or two as the arriving charabanc struggles up the drive towards the house. It finally grinds to a halt, disgorging eight very pissed thesps. The men, their arms out wide, are pretending to be Spitfires. The women can barely walk. Husband and wife exchange glances, then grin. In front of our eyes is the promise of five more episodes. They, and we, can hardly wait.

'How did she fucking pull it off? She's Afghani, for Christ's sake. She's not supposed to know about the Battle of Britain.'

Rosa, as I know only too well, only uses the F-word under extreme duress, either rage or delight. Happily, it's the latter.

'Amazing,' I agree. 'Maybe we should start watching *Hollyoaks*.'

Rosa tells me she's already despatched the script to her three favoured commissioning editors, and is using the word 'auction', which is a very good sign indeed. I, meanwhile, am still thinking about Haj. In the shape of both offerings, we appear to have something of a prodigy on our hands. *My Place or Yours?* at first convinced me that Mr Big really existed. No one could have caught a guy like him so perfectly, no one could have got those little details so right. And now her first stab at Rémy's epic idea has taken me straight back to the world of thin beer and frenzied coupling. She's called it *Their Finest Hour*, yet more evidence that she utterly gets it.

That afternoon, after despatching a herogram to Haj, I invite Dessie to read the script for himself. The format throws him a little at first but it's a tribute to the sheer force of Haj's writing that he so quickly gets beyond the capitalized scene intros and the blocks of stage direction to wallow in the sheer abandon of this long-ago culture clash. Like me, he finds himself wrestled to the mat by Haj's playful talents, and like me he also draws a conclusion of another sort.

'To write like this,' he says, 'you have to know how to lie.'

He delivers this conclusion with an air of faint wonderment as if it's a truth that's only just occurred to him, while I – long used to the promise and rewards of clever fiction – can only nod in mute agreement. Haj is undoubtedly a liar of genius. And the cleverest thing of all is that it never shows.

Within a couple of hours, Rosa is looking at two reactions from her chosen commissioning editors. Both are extremely positive and while we're still on the phone she gets a text from the third editor, the youngest, telling her that she's totally hooked. 'Wonderful,' she's written. 'Let's talk soonest.'

The likelihood that we might be moving into proper development rather more quickly than we anticipated makes it all the more pressing to pay Tony Morse a visit. A useful lesson I learned in showbiz early on is never to be overtaken by the passage of events. Scoping for the deeper potholes in the road ahead is the key to a successful production, and given that I'll be sitting in the director's chair, I want the shoot itself to be a pleasure, as well as a source of brilliant daily rushes. Already, on the strength of those reactions to Haj's trial script, I'm starting to think about casting and crew choices, drawing on decades of admired performances and remembered faces, and by the time I finally get through to Tony Morse, evading his fearsome PA, it takes me a moment to realize that my call is far from welcome.

'Bad time,' he says at once.

'Bad how?'

'Don't ask. I dare say you remember Pompey. Ugly can sometimes be wide of the mark. Try vile and you might be a little warmer.'

'So what's happened?'

'You don't want to know.'

'But I do, Tony.'

He tells me it's not a subject he can discuss, not in the office. If I care to phone him this evening, he may still be at liberty to let me into a secret or two.

'At liberty?' Tony Morse, like all lawyers, has a lifelong respect for language.

'At liberty,' he confirms. 'By this evening, they may have banged me up. In my trade you get to know a thing or two about the Men in Blue. Not all of them are stupid, alas. Do you happen to know where Dessie Wren might be?'

'He's here. With me.'

'Really?' He sounds surprised, even aghast. 'You're not . . .?'

'I'm afraid we are, yes.'

'Two fucking disasters in one day? This is more than any man deserves. Oh, Christ, tell me it's not true.'

'But it is, Tony.'

'*Really?* Scout's honour?'

'Really.'

'Lucky man.'

'Lucky girl, too.'

'OK.' He's trying hard to take in this news. I can hear the distress in his voice, and I'm doing my best not to be flattered. Tony Morse has always talked a good game as far as I'm concerned but this is the first time I've realized that he might have meant it. 'Listen,' he says, 'forget phoning tonight. Drive over with Dessie. I'll still be allowed one call from the custody suite, so you'll be the first to know if you need to turn round and head home again.'

'You really mean tonight? Now-ish?'

'I do, yes. Must fly, my darling. Laters, eh?'

I pass on the essence of this call to Dessie. I've known since last year down in Southsea that the two men are still close and when I tell him that Tony's expecting imminent arrest he offers at once to drive us all over there.

'Us all?'

'H comes, too. I think Jess and Andy have had enough. What else can we do?'

Tony Morse works long hours and a text from his Pompey office tells me he'll be through by seven o'clock. He doesn't want to meet in a pub or a restaurant and he offers to order any takeout of our choice if we can make it to his house. He also offers to put us all up but I'm not at all sure this is a good idea. A big, refurbished hotel on the seafront overlooking the pier has always been an H favourite, and I book two rooms.

We pass the journey listening to Russia vs Denmark on the car radio. By the time we're on the edges of Pompey, peeling off the M27, the Russians are staring at a bad defeat which evidently means that we might – a little later in the tournament

– be playing the Danes. The feeder motorway that crosses the upper reaches of Portsmouth Harbour offers a dramatic view of the city's skyline. Tonight has laid on the bonus of a spectacular sunset, the Spinnaker Tower etched against an explosion of scarlets and yellows, but the real fascination for both Dessie and I is H's reaction. He's sitting in the back of the car, gazing out at the view.

'It's Pompey, H,' I say.

'Yeah.' He nods. 'I hear it's a shithole.'

Tony Morse lives in a big Edwardian spread in Craneswater, which is the closest Pompey gets to posh. It's a lovely house, red brick, huge windows, lovely garden, the kind of family residence built for an age with more time on its hands. Dessie parks up outside, and walks H to the front door. He must have come here lots because he's always rated Tony's advice, legal or otherwise, but once again he shows absolutely no sign of recognizing the place.

Tony opens the door. He looks terrible. For a heavy drinker, he's still a handsome man. He's Dessie's height, but without the extra poundage, and he's always had exquisite taste in clothes. His suits are made to measure and I happen to know that his leather shoes are also bespoke, shaped and stitched on his own special last. None of this has ever come cheap, one of the many reasons I've always adored him, but this evening he's wearing a shell suit in worn polyester that might have come from Oxfam, and it doesn't suit him. His face looks drawn, and his eyes are red and a tiny twist of cotton wool on his chin hides where – unthinkably – he's cut himself shaving.

He stares at us for a moment, gives Dessie and H a cursory nod, and then succumbs to a long hug from yours truly. Mercifully, he's yet to abandon a dab or two of Terre d'Hermès, my all-time favourite aftershave.

The house feels cold for June, and somehow abandoned. Tony takes us through to the big lounge that overlooks the garden. There's a nearly empty bottle of something red on the table beside the armchair, and a single glass beside it. While he fetches more glasses and another bottle from somewhere deep in the house, we all linger in the big bay window. I can't recall whether the croquet hoops were there last year, but I can remember Corinne serving us Armagnac on ice in the garden and fussing with the parasol to keep the sun off her *amour*.

Tony's back in the room now. There used to be show-off shots of Corinne everywhere, photos that Tony adored, but now – with a start – I realize that he's turned every single one of them around. It's a stagey little gesture, very Tony Morse, but it suggests he's in a very bad place. Our favourite lawyer is in despair.

It's Dessie, bless him, who gets us down to business. 'So what's happened?'

'I screwed up,' Tony says at once. 'Of all the people in this city who should be careful who they trust, you're looking at me. I vented. I lost control. Mea culpa. I hold my hands up. Me. My fault.'

'So what's happened?' Dessie asks again.

'I found messages on Corinne's phone. This was last week. I shouldn't have been looking but I was. She's been odd recently, trying too hard. That's always a tell.'

'And?' Me, this time.

'The guy's surname is Windsor. His mates call him Prince, including me. He's funny, and he's great company if you're in the mood, and he knows how to listen. Women love that, which should have wised me up.'

'We're talking about Corinne?' Me, again.

'Of course we are. I knew he fancied her from the start because I know him, and I'm not blind. My mistake was assuming she took it in her stride. Corinne is a looker. Scaffolders give her a whistle in the street. I watched her at a cathedral drinks party before Christmas. Gentlemen of the cloth who should have known better wanted to get inside her knickers. I knew that. I've always known that because I was exactly the same way. The moment I laid eyes on her, she was mine. Must have. End of.'

'Except . . .?' Dessie's taken over the running.

'Except I didn't reckon on the Prince. When it comes to texting, he's an artist. If he's got those talents in the sack, I'm royally fucked. And I was. And so was she. And after not very long she wanted all of him, all of the time. That's when she left me. We'd had words. The moment she realized I'd been checking her phone, she was gone. She didn't even bother to pack.' Tony is looking at me. 'If you fancy anything from Reiss, help yourself. Her frocks are all still upstairs in the wardrobe.'

'So where did she go?' Dessie asks.

'She's never said. Not then, and not now. But sadly, ladies and gentlemen, this is where the real story begins.'

At first, he says, he was in denial. He was sure she'd be back any minute. It was all a nightmare. He'd even rung the Prince on his private phone but he wasn't picking up. Then, as the days went by, it began to dawn on him that this was for real, that she'd never be coming home, not even for those precious Reiss dresses, and at that point the only true friend he had left in the world was an even stiffer drink than usual.

'Alone?' I enquire.

'Christ, no. I'd have topped myself. I have a sort of mate called Den. Worst mistake I ever made. This is a guy with connections on the dark side. I've known him for years. We have a great relationship. He's never short of a story and he makes me laugh. I always told myself he'd look after me if things got sticky, and God knows I wasn't wrong. His fault or mine? *Moi*, I'm afraid.'

Den, he says, took him to the back room of a pub off Albert Road. This was Saturday night and Tony was looking for a shoulder to cry on. When the landlord closed the door and stood guard for a bit of privacy, Tony should have got the hint but didn't. He poured his heart out to Den, the messiest emotional dump you could ever imagine, and the evening ended – as far as he can remember – with my all-time favourite lawyer passing contact details for Prince across the table.

'They must have included his address,' he says. 'Big mistake.'

The next thing he knows, it's Sunday morning and he's fighting the grandmother of all hangovers. Then comes a message from Corinne.

'She wanted to know what the fuck I'd done to her man.

Just that. *What the fuck have you done to my man?* To be honest, I hadn't got a clue. I could remember the pub, I could remember Den being there, but that was it. What the fuck have you done to my man? *Nada.* Nothing. *Rien.* Little me? Blameless.'

Tony has built a career on defending the wicked and the wilful, and once again he's making his case, but this time it's in his own defence.

Dessie isn't entirely convinced. Neither am I.

'This Prince guy got hurt?'

'I'm afraid so. He's in the QA.'

'How come?'

'Someone paid him a visit. Beat him up. Then kettled him.'

'Kettled him?'

Tony nods, then gestures wordlessly at his groin. The Queen Alexandra Hospital is the city's biggest. All emergencies go there.

'And Corinne?' I ask.

'She spent yesterday with him. She hasn't spared me the details, as you might imagine. She's also been to the police. If you're thinking motive, it's not the hardest case to crack.' He shakes his head, and then offers us a refill. Dessie says no, as do I. H is staring into nowhere, his face a mask.

'They'll pay you a visit.' This from Dessie. 'I'm surprised they haven't already but everyone's stretched tight and Covid hasn't helped. They'll statement Corinne. This pub you went to. Was it the Tallyman?'

'Yes.'

'And she knows you use it?'

'She knows I go there sometimes, mainly with the dodgier clients. She thinks it's a dive.'

'She's right. My guess is they'll talk to the landlord. Look at the CCTV. If we're talking about the same Den, you might have a very big problem.'

Tony's gazing out of the window at the last of the daylight. A big seagull has just shat on his croquet lawn.

'I know,' he says. 'I suspect the phrase is damage limitation.'

THIRTY-THREE

We leave an hour or so later, having done our best to offer Tony a little comfort, but I think he knows his career may be over. He's definitely expecting a knock on the door and a summons to the custody suite, and after we've said our goodbyes, and I've given him another hug, he watches us make for the street before lifting a weary hand in farewell. According to Dessie, Tony Morse has made a decent living from the darker corners of this strange city, and he knows exactly what to expect.

The three of us have a cheerless curry in an empty restaurant behind the seafront, and then make our way to the hotel. While Dessie finds somewhere to park, I take H across the road and onto the promenade. It's a cloudless night and a waning moon hangs over the blackness of the water. Across the Solent, the faint outline of the Isle of Wight is pricked with lights, and seagulls are fighting for scraps on the tideline.

It was here last year, on a very similar night, that I found Malo unconscious on a bench barely half a mile away. He'd been ambushed and beaten up and for a minute or so I thought he was dead. It was Dessie who took care of me that night, but the memory of Malo's broken face as the paramedics lifted him into the ambulance has never left me. I reach for H, and slip my arm through his. I'm shivering now, and he gives my arm a little pat. Lights down, I think, gazing into the darkness once again.

At the hotel, Dessie puts H to bed in the room next door, while I use the bathroom. By the time Dessie's through, I'm in bed myself. We talk for a while about Tony Morse but Dessie's honest enough to admit that there's little he can do. Tony's clientele, to his great credit, largely come from the city's less favoured areas. They're young and feckless and never much care who they upset, and some of Tony's more outrageous pleas in mitigation have won him few friends amongst the Men in Blue. The fuss about the Prince, says Dessie, will be a fine opportunity to level the score and if money's changed hands, then Tony might end up inside.

'You think he might have paid to have this man beaten up?'

'It's possible. He says he can't remember, which doesn't help, but he can be reckless sometimes, especially when he's upset.' Dessie shrugs. 'I'll make some calls tomorrow, find out exactly where we are with this. I doubt we'll be gone before midday.'

Unlike Dessie, I have trouble getting to sleep. That tiny interlude on the promenade with H has revived far too many memories from last year, and I lie in the half-darkness, debating whether to pay a sentimental visit to the flat where Malo and I helped nurse H through Covid. The flat, which was unloved, had belonged to Tony Morse's father before he died and is a bare ten-minute walk away. Tomorrow morning, I think, as I finally drift off.

I awake hours later. It's still dark, still the middle of the night, but I feel an overwhelming need to check on H. I tell myself this is crazy, that he'll be asleep, but the urge won't go away and in the end I slip out of bed, wind a towel around me, and step into the corridor. H's door, thankfully, is unlocked. I ease it open and peer inside. H's breathing has been laboured since he contracted Covid and he's a noisy sleeper, but I can hear nothing. The sheets on the bed have been thrown back. There's an abandoned towel on the floor and of H's clothes I can find no trace. The smell of last night's curry hangs in the empty en-suite.

'He's gone, Dessie.' I'm back in our room, trying to wake him up. 'He must have walked out.'

'Who?' Dessie is peering up at me, shading his eyes against the lights I've switched on.

'H.'

Dessie shakes his head. Can't have happened. Shouldn't have happened.

'I put the deadlock on the door,' he says. 'What the fuck is he up to?'

We get dressed. Downstairs, the night receptionist is buried in a copy of the *Portsmouth News*. When we ask about an old guy from Room 217, he nods towards the big revolving door.

'A couple of hours ago,' he grunts.

'Did he say where he was going?'

'He didn't say anything. Just left.' He abandons the paper to check his screen. 'You've pre-paid both rooms, right?'

'Right.'

'Then what's the problem?'

What's the problem? We're the problem. H is the problem. Tony Morse is the problem. And now this unforgiving fucking city is the problem. One way or another we have to find H before Pompey – or something even worse – reclaims him.

Outside, the first faint glimmer of dawn has appeared away to the east. The wind has got up during the night and I can hear the growl of waves breaking on the pebbles across the road. Dessie leads me to his car, which is parked around the corner.

'Where are we going?'

Dessie doesn't answer. This I'm beginning to recognize as a sign of anger. He's angry at H for doing a runner, and angry at himself for letting it happen. I put a reassuring hand on his thigh.

'It'll be fine,' I mutter hopelessly. 'Everything will be fine.'

Dessie ignores me. We drive away from the seafront, leaving Southsea. There's no traffic but the streets are choked with parked cars. There are lights behind the curtains in one or two bedroom windows, but no signs of movement. H's beloved Pompey, that term I've learned to dread, has once again turned its back on the world.

Soon, I begin to recognize where we are. This is Fratton, street after street of terraced houses. I've been here before, again last year, and as Dessie begins to slow, looking for a parking space, I recognize the house.

'That's where Wesley lives,' I say quietly.

'You're right.'

'You think . . .?'

'I do. I hope not, but I do.'

'Settling accounts? Doing Tony a favour?'

'Yeah.'

Dessie abandons the hunt for a parking space and leaves the car in the middle of the street, the hazard lights flashing.

The thin wash of dawn light has brought a face to the window of the house opposite, and the woman is peering down at the car as we get out.

Dessie pauses in front of Wesley's front door, then presses the bell push. Nothing happens. He tries again. Still no sign of movement inside. Then he steps back from the door and peers up at the curtained bedroom windows before fetching out his phone. He has Wesley's number on speed dial. I can hear it ringing. Finally Wesley answers. I recognize his voice.

'Fuck off,' he says. 'It's four in the morning.'

'Open the door, Wes.'

'Why should I?'

'Just open the fucking door and stop dicking us around.'

Wesley grunts something I don't catch and the phone goes dead. Moments later, the door opens and he's standing in his boxers. His hair, a winsome Afro, is as wild as ever and he looks fit and intimidatingly trim. Wesley is manic about working out, and it shows.

'What's this about?'

'Are you going to let us in, or what?'

'I asked you a fucking question. What is it with you guys? Are you all fucking deaf?'

So far I've been standing behind Dessie, half hidden from view. Now I step into the throw of light from the hall, and for the first time I spot the bandage wrapped round Wesley's right hand. Blood is still seeping through the whiteness of the crêpe.

'You.' He's staring at me. 'What the fuck's going on here?'

Dessie looks at him for a moment, then pushes him hard in the chest. Wesley staggers backwards, then recovers his balance in time for Dessie to floor him with a knee to the groin. The fight is brief and ugly, constrained by the narrowness of the hall, and I'm inside with the door shut by the time it's over. Dessie is astride Wesley, one knee on his chest pinning him to the carpet, his big hand clamped around his windpipe.

'H,' he says. 'Where is he?'

Wesley tries to shake his head. Dessie is squeezing and squeezing.

'I'll ask you again, Wes. Is he upstairs? All you have to do is nod.'

Wesley's eyes are starting to water and his face has reddened. Any minute now, I think, he'll go pop.

'One last go, Wes. Let's make this thing really simple. H knocked on your door. Am I right? Just tell me yes. Just nod.'

At last comes a movement, the faintest nod. Dessie eases the pressure and I watch Wesley's chest swell as he fights to get air back in his lungs.

'Which room, Wes?'

Wesley's trying to clear his throat. Finally, he manages the beginnings of a conversation.

'He's a mad old fucker.' His voice is croaky. 'He tried to kill me.'

'How, Wes? How did he do that?'

'He came at me with a knife. Out there on the street. Tapped on the door and then tried to do me.'

'And you?'

'I whacked him.'

'Is he hurt?'

'No. He's gone. He's past it. Once, maybe . . .' He shuts his eyes and shakes his head, the sentence uncompleted. 'Just get off my fucking chest, yeah?'

'You're going to behave?'

'Whatever.' Wesley, it's obvious, has had more than enough of DS Dessie Wren.

Dessie gets to his feet and extends a hand, which Wesley ignores. Dessie nods at the bandage.

'How bad?'

'Deep, two cuts, bled like a pig.'

'You want us to take you up the QA?'

'I want you fucking gone. Door at the top of the stairs. First on the left.'

Dessie throws me a glance, and I mount the stairs. I'd forgotten how pink the place is. Pink stripey wallpaper. Pink highlights on the coving. Dainty rings of pink on the bannisters. The bedroom door is shut, the key in the lock. I knock twice.

'It's me, H. Enora.'

I can hear nothing. Downstairs, Dessie wants to know how much Wesley charged for the job on the Prince. Wesley won't tell him, denies all knowledge, then says the cunt had it coming to him. Pink, I think. Psychopathic or what?

I turn the key in the lock. The room is in darkness but in the light from the hall I can see the faintest shape of a body under a quilt. I open the door a little wider and then turn on the light. H is asleep, and I recognize the rattle deep in his chest as he draws breath. I step across to the bed and look down at the face on the pillow. H must have sensed my presence because his eyes flick open.

'You're OK?'

'Yeah.' When he reaches for my hand, I give it a squeeze.

'Not hurt at all?'

'Never. I killed the fucker. Twice.'

'Twice?' I'm looking at the quilt, at the pillow, at the crumpled fold of sheet. More pink. More madness.

THIRTY-FOUR

We're back at Flixcombe by late afternoon. Dessie has spent most of the morning dropping into various offices at Pompey's biggest police station and confirms that Tony Morse will shortly be invited to present himself at Kingston Crescent for a formal interview. Various leads have been chased up, and there are plans to arrest Wesley Kane on suspicion of GBH. Should proof emerge that money from Tony triggered the assault, then he – too – will be arrested and charged with conspiracy. Given the circumstances, there's every chance that the case would go to Crown Court, and even a non-guilty verdict would have – for Tony Morse – profound consequences. The Prince, meanwhile, will need a great deal of dental work and may require a skin graft in his nether regions.

No one understands the gravity of this incident better than Tony himself, and H and I pay a visit to the house in Craneswater on the off-chance that he may have taken the day off. We find a new-looking Mercedes in the drive, and when we ring the bell, it's a woman who comes to the door. She looks me up and down and it takes me a second or two to recognize Corinne. There's a neat pile of her belongings behind her in the hall so I assume she's used her key to collect all those frocks.

'Tony?' I enquire.

'At work,' she says briskly. 'Didn't you come round last year? When he was poorly?'

'I did.' There's an awkward pause before I can think of anything to break the ice. 'I'm sorry for both of you, by the way. Am I allowed to say that?'

'Maybe you mean all three of us.' A cold smile. 'Tony never did things by halves.'

Did, I think. Past tense.

*   *   *

We leave the city within the hour. Back home at Flixcombe, minutes after we've settled H back in, I get a call from Rosa. First – with apologies for the short notice – she tells me that Rémy's funeral is now to take place the day after next, in Paris. The service will be followed by a wake. Rémy was always the master of the sudden swerve when it came to changes of plan, and in death nothing appears to have changed.

'Where?'

'No one knows yet. I'll keep you in the loop.'

'But you're coming, too?'

She says she doubts that will be possible. Negotiations over *Vlixcombe* are starting in earnest with one of the three commissioning editors. The Beeb have scented the possibility of a four-way partnership with French, German and American participation. This will spread the financial risk and offer guaranteed access to important foreign markets. Better and better, I think. Thank God for the Second World War.

'So what happens next?'

'The Beeb girl wants to come down to take a look. Her name's Becca. If I brought Haj down as well, we could have a party.'

This sounds more than promising. I'm looking at H asleep on the bench in the kitchen garden. I don't think he remembers anything about leaving the hotel and trying to kill Wesley, and physically he seems pretty much intact.

'Some time next week?' I'm back on the phone. 'After I get back from Rémy's funeral?'

'We were rather thinking tomorrow, my angel. Maybe a little lunch? This is showbiz, remember. Time, alas, waits for none of us.'

Tomorrow? A little lunch?

Rosa, having taken our postcode for her satnav, has already rung off, and after a moment or two of blind panic I'm left to draw up a list of goodies to christen our new baby. It starts with champagne, which sounds a bit splashy, but I don't care. Rosa will doubtless be down in time for lunch and I'm listing the ingredients for a New England fish chowder when Dessie appears in the kitchen. He has more news from Paris, none of it good.

Jersey police, it seems, are pushing for the extradition of Ratko to the island's jurisdiction but Dessie thinks it is unlikely to happen. So far, the presiding *juge d'instruction* has failed to mount any kind of case that would warrant proceedings in a French court, and Ratko's legal team are pushing aggressively for early release. Whether or not this will happen any day soon is anybody's guess but Dessie's latest conversation with the woman in charge of Palliser suggests the game's up. No one doubts for a moment that Ratko is a key player when it comes to Class A drugs, but at his level every risk is carefully assessed and dealt with before it appears on anyone else's radar. Narco money, in short, can buy anything.

'I think we're fucked,' Dessie says. 'And if you're asking, I have to tell you it's not a good feeling.'

I try and cheer him up with Rosa's news about *Vlixcombe.* The imminence of Haj's arrival prompts him to delay his return to Palliser.

'You're leaving me?' This comes as a bit of a surprise.

'I'm going back to work.' He smiles at last. 'There's a difference.'

'Forever?'

'Christ, no. I'm on a short-term contract already. Everything in my trade is a moving target. The work is demand-led but if Palliser is dead in the water, it might be a different story. Either way, H will still need his hand holding.'

'And me?'

'You, too.'

We're standing beside the kitchen table. This man suddenly feels very close, both physically and in a number of other ways. We hold each other's gaze for a long moment.

'Are you asking me to move in?' He asks at last.

I do my best not to smile. Oddly enough we've yet to raise this possibility, let alone discuss it. On the bench outside, H turns his face to the sun and smothers a yawn.

'I am,' I say at length. 'I think we can find room for you.'

I drive to Waitrose in Bridport and stock up on goodies for the chowder. I'm aware that Haj doesn't drink, and younger recruits in BBC drama have a tiresome reputation for taking care of their livers, but I know exactly how thirsty Rosa can get when a major deal's in the offing, and I absolutely want Dessie to be part of this. If he necks enough of the Waitrose Stellenbosch Chenin Blanc there's a decent chance he'll have to stay the night. My shopping done, I find space for a case of champagne in my trolley and I'm trying to make the bloody thing behave in the car park when I feel a presence behind me. It's Simon, my ex-thesp estate agent. He, too, is being stern with his trolley.

He apologizes at once for not getting back to me. Planning permissions around paragraph seventy-nine are more arcane than he'd expected, and he doesn't want to risk a conversation when he has nothing definite to say. I tell him it isn't a problem. The Flixcombe estate will be there for a while yet and we have plenty of time to decide whether part of it should become a posh housing estate.

'I'm not sure that's the phrase we should be using.' He's looking pained.

I put my hand on his arm and tell him the word 'arcane' has made my day. I haven't the first idea what it means in this context, but I'm curious to know how he'd ever market his twenty paragraph seventy-nine houses.

'Very good question,' he says. 'We think *Fine Country Living* might do the trick.'

'We?'

'There's talk of me becoming a partner in the business. Early days yet, of course, but I seem to be closing the right kinds of deals.' He's looking at the contents of my trolley. 'Someone's special birthday? I know I shouldn't be asking.'

'Better than that,' I say. 'The Beeb are down tomorrow. Maybe you should be working on that French accent of yours.'

I spend the evening getting everything ready for tomorrow's visitation. Dessie and H watch England beat Czechoslovakia to take us through to the knockout stage, and after a modest celebration they settle into a viewing of *Top Gun.*

Back last year, when he was beginning to recover from Covid down in Southsea, H made Malo watch this movie at least three times but, as ever, he's discovering the world of

Maverick and Goose and the gum-chewing Iceman anew and whenever I put my head round the door of the den, he's on the edge of his seat. Towards the end of the movie there's a big aerial shoot-out that still does it for me and I linger behind Dessie's chair, waiting for the moment Maverick finally bonds with Iceman and obliterates everything in the sky that moves.

'This turns you on?' I'm running my fingers through Dessie's greying curls.

'Always.' Dessie finds my hand. 'Especially the bit when he gets that third MiG.'

Being back in our own bed is bliss after the traumas of last night, and I rise to next morning's challenges with a song in my heart. By late morning, the cooking is done, and the champagne is on ice. All I have to do now is help persuade the BBC to stake millions of pounds on Rémy's little fantasy.

Thanks to the weather, we get off to a fine start. The sky is what the French call *moutonneux,* the intense blue of mid-summer flecked with tiny sheep-like clouds. It's very pleasantly warm, rather than hot, and the house – I know – is looking its best. Dessie has been at the wilder corners of the kitchen garden with the secateurs and has made space for a table with five settings so we can eat and drink *en plein air.* I've lived for most of my life in West London, and even if you can afford a place with a garden, I know that nothing can hold a candle to the drowsy peace of a setting like this.

After a brief tour of the house, Dessie has settled our guests at the table. Becca turns out to be a rangy girl in designer jeans and baseball boots and a Harlequins top. She exudes a fidgety intelligence, gazing around, taking everything in, asking question after question, while Haj, sporting an enormous pair of sunglasses, excuses herself to take photos of the rear of the house from various angles. When she returns to the table, she shares the images on her iPhone with Rosa. Every next view, she says, sparks a new plot opportunity. Her hand on her heart, she never expected a property as beautiful and rich as this.

As beautiful and rich as this. I catch Dessie's eye and raise my glass.

'To *Vlixcombe*,' I murmur. 'And all who may sail in her.'

'May' is *le mot juste* here. Everything in the early stages of any showbiz negotiation, as I know only too well, must take place in the subjunctive mood. May. Might. No assumptions. Nothing taken for granted. Becca seems to have taken a shine to Dessie.

'You were in submarines. Have I got that right?'

'You have. A thousand years ago. Who on earth told you?'

'Rosa. Only we're doing a series for the autumn. It's in post-production just now. It's called *Vigil*. The coldest bits of the Cold War. It's a boys' watch. I'll send you a disc if you fancy a look.'

Dessie looks suitably impressed and reaches for his glass.

'To *Vigil*,' he says. Another toast.

After the Laurent-Perrier, with Rosa's help, I serve the chowder. She traps me briefly in the kitchen and wants to know more about Dessie.

'He's something else, isn't he? So bloody real. And so bloody *hot*.'

'You think so?'

'I do, my precious. If all else fails, and it won't, at least you've got a proper man in your life. What have you done with H?'

'He's with Jess and Andy in the cottage over the way. You might get to meet him later.'

She looks at me for a moment. She's carrying a dish of lightly sautéed courgettes, ready to take them outside.

'What an amazing *ménage*.' She's grinning. 'An ex-submariner, a loony drug baron, and your lovely self.' She nods outside. 'The pair of you are knocking them dead. What a team. This can't not work.'

A couple of hours later, I'm beginning to think she might be right. The meal done, we've embarked our guests in a couple of cars for a tour of the whole estate. Haj is riding alongside Dessie in his VW and once again she asks for frequent stops so she can dart out with her iPhone to capture another location shot.

Rosa and I, meanwhile, are sharing my little Peugeot with

Becca, who seems less interested in the view. Like the rest of us, she's been super-impressed by Haj, not just the standard of the script she offered, but the speed at which she seems to work. All three of us agree that she's a genuine find, and when Rosa confesses that Haj's hands-on experience at the coal face has been limited to a couple of episodes of *Hollyoaks,* she shakes her head in wonderment.

'Does she write anything else at all? Plays? A blog? Something longer?'

Rosa and I exchange glances.

'No,' I say. 'At least not to our knowledge.'

At the very top of the estate lies a copse of trees that offers probably the best view of all. The house nestles in the soft green folds of the landscape below us, and there's nothing to suggest that we might not be in the summer of 1940, with France overrun, and the *Luftwaffe* getting ready to set about the RAF. Ageless is today a word that sadly belongs to estate agents and other hucksters, but in this context it's near perfect. Dub on the distant whistle of a steam train, and perhaps a Spitfire or two, and we could be awaiting the arrival of the French thesps.

This, I know from experience, is the kind of moment when Rosa likes to pounce.

'So what do you think?' she asks Becca. 'And I mean *really* think?'

'About Flixcombe?'

'About *Vlixcombe.* To little me, that first script is a proper come-on, in fact it's irresistible, but the real gift is the location. It couldn't be more perfect.' Rosa is beaming. 'Could it?'

Thankfully, Becca appears to agree. We return to the house for a Dorset cream tea, and Becca quizzes Haj at some length about her forward ideas for the series as a whole. Haj has wisely anticipated this question, and as I watch her pitching to Becca my admiration can only grow. She has a fountain pen and a pad of paper, and she's sketching out plot pathways for each of the major characters. This might seem mechanical, the magic of the series becoming the prisoner of straight lines and squirly question marks, but in Haj's elegant hands it's anything but. She leans into the conversation as if she's confiding a bunch of family secrets, her sunglasses abandoned on the table, and I can tell by the fierceness of Becca's attention that she has our commissioning editor totally hooked.

And so it proves. She must have taken Rosa aside for a personal word before all three of them leave because, as we exchange hugs and they clamber into Rosa's BMW, my lovely agent is looking beyond radiant.

'Super, super day, my precious,' she calls as the big car purrs away. 'Take great care of that darling man of yours.'

That darling man of mine. I lead Dessie at once to bed. H, I tell him, is in the very best hands and we'll sort out a treat or two for him later, but for now I can think of no better way of celebrating.

'So you think it's really in the bag? You're that sure?' We're halfway up the stairs.

'You're never sure of anything in this business. Never. But it went incredibly well, and a lot of that, my darling man, was down to you. You played a blinder and now I'm going to say thank you.'

In bed, moments later, I disappear between his thighs, lapping softly until he can hold on no longer. He tries to pull away but it's too late and anyway I don't care. Everything today has been a feast and I see no reason to stop.

'MDM,' I murmur afterwards.

'MDM?'

'My darling man. I might patent you, turn you into a brand.'

'Me?'

'Us.'

Dessie likes that. We lay entwined, picking at the day the way you might take your fork to the remains of an epic meal. What he made of Becca. The many rude talents that make my lovely Rosa so formidable. How loud she is. How big her spirit. And how she can mug you blind with that winning smile on her face. And last of all, we come to Haj.

'You were together for the best part of an hour in that car of yours,' I tell Dessie. 'I was timing you.'

'Why would you do that?'

'Sexy scribe? MDM? The man who hunted all those Russian subs? The script writes itself.'

'Very funny. I'm twice her age. Probably more.'

'Exactly. Women love experience. It saves wasting so much time.' I kiss him. 'So what did you make of her? What did you talk about?'

'That book of hers, mainly.'

'You lie.' I'm up on one elbow now, gazing down at him.

'Alas, no.'

'Alas? Am I hearing disappointment?'

'Not at all. It's what I thought. She runs with the Russians, and I gather she's having an affair with one of them. His name's Yuri, and he's big in aluminium. He's also married with three kids but that doesn't upset her enough to ask for her key back.'

'He's a regular?'

'Has to be. She says she loves him, but I suspect that's her conscience speaking, not her heart.'

'And you're telling me that he put her up to *My Place or Yours?*'

'I am, yes. Her and a woman called Anoushka. Name ring any bells? I gather she works in PR and is thick with the Russians. These guys are all resident in London. That makes them legal. They come for the schools and the law courts. They know their money's safe, and their kids, too. But in the end they take their marching orders from Moscow. Putin loves kicking doors in and Haj has done her best to help.'

I nod. Anoushka, at last, has slipped into place. As I'd suspected, her role was simply to muddy the waters around *My Place or Yours?* When I ask whether Haj got well paid for her little fiction, Dessie shrugs.

'She wouldn't say.'

'But what do you think?'

'I think her Russian mates must make life very sweet for her so in the end I'm guessing it's down to the same thing. This guy Yuri has his own helicopter, by the way. And he's crazy about sky diving.'

I smile. Only this afternoon I found a text on my phone from the Jump School. They're offering a date for me and H to turn up at their airfield and learn the truth about gravity.

'July the fourth,' I tell him. 'They might have room for three.'

'You mean jump?'

'Yes.'

'Why would I ever want to do something like that?'

'Because you love me?'

When Dessie means it, he has the softest laugh. He's licked his big finger and now he's tracing the curve of my lips.

'I'll come and watch,' he says. 'You can call it moral support.'

I nod. This is good news but something's bothering me and I've just realized what it is.

'So how come our Haj was so frank with you?'

Dessie has disappeared towards the foot of the bed. He's decided it's my turn to be pleasured. He definitely hears the question because he lifts his big face for a moment, moist and shiny, and smiles.

'It's a gift,' he says. 'Ask the right questions, find the sweet spot, and you'd be amazed how people open up.' That chuckle again. 'Never fails, I promise you. Relax just a little bit more and I'll prove it.'

I talk to Rosa that same evening. She's back in town now, tucked up in the little pied-à-terre which is her workaday London home. The return journey, she says, was a delight, a non-stop meeting of minds on the rich possibilities awaiting us down the line.

'Becca's happy for me to direct?'

'With input from that dreamy man of yours? Very. That's a joke, by the way, my precious. These kids in the biz are so savvy these days. They know the value of the right headlines and a thesp like you in the director's chair will play better than well in the trade press.'

'But does she think I can do it?'

'She hasn't a clue, and to be frank neither do I, but you've been around some great directors in your time and I can't believe you haven't picked up a trick or two.'

This, we both know, is a million miles from the brutal slog of a six-ep location but I don't bother to argue. More pressing is another issue.

'Is she talking money at all? Becca?'

'Not yet, but we'll get there soon. First we have to find a producer you can work with, and get all our heads together. We're going to need detailed costings, a stage payment schedule, insurance provision, the whole nine yards.'

'And the location fee?'

'That too, of course. Goes without saying.'

This, I know, is where the real problem might lie. I explain again about H's unfitness to sign anything. I've been hoping for some elegant legal finesse that Tony Morse might have shared with both of us but just now he has other things on his mind.

'Like?'

'Like getting himself arrested. He may have paid to have someone beaten up but he can't remember.'

'This is bloody Portsmouth again?' Rosa makes it sound like an affliction, something against which you might be wise to vaccinate.

'I'm afraid so. But even down there a jury would take a dim view of hospitalizing someone you don't happen to like. Not to mention the judge.'

'I see.' Rosa's gone quiet. She's obviously having a think. 'Ironic, isn't it? That estate of yours probably swung the whole thing today. It looked totally fabulous, period fucking perfect, yet it might turn out to be a deal breaker.'

'You mean that?' My heart is sinking.

'Never.' She brightens again on the phone. 'There's always something clever and witty we can do. Depend on it. Have a great funeral, by the way. And send him my love.'

'Him?'

'Rémy.' She laughs. 'He'll understand.'

THIRTY-FIVE

I depart for Paris very early the following morning. Dessie drives me to Yeovil Junction first thing and I take the train to London. I'm flying from Gatwick. Getting into France used to be easy but these days it's turned into a nightmare. You need evidence of a double jab, plus a PCR test, plus a special *attestation*, signed and dated, pledging that you haven't been anywhere near a Covid positive over the last few days. Happily, thanks to a pop-up centre in Bridport, I have all of the above.

But Covid can be a blessing, too, and I've never seen Gatwick so empty. I have time for a coffee and a quick call to Dessie before I stroll to the boarding gate. He has news, alas, about Tony Morse.

'He's just been arrested,' he says. 'No charges yet, but I suspect they've got him kippered.'

'How?'

'Money changed hands. Quite a lot of it.'

'Shit.' I'm staring at one of the departure screens, haunted by the thought of Tony Morse banged up in some custody cell. He probably knows the routines better than any serving policeman, and it isn't hard to picture the kind of reception he'll be getting. As a matchless defence brief, he's spent the last umpteen years getting in these cops' faces, teasing them in the interview room and the magistrate's court, and now will be payback time. Poor man.

Dessie wants to know a little more about the funeral.

'It's in a lovely church called Saint-Étienne du Mont. It's hidden away in the Fifth, near the Pantheon. I went to a wedding there once. It's a perfect choice.'

'And afterwards?'

'Afterwards will be raucous, and I hope funny. Rémy collected some very odd friends. I think the posh word is ungovernable.'

'Sounds like *Vlixcombe.*'

'You're so right. I was thinking that, too. Maybe that's where the idea came from in the first place. Are you missing me, by the way? Just a yes would be fine.'

'I can do better than that, but you need to wait. *À demain*, isn't that right?'

See you tomorrow. He most definitely will. I blow him a smoochy kiss on the phone, raising a smile from an elderly lady on the row of seats opposite, and then join the queue to file onto the aircraft. I have an entire row of seats to myself, and minutes later I'm staring down at the grey waters of the Channel. So much has happened, I think. Rémy gone. *Vlixcombe* in the rudest health. My darling man about to join me at Flixcombe while H shuffles ever deeper into the twilight. I was looking at him last night, after I'd tip-toed into his bedroom to say goodbye. Already, he seemed to have worked out that I was off again, and he looked totally bewildered. No man could fake that kind of lostness, I've decided. Not even H.

From Charles de Gaulle, I take the RER and Metro to Jussieu and walk to the church. Paris, like London, is still waiting for the tourists to return and the half-empty streets feel strange as the clouds part for a burst of late sunshine. I'm a little early for the service and getting served within seconds at a pavement café in the middle of summer is unheard-of, but I feel the need for a decent coffee, and a bit of a think.

My phone lies on the table in case Rosa wants a chat, but she doesn't ring. The weeks and months to come, I know with absolute certainty, will be very busy indeed and one of the many reasons I've fallen in love with Dessie is the knowledge that he'll be happy to look after H in my absence. He told me last night that he'll be there for both of us and what made it all the sweeter was the smile on his face. The irony, I think, would have amused Rémy no end. First you spend half a lifetime trying to put Pompey's top criminal face away. Then you end up nursing him. Very odd.

I leave the café shortly afterwards and make my way to the church. Saint-Étienne is one of this city's hidden gems. It lies in the fork of two roads, neither of them busy. The exterior is a bit of a muddle, the impact unbalanced by a soaring campanile which looks like a bit of an afterthought, but I've always had a taste for quirkiness like this, and I pause before I cross the road. Faces I recognize from long-ago shoots are gathering in the fading light outside the west door. Nobody appears to have bothered with dressing in black which comes as a bit of a relief because I, too, have gone for something I know Rémy loved. I've had this summer dress half my life. It's a cheerful combination of bright daubs that Miró would be proud of and it's always been fun to wear. The neckline is slightly immodest and when I modelled it for Dessie last night he, like Rémy, fully approved.

The dress draws applause from a couple of actors I meet beside the door. We exchange kisses and try, unsuccessfully, to work out when we last met. Rémy, we agree, was far too young to deserve such an early exit and our little group thickens with the arrival of two women I don't know. One is an actress, the other her agent. Everyone is smoking, and I slip away into the church as yet more of Rémy's many friends appear.

The interior of the church, artfully candlelit, is already half full, and I take a seat near the back. I'm anticipating a eulogy or two, and from here I have a perfect view of the pulpit. Soaring columns reach dimly for the vaulted roof, and the altar is framed by matching stone staircases that spiral upwards. Inside and out, as Rémy might have said, Saint-Étienne has done its own thing.

The service starts late. It can't be the traffic because there isn't any but by the time the cortège arrives at the west door the show is running fifteen minutes late. Thesps have never had any time for decorum or good manners, and neither have the cameramen and other techies that I've recognized. Of Claudine, strangely enough, there's no sign.

The coffin has appeared now, carried on the shoulders of a rich array of French acting talent, and we all peer round as it makes its way down the aisle. Rémy was born in the south and was always proud of his origins, and the coffin is draped in the scarlet-and-yellow flag of Languedoc, which is a nice touch. Ditto the music, the sublime opening from 'La Grande Messe des Morts' that Berlioz wrote in this very city. Berlioz was another Rémy passion, and one day he swore to put this haunted man on the big screen.

The priest gets the funeral mass underway, and we listen to the choir singing an excerpt from the Rachmaninov *Vespers*. Their unaccompanied voices fill this huge space and already some of the women are dabbing at their eyes. Saint-Étienne houses the tombs of both Racine and Pascal, which means that Rémy has found himself in good company, probably no accident because Pascal was another of his heroes. He once told me that a hunger for knowledge was the true measure of any human being, and that Pascal – scientist, inventor, scribe, and philosopher – puts us all to shame. His insistence that imagination shapes everything, much quoted when script editors got difficult, became one of Rémy's lodestars, and when Habeeb mounts the steps to the pulpit I'm wondering exactly how anyone can do justice to the man who has left us all.

Rosa has already told me that Habeeb, a Muslim, is far from comfortable in a setting like this, but it's a tribute to both he and Rémy that none of that potential awkwardness shows. His eulogy is both graceful and perceptive. He tells us it was an honour to be asked to help steer Rémy's career all those years ago, and a blessing to feel representation turning into a deep and lasting friendship. He had an enduring respect for Rémy's many talents, amongst which he included a limitless appetite for earthy Languedoc reds and long nights of even better conversation.

This happens to be true and stirs both laughter and a brief flutter of applause, but as Habeeb moves deftly amongst many of the high spots of Rémy's career, referencing this feature film, and that TV series, I'm beginning to wonder how he'll manage the tricky segue to the field in Jersey where our cherished and multi-talented friend met his death. As I know only too well, Rémy had briefly ceased to be a director of genius and had become a novice drug dealer with none of the street skills he needed to survive. On the evidence of the last ten minutes, I have every respect for Habeeb's judgement, but how on earth will he explain the past few weeks?

In the event, wisely, he declines the challenge. He wraps

up the eulogy in a soft mist of nautical metaphors. How Rémy loved nothing better than to be sailing alone at the helm of his beloved *Caspar.* How he knew every millimetre of those treacherous reefs off Brittany, and every waiting ambush in a busy production schedule. How he could sniff out a false note in a script or a performance and put things right in a moment's conversation. How his instincts and his navigation never let him down in all the many corners of his busy life, and how blessed we all were to have known him. Rémy's talents and his judgement, he suggests finally, have helped us all when it really mattered, and we'll all be the poorer now he's gone.

We all adore a good performance, and this is one of the best. Murmurs of congratulation and thanks greet Habeeb when he descends to the floor of the nave, and an actress I've never much liked gets to her feet and embraces him. This is totally unnecessary because Habeeb doesn't need this stagey little gesture but we're near the end of the service now and there's a genuine sense of relief – or perhaps release – when the priest crosses himself and intones the final words of the mass. We've said goodbye to Rémy in a proper and fit manner, which is exactly what he deserves.

After the cortège has departed, mourners make their way down the aisle and out into the falling dusk. I've yet to gather my thoughts, and within minutes I'm alone in the church. I can't rid my mind of the quote from Pascal: imagination shapes everything. Is that why nothing is ever quite the way it seems? Is that what took Haj to write a pack of lies about a man she's never met? Is that why I found it so difficult – until now – to take Dessie at his word? And might that explain why Rémy wrote a final part for himself that he simply couldn't fulfil?

'Great dress. I love it.' I've heard this voice before, thickened by too many cigarettes. Balkan accent, too. Another clue.

I look round, already aware of a feeling of dread stirring deep inside me. I'm right. Ratko is standing behind the chair, looking down, not bothering to hide his interest in my cleavage. He's wearing a dark suit, which is ironic given the way the rest of us turned up. The undertaker, I think. Here to bury the man he probably killed.

'You came for the funeral?'

'I did, yes.'

'You wanted to make sure he'd really gone?'

'I wanted to meet you.'

'Why?'

'It's a business proposition. We need to talk.'

Business and Ratko don't belong in the same sentence, not unless you're contemplating a new career in the narco trade, and watching Rémy being carried off to his grave is a very timely reason for me to decline.

'I think not,' I say. 'Aside from everything else, I've got a wake to attend. We're saying goodbye. It might take a while.'

'I'm sure it will. Ten minutes. That's all I need.'

'Here?'

'Wherever you like.'

I gaze up at him for a moment, trying to make a decision. Somehow or other I have to get rid of this man.

'Outside then, on the street.'

'Where everyone can see us?' Ratko's smile seems unforced. 'Rémy always said you were the smartest of them all.'

Every girl loves a compliment, which is my excuse for following him out of the church. Of the mourners I can see no trace. It's mid-evening now, and the shadows are beginning to lengthen as the sun sets, but a comforting scatter of people are hurrying here and there. In what's left of the daylight, I tell myself, what can possibly go wrong?

There's a bench on the apron of *pavé* in front of the west door, and at Ratko's invitation I sit down.

'Just a couple of questions before we start,' I say. 'How come you're a free man?'

'Because I haven't done anything wrong.'

'Rémy? Shot dead? Didn't murder used to be a crime?'

'I didn't kill him, and I have no idea who did. I was on a boat, miles away.'

'So why did he die? Who did he upset? You, maybe?'

This time he won't answer. Instead, he wants to talk about Flixcombe.

'I came and took all those photos. Do you remember that?'

'I do. You said you were going to be Rémy's location manager. That was a lie.'

'A small one. Rémy definitely needed the pictures and I wanted to look round the house.'

'Why?'

'Because I'm going to buy it.'

'*Buy* it?' I'm staring at him now. This is something I definitely haven't been expecting. One drug baron buying the other one out? Surreal.

'What makes you think it's for sale?'

'I know your partner has problems, financial problems, big financial problems. It's a lovely house. I can make those problems go away and that's a promise.'

'You're right about the house, wrong about H.'

'He doesn't need the money?'

'He's not my partner. We're friends, and as I'm sure you saw, he's not very well. As for the house, it's not for sale.'

'You've applied for planning permission?'

'You know about that?' Here's another surprise.

'Of course.'

'Then the answer's no. Not yet.'

'Good.' He nods. 'Fifteen million dollars US. No planning permission. Nothing to spoil those views. The money will be in cash, in any currency of your choice, and my solicitor will be in touch within the week.' He's on his feet now, looking down at me. 'You're going back tomorrow?'

'Yes.'

'Then expect her call. I've retained someone local.' He names a firm of solicitors in Bridport. I'm beginning to think this offer of his might be for real.

'One more question,' I tell him. 'Just one.'

'Why do I want it?'

'Yes.' I nod, almost impressed at how quick he is, and this time I'm not bothering to hide my chest.

Ratko appears to be giving my question some thought. At length he gestures back towards the church.

'I've been to far too many funerals lately,' he says. 'I guess you might call it retirement. One day God tells you to cash in and I'd be a fool not to listen.'

With this *adieu*, he shrugs, and then turns away. Watching him cross the road and round the distant corner, I begin to wonder whether Rémy ever really meant *Vlixcombe* to happen. Was sending Ratko to West Dorset and letting him take all those photos simply a way of trying to settle his drug debts? Was he aware that Ratko wanted to buy H out? Either way, I realize that it doesn't much matter. Whatever Rémy's master plan, it didn't work.

The wake is to be held in a suite of rehearsal rooms off the Boulevard de Belleville in the Twentieth arrondissement. This part of the city is also rich in post-production studios and the choice is inspired. I make my way north, riding the Metro again, glad to be wearing a mask. No one has any right to the broadest of grins, especially on the day of a funeral, but my conversation with Ratko was beyond surreal. I've been on my phone, punching in the figures to do the conversion. Fifteen million dollars is eleven million pounds, and all this without months of tiresome haggling with the planners. There will, of course, be drawbacks. A sum of money that large, given Ratko's track record, will be hugely tainted, but I'm still in one piece, no one's so far put a gun to my head, and in the shape of Dessie I have someone to tell me what to do next.

The rehearsal rooms are above what used to be a garment factory. These spaces are never pretty but mounting the stairs to the swelling promise of much conversation and much laughter I know I'm in for a treat. Walking into the biggest of the rehearsal rooms is to walk into Christmas. Someone's worked miracles with decorations of every kind, and a scrum of faces from the church have gathered round a montage of blown-up photos that nearly covers an entire wall. A trestle table beneath the window is already littered with empty bottles but there are unopened cases of wine neatly stacked on the floor, and two of those huge portable fridges we use on location are full of chilled Stella and 1664, plus a nest of white wine.

I help myself to a glass of Albarino, which happened to be one of Rémy's favourite tipples, and join the crowd around the photos. Naturally we're all hunting for shots of ourselves, memories of our days in Rémy's sun, and the wake has become a blur of pointing fingers and remembered anecdotes. The night shoot on the wasteland that used to be the Ocean Terminal in Le Havre, when a band of feral druggies tried to steal half our equipment. The morning Rémy descended to breakfast on a shoot in Tours and fell in love with the pretty journo from *Le Nouvel Observateur* who'd come to interview him. The car chase in a long-ago movie that nearly killed the stunt man who'd insisted on driving.

The latter incident was on a location I'd shared with Claudine, and I try and find her in the teeming chaos that seems to have enveloped us all. Rémy was always brilliant when it came to crowd scenes and I know he'd relish this one, and I share this thought with a woman half my age whose face looks familiar but I can't quite place. She's concentrating hard on a glass of Pernod, trying to avoid spillage. It's an impossible ask, and she seems grateful when I steer her to somewhere a little less manic. Naturally we talk about Rémy and it turns out she had a big break-out role in his most recent offering for France2. She played a reformed junkie under siege by a senior French politician, and she was in awe at the quality of the daily rushes that Rémy was able to conjure from a script she regarded as mediocre.

'It was like magic,' she says, running her finger round the edge of the glass. 'I never worked out how he did it.'

'Was he good to be with? Relaxed?'

'He was lovely.'

'No pressures? No signs of angst?'

'None.' She's looking at me harder now. She's a very pretty girl and I expect she's a fine actress but she can't hide a suspicion of where all these questions might be leading.

To change the subject, I ask whether she knows Claudine.

'Of course I do. Everyone knows Claudine.'

'And is she here?' I gesture round. 'Only I can't find her.'

'You haven't heard?' She's staring at me now.

'About what?'

'Claudine. She left Rémy for some shit Serb gangster. From what I can gather, it broke his heart.'

THIRTY-SIX

This is news I realize I've half-expected and it puts Rémy's death in a totally different light. If you knew him really well, and I like to think I did, you'd sometimes glimpse the darkness that lurked beneath the *calme* that – on and off set – became his trademark. Rémy was a man who never shirked difficult decisions and the sudden absence of Claudine would have hurt him badly. I'm thinking about her this morning as I struggle with a major hangover after leaving the wake past midnight. When she gave me the news about Rémy's death on the phone, she was crying. Does that make her a good actress? Did she know what she'd done to him? Or was she genuinely shocked?

By the time I get to Charles de Gaulle for the flight home, the worst of the headache is beginning to subside. I put a call into Dessie and tell him about Claudine. He seems unsurprised, and when I go on to explain about Ratko's offer for Flixcombe he warns me that fifteen million US dollars will be narco money. However well washed, he says, there's no laundry in the world that could get all the stains out. This isn't the news I want but it's still nice to hear his voice. When I ask him about Tony Morse, he tells me he's heard nothing.

'So he's still banged up?'

'Yes.'

'Until when?'

'My guess is today. I've got to go to a Palliser meet this afternoon. It turns out there's still stuff to do. If I get time, I'll pay him a call.'

'When are you home?'

'As soon as. Sunday at the latest.'

'Miss me?'

'Always.'

* * *

The Gatwick departure is delayed by nearly an hour. I manage to sleep during the brief flight and a call to Andy brings him to Yeovil Junction to meet my train. The hot news from Flixcombe is that H this morning insisted on watching a replay of the England game against Czechoslovakia, apparently in the belief that Harry Kane might slot a couple of extra goals. Quite how this might have happened had baffled both Andy and Jess, but the moment the referee blew for extra time H was on his feet celebrating, as he put it, Harry's fucking hat-trick.

'You're making this up, Andy.'

'No way.'

'And the real result?'

'One-nil. Just like last time.'

I nod, oddly comforted by this latest outbreak of H's craziness, and when we get back to Flixcombe and he's there at the kitchen table he shows no signs of realizing I've been away.

'Kane just banged six in against Peru.' He's beaming. 'Can you believe that fucking man?'

Dessie phones in the evening. He's been making further enquiries about Claudine. It's hard to believe but it appears that the massed ranks of Operation Palliser have misjudged her abandonment of Rémy in favour of Ratko, and only now is the crime scene in that Jersey field beginning to make sense. The single bullet to the head. Rémy's prints on the butt of the automatic. Not a drugs hit dressed up as a would-be suicide but the real thing. The gun has at last been traced to a consignment stolen from a gun shop in Malaga, though it's still unclear how it ever got to Jersey, and into Rémy's hand.

'We're thinking acute depression,' Dessie says. 'Life ganged up on him. He'd got into trouble with Ratko, owed the man a ton of money. His woman pushing off probably did it for him.'

'Despair,' I'm nodding. 'It was always in him. Deep down he was ultra-sensitive, there for the taking. Maybe that's what made him such a fine director. You have to have feelings in the first place, and in the end they killed him.'

I shake my head, and then stare into nowhere. It all sounds far too neat, far too perfect, but I've a feeling we may have tripped over one of life's more brutal truths: that the worst things happen to the best people.

I tell Dessie I love him, and hang up. When H comes into the kitchen to find out what's going on, I'm in floods of tears. I dry my eyes and tell him I'll be fine, but I can tell he doesn't believe me. Very sweetly, he escorts me to bed and even tucks me in. When I lift my head from the pillow to say night-night and well done to Harry Kane for all those extra goals, he's gone.

Next morning, I'm sort of better. I have Rosa on the phone for far too long because she's insisting on a full account of the Paris revels. I describe the scene in the church, tell her Habeeb was magnificent, and skip my little tête-à-tête with Ratko.

'And the wake?'

Again, she wants full details. I tell her about the rehearsal rooms, and the scrum around the photo boards, and name a few luminaries I know she will recognize, but then I get to Claudine and I lose it again.

'What's the matter?' she's saying.

'It's Rémy. He committed suicide. No one shot him, he did it himself. Claudine walked out on him and it was all over. A wrap. Finished. Done. Shit. I'm sorry. I should be better than this.'

She tells me not to apologize. She says she feels my pain. Then she asks about that darling man of mine.

'So where is he?'

'I don't know. Pompey, I expect.'

'Then get him down. That's what he's for. Don't put up with any nonsense.' She sounds really angry, and when I realize she means it, I start to laugh. 'That's better,' she says at once. 'Now, let's change the subject.'

The Beeb's drama department, it seems, want to start formal negotiations. Rémy's little orphan is already up and running, and the whole wild adventure is proceeding at unheard-of speed. Never before has Rosa known a project gather so much momentum so quickly, but neither can she remember a trial script episode that read so perfectly.

'And Haj?'

'She's working on episode two. By teatime I dare say she'll have the entire bloody series in the bag. You may have a rival, by the way. That darling man of yours made a real impact. Nip this in the bud, my precious. Do something really lovely to him.'

'I have done.'

'Then do it again.'

She breaks off to take another call, and then she's gone. That same afternoon, I have a conversation on the phone with Dessie. He says he's been in touch with the Jump School and managed to nail an earlier slot.

'For H's sake?'

'For yours.'

'Like when?'

'Like Tuesday.'

'*Tuesday?*'

'Yeah. They had a cancellation. We were in luck.'

'And you're jumping, too?'

'No way. It's the Germany game on Tuesday night so I'm taking no risks. I'll be down tomorrow afternoon. You might have a word with H, explain what's going on. I doubt he'll understand but bits of it might stick. The other thing you'll both need is a medical certificate, which might be a bit tricky when it comes to H. Talk to his doctor. Use that famous charm of yours, yeah?'

The line goes dead and I'm left staring at the phone. Conversations this brisk have never really done it for me, so I go to the Jump School website to check out the medical requirements. Dessie's right, of course. High blood pressure, recurring injuries, and something termed 'neurological conditions' are no-nos for jump candidates but there doesn't appear to be any age restriction, and neither is there any mention of Long Covid or dementia. This is heartening but anyone over the age of forty has to turn up with a medical certificate signed and stamped by a registered doctor.

I linger on the Jump School website to watch a couple of

jumps filmed by the school's cameraman. They both feature women jumping for the first time. Both are harnessed and the instructor rides on their backs. On the ground, I can imagine this configuration, one body anchored securely to the other, to be awkward and a bit ungainly, but in free fall, before the parachute opens, the two figures appear weightless as they plunge towards the airfield below. Both women are obviously having the time of their lives and the mike on the camera picks up their screams as the parachute suddenly blossoms above them, but there's something mesmeric about that forty-five seconds of free fall, and before I ring the medical centre where both H and I are registered, I take a second look at both sequences. This is for me, I think. No matter what happens.

When I finally get through to the doctor who normally deals with H, it's gone five. Thanks to Covid, doctors are used to consultations by Zoom and I quickly explain what I need for Tuesday's excitements.

The doctor, a lovely woman with a soft Irish accent, is looking puzzled.

'Mr Prentice is anticipating a parachute jump? Is that what I'm hearing?'

'That's right.'

'But he has Long Covid. Are you telling me the symptoms have gone?'

'No. He's still breathless.'

'And walking?'

'Difficult some days. Better on others.'

'I see.' She's studying his notes. 'And his dementia?'

'Probably worse. I wouldn't be having this conversation unless I thought it might do him some good.'

'How? How could that possibly happen?'

Here, I'm in real difficulty. I know Sayid would never have recommended extreme sports unless there'd be a definite possibility of improvement, but for the life of me I can't understand why. Maybe I should have quizzed him harder.

'I'm afraid I can't tell you,' I say. 'Would it help if I brought him in?'

'I doubt it. This is a tandem jump?'

'Yes.'

'Then we have to think of the instructor's interests as well as Mr Prentice. I'm sorry to disappoint you, Ms Andressen, but the answer's no.'

I nod, tell her I understand. When I say that I, too, want to jump she brightens immediately. I tell her my age, and answer a couple of lifestyle questions, and she books me in for a blood pressure test with the practice nurse on Monday morning. Given an OK result, she'll be happy to sign a certificate.

'Good luck,' she says. 'And consolations to your Mr Prentice.'

My Mr Prentice. That evening, as a break from yet more football, I find H's copy of *The Italian Job* and settle him down in the den to watch it before I retire to the kitchen to start making to-do lists for *Vlixcombe*. Being around actors again in Paris has whetted my appetite for the specialness of location work and I'm keen to build an on-set chemistry that will withstand the test of a long shoot. When I check briefly on H, he half-turns on the sofa to look up at me. I'm not sure he's got any real interest in the movie but he doesn't seem to care.

'You OK?' he grunts.

I nod, say nothing, go back to my list.

Next day is Sunday and Dessie, alas, doesn't turn up. On the phone, he's blaming what he calls 'the fag end of Palliser', a mountain of paperwork he still has to shift, but promises to appear tomorrow. H and I share a quiet evening watching Belgium beat Portugal, and next morning I get an early call from Ratko's solicitors in Bridport. At first I mistake the woman on the line for a secretary but she turns out to be the partner assigned to handle Ratko's offer. She's after a meet, which comes as no surprise, but when I ask about the origins of such a huge sum she's less than keen to discuss it.

'We'll be taking all the required steps to check our client out, Ms Andressen, and that applies equally to the provenance of his money. What we need to ascertain at this point are your views on the possibility of a sale. I'm not asking for a decision now, of course, but it might be useful for us to get together.'

Indeed, it might. I shan't be making any decisions of any sort without Dessie's input, and there's still the problem of H being unable to sign anything, but the moment I put the phone down I'm thinking of Haj, and her Russian friends, and the wider circles she probably moves in. All that money sloshing around, and so easy – begging Dessie's reservations – to turn it into 300 acres of prime Dorset real estate. If we were to find a way to sell, I'm already thinking about some temporary lease-back deal on Ratko's part to enable the *Vlixcombe* shoot to go ahead.

This, I suspect, will be complicated and doubtless take forever to sort out. More pressing is my imminent date at the Jump School. I do my best to explain the issue over the medical certificate to H but this turns out to be much easier than I'd imagined because he has no memory of me mentioning it before. As a taster for tomorrow's excitements, I fetch my laptop and show him the footage from the Jump School website. He gazes at it, enraptured.

'You want to come with us, H? You want to watch me do it?'

'You?'

'Me.'

'Doing that?' He's nodding at the screen.

'Yes.'

'Fuck me.' He's in awe. 'What was it like?'

After lunch, I drive to the medical centre in Bridport and park H in the waiting room while I have my blood pressure taken. To my surprise, after the events of the last few weeks, I appear to be in the rudest health, and within minutes we're heading back to the car with my precious certificate. As soon as we're back home, I phone the Jump School and cancel H's booking. I'm to appear tomorrow around nine o'clock for a full briefing. The jump itself is scheduled for late morning, and the gods of the weather appear to be on my side. A light wind from the east, and a thin scatter of high cirrus. In other words, near-perfect conditions.

'How high do we go?' I ask.

'Ten thousand feet, give or take. We're talking six minutes you'll never forget.'

*   *   *

Wonderful. Dessie arrives in mid-evening, rather later than I'd expected. There's a special on TV in anticipation of tomorrow's game against Germany and he settles in the den to watch the end of the programme with H. He's looking exhausted but he tells me that Palliser has been put on the back burner, and that his services will no longer be required. This, I hope, is the best news for all of us but there's another question I have to ask.

'Tony Morse?'

'Conspiracy to wound. They charged before they released him, poor bastard. Losing that woman's one thing. His whole fucking career down the khazi, quite another.'

'But he's back in Craneswater?'

'Yeah.'

'And?'

'I never got a chance to pop round. He's on police bail so he'll have to report at least weekly. Always kick a man when he's down. Spiteful, believe me, doesn't begin to cover it.'

I say I'm sorry. Tomorrow, I tell myself, I'll try and give Tony a ring and do whatever I can to cheer him up.

'How did he take it when you explained he wouldn't be jumping?' Dessie nods at H.

'I don't think he understood. I showed him some footage but he just got confused. I thought you might have better luck, you know, man to man.'

Dessie eyes me for a moment, then shakes his head before smothering a yawn.

'Thanks a bunch,' I think he says.

THIRTY-SEVEN

Next morning, the three of us leave Flixcombe before eight. The airfield at Dunkerswell is busier than I'd expected and after we've parked up and got out, every passing conversation seems to centre around tonight's game. Might our luck at last turn against the Germans? Might we avoid sudden death from penalties?

I spot Cleggie from a distance. He's wearing his Red Arrows flying suit and he's standing beside a biggish aircraft with high wings, peering up at a smear of oil trailing from one of the engines. He looks a little older, with crinkly new lines around his eyes, but he's no less cheerful. He gives me a hug, and I introduce Dessie and H. Cleggie has a bone-crushing handshake but it doesn't seem to worry H in the slightest. When Cleggie asks him how's he doing, he smiles.

'Great weather.' He gestures vaguely upwards. 'Lovely job.'

Cleggie shows us the way to the Jump School. There are two parachuting outfits on the airfield, and judging by the cars parked outside, the other one – Skydive Buzz – is equally busy. We're walking fast now because I've misjudged the time, and H trails in our wake. He's out of breath again and for some reason he's brought a little rucksack he's unearthed from somewhere. Dessie has taken a look inside before we left and found a pullover and a single sock. Evidently H thinks we've all come for some kind of picnic and thinks it might get nippy towards dark.

At the Jump School I sign in. The doors to the briefing room are open and I can see at least half a dozen people waiting for the morning's session to start. When I enquire whether it might be OK for Dessie and H to listen in, the girl handling registration sees no problem. There's a coffee machine down the corridor and a big plate of hot pastries if we've neglected to have breakfast.

The briefing starts with an overview of what awaits us. We'll all be jumping with our own instructors from the back of Cleggie's Skyvan. The exit, says the guy in charge, is to the rear of the aircraft, off a ramp that folds out and down. This offers the school a perfect platform for mass formation jumps but this morning we'll be leaving the aircraft at carefully timed intervals, on his cue. Jump altitude remains 10,000 feet. Forty-five seconds of free fall and then a five-minute descent beneath the parachute. There is, he says, plenty of airfield to take us all when we land.

This sparks a ripple of slightly nervous laughter, mainly because we're gazing at a slide on the A/V presentation. From 10,000 feet, the airfield looks tiny, three runways on a postage stamp of grass, but the class leader assures us that it gets a whole lot bigger as we fall. He's a beefy thirty something with a brutal buzz-cut, and I suspect he probably has a military background. Henceforth, we're to call him Meredith.

The morning's important business, he says, is getting to trust the harness. For whatever reason he chooses me to step forward and play the guinea pig, and I'm introduced to the instructor with whom I'll jump. To my slight surprise, this turns out to be a tallish woman called Darcy. She must be half my age and twice as fit, but I'm comforted by the firmness of her handshake and her effortless command when it comes to fitting my harness. Under her guidance, as Meredith supplies commentary, I step into a cradle of webbing, heavily stitched. The harness loops over my shoulders, up around my crotch, and Darcy gently tightens it until every spare bit of me feels supported. Four steel anchor points will glue me to my new buddy once we're in the aircraft, readying for the jump, but for illustration purposes Meredith insists on showing everyone exactly what we'll look like when we step into the void together.

Darcy gets harnessed up, and then beckons me into a kind of backwards clinch. I hear the steel fixings snap into place, and the two of us are suddenly one. The key, says Meredith, is the landing for which I must draw up my knees. Hampered by the harness, this is easier said than done but after a couple of adjustments I manage it. From time to time, summoning a brave smile, I look for H and Dessie in the back row of seats.

Dessie is studying his phone while H appears to be asleep. Every actress depends on an audience but oddly enough I find this reassuring. Jumping into nowhere from two miles up? Just another day at the office.

The briefing complete, we await a distribution of both harnesses and instructors. The dish of pastries passes from hand to hand, but interestingly there are very few takers. I've decided already that my Darcy is beyond competent, and I demolish a *pain au chocolat*, which is delicious.

Back in the sunshine, at last, we gather herd-like and make for Cleggie's Skyvan. I'm deep in conversation with Darcy, who turns out to be a third-year physics student at Exeter University. She rows, as well as skydives, and by the time we make it to the Skyvan, we've properly bonded. Mustered in a loose semi-circle, we listen to a second, far shorter brief from Cleggie. He's always had a slightly rogueish charm, and this – together with his Red Arrows flying suit – makes a very definite impression on a couple of the older women. On the way over the airfield, I've been aware of Dessie and H with their heads together, and when Cleggie has finished with his list of do's and don'ts once we're in the aircraft, Dessie appears beside me.

'H wants to go up.' He nods at the aircraft. 'Can you make that happen?'

I tell him I can at least try. Getting H airborne may not be the same as a parachute jump but it might help bring just a flicker of light to the deeper shadows in his failing brain.

I walk across to Cleggie, who's about to get into the aircraft, and explain about H. He looks a little doubtful to begin with but after I mention our disappointment over the medical certificate, he sees no problem.

'And your other friend? Dessie? There's room for him, too, if he fancies it.'

'Perfect,' I say.

I return to Dessie. Novice jumpers and their instructors are already clambering into the aircraft. The news that both he and H are welcome aboard, earns me a brief hug.

'Enjoy,' he whispers.

The four of us, including Darcy, are the last in. Meredith

has already drawn up a jump order and Darcy and I are to exit first. There are fold-down seats along both sides of the fuselage, but there's no way we can use them, and I count eight instructors making final adjustments before mating with their novice jumpers. Most of the jumpers are toting wrist and helmet-mounted cameras, and I curse myself for not bringing something similar. After Darcy and I are safely an item, she tells me it won't be a problem.

'I've got a smartphone with a big wide-angle lens,' she murmurs. 'I'll grab some selfies on the way down.'

Next I hear the cough of first one engine and then the other. There's a noisy minute or two before he lets both engines settle, then Cleggie opens the throttle and we bump over the turf towards the runway. Meredith has warned us that the aircraft is no spring chicken, and that the climb to ten thousand feet might take longer than EasyJet. By now the busy hum of conversation has died. People, especially the novices, are exchanging glances, and as we roll down the runway and lift off, I catch one of the older women towards the front of the aircraft crossing herself.

There are smallish windows along the length of the aircraft, and I watch copses of trees in the greenness of the Devon countryside growing ever-smaller as Cleggie circles, climbing for height. After what seems an eternity of waiting, I can feel myself beginning to cramp up and I catch Dessie's eye in time to blow him a kiss. He and H have found seats at the front of the plane, and Dessie points at H, who is glued to the view from the nearby window, and circles his thumb and forefinger. This, I know, is his way of signalling that all is better than well, and I raise my thumb in acknowledgement before trying to ease the cramp from my right thigh. Then comes a blast of cold air as Meredith lowers the exit ramp at the rear of the aircraft, and peers down to gauge when to despatch the first pair of jumpers.

That, of course, is Darcy and little me, and for the first time I feel a knot of something very unpleasant in the pit of my stomach. So far, I haven't felt the least bit frightened. Not when I was watching the Jump School videos, not when I was listening to Meredith's morning brief, not even when we stepped into the belly of the Skyvan and prepared for take-off. But now, staring out at the distant green jigsaw of fields that is this part of Devon, it's impossible not to recognize that the next few minutes will be very black and white. Either the parachute works, or it doesn't. Either we land in one piece, or we die.

Feeling slightly ashamed of myself, I try and bury this feeling under a blizzard of half-remembered statistics. How many skydivers jump every second of every hour all over the world? How infinitesimally few of them ever come to grief? This is a bid to comfort myself and to be frank it doesn't work. I know that mankind was never designed to fly. I know that gravity is God's way of settling debts. Alarm has become dread. For whatever reason, I'm seriously frightened.

Meredith appears to be happy with the position of the aircraft. He's wearing a pair of headphones and is – I assume – talking to Cleggie at the controls up in the cockpit. Then he looks directly at Darcy and holds up all ten fingers, counting off our jump-cue second by second. Darcy gently guides me onto the ramp. In five seconds we must jump. I try to resist peering down but it's impossible, and for one terrifying moment, I'm thinking of tapping Darcy's leg and calling the whole thing off.

Three.

'Ready?' I can feel the warmth of Darcy's breath in my ear. I nod, fighting the urge to close my eyes.

Two.

We're right on the edge of the ramp now, waiting for the cue. Then, inexplicably, another figure has appeared beside us, a little unsteady, not strapped to anything. He shoots me a look as Meredith abandons the countdown and makes a lunge for him but it's too late. To this day, I swear he had a smile on his face.

H steps into nowhere. And then he's gone.

THIRTY-EIGHT

Darcy and I stand rooted to the ramp and for a long moment no one apart from Meredith appears to have a clue what's going on. A stir of movement at the front of the aircraft. An old guy making his way towards the ramp at the back. And the softest gasp from Darcy as he just kept walking.

By the time Cleggie drops a wing and heads back to make a landing, Meredith has closed the ramp. As we later learn, Cleggie has already put out a Mayday and a smallish crowd has assembled to help us out of the aircraft. The Jump School are commendably efficient: cups of tea, and blankets if needed, plus the promise of counselling once the implications of the incident have sunk in.

Dessie, too, is a tower of strength. His support is largely unvoiced. He's offering the only comfort I want, which is rudely physical. He puts his arms around me on the bareness of the airfield and gently rocks me back and forth. What I've just witnessed is beyond the reach of words. In any language, it makes absolutely no sense. At least, not yet.

Both of us, Dessie and I, are asked to wait at the Jump School for the arrival of the police. H's body has already been spotted in a neighbouring field and the farmer is removing his dairy cows before paramedics attend to slip his broken remains into a body bag. The police are with us within the hour, summoned from Exeter, a uniformed sergeant at the wheel of the marked car, a young female PC beside him.

The Jump School have an office available and both Dessie and I make full statements. We explain about H's dementia, and his ongoing battle with Long Covid. When the sergeant enquires whether he might have been depressed, we both shake our heads. A little lost? Yes. Not quite the H he used to be? Definitely. But not depressed. Never.

'And he was sitting beside you at the front of the aircraft?' The sergeant is looking at Dessie.

'That's right.'

'And he just got up?'

'Yes.'

'Why was that? Did you ask him?'

'I tried. It was very noisy. I think he wanted a better look.'

The two officers exchange glances.

'So why do you think he did it?' The young PC has put her pen down. 'Why did he jump?'

Dessie says he doesn't know.

'Ms Andressen?'

'It's the last thing in the world I ever expected,' I mutter. 'He was never a loser, never a quitter. He was always so much bigger than that.'

It falls to me to make the official identification. H's body has been taken to the mortuary at the big Exeter hospital in Wonford, and Dessie drives me there in convoy with the police car. Mortuary technicians have had time to tidy him up, and his shrunken body is covered in a sheet. The sheet is pinked with blood around the area of his chest but when I draw it back, his face is mercifully intact.

I study him a long time, not because there's any doubt who he is, but because I want to remember the expression on that face, which is remarkably peaceful. Finally I stoop and briefly remove my mask to kiss him on the forehead. His flesh is already cold, not H at all, and when the sergeant asks for a formal ID, I confirm his name and date of birth. Then I turn back to the technician.

'So how did he die, exactly? What killed him?'

This is a very silly question. Ten thousand feet killed him. Not wearing a parachute killed him. But part of me needs the anatomical details.

The technician is reluctant to hazard a guess. The post-mortem, he says, won't happen for a while but he thinks both his legs were broken, and his pelvis too, and there's obviously been massive compression of the spine. Most jumpers, he says, impact headfirst but the evidence suggests that H was spared disfiguring injury.

'And on the way down? Would he have been conscious? He'd know what he'd done?'

There's an awkward silence. Neither the technician nor the police sergeant know what to say and it's Dessie, as ever, who comes up with a kind of answer.

'Dementia may have been a blessing,' he says quietly. 'I think we should leave it at that.'

Very sensible. We drive home. En route, I put a difficult call through to Malo and do my best to cope with the flood of tears which follows. This is bad enough but after we arrive back at Flixcombe it gets worse. H's death is lead item on the local news and Dessie and I sit numbly on the sofa holding hands, staring at shots of Cleggie's Skyvan and then of the field where H met his death. A text from Cleggie has already arrived saying how sorry he is for both of us, and for H too, which is kind, but when a reporter from a national paper manages to get a call through, Dessie hangs up on him.

I open a bottle of Bombay Sapphire and pour two large gins. Process is a truly ghastly verb when it comes to an event like this but when shock begins to turn to grief, I recognize how important it is to try and unpick what's just happened. H definitely wasn't himself, hadn't been for many months. Maybe he understood that money troubles were looming. Maybe he missed his beloved Pompey. Maybe Long Covid had touched him in places we'd never suspected. But would any of that drive him into taking that last fatal step?

Dessie and I debate this for a while, prowling around those last months of his life looking for clues, and the longer we talk the sadder I become at what H missed by bringing his own story to such an abrupt end.

'*Vlixcombe*,' I say. 'It might have changed everything. And there's all that money in the offing from Ratko. And I keep reading about new treatments for Long Covid in the pipeline. We could have sorted all his troubles out, every single one.'

Dessie listens hard to all this but doesn't offer an opinion. I'm really getting to know him now and I've a feeling he's reserving his judgement. After a while, on our third gin, he asks whether I'd mind if he watches the England game.

'Not at all,' I say. 'We should do it for H.'

And so we huddle together on the sofa as Raheem Sterling's early shot tests the German goalie and the Wembley crowd erupts. The gin has kicked in by now and at half-time, still nil-nil, I wander upstairs to H's bedroom looking – I suppose – for any clues he may have left. Might there be a note of some kind? Had he pre-planned this final plunge? I look very hard but I can find nothing except an old Pompey football top, balled beneath his duvet. When I feel it, and then lift it to my face, it has an earthy smell that makes me think at once of H. It carries the number 9, which may signify something for hardcore Fratton End fans but, alas, not me.

Downstairs, I can hear a roar from the crowd as the game against Germany kicks off again. At the top of the stairs, about to rejoin Dessie, I hesitate, then turn round, still convinced that H must have left some sort of *adieu*.

I find it beneath my pillow. It's a very old photograph I recognize at once. A much younger Enora Andressen is posing on the deck of a big motor cruiser. The boat is called *Agincourt* and it belonged to a Pompey mate of H's and beyond the forest of masts, dusk is beginning to settle on the waterfront at Antibes. This is where I first met H all those years ago, where he mixed me a series of killer margheritas, where we took each other to bed and fucked a little and made the tiny speck of DNA that became our son. I turn the photo over and take it to the window to read the message on the back. H's handwriting was always terrible but this time he's used capital letters. MY GAL, he's written. Just that.

This is the second time I've lost it in the past few days. First Rémy, now H. Both gone. I sit on the side of the bed for a very long time, glad that Dessie can't see me this way, then I dry my eyes and blow my nose and take the photo downstairs.

'This,' I say, giving him the photo. Dessie studies it a moment and then nods, as if it comes as no surprise.

'Where did you find it?'

'Under my pillow.' I'm staring at the score in the top corner of the screen. We're winning two-nil. Against Germany. The figures mean nothing. Then I turn to Dessie again. 'Do you think he was jealous? Of us? Might that explain it?'

Dessie looks at me for a long moment and then shakes his head. 'He wanted all of you to begin with,' he says. 'Then he thought it better to leave us to it.'

'How do you know?'

'He told me.' He gets to his feet to give me a hug. 'Last night.'

AFTERWARDS

Every decent story has a twist in the end, and this is mine. It's over a week later. The media circus has moved on, I've taken numberless calls from well-meaning Pompey mates of H, and we've been joined at Flixcombe by Malo and Clemmie. Rosa is deep in detailed negotiations with senior honchos from the Beeb's drama department, and Ratko has increased his offer to seventeen million US dollars. Only this morning, the coroner's officer paid us a visit and took yet another statement ahead of the inevitable inquest. The pathologist who conducted H's post-mortem had trouble, it seems, locating a single unbroken bone below his neck. This, in a way, is vintage H. Malo's dad never did anything by halves.

This morning, I took a call from Harry, H's father. He'd been one of the first people I'd contacted the day after H died, and now he wants to pay us a visit. On the phone I tell him we'd all be delighted to see him.

'*All*, pet?' Harry is a Geordie.

'Me, Dessie, Malo, and Clemmie of course. She's pregnant, as you know.'

'Dessie?'

'He's a friend of mine. Actually he's more than that. I know he'd love to meet you.'

Harry drives down that same afternoon. I've only met him once, back last year when he came to our borrowed Southsea flat where we were all nursing his very sick son. I could see H in his face then, and nothing's changed.

We all make a fuss of him, and I've roasted a big chicken in his honour because H always said it was his favourite. After we've eaten, I break out the port while Harry disappears to the bedroom we've readied upstairs. When he returns, he's carrying a sizeable manila envelope.

'Hayden's will,' he says quietly. 'He gave me a copy for safekeeping. I think you ought to take a look.'

Conversation has died around the table. Three pairs of eyes watch him slip the will from the envelope while Dessie fetches my glasses. Legal documents, as I've explained before, have never quite been my thing. I'm comfortable with scripts, and even better in the company of certain novelists, but freehold assignments, and royalty agreements and legalese in more or less any form have always been hard going. I read the preamble and begin to labour through the second page.

'See the little yellow slip?' Harry murmurs after a while. 'That's where you need to go.'

I follow his instructions. The meat of the will is on page seven. I read it twice, and then a third time just to make sure. Then I look up.

'He's left me Flixcombe,' I say. 'The whole bloody lot.'

Malo is the first to kiss me. Then Clemmie. Then comes a long hug from Dessie.

Harry watches us all, and then smiles.

'Cheers, pet.' He raises his glass. 'Young Hayden thought the world of you.'

One postscript. Haj's cheeky little masterpiece, I'm very happy to report, has just been bought by a Paris-based publishing house after brief negotiations with a Russian middleman called Sergei. The publishing house belongs to Georges Monsault, who is very happy indeed to add to the gaiety of one nation and the sorrows of another. Dessie believes Russian money, lots of it, swung the deal.

My Place or Yours? The simplest of questions.